Andrew Sanger was born in London in 1948. He attended the Lycée Français Charles de Gaulle in London, and Colchester Royal Grammar School. He abandoned a degree course in anthropology at University College London to spend most of 1967 and 1968 as a dropout in and around San Francisco, followed by several years drifting in the US, Europe, the Middle East and Asia. He settled in the Languedoc region of France, where he worked as a truck driver.

In 1978 Andrew Sanger returned to England and became a freelance journalist contributing to a wide spectrum of British national newspapers and magazines, winning awards for his travel features and for ten years editing French Railways' travel magazine, *Top Rail*.

Andrew Sanger is the author of more than forty guidebooks, and two other novels, *The J-Word* (2009) and *The Slave* (2013). He lives in London with his wife Gerry.

For more about Andrew Sanger, see www.andrewsanger.com.

LOVE

ANDREW SANGER

FOCUS BOOKS
London, England
www.focus-books.co.uk

Copyright © Andrew Sanger 2015
This edition published by Focus Books
ISBN: 978-0-9558201-3-7
All rights reserved worldwide
www.andrewsanger.com

―――――

The right of Andrew Sanger to be identified as the author of this work has been asserted by him in accordance with the Copyright, Designs and Patents Act 1988.

―――――

Historical events are described and real people mentioned, but the story and all its characters are fictitious. Any other resemblance to real persons is coincidental.

―――――

Proper names are spelled as was usual in 1967-1972 (list at end).

―――――

THANK YOU
Peter Shenai, for creating the cover of this book.

FOR GERRY AND JOSH

I need to know who lays claim to my past.
Who, of all those I was?
I am those that are no more. For no good reason
I am, in the evening sun, those vanished persons.

Jorge Luis Borges

* * *

For this is all a dream we dreamed
One afternoon, long ago.

The Grateful Dead

* * *

There just ain't no percentage in
Remembering the past.
It's time you learn to live again
And love at last.

Taj Mahal

* * *

You, who are on the road
Must have a code, that you can live by
And so, become yourself
Because the past is just a goodbye.

Crosby, Stills, Nash & Young

Prologue and Epilogue

Yesterday Angela stepped back into his mind as though she'd never been away. That knowing smile, the sardonic expression, her steady gaze; he even half-heard her voice, saying his name.

All the windows had been wide open. An exquisite current of summer air passed through the room. A single, cooler gust flicked one corner of an Indian wall-hanging. Dozens of tiny mirrors woven into its fabric caught the sunlight, scattering a confetti of reflections around the room.

Simon's eyes followed the speckles of light as they flew like a flock of tiny birds over the pale wooden floors and white walls, and vanished. And as he looked, there she was, as if right beside him.

He bought it for Angela, that hanging. In the end he had to keep it for himself. He shook his head as if to deny the memories. In his mind he could see the water of the lake, the carved wood of the houseboat, a mist in the distance hiding the Himalayas. He heard the splashing of oars:

This guy rowed up alongside my boat and called out. He offered me some wall-hangings. He had a whole stack of them, brightly colored, each one patterned with imperfect geometry. I bought the best of them for Angela and he rowed away. Then I realized it was too late to give her anything.

Those acid days passed long, long ago. Burned off like a California fog, and we came down at last, down and down. And the hair was cut and dried, and babies born, faces lined, and that endless summer ended, and was forgotten, or remembered, or mis-remembered, and became legend.

Oh, to hold on to time! And keep the days, the years that belong to us, and never lose them. A whole life is but a single moment, the present day a mere shimmering surface.

Dark, dripping foliage overhangs the path. Simon puts his hand in Milly's, and they walk like that, hand in hand, slowly between the stone columns. On every side, heaped white cloud froths above billowing treetops. Thanks to the downpour, they have it all to themselves, this dreamlike place, the high walkways of a pergola hidden in Hampstead Heath. Roses and jasmine twine around its pillars, spreading leafy tendrils. Underfoot, big puddles lie on the brick pathway, pink and white petals floating in the water.

'I remember when this was in ruins,' Simon murmurs. He knows, of course, that they both remember.

'They made a lovely job of restoring it,' Milly says as she has said several times before, and Simon as usual agrees.

'I used to come here to draw,' he tells her lightly. This too she has heard before. 'And I used to walk here with Angela.' At once he wishes that name had not slipped from his thoughts and been said aloud.

Milly looks at him surprised. She knows well enough that Simon lived with Angela in a little cottage nearby. She called on him there once, a disastrous occasion. Normally they do not refer to that time, nor to that name.

She sees the same young man beside her still, as if old age were nothing but a guise, though his youthful slimness was lost long ago, and the last of Simon's long blond tresses are these days clipped as short and silvery as steel pins.

'Something must have reminded me.' Simon takes Milly in his arms. He touches her forehead with his lips in silent apology. Her face, too, is only a reminder of the young and pretty face it used to be. The brown eyes, though, cautious as a doe's, are the same; and the dark, straight hair, although now cut in a neat bob streaked with grey; and she remains always and always the girl he once knew. No more is said about Angela.

Reaching a little footbridge, they pause again. Simon leans over its carved parapet and looks down. There is no one on the path below.

Yet he sees a young man there, wearing bangles and beads and patched, flared jeans, and with long hair and a full, wild sandy beard. Beside him, a young woman in flowing ankle-length skirt, with hair even blonder, golden. Now the young man looks up and catches his eye. For an instant, neither knows which is the ghost.

On the bridge, Milly turns to Simon. What is he staring at, down there? She looks over the parapet, but sees no one.

On the path below, it is Angela who glances at Simon curiously. She follows his gaze up to the parapet. But there is nothing.

Summer 1968

Ragged crescents of eucalyptus leaf lay on the narrow trail, and eucalyptus scent burned the air. Between the trees, long grass grew brilliant and golden. A few rocks, half hidden by bushes, jutted into little Lake Anza. On one of them a girl sat facing the water.

Everything glowed in the sun's bright light. Shimmering blue silk sky cast iridescent reflections in the lake. Two ducks flew past, their wings creakily beating, almost touching the surface, and were gone. Blue dragonflies silently weaved patterns over the ripples.

I stood concealed in cool shade, my feet bare on the earth. She gazed with rigid, determined immovability. Her great mass of wavy blonde hair really was flaxen – as yellow as the grass – and her blue jeans, faded and embroidered, tight across thighs and hips, were rolled up over wet ankles. The loose shirt was of some gauzy cotton voile, tie-dyed or batiked with circles of color.

For a moment I lingered, looking, wondering how to make an approach. Clearly she wanted to be alone. I walked away, the ground moist underfoot. Then all at once I halted, for ahead of me a majestic dog, a huge German Shepherd, stood pulling, gnawing savagely, at a massive log that lay across the path. His ruddy mane swung from side to side as the powerful shoulders labored, and his white fangs tore at the wood, yet he could not move it.

Sensing my presence, he turned, without menace. There was even something of a good-humored smile in his canine features. He seemed safe, I judged. Stepping over his log, I gave it a tug, as if to help. Suddenly the great jaw had moved onto my hand, a sharp tooth ripping the flesh on one finger. I cried out and jumped back in pain and horror as blood gushed out.

'Sirius!' A quiet, forceful, female voice. The girl stood right beside me – I looked up, startled. It was thrilling that she had come so close, but now I saw that she was not as pretty as I had imagined, though her nipples visible beneath the thin cotton compelled glances. The face was rather round, the cheeks dimpled, with a small chin, but the mouth was drawn too tight, as if touched with contempt. The hair, a cascade of golden threads, looked as if it had been shot through with electricity. She was a lot older than me, well into her twenties.

It was just a gentle rebuke, and she patted the dog. Our eyes met, hers arresting, half-mocking, blue as cornflowers, disconcerting. I did not want them to turn away.

'You OK?'

'Yah. Could get infected though,' I declared.

She turned to look at my hand. 'Oh, I doubt that. Cover it up, keep it clean. It's just a graze.' Her perfect white smile brought Sirius' pointed teeth to mind. The dog pressed his nose to drops of my blood on the ground, sniffing with interest.

'I tried to help him shift that log.' I heard a note of apology in my voice, and could have kicked myself for it. It was she who should be saying sorry. Sirius moved away and again pulled on the log with his great jaws.

Her deliberate stillness and calm made me feel foolish. 'Yeah, I was watching.' That pleased me: she had been watching. I imagined myself through her eyes. 'He's been working on that for months. I've never seen it budge an inch. He didn't mean to hurt you. You shouldn've put your hand there.'

That was probably all the apology she would give, which was none. I dabbed at the bite with a blood-soaked handkerchief.

'He's had all his shots,' she added. Now her gaze rested longer on the cut, a glistening red line from knuckle to tip along the fourth finger of my left hand. A slight frown; and she hesitated. 'That actually does look sore.' Then, 'Call me if there's a problem, and we'll deal with it. There won't be, but you know, just in case.' My heart leapt. She wrote on a scrap of paper.

'What's your name? I'm Simon.'

Without an answer, she had already turned away. Sirius followed with bounding energy. On the paper was the word *Angela* with a number. I slipped it into my jeans pocket, and continued to walk. Under the handkerchief, the blood on my finger had already dried.

* * *

The delicate mist that afflicts San Francisco on summer mornings hung over the rooftops. Slowly it lifted and cleared, revealing the radiant blue of another fine day. I sat in a rocking chair on the porch, the sketchpad on my lap. To capture the translucent fog in pen and ink proved beyond me. Watercolor might work better, I thought, if I were any good with watercolors. The air in the shaded street was exquisitely cool with the promise of warmth to come. Windows and doors stood open, the scent of marijuana drifting.

I went back inside, the screen door banging shut. The rooms of the house were spacious, almost unfurnished, and the wooden floors uncarpeted. Paint peeled from the woodwork.

Around the breakfast table there was idle, dreamily ill-informed talk about events across the country and in Europe, the straight world, as we called it then, the unhip world, the world outside. All the upheaval, in Paris, in Berlin, in Prague, I pictured in waltz-time, in formal dress, danced in crumbling baroque ballrooms. From this kitchen it's seen as a whole planet engulfed by a wave of freedom and imagination.

Someone said they liked the look of Eugene McCarthy, the anti-War Democrat senator campaigning to be elected president in next November's elections. Some laughed at the idea of believing his promises. Meanwhile, the Peace and Freedom Party sprouted and blossomed like a surreal hybrid of flower power, people's power and Black Power. That too brought a smile. It didn't have a hope. Nobody would vote for such a bloom except people like us, and people like us wouldn't vote, or were too young, or had burned our ID. I was a foreigner in any case, so had no vote to cast. In the end peace and freedom would win anyway, we argued, win the entire earth, not just the State of California. In the meantime, the only sort of party we supported was the kind with plenty of dope, music and sex.

The house phone was in the living room. I struggled to clear my head, to stop being stoned, and dialed the number.

Angela asked if my hand was OK.

'It's fine. But I'd like to see you again,' I said.

'I knew you'd phone, man.' Of course she did. Guys always phone.

'Did you know what you'd say?'

A long instant of silence before she answered.

'That it'd be cool.'

'I thought you didn't want me to call.'

'Yeah, well, I changed my mind.'

During the afternoon she drew up outside the house in a big old Chevrolet, a huge expanse of ornate 50s Americana like a cinema organ. Sirius stood across the back seat and gave me a toothy smile.

I slid onto the seat next to Angela and frankly felt awed. She was much more mature, more self-assured, more experienced, quite out of my league. Her Californian tan and easy physicality almost scared me. No girl-next-door this, but a very adult woman. I was excited like a lion tamer entering the lion's cage.

Cool, man. Pull back that dressing, let's see where Sirius bit you. Shit, man, there isn't a mark there – you faked the whole fucking thing, man. Hey, there's gonna be a fucking scar there, man. Scarred for life, yeah. Really. Anywhere you wanna go? Just ride through Berkeley. See what's happening on Telegraph. Cool, man.

It struck me that she was just about the only American I'd met who hadn't remarked on my English accent.

Her every word and every movement seemed calculated and hinted at something obscure, a deeper meaning. Something about her made me nervous. It was some trick of the voice. Everything, even the changes of mind, felt planned. As if she had planned it when the wind blew strands of her hair onto my cheek.

'What's your sign?'

She grinned at the predictable question. 'Scorpio.'

'I knew it! The worst,' I grimaced.

Angela chuckled. 'Wow! Shit, man – Scorpios ain't so bad. We're just misunderstood! What's *your* sign?'

'Scorpio.'

Again she laughed, with real mirth. 'Jeez, fucking Scorpio! What d'ya have rising?'

Oh, we all knew about such things. Sun in Scorpio in the twelfth house, Moon in Taurus in the sixth, Libra rising…

North on Telegraph Avenue. Teeming, exuberant life, musicians, dope hawkers and peddlers, people calling out their wares, the sound of flutes, drums. She turned past the campus. UC Berkeley had basked in radical cachet since the Free Speech Movement, but things were racing forward now, and had taken a strange turn away from political debates and activists' meetings. Some of the longhaired students looked scholarly, just youthful Americans in school. But acid was changing that. Others didn't know any more where school began and ended.

Angela turned a corner. Along Bancroft, beside the campus. Up Shattuck. Now we climbed into residential hills that rose above Berkeley. Here professors, not students, made their home. The neighborhood was respectable, peaceful, restrained. No riotous children played alongside heavy traffic. Instead, sprinklers sprayed, irrigating flowerbeds and green lawns. Angela's car, broad and stately in the tinny American style, swept along nearly empty roads.

Her house was square and solid, surrounded by a garden. Sirius bounded out of the car, barking with frenzied eagerness as he ran to a side door. Angela and I followed, a little too close together on the narrow side path. Though we had not touched, not so much as shaken hands, the possibility of intimacy crackled between us. I longed for it, yet had a sense of getting far out of my depth. I walked into her domain. Inside, the decoration and furnishings were shockingly expensive and unhip, as though she were in disguise, a spy in a safe house.

She put on some music, a folksy zither version of *Pack up your Troubles*. 'What is that?' I asked.

'Don't you know them?'

I didn't. 'Richard and Mimi Fariña. They played a lot of open-air, free stuff. I knew Dick – Richard. He was half Irish, half Cuban. What a mix! Not surprising he was heavy into politics. He wrote a great book, too, called *I been down so long it looks like up to me*. You *must* have heard of that. But he got killed in a bike accident a couple a years ago. He was a great, great guy, a genius. I loved him. Mimi is Joan Baez' sister,' she added. 'She's far out too. She lives over in Mill Valley. I like her a lot.'

'So, I mean – do you know Joan Baez as well?'

With a laugh, she said she did. 'We'll go over there sometime.'

'OK.' I tried to sound nonchalant. We sat at a kitchen table with cups of weak tea and slices of a cake she'd baked. That *sometime* meant she and I would be together on another day in the future. It took me a while, talking over tea, to realize she knew everyone. Everyone on the West Coast music scene.

Whenever her eyes met mine, they peered with unnerving steadiness. I could not look, yet could not look away. Even at this stage, in our first hours together, I was thinking of Angela as an 'experience' rather than as a girl or a woman. Certainly this was not like any previous encounter. Though wary, I wanted to go on at least until we had slept together.

Maybe she could see what was in my mind. Suddenly she got up from her chair and went to a work surface, as if to prepare a meal, though she just stood there lost in thought.

'Leave me alone for a while. Take a look at the garden. It's lovely.'

I opened the back door and stepped outside. The late afternoon air was still, clear and mellow. A tiny square near the door was paved in red stone. Three small trees stood crowded together. They bore some citrus fruit: one might have been a variety of mandarin, one looked like a cross between orange and grapefruit, and the other I recognized as a lemon tree. Some of the lemon's yellow leaves lay scattered on the red paving.

Beside the trees, in their shade, a rough wooden table with benches made a rustic scene. Impossible to believe this was an American city! I sat, then lay, on the dry grass and squinted into the shining sky.

At last Angela emerged from the house and sat on the grass beside me. She asked, very brightly, about the journey across America, and about my life. 'What are you into?' 'I don't know. Just hanging around. Drawing pictures. Traveling. Music 'n' stuff.' In good humor, she asked about England. She knew it as a place supposedly resounding with great music. It brought the Beatles, the Rolling Stones, Pink Floyd, Cream to mind. She had not heard of the dozens of lousy bands who, I told her, filled the British charts. She had heard of Carnaby Street, of Swinging London, of Liverpool and the Mersey Sound and thought it meant something – something more, that is, than mere commerce (didn't know, of course, where Liverpool was).

As the first months of 1968 turned to spring, the upheaval on the West Coast – bright, amazing flares of liberation – had drawn me forward like a grail. At last I reached San Francisco, and it proved no disappointment, a forest fire was igniting here whose the flames must engulf the whole world. More than that, another liberation promised to be greater than all, a liberty beyond politics. For a while, I drifted in and out of the Bay area, breathing the exhilarating air of a revolution of mind.

There was a party mood, musicians on the loose, longhairs, dope heads, acid freaks, greeting each other, friends and strangers, with a sign, an understanding, a recognition in guileless eyes.

Love 15

A girl in the street put a tab – of acid, she said – into my mouth, and I swallowed. I met another girl and told her I was tripping: she walked with me, held my hand, protected me, as we went wide-eyed through the city, until at last she took me home and put me in her own bed, in her house, the house where Angela had just picked me up.

In the garden, Angela told me about herself. It was all unremarkable: her name was Angela Olsen, she was born in 1944, grew up in Los Angeles, majored in Spanish at a private college down there. Then she mentioned someone called Jesse. Pronounced 'Jessie'. She had lived with him for years in Berkeley. 'I loved him. Man, I loved him.' Then last year he had gone, rejecting her, to India, where he intended to remain forever.

'What's he like?'

'So sweet and nice. And unusual. I can't say what it is about him.'

Especially since the Beatles moved in with the Maharishi this year, India meant the spiritual way to turn on, tune in and drop out of a hung-up, fucked-up West. Jesse's case, Angela told me, was different. He was not at an ashram, not meditating, not in thrall to any guru, not lost to drugs nor repudiating them. He simply wanted to get away from her, had quit the States to get away from the draft, was interested in India and ended up on the staff of a university out there.

'Are you still in love with him?'

'I guess I am.' Angela said she missed him terribly, and longed to have his child. That was the thing she wanted most in this whole world.

I did not quite believe this tale of fidelity and devotion. If Angela really could look into my mind, she knew that I had already started calculating how to tempt her to spend at least a single night with me. My own nerves were taut with anticipation. Surely she had indeed seen my thoughts, for now she added that she did not 'feel ready' to sleep with 'someone else'. Jesse was too close.

'All right,' I agreed.

Afternoon turned into evening, a change barely perceptible at first, the evenings being without the chill I had grown up with. A delicious aroma of cooking drifted from the open door of the kitchen.

As we walked into the house, Angela opened a cupboard, took out a large brown-paper bag (of the sort given to customers by American grocery stores) and dumped it on the table. With a smile she proposed, 'Hors d'oeuvres?' My nose knew before my eyes that it was full to the top with marijuana.

'Wow, man. Fucking wow. Where d'ya get this?' I asked. According to the Berkeley Barb, a shortage of dope had struck the Bay Area. Now I could see where most of it had gone.

'From my friendly neighborhood dealer – where else?' She sat at the table to roll a joint.

'It looks like you're dealing the stuff yourself,' I ventured. I had not been able to understand how she came to have so much money, and it was uncool to ask. With a whistle at the mere idea, she replied, 'No! All for personal use.' She grinned. 'Of course, every woman has her price.'

It struck me that we would indeed be sleeping together this night. It was a certainty.

'And by the way,' she said, 'if ever you want a tab of acid, just ask.' She opened the fridge and took out a big plastic tub. Inside were hundreds – no, it looked more like thousands – of tiny orange tablets. 'Recognize it? Genuine California Sunshine. One hundred percent Good Stuff. This lot's fresh off the press. We'll take some together one day.'

Again a promise of being together in the future! At that moment the thought of an acid trip with this scary woman alarmed me. If she could already look straight into my mind, she'd certainly be able to if it were stripped bare by LSD.

Angela took out a single tab, wrapped it in foil and handed it to me before putting the box back in the fridge. 'Remember there are two trips in those tabs. That's two hundred seventy mikes. Cut it in half, unless you're ready to lift the top right off your head.'

She had made a rich and succulent vegetable casserole and a pan-full of brown rice. Food, too, had started to become an issue. The meat industry, chemicals, profits, farming, additives, people were taking up new positions, asking new questions, finding new answers. *You are what you eat* was the cry. *Natural* was news. *Organic* was news. *Yin and yang* was news. *Whole foods* were news. Ours was to be a revolution of neither ballot nor barricades, but of body and soul. It was to be fought in private, between the sheets, at the dining table and in the supermarket, even inside ourselves. We were the battleground, uncertain what might be won or lost.

Music I didn't recognize was playing, she put on records I'd never heard, folksy stuff, jug band sounds, beautiful jazzed-up blues.

After dinner, Angela suggested we drive into the hills and take a look over the Bay. She said it was 'like a jewel box' at night. The last, faint light of evening lingered in the air, and by the time we reached Angela's high point, it had become dark. Below us the thousands of streetlights in Berkeley and Oakland looked indeed like sparkling luminous strings of shining pearls and diamonds, and the Bay as black as velvet. Lights on the hills of San Francisco flickered through mist over the water.

Around us hung a silence that actually seemed to muffle sound. We stood for a few moments beside one another, almost like an old couple, though we were still strangers. It might have been a moment to touch her, but I held back, uncertain.

We were close to Tilden Park, and drove to the entrance. Leaving the car, we took the very same path I had followed the day before.

Lake Anza was perfectly still tonight. Frogs croaked in some cryptic sequence, and splashed into the water as we came near. Now we saw that it was not dark after all: the moon had risen, casting a pale whiteness over the leaf-laden branches of trees ahead and behind us.

We came at last to the rocks, those on which she had been sitting when I saw her for the first time, yesterday. The scene was reconstructed in a dreamlike night setting, this time with me in the picture, not merely watching. Angela stepped with care to the furthest rock and sat down. I followed and placed myself alongside her.

She stared into the water, then into the silver sky, as if she had forgotten me. Like yesterday, I did not want to disturb her meditations. The pale darkness like a blue fabric enclosed us. The rich silence too seemed something close and physical. There was a gust of wind and the movement of some small animal. A leaf fell – and by chance landed on her knee, balancing there on her jeans. We both glanced at it with surprise. I touched the leaf with one finger.

Angela looked up, cautious. 'Trying to cop a feel?' she whispered.

At once, before the impulse could be halted, my hands held her. Without hesitation she acquiesced, and in an instant we were caressing, tasting, exploring, thrilled, reveling in one another.

At last our mouths parted. She stroked my cheek with her fingertips. '*That's* the way to cop a feel.'

No mention was made of not sleeping together, or not feeling ready. We drove back to the house and she simply led the way upstairs to her bedroom. Later, we lay close together, warm and satisfied, the sheets thrown back. A strand of moonlight reached across the room.

Into her ear I murmured 'I thought you said you didn't want…'

I could see her smiling to herself in the dark. 'Yeah, well, I changed my mind.'

Sunlight streams in a golden haze through half-drawn curtains. The bed is warm, the pillows soft. I put one hand over Angela. She is still sleeping. I close my eyes and see California's great fields of yellow, great skies of blue. This is purest, unimaginable summer, a summer to last forever and ever.

All the past seems remote. London I remember as if seen in darkness. All Europe appears as some dusty Gothic mansion, its ancient east and west wings, alike vast, within walls of centuries. Each room a nation, piled high with decay, laden with rich waste, rags and torn scraps, unreadable pages of the past, airless with the odor of time. Now a dazzling light from the West pierces its narrow windows, and through the grime can be seen – a new world, a new life, Outside.

This is the very place, this town where I lie in bed beside Angela in the late morning, from here the light comes, here everything new is being tested and made. Acid, acid, seven, eight, nine, ten trips since I arrived here – I can't remember them all – Window Pane, White Lightning, Microdot, California Sunshine, blue tab, white tab, yellow tab, drops on blotting paper, they melt together in my memory – though none with Angela yet. If everybody does this, the world will change totally. And it looks like everyone will do it. The acid summer begins to burn.

Strangers' glances in the street, eyes open, instant translucent bonds of understanding, I'm tripping, you're tripping. The acetylene of acid will torch away the trash, the cluttered past. All time will be one moment, the long moment of a life, of all our lives. We will burn politics with acid, wash away the twisted emotions and baby frailties at the core of society. Every one of us, struggling with our own dizzying acid revelations, eyes forced open on the stark page of… one's self: inner conflicts and unconscious obsessions, will one day finally get our heads together – grow up and away from all this, and be at last what a human being can be. Cut away the layers of hypochondria, paranoia and egotism. Scour out our insides, source of this emotion. Scorch all that stuff away and let in a light like there's never been.

To have no past, what freedom! Yet we are the past, every cell the living past. Sunlight makes a warm glow through closed eyelids. At London's anti-war, anti-American demonstrations, in great crowds we still move under moist skies in Trafalgar Square or outside the fortress American embassy in Grosvenor Square guarded by its phalanx of horsemen. Chant and yell, stop traffic, pelt police, draw blood.

Name? Simon Shaw. *Age?* 19. *Are you now or have you ever been a communist, a homosexual?* No, I just lie around in my room listening to music, or discuss politics in other people's dim, dirty bedsits. Socialism, nihilism, anarchism. Homosexual? Nah! For a laugh once, my friend Paul and I, we sucked each other's pricks. Is that homosexuality? Never again, though! Ugh! I discovered that come tastes like rotting fish. Not that I've tasted rotten fish. *Have you ever taken drugs?* Taken drugs! Perish the thought! No, no, no, no. *Will you seek employment in the United States?* No fucking way, man. I'll scrounge and beg, I'll borrow, call on friends of friends. I'll do a little mild wheeling and dealing.

The richness of the life here is new to me. I have never lived in such a house. With such a bathroom, such sumptuous bedrooms. We eat breakfast in the garden. The shade of the lemon tree rests over us. The dry yellow-green leaves against the blue sky, the red tiles by the door, our glasses and plates on the wooden table. There is no sound. Is this anything more than a long, luxurious holiday, my own American dream? She, though – Angela – is not a holiday from which I shall ever return home, nor a dream from which I shall ever awake.

Angela's influence cannot be resisted. I yearn to please her, with no idea how. Even as we lie half-uncovered in the warm mornings, she seems controlled and self-assured. She speaks quietly, often wry or amusing, never chatters. Her composure is frightening. All she says and does is weighed, considered in an instant. She seems to watch every muscle as I move, as I walk, stand, wash, sit, dance; scrutinizes my face as I talk; listens attentively to subtle, unheard undertones. I sense her constant disapproval. She disapproves of my behavior but says nothing. I try to check myself. To be as dignified as her. For Angela to consider me an equal, this is my goal. What on earth can her goal be?

I try to see myself through her eyes: slender English boy in blue, a naïve visitor with a sketchbook and all the time in the world. Long, long pale hair flows over my shoulders, and a tawny mustache over an innocent white smile. She says I look a lot like him. Like Jesse.

Jesse, she says sometimes. Jesse. It's Jesse she loves, loved, will always love. But Jesse went away and left her behind.

At first she wore a shirt and Levi's. As weeks and months have gone by, more and more, flowing skirts, long smocks, tee shirts, everything swirling with color, tie-dyed, batik, printed, painted, embroidered, appliquéd, crochet, hand knitted.

Angela lets colored cloth into my jeans to flare them, and colored cotton patches where the denim has worn through, and patches on patches where *they* have worn through. She has embroidered leaves and curling green stems and bright flowers onto my cotton shirts. The Old West chic of American denim, blue as the summer sky, and pale leather like the horizon of dried out grass, fringed jackets, embossed boots, wide belts, broad-rimmed hats, was giving way to the acid kaleidoscope.

Angela was already nostalgic for an even more golden age two years ago, when acid was so new it was still legal, and she with her friends had taken it like explorers taking the first steps on another planet.

No politics discussed, no angry plans made, no Utopia mapped out. Just dope and music, dope, music, and a heady knowledge of being in the forefront of history while suspended motionless in time.

The war, the war, the war, the war, the war, was the mantra here. Vietnam. Vi-et-Nam. Nam. Nam. Nam. Nam. I picture rich, heavy foliage, thick green leaves dripping with tropical rain. All the young men would be drafted. They would all be sent to Nam. From these paved streets and wide cars and big supermarkets they would depart to fight the Vietcong. The Cong. The Cong. The Cong. I picture taut, determined yellow-skinned men with expressionless faces. 'Hell no, We won't go' was the great shout of rage and fear rising from American guts. As a foreigner, I did not have that to deal with, but then, nor did the women.

Men faked draft exemptions or burnt draft cards. For their 'protest', men could go to prison, but instead they became anonymous, disappeared, drifted, dropped out. Police stopped cars, every day hundreds of times, asked to see men's papers – their 'Ah Dee'. But they had no ID, no social security number, no papers at all, or false papers. No young man was anyone any more.

Then time began again, in an explosion of dope and street life, color and tangled threads, wild fringes and flares and patches and batik and beads, headbands and bells, transparent voiles and naked skin and the scent of patchouli. The pedigree is pure American: half Indian Nation, half Hollywood Western, but worn and ripped and splashed with rainbows. Like an acid trip seeping out of the privacy of the brain, running into the fabric, into the streets themselves.

* * *

We drive to the supermarket in downtown Berkeley. The light is too sharp down there, the heat moist and oppressive, sidewalks too crowded, too many cars, madmen, policemen. Yet there's a wild, steamy good-time feeling, black and white street musicians together, exuberant, classless, race-less, anything-goes sound of drums, clarinet, saxophone, the air hanging with the fragrance of dope, men and women half-dressed hand in hand, kissing, dancing, laughing. We return to our cloistered world in the hills. In the tree-lined roads of Kensington a cool silence seems to have settled permanently.

Rolling joints: not tea-ceremonies of dope in dark rooms, as in England, but quick and easy, a twist of dry, fragrant greenery. In the car, in the garden, in the street. Just sprinkle the grass onto the paper, roll it and light up, inhaling deep, deep into body and soul. At once there's a smile in the air. Or for something stronger, crumble hashish into the grass, break up the soft brown lumps with your fingertips.

More grass and more music, each note alive and separate, background harmonies jumping to the foreground, rhythms insistent, repetitions vivid, the sounds inwardly visible and tactile. Not just rock, even mellow folksy singers, or country and western, classical as well, all music is evolving and mutating. Popular songwriters' banal lyrics trail behind the explosion of creativity, unable to keep up with the mood and mind of the times. *You don't know what is happening, do you...* From the saliva-soaked roach end of a joint, held with ornate silver 'roach clips' like a pair of tweezers, we extract the last breath of grass.

What a day for a daydream... We breakfast on the Lovin' Spoonful, move on to Jefferson Airplane, the Incredible String Band, Dylan, the Dead. Lunch on Country Joe as he sings cheerfully *One two three, What are we fightin' for, don't ask me I don't give a damn. Next stop is Vietnam. And it's five six seven, Open up the pearly gates. Ain't got time to wonder why, We all gonna die.*

Captain Beefheart, yelling messages of mayhem and mysticism, Frank Zappa's surreal rip-roaring madness. Later in the evening, though, Angela may succumb to Leonard Cohen's soothing melancholy. In bed before and after sex we tune in to FM radio stations broadcasting endless rock music without comment or ads – occasionally an address is given for cash contributions.

Acid freaks read messages in McCartney's ditty about *Strawberry Fields*. Then the Beatles too got into acid... yes, the whole world is coming our way: *All you need is love, Love is all you need.*

At this great party in history, a man and a woman catch each other's eye. And Angela's embroidery springs up on my shirts – flowers over a pocket, the sun and moon on left and right shoulders – and my jeans – scorpions, marijuana leaves, rambling wildflowers winding over the denim, around the crotch.

A part of me wants to leave, and be as I used to be. I am becoming her creation. Angela is weaving a web of silk around me. I remember the life before I met her – as if it were long ago! Although I may wish to leave, that cannot be. There is no going back to those days.

I was free then, before Angela, unburdened, in every sense unattached. That was another kind of dream, a glorious escapade, too good to be true. From the small world of an English childhood I stepped into the greatest adventure of our age. Soon, said tight-lipped voices in my head, we would be disciplined: we would tread again the narrow way, between the high fences of what is possible and impossible, and take our place in the eternal relay of lifetimes, each passing the baton to the next, normal-living and normal-dying, living-dying endlessly forward into nothing, just one among the uncountable dust of humanity, indistinguishable, infinite in number, in time, infinitely similar, infinitely repeating in unison, unanimous voices, radio and newspapers and television marching in time. Infinite souls born and spirits broken, neat haircuts, checking creases, brushing dandruff, clinking glasses, waving flags, supporting teams, taking loans, repaying loans, and buried under a normal, polite epitaph. Polite smiles and forms of words and the asthma of normality, the world built on conventions as strong as concrete and steel, fixed masks, shackles of culture. Routine and habit, prejudice and ignorance, the sins of the fathers and mothers learned and relearned unto the thousandth generation.

Now the concrete is cracking, the metal twisting. We are breaking our shackles, breaking out like weeds through the pavement.

Bedroom door closed, a teenage schoolboy in England lies naked under the blankets listening to Radio Luxembourg. Bob Dylan sings like an air raid siren and says the times are a-changing. Terse, drumbeat verses hammer out a warning. *Come gather round people. Come writers and critics. Come senators, congressmen. Come mothers and fathers. The line it is drawn.*

Kids at school look at each other and discover they are not the only one. And indeed, that it has happened to kids all over the world.

Something in the human heart wants a big change. It's started happening and we are the first to know. Everything must be torn away, ripped down from the windows like worn fabrics heavy with dust. Let the light and air pour in, the limitless light.

In waking hours, the present tense sweeps all before it. Whenever I sleep, people from the past meet together in my dreams.

The past is in London. There I am lying on cushions, reading Oz in a dimly lit bedroom, smoky with dope, the curtains drawn to keep out peering eyes. Frantic illustration and swirling text overlays color-sprayed columns: *THE LIFE .. I am trying TO GRASP – is the me – that is – to GRASP – is the me – THAT IS... grasp it...*

On the cover of Oz, 'new easy-to-read for over-thirties', a photograph of an execution in Vietnam. Blood runs down the page. It's the picture of police chief General Nguyen Ngoc Loan summarily executing a supposed Vietcong officer in a Saigon street, last February. But there's no caption. It's pure, timeless image, an icon.

Demonstrations every weekend in Hyde Park and Trafalgar Square. We go out just looking for one to join. Vietnam is the password to every protest. The war is full of symbols. *Defoliation.* News footage takes us face to face with a pre-industrial society, whose population work the land and are communists – so *they* can't get an American visa. *Please give blood for the Vietcong.* The Vietnamese are walking around with our blood in their veins. Bombed and dying, they shed our blood, it seeps into the soil. Runs down the page.

An epic for our times. Playing now on the stage of history. American soldiers in a major movie, a popular soap opera. We interrupt this war for a word from our sponsor. An episode shown every night all over the world. Who is the star of that execution on the Oz cover? Who played the victim? That's not real blood on the page. Vietnam is not a real place, it's an issue, an idea, our weekly street party. A parable we are telling. Vietnamese peasants in their attractive, chic loose cottons are artworks. Their suffering appears, Christ-like, the vicarious suffering of all. The straight world dances the dance of death, America destroys lush greenery, uprooting hidden fears in dark, shadowy undergrowth.

The Vietnam Courier and other Chinese bulletins on airmail paper lie on the floor alongside Oz. *Introduction of US and Puppet Troops into Demilitarized Zone another extremely serious war extension. 2,000 US troops wiped out in demilitarized zone in 4 days. Demilitarized zone turned into a battlefield. Chairman Mao receives military cadres. Situation is fine.*

I don't know what 'cadres' are; like 'intellectuals', they exist only in Peoples' Republics and are hard to visualize. But Mao is cool. He's hip. He's together. Shit, man, Mao's a poet! He's one of us, he wants to free us from the tyranny of the past. We like his snappy, scary phrases: Power grows from the barrel of a gun. Right on, Mao, man. All the same, he's a little off beam with that one. And with the barrel of a gun, you generally miss the target. Only drugs and love are sure to hit the spot. That's what will change the world. Still, *Cultural Revolution* is a great phrase.

Soon 'Vietcong' becomes 'National Liberation Front', and a dozen closer-to-home Liberation Fronts signal the war for all our freedoms, as though Vietnam and our movement were one, all of us on the same side. A hurricane rises from the Pacific. Yet in the background someone is singing a catchy Top Ten tune: *If you're goin' to San Fran Cisco – be sure to wear – some flowers in your hair – If you're goin' to San Fran Cisco – you're gonna see – some gentle people there...*

* * *

From London I arrive at San Francisco and wander amazed in the hilly streets. Across the whole city from Bay to Ocean, not one person wears a flower in their hair.

Golden Gate Park is pretty much a rectangle except for the long narrow strip which pushes into the Haight-Ashbury district, making the park look like a cooking pan. Haight-Ashbury and the pan's long, narrow handle is the stoned, sunny heart of the movement, the underground, the revolution. A lot of people hang around in that part of the park asking for spare change.

Lying on the warm, worn-out Golden Gate grass, I read Zap Comix. Crumb's cartoon-strips are alive. Everything is acid-hallucination real, rounded, three-dimensional. I move in closer and closer, discovering worlds within particles, particles within worlds. Mr Natural is my guru, he knows everything worth knowing. I would love to meet R. Crumb, the cartoonist, the real Mr Natural. Or is Mr Natural his guru too?

I fall asleep in the park, then stroll, yawning and waking, along Haight Street to pick up some copies of the Berkeley Barb. There's thirty cents to keep for every copy sold. The office, up some dark stairs, is filled with hair – guys with huge hair, two feet long, beards two feet across. One of them hands me a stack of Barbs, and I head back along the street with the papers over my arm, offering copies to passers-by.

On the corner of Ashbury, a guy is almost horizontal on the sidewalk. All around, dealers, merchants of the new consciousness, call out 'Acid, lids...' (a lid was a little bag containing an ounce of grass) and there is music in the air from sidewalk players. I grin at the guy on the ground, and he says: 'Wha's happenin'?'

I shake my head. 'Just... everything, man.'

'Yeeaah, man. Far out.'

'You seen the news?'

'Wha's 'news', man?'

I laugh and nod. 'Right on, man.'

'Yeah, keep clear a that shit,' he says. 'There's no news but what's happening right a-here where we're at right a-fuckin' now, man.' He smiles but I can see he is serious.

'So you don't know the whole of Europe is exploding, man?'

'Europe?' he frowns, as if to say, what's that?

'The whole population of the world smashing the whole fucking system,' I tell him. 'France, man – Paris – amazing – the whole business district burned out – yeah, it's the real thing, man. The workers in France are on strike – forever. The whole of France is with us. Wow. It's happening all over the world, man. Germany. Amsterdam. Poland, man – yeah, even places like that. China – you don't know about the Cultural Revolution? People rising up! Their thing is "Destroy the Old World, Forge the New". You dig that? Kids throwing teachers out of classrooms?' I laugh with glee at the thought. 'So far out.'

He gives a wry, patient, skeptical smile. 'That's cool, man. That's cool. *But do they do acid*? 'Cause, man, if they don't – all that Street Fightin' Man stuff is fucked. It's part of the system.'

'Yeah, cool. That's true. You're right, man,' I admit, chastened. 'So you don't want a Barb?'

'Yeah, I'll roll ya a joint for it.'

A dozen hippies, patched and unkempt, spaced-out and longhaired, the women in full, long skirts of thin cotton, park their bus near Fisherman's Wharf. I climb in, welcomed with smiles and a joint.

Traveling from farm to farm, picking fruit for a living, we sleep under the stars, swim in rivers cool under the inland Californian sun. In the bus are blankets on the floor and curtains at the windows, and here or on the ground outside we make love in assorted couples. Across the back of the bus are painted the words *In Love We Trust.*

We know what the driver in the Oldsmobile or Buick behind is thinking. Some people feel so strongly that hippies should be shot that when they hear the word *Love* they take their handgun out of the glove compartment, aim and pull the trigger.

An echoing metallic crack, a sharp whine of rushing air beside the face, and ringing like a church bell as the bullet strikes the pavement. But what a liberation to be able to believe in something not man-made, even if it is only Love.

Wearing few clothes, or none if farmers allow it, we pass a few hours each day picking the first cherries of summer. In the evenings we rest under the night sky, faces lit by the dark red glow of a fire. Someone plays a guitar. I lie with one of the women, slender and dark, staring into the deep well of space, watching the falling, shooting stars.

When we take acid together, the whole group, the mundane realities of their life vanish like a mist. The thin lines which describe them, us, as hippies or as fruit-pickers, are whitened out. These are no fruit-pickers – except on the other side of some looking glass where dreams are real and reality is dreams. Instead I see something like a religious service – a tight web of humanity, binding relationships, mutual confidence, shared belief shining bright.

And I see, just as clear, that their life isn't mine. I want to go further than the next fruit orchard. I don't belong here or anywhere, am merely passing through, and won't be staying – nor going back home, either. My destiny is elsewhere.

Their bus pulls up on Highway 80, the dark, starlight girl kisses me goodbye, and I hitch back to the house in San Francisco. What now? Tomorrow I might head over to Berkeley, check out what's happening there, maybe get a ride up to Tilden Park, take a walk round Lake Anza.

Angela's house is on one of those pleasant old streets where, for some reason, mail is delivered through a front door mail slot, instead of a curbside mailbox. A letter, addressed to me, lies on her doormat. My old school friend Paul sends a sporadic chronicle of the events in Europe. He seems to be at all of them. His bulging envelopes are decorated with stamps from different countries. The handwriting falls out, excited, on torn scraps, hasty dispatches as if scribbled while sheltering from the fire of battle. The very paper seems to give off teargas, jabbing mucus membranes.

Hurried, staccato phrases bring news, several weeks late, of the uprising in France, slogans, snatches of history. 'The spirit, the mind, the imagination are in revolt, walls covered with graffiti. People digging up cobbles to throw at the police. The French love the idea of Revolution – their finest hour. Heard a good speaker, Daniel Cohn-Bendit, a student at Nanterre. The press call him Red Danny.'

There's nothing about love and peace and acid. Paul is straying away from me, far along another path.

A page torn from a notebook: 'Bourse on fire. Cohn-Bendit back in Paris with black hair! Will press call him Black Danny now?'

Another envelope arrives from Berlin a month later. Pamphlets and leaflets, bizarre and alien in this quiet, sunlit room, tumble out onto the table, with pages of debate, theories, ideas, prophecy and visions, a meditative, mantra-like, stream of acronyms and abbreviations, word-game fractions of factions. Huge demonstrations chanting *Marx, Mao, Marcuse*. 'Marcuse says Americans and Europeans are rebelling not against the ills of modern society, but its benefits. The Situationists argue that what people are rising up against is not poverty or oppression, but boredom.' The Situationists have become entertainers in their own right: avant-garde vanguard of a TV-watching proletariat.

I see that political types like Paul are aiming, as we are, not for a change of government or even a whole new system, but for some meta-freedom, a transcendent fulfillment, perfect liberty of the heart.

On the next sheet, 'Something's going to happen in America,' he predicts, as if nothing has happened yet, while news bulletins show city streets lurid in flames, fast-moving youths starkly lit, crowds in flickering shadow, and a parade of stuffed shirts openly voice their fear of revolution. That, I suppose, is what Paul hopes is about to happen.

Then we learn that France has just had a general election, and the Gaullists, the rightist governing party almost toppled by the May uprising, has been re-elected with a bigger majority. So France is *not* full of revolutionaries after all! The strikes were not crushed, they were outvoted. All the politics of poetry and dreams have been brushed away, into the margins, the prisons, the graveyards or university lecture halls. Its heroes and guerrillas are back in the classrooms.

For some freaks, the news from France is an irrelevance. The unrest in America is what counts. For some of us, even that is remote. For the politicos, more disappointments are coming. It turns out China's Cultural Revolution is more complicated than we knew. In Eastern Europe, Russian tanks have turned the Prague spring back into winter. In California, the police are picking off the Black Panthers one by one, arresting them or shooting them dead. Around the world, the System is shoving back. All those who take up arms are gunned down. That Haight hippy on the sidewalk was right: Street Fightin' Man is just some straight on a dead-end ego trip.

Yet in the streets the real movement seems to be surging forward like a flood tide. Berkeley is its capital. Yes, Timothy Leary had the answer:

turn on to LSD, tune in to what's really happening, drop out of the system. Let the whole charade grind to a standstill. Mr Natural has the answer. Acid, dope, music.

And sex, yes, that is the answer, the only thing that makes Angela let go. Or maybe even then she is controlled, calculating. In clothes or naked. In mid-morning sunshine or by moonlight. The whole of one night was spent in the bathroom, long and slow, on the floor. At dawn we reeled like two drunkards into the bedroom. Soft, still morning, as fragile as fine china, was beginning to lighten the room. We crept under the sheets and slept.

* * *

Often there were drives out of the city to call on her friends, most of them not far away, up or down the coast, along Highway 1, skirting dry cliffs streaked with tough greenery. Sometimes we drove further, down to Los Angeles, to Laurel Canyon, to Beachwood Canyon. Most of the time I didn't know where we were, and it made no difference, only that the houses were astonishing, full of space and light and people and music, opened onto huge outdoor platforms and decks and verandas, and swimming pools and dreamlike settings, and belonged to pop stars and rock stars who greeted Angela with delighted hugs and kisses. We'd drift from one to the other. She was in fact making deliveries.

The hills reached long fingers into azure seas flecked with white, azure skies flecked with white. Headlands made barriers along the wild sunset-facing ocean. Once we stopped to strip off and run into the waves on Carmel's vast, flat beach, pelicans diving and scooping beside us.

Or head north on Richmond Bridge across the Bay into Marin County. We pulled up at drive-in diners and restaurants and ordered over a microphone, happily obliged to abandon our right-on food philosophy, and sat in the car with burgers loaded 'with everything' so my hand ached from stretching to hold them and my mouth could hardly open wide enough to take a bite, and sucking from two straws pushed into malted shakes as thick and sweet as treacle, like a trip to heaven when dope had given us 'the munchies'.

Everything Angela showed me came as a surprise. We drove over to Mill Valley to meet her 'dearest' Sasha, tense and wired, tall and tanned, restless and forceful, with cascading bright auburn hair; and Sasha's 'old man' Jack, who truly *was* old to my eyes; big, loud, swaggering, with ponytail and droopy mustache, the picture of a rangy West Coast neo-cowboy in high-heeled leather boots, fringed jacket and blue denims.

We were well into the visit before I realized who Jack was. Jack – Jack Hitchins – was the mysterious, legendary, elusive figure known to the underground press and the rest of the world as Doc, or The Doc, the hip super-chemist of whom I had reverentially heard and had no expectation ever to meet. To Sasha he was Jack but by anyone else, it seemed, he had to be called Hitch. It was never to be Doc in his presence. I was introduced to Jack's brother, Don, quite unlike him, incongruously retiring, fey, neat and conventional, almost straight-looking. It was they who, since the great Owsley went to jail last year, now manufactured the acid everyone was taking, the acid we would all take one day, the acid thrown from the stage at concerts, the best acid in America, the acid which was changing the world.

Sasha, I saw, was some sort of benefactor to Angela. Either that, or Angela was being paid for something. Sasha handed her great wads of banknotes and embraced her lovingly. Her view of me was that 'any friend of Angela's is a friend of mine'. I sensed secrecy and discretion, things I wasn't to be told or find out. They all knew Jesse, and looked me over in that light, comparing us. Yep, Simon *is* sorta like Jesse to look at. Younger, though. Skinnier. And the coloring, of course. And English. His eyes don't have that… and… well, Simon ain't Jesse.

The three of them, and others, and a dozen visitors, were all living at Jack Hitchins' ranch, hidden away in a fold of Marin County hills. I had never seen anyone, let alone freaks, living in such a way – with parkland and stables and paddocks, swimming pools and music rooms and dope rooms and private cinemas, and security gates at the end of long driveways. Where did the police think all the money came from? 'The music business,' answered Hitch.

From our first conversations Jack Hitchins suggested he was involved in some way with Jefferson Airplane and the Grateful Dead, and that they also spent time on the ranch, and he played guitar himself, and that one day he would cut a record in his own right. 'Hitch,' I said tactfully, 'the pigs must know you aren't a recording star – yet'.

'That's right, man. But you know, I also have my financial advice business, and a lot of bands, a lot of big names, they're my clients.'

'No, man, I didn't know that.' I could only guess what sort of advice Hitch would give, or whether this was even true. I didn't bother to ask anything more. The ranch lands extended to a cliff top overlooking the Pacific. Waves broke on rocks far below. A morning mist cleared by early afternoon, revealing wide, rough, beautiful ocean views.

On a shaded lawn by the house I lay naked alone. Sasha, in a slinky wrap-around like a sarong, approached with a package covered in silk. She sat beside me in the shade and said nothing. Unwrapping the bundle, she revealed a thick book and three strange coins. Tossing the coins onto the grass, she studied them and drew lines, continuous or broken, on a scrap of paper. Eventually she consulted the book, finding the same pattern of six lines illustrated. She read avidly.

'What are you doing, Sasha?'

'You don't know the Ching?'

'Nope. There's plenty I don't know.'

'True of us all, man,' she confessed. After a moment's hesitation, Sasha handed me the book, heavy and dense between hard covers. 'It's the I-Ching,' she explained. 'A Chinese oracle – you ask it questions. It can solve your problems, give you answers.'

'OK, I'd like to consult it now, show me how,' I said, sitting up.

She was curious. 'What do you want to ask?'

'Shall I leave Angela and go back to England? Or travel?'

Taken aback, she looked tempted to give an opinion of her own, or perhaps to ask if Angela knew about these thoughts. Instead, she said, 'That's two questions, or three,' and took me step by step through the I-Ching. The coins were copper or bronze, circular and thin, with a neat square cut from the center, and embossed with Chinese characters on one side. I threw them on the ground.

Sasha told me the side with the Chinese writing was yin and gave a value of 2. The other side was yang and gave 3. There were three yins, giving a total value of 6. Sasha drew a broken line. I threw again. Above the first line, Sasha now drew a solid line. Now a broken line, and another and another. The sixth throw gave a solid line at the top. Sasha looked up my hexagram in the book. It was shown there with the name Youthful Folly.

Youthful folly! I read the cryptic 'judgment': *It is not I who seek the young fool, the young fool seeks me.... Perseverance furthers.* Beneath it, a passage explained: *In the time of youth, folly is not an evil. One may succeed in spite of it, provided one finds an experienced teacher.*

The first and third throws both came up with a total of 6, so they, Sasha explained, were 'changing lines', providing their own judgments. The first said, *To make a fool develop, it furthers one to apply discipline. The fetters should be removed. To go on in this way brings humiliation.* The third added, *Take not a maiden who, when she sees a man of bronze, loses possession of herself. Nothing furthers.* And then, *A weak, inexperienced man, struggling to rise, easily loses his own individuality when he slavishly imitates a strong personality of higher station...*

Disturbing ideas, strangely relevant, yet they reached no conclusion at all. Was Angela the 'experienced teacher'? Was she the 'discipline' that should be applied, or was she the 'fetters' that should be removed? I recognized a warning in the lines about imitating a stronger personality, but in this imagery, who was the 'maiden' – Angela, or myself?

'What does it mean – should I go or stay?' I asked.

Sasha looked thoughtful. 'I can't say. The Ching speaks in riddles. Years later, you can see that a hexagram made sense. That's how you learn how to interpret what it's saying. It's a matter of following your own intuition. The I-Ching helps you with that.'

'Oh. So, when the problems have all been resolved anyway, you discover what the I-Ching was trying to tell you.'

She didn't catch the note of irony, nodding in thoughtful agreement. 'Is that your only choice, man? Stay with Angela, go back to England, or travel? What about, leave Angela and stay here in California? Or, travel with Angela? See, you didn't ask the Ching a correct question. Do you really want to leave her?'

'Well – she loves this guy Jesse, doesn't she?'

'We all do, man,' Sasha said wistfully. 'Beautiful guy. Artistic. Virgo, moon in Aquarius, Taurus rising.'

I assumed she meant he had a beautiful personality. 'Why doesn't she just get on a plane to India?'

'How can she? Like, chase him across the world? On her own? She'd be scared to do that. All the while knowing he doesn't want her? And then come back again? That's not the way. She's suffering inside.'

'*Exactly.* She wants him, not me. So I might as well split.'

'And go where? Back to England?'

'I don't know. Anywhere.'

'Want my advice?' Sasha offered. 'Yah, be with Angela awhile. Learn from her. Just don't try to become like her.' Having ended her I-Ching interpretation, she paused, then added, 'And don't get in too deep, man. She could break your heart like that' – she flicked her finger and thumb apart in a contemptuous gesture. 'I'm her friend, but I'm telling you that's the type of chick she is. And another thing: I would have had Jesse myself if I could. Except me and Hitch have a destiny. My place is with Hitch. Angela has a destiny, too. So do you.'

'What, you mean our destiny is together?'

'That's not what I'm saying. It's complicated.'

Maybe she thought she had hurt me, because now Sasha knelt down and put a hand on my shoulder. She began to stroke the back of my head – I supposed it to be a soothing, sympathetic gesture. 'Maybe you're already in too deep. Do you love Angela very much?' I did not reply, because I did not know the answer.

I remained silent. At first running through my hair, then her fingers were caressing it suggestively. Her eyes held mine, and as she turned, all at once our faces were close, our mouths almost touching. Her tongue shot out to my lips. She put both arms right around me. I put my arm around her slender waist. Her body through the cotton was soft, her breasts touched my bare chest.

'Kiss me. Kiss me, Simon. You do want to lay me, don't you? You want to fuck, don't you? I can see that you do.' she asked.

If she had said nothing, it might have happened. Now, alarmed, I shook my head. 'No, no, I don't, not right now. But we will do it – someday.' My guess was that Angela wouldn't like this, me with her good friend. I moved away and tried to put sex right out of my mind. 'What else do you know about, that's like the I-Ching?' I asked.

She laughed bitterly, 'Cool, man. You don't wanna, you don't hafta,' then stood and straightened her sarong. 'Find me in my room 'n' I'll teach you about Tarot. Really.' She went away with her book, and I lay troubled on the grass, hoping I hadn't annoyed her.

I tapped on the door. Sasha, now wearing a clinging silk dressing gown, answered with hair unkempt, nose red and running and eyes swollen. Had she been crying? 'You OK, Sasha?'

'I'm just great.'

'You sure? Is this a good time to look at Tarot?'

'Lousy time, but come on in.'

The room was hung with Oriental prints and full of delicate, exquisite objects, fine fabrics, hard to comprehend in a single look. There were pretty bedside lamps. She sat on the side of her bed, and the robe fell open high up her thighs. On a varnished bedside table a small pile of white powder lay on a piece of card, beside a razor blade. Without further conversation, she took up the blade and worked at the powder, cutting any larger pieces. Using the blade, she divided the pile into two, and made each into a long narrow line of powder.

'What's that, Sasha?'

'My medication. My pain killer. My wings of wax. My dreams of happiness.' As she worked, the robe opened further, to the patch of hair.

'Is it cocaine?'

'It is.' I had wondered if it were heroin. She took a banknote and rolled it into a tube like a drinking straw, and holding it to one nostril while she pressed the other shut, she breathed in sharply. The powder disappeared into her as if scooped up by a vacuum cleaner. She switched nostrils and breathed in the other half of the line.

She handed me the banknote and made space for me to approach the little table. I sat down beside her and breathed the white powder deep into first one nostril, then the other.

'You do much coke, Sasha?'

'Three times a day after meals. Or instead of meals.'

'Is that true?'

'No,' she said, 'it's not true. Here, give me a kiss.' She grasped the side of my head and leaned back on the bed.

Surprised, I kissed her lips and pulled away again, but her hands moved to my shoulders and urged me down. 'Whoa, now, Sasha. I'm not sure about this. What will Angela feel about it?'

She tugged at the buckle on my belt, but I held her hand to stop her.

'No, Sasha, not now. I'd love to learn about Tarot. That's all.'

'Wow! Playing hard to get! A guy that doesn't want to get laid! Far fucking out!' She laughed, unamused. 'I *want* Angela's English boy to fuck me.'

I thought to ask why, but stopped myself. A man's desire is never questioned. Why should a woman's? A man's desire is seen as healthy, and instinctive, a woman's as unhealthy. Wondering why I didn't just take off my jeans and have sex with her, I said, 'Sasha, Sasha. We will fuck a hundred times. It'll be far out, it'll be beautiful, but... not yet.'

'Promise?' she pouted.

'I promise.'

She rolled on the bed and turned her back to me. 'I'll talk to you about Tarot tomorrow morning.'

I slipped out of the room. Jeez, she's weird. The stars looked super-bright and super-sharp like shiny pieces of tin.

In the morning Angela gave Sasha a big hug, and to my surprise we said goodbye to Jack Hitchins' ranch and drove away.

'Where to now?' I asked her in the car.

'Anywhere. I need to get away from...'. She didn't say what, finishing vaguely, 'Get my head together.' She drove onto Highway 101, heading north through a hot, broad landscape, sometimes flat and dusty, sometimes jagged rock, sometimes soft, rolling pale green, that all added up to something like a bigger, emptier South of France. After a long spell of tight-lipped silence Angela asked, 'Did Sasha try to make out with you?'

'Yeah. But I told her I didn't feel cool with it.'

'Good, good. She used to do that to Jesse, too. I love Sasha dearly, but... yeah. She has some hang-ups. And a heavy coke habit.' A big sigh, a pause, a click of the tongue. 'Yup. Difficult sometimes, friends. All of 'em. Sometimes I hate my friends. Do you ever get that?'

In truth, I did. After several moments of silence, she added, 'She's had a whole slew of problems.'

I didn't ask what Sasha's problems were, and never found out. We smoked a joint and listened to the radio, a head music station. For no reason I could see, Angela suddenly turned off the highway, taking a narrow road through wooded hills down to a small town by a river, a picture-book American village. It wasn't till later that I figured out we were somewhere on Russian River. Some freaks had opened a funky old-fashioned country-style restaurant, spacious and airy with bare clapboard and floorboards and big wooden tables. Inside the fragrant air was warm and sweet with baking, and laid-back ponytailed hippy waiters brought bread fresh from the oven, huge portions of home-made pies and pancakes, thick and creamy ice-creams.

Tall, immensely wide redwoods, their fibrous wooden flesh flaking like roast meat, hid the river from the road. We strolled beside the band of water as it flowed shallowly over rocks and yellow sand. The sun shone warm in the soporific silence; there was an air of secrecy. Angela lay back sensuous as a cat on the soft bank and reached an arm round me for a long kiss. Afterwards we lay sleeping in the shade while a sweet breeze touched my back. Our clothes made a pretty heap of patched blue cotton. The clear water, the giant trees, made something trivial of us and our concerns, all history just a mist on their enduring world.

Returning towards the city, again with an FM station playing non-stop music, late afternoon sun glinting from the cars ahead of us. 'Angela, stop, stop! There's a couple of hitch-hikers.'

'Too bad,' she replied as we passed them at the edge of the tarmac.

'Hey! Those guys'll get busted for hitching while you just drive by.'

She laughed at my concern. 'Look, Simon, it was their idea to hitch somewhere. I don't owe them anything, and they don't owe me anything. We're free of that shit. Forget them.'

Through the ugly and the beautiful garbage and billboards, winding into American communities of gas-stations and burger drive-ins, and winding out again, Angela's big Chevrolet cruised between the eternal heaps of trash, used tires, American flags, grossness and waste.

There is a moment, when the beer can is still in the air, thrown from the car window to lie rusting beside the road. In that moment between consumption and conscience, there is the American Dream. The car has moved on, the hills in the distance are green, the roadside grass black with dirt.

* * *

Angela complained that the scene was *so* losing its way. People getting into speed, dealers dealing bad acid, too many *weekend hippies*. 'When even freaks are fucking straight, isn't that the fucking end?'

Worst of all, viewpoints were becoming fragmented. A slumbering nest of forgotten anxieties, nursery grievances and dangerous questions was stirring – about men and women, lust, power, love, biology, instinct, conditioning, stereotypes, children, parents.

Is it true that everything *ain't nobody's business but your own*? Is everything a free choice? Is nothing a free choice?

Women's liberationists were taking up Black Power's enraged call for separatism and self-interest. In June, Valerie Solanas had shot Andy

Warhol, and the bookstores had re-stocked her weird *SCUM manifesto, the Society for Cutting Up Men*. Plenty of women were already saying a man and a woman could never meet as equals, fucking is oppressive, all men are into rape. I noticed "No Men" painted onto a few doors.

Angela was dismissive. 'Mind games and power trips and politics! I mean, shit, man, what's happening to love and peace?'

Until now, men and women had welcomed the Women's Movement with equal joy. The real revolution at last: in psychology, not politics. Everything, everyone, everywhere without barriers or differences or hierarchy. Angela said, 'Drop acid and forget which sex you are.'

Sasha, Hitch or Don sometimes arrived without warning. These were not mere social calls. I understood now that Angela provided them with a warehouse and a safe house, a bed for the night, and a home from home hidden from view.

On one of his visits, I happened to mention to Hitch that he was lucky to have made so much money. He chuckled, 'Gree-een Power, man. Greenback Liberation Front.' Then he assumed a sober expression as one discussing weighty matters. 'That's cool, spare change to ease the way. But, no, the bread is only a consolation prize. It doesn't change anything. I mean, how much would it take to make *you* happy?'

'Uh, couple a hundred dollars?' I suggested, not quite in jest.

Laughing loudly and shaking his head at such a modest figure, he reached into his leather jacket, pulled out a bundle of notes and handed me two one-hundred dollar bills. 'Yours. Happy now?'

In truth, I was astounded and utterly thrilled. He insisted he was right: 'By tomorrow, that'll make no difference!'

Once, we stopped by at their 'acid house'. It was an unremarkable, tacky, wood-clad town house near a gas station on busy West Berkeley Avenue, the kind of quick-turnover neighborhood where people work on cars in the street and don't know or care who's living next door or what they're doing. There were curtains at the windows, a TV aerial, and a convincing kitchen visible from the street.

Inside, though, beyond the kitchen, the rest of the place was like a little factory, with wooden crates, glass jars and tubs of chemicals. Unused furniture had been pushed aside like items in a surreal artwork. It was hard to figure out which was more incongruous, the spotlessly clean worktables, spotlights, gas canisters and chemistry equipment, or the armchairs in the sitting room and beds in the bedrooms.

Out of that ordinary-looking front door came thousands of tabs of acid which reached every part of the world, or every part where hippies roamed. Most of it passed a few nights sealed in Angela's refrigerator. No acid was stored in the acid house, which would soon be dismantled and replaced with another.

Back at home, just the two of us again, Angela joked 'Come up and see my Tarot cards sometime, honey,' in husky come-hither tones. There was no suggestion now that she minded Sasha's behavior. 'Anyway, I can show you Tarot just as well as Sasha. Really,' she said. 'You want to learn about Tarot? With no strings? But – it's heavy. It's not a game.'

She worked through how Tarot cards can be used to see someone's destiny, but it seemed implausible – adding the numerical values of the letters in a person's name to their birthdate – and, then, like the I-Ching, the results were too obscure. It was all maddeningly indifferent to the strictures of ordinary common sense. Compelling pictures on the cards hinted at enigmatic truths, yet the dreamlike symbolism eluded me.

Angela had no such problem. She said she could see my future in The Tower. She handed me the card: a tower struck by lightning; falling with the masonry were droplets of light, a mighty crown and a man and woman. They fall haphazardly, helpless, hopeless, towards jagged rocks below. What could it mean? Was I, were we, heading for a fall? Now, or in life generally?

Angela's own destiny was the Three of Swords. We gazed at the grim image, a heart pierced by three swords. The meaning – heartbreak, pain, loneliness – seemed horrible and obvious. Why three, though? Why storm clouds gathering? Why no people in the picture, as in nearly all the others? Was Angela destined for loneliness? It seemed unlikely.

As I wondered aloud, Angela replied, 'Maybe it's better not to know. Keep our illusions a while longer.'

Abruptly she suggested we 'drop that Sunshine now.' I was caught unawares and unprepared.

Dropping acid together had remained for months the landmark which we must reach. No relationship was complete without that. It was an unnerving prospect, though. Angela would be able to handle whatever acid could do, and would see me stripped of all my own hopeless efforts to be cool, or calm or collected. We'd both be able to observe with horrible clarity how childish and foolish I was compared with her. (No doubt Angela could see all that in any case, with or without acid.)

She knocked one of the pills out of a container. Tiny, bright orange, the tablet lay alone on the kitchen table, dwarfed by other less powerful objects. Taking a razor blade from a drawer, Angela then divided it into two equal sections, working slowly and carefully. As the tab split, she picked up one of the halves and placed it in her mouth.

'Cheers!' she said.

I picked up the other half and swallowed it. 'You want to go up to the Park or something?'

'We'll get moving in about half an hour. Sure, we can go up to Tilden Park. Take it easy,' she said. 'Just relax. Ree - lax. You know.'

She went up to the bathroom and I remained in my chair at the table to compose myself.

The kitchen became increasingly cool and dark to my mind. A cavern. People still live in caves, I told myself, they haven't changed. In lots of other ways, too. Nor will they. Humans will always be human.

I called to Angela from the bottom of the stairs, as if from the bottom of a well. 'Hey, you ready?'

She called back, 'No. Wait a minute.'

I stood in the middle of the cave-kitchen and looked around, as if for inspiration or clues.

Why do I have to wait? Why can't I just go?

I began to move towards the door, then stopped myself. I'd need the car. Anyway, it would be bad for Angela's trip if I went out on my own.

Still, I felt too cramped in the little kitchen. The corners of the walls seemed to become more geometric and closer to me. A picture hanging on the wall above the kitchen table – a picture which I didn't recall even noticing until now – looked lurid. It was an artless display of color. I could feel the personality of the painter, his talentless frustration. As the room seemed to become smaller, the picture became larger. 'I must leave,' I said to myself. I hurried to the door and went out.

In the open air, I felt the mood of the kitchen subsiding like a wave drawing away. It was some moments before I again remembered I could not leave without Angela. I returned to the hard angularity of the house and went upstairs – like rickety, uneven steps in a Van Gogh painting.

The staircase was like a dark, low tunnel. It amused and frightened me. As I climbed, the sense of ascending from the ground was dizzying. Stacking rooms on top of each other struck me as impossibly, comically ludicrous. At last I reached the bedroom, strangely small and high above the ground. Angela was in there, not quite dressed, like some fleshy female animal, some human animal in her lair, soft rounded inviting shapes draped with thin cloth. So what did I look like? A male animal? How does that look? I glanced at my arms, my legs. Was that me? I stared in stark disbelief at a lean, hairy limb for a second, then glanced back at Angela. She was wiping a skin-cleanser on her face. It made her appear grotesquely self-absorbed. The biting aroma of the cleanser pierced the skin inside my nostrils.

'Hey, when you gonna be ready?' I asked her, startled to hear a note of anxiety in my voice. I looked to see if Angela had noticed it. Moving with an irritating slowness, continuing with what she was doing, she seemed hardly to have heard me at all.

So I tried again: 'I hate waiting around.' I realized that I did not know if it had been an hour or five minutes. Perhaps, after all, it *was* only five minutes. My voice sounded dry and strange in my ears. I heard the words re-echo in my thoughts, and wondered if I had said some of them twice. They seemed ambiguous.

With bovine docility, Angela turned and looked at me curiously.

'You getting off already?' she asked. 'OK, let's go, huh?' She grabbed my arm, pulled me into an embrace. I looked over her shoulder at the bedroom. It was peculiarly misshapen, the window tiny, the dim light transformed into a multitude of soft shadows. The fabrics, the textures, were rich and dark. The appearance of the room changed as my mood became more positive, the colors becoming warmer, more golden, the shadows lighter, even as I watched.

Leaving the house was truly like stepping through some insubstantial veil into another world, another era, and another state of mind. With Sirius standing across the back seat, Angela drove to Tilden Park. The orderly streets, retired people working as if motionless in their gardens, the cruising American cars, were a picture in colors impossibly real. Because, of course, as I reminded myself – they *were* real. This was life, not a painting, nor a film. There came a point where I could not think about it, just gasped, my mind reeling, like fuses blowing in slow motion, overwhelmed by impressions.

Angela's voice: 'Phew! Good stuff!'

I was drawn back from reverie, amazed to see that she was still driving the car, still *capable* of driving it.

'How you doing?' I asked.

'Coming on strong,' she said. 'You?'

'Just wow.'

'We'll be at the park soon – there may be quite a lot of people.'

'I don't think I could handle talking to anyone.'

Angela laughed. 'They couldn't handle talking to you, either.'

We walked in slow motion along a path I did not know, or did not recognize. I felt a euphoria complicated by butterflies in the stomach. The path wound into trees and around a corner, like the romantic picture-book ideal of a perfect little pathway. *Now I am awake in dreams.* Yellow slopes came down on either side, the long grass like delicate golden flowers. Ahead, trees in a million shades of green seemed to swell and swirl while motionless, vibrating. I took off my sandals and felt the cool dampness of the earth on the soles of my feet as if touching it with my fingertips. It was hard to believe that this bizarre, moist, springy substance was any more natural than the concrete I was so accustomed to. Or unnatural. Sirius ran ahead, as usual holding a long heavy stick in his toothy jaws. His head was held up boldly and proudly, his strong animal body sleek and handsome. Sometimes people would be coming the other way. None of them looked as fine an animal as Sirius. Many were laughable and pitiable, like characters from R. Crumb's Zap Comix. *Maybe I look like that too?* They walked stiffly, strutting like mechanical toys. *I am alive in a cartoon strip.* Sirius would always give people a start, and they'd make some comment and greeting – which I feel, see, imagine or think is a sort of speech-bubble rising in the air. I concentrated on making the correct smile. All the women wore clown's make-up.

For an instant I thought their make-up looked unnatural. A confusion of counter-arguments welled up. *Un*natural? It's natural, rather. People pit Man against Nature – they're all shouting for Nature. Down with Man! But what is Man, what is Nature? We are it, obviously, we grow from it like mushrooms, like weeds from the earth. Physics and chemistry turning in space. It's all part of the same place – the one great big Here. Nature is all. Trees, concrete, grass, make-up, guns and rockets, burger and fries, our tender flesh and the hard, shining metal of our car. Nothing is unnatural, nothing defies Nature.

My eyes met Angela's with ease. Her pupils were extremely dilated. Sharing these seconds together, or this second. Time, the sense of summer passing, life slipping away in a stream of moments, like a current of air blowing on me. I lay back on a bed of gold among silvery shafts of light. The sky shattered into a kaleidoscope of patterns. Concentric pentagons in the blue moved in and out as if breathing. Birds traced marks in the air, double, triple images, as if the bird were still there. Faint, remote sounds of faraway voices and cars hung in the background. I moved over to Angela and put a hand on her leg.

'You trying to cop a feel?' she whispered. My mouth was dry. She held out a hand to mine. It seemed to come from another world. As our hands touched and grasped each other, the two worlds united. She squeezed my hand and smiled. I remembered that Angela often seems to be critical of me, and I gazed at her: she did look very imperious and dignified. Perhaps, after all, this dignity of hers was just a fantasy of mine? No... I... It was just a fantasy of *hers*.

Realizations moved in endless mirror images, in spirals, in circles. I tried to take hold of the mind's spinning top and bring it to a stop.

Be quiet, take it slowly. Here... I... am. Simon in Berkeley. Now it's starting again, my thoughts are racing around, I can't keep up. I am not "Simon in Berkeley". I am not anything. Not a traveler, a hippy, an English boy. That's the straight way of thinking. I'm not even Simon, that's a word, not a person. I begged myself: stop racking my brain.

Angela was still giving my hand that quick squeeze and smiling. Less than a second had passed.

'Shall we walk some more?' I suggested.

Sirius became absurdly excited as soon as I got to my feet. I threw a stick he brought me, and he raced after it with imbecilic determination. I took a single step and found I was moving along the path. Angela caught up and we walked beside each other, the moronic dog dashing on ahead.

People we passed lurched forward in exaggerated, uncomfortable movements, their faces like plastic caricatures. *What strange grimaces do I have? How foolish I probably look! For I am no different from these others.* I glanced at Angela: her face too was marked by some long-held emotion. I resolved to put the detritus of the past behind me, where the past belongs. To outgrow it, and unhook myself from it at last. As we skirted a grove of eucalyptus, their scent swept through me like a gale.

Angela drove us away from the Park on winding, hilly roads. I looked out of the window, happy to be taken anywhere at all, gliding effortless over the contours of a land laid out to dry. Suddenly she slowed and pulled into a roadside parking area from which was an immense view. I left her in the car and climbed up among rocks to reach an even higher panorama. I found myself surrounded by large lizards, leathery and foreign-looking, each one perfectly motionless. Within thick, heavily ridged skins they seemed, like us, well armored for survival. Their huge eyes stared obliquely at me. I thought, I'm in America, I don't know what these lizards are. They may be poisonous. I might misjudge the situation. What should I do? I inspected them. They obviously enjoyed basking in the sun. I jumped over them and scrambled down, keeping my eyes open for other American hazards, and did not stop looking until I reached the parking area – a hazard in itself. There I found Angela. Was she another American hazard?

At last towards the calm streets of Kensington. The dusk was streaked with daydreams, projected onto the windscreen. At the house, Angela regained her normal cool, an amused-but-critical frostiness. I went up to take a shower – the stairs, I noticed, looked quite normal. The water ran in warm cascades over my back and shoulders. It was the best shower of my life. As I stretched out on the bed, dark sleep poured down from the heavens, sweeping everything away.

Breakfast finished – juice, cake, granola – we lingered at the garden table under the lemon tree, idly talking in dappled shade. The back door stood wide open; from inside came the sound of Canned Heat's latest album. The phone rang and Angela went into the house to answer it.

'It's for you,' she called, eyebrows raised as we passed one another in the doorway. I rarely received a phone call. 'British,' she added.

After the first shock of recognition and pleasure, Paul's posh English voice jarred like a splash of cold water, as if someone were trying to sober me up. 'Hold on, Paul, I'll turn down the music.'

'I'm in Chicago,' he explained.

'Chicago!' I tried to understand. Chicago was the main story on the news. 'Were you in the riots?' Footage had been seen everywhere, of police cars driving at and over demonstrators.

'Yes, of course.'

'Wow. Are you OK?'

'Yes, of course. It would be nice to see you if you're around.'

Angela was not pleased at the prospect of a stranger staying in the house. She offered to collect him at the bus station in Berkeley, but I wanted first to meet Paul on my own. He emerged from the Greyhound gingerly, looking this way and that, in torn and dirty jeans and bare feet. His thick mat of dark brown hair, greasy and unbrushed, threw itself back with exquisite abandon from the defiant, thoughtful face I loved.

In an instant my mind sought and found the good, solid ground of the years before Angela. The sight of Paul stepping, as it were, straight out of that past into the midst of my present Californian dream, incongruous sight, surreal and impossible as an iceberg on a Caribbean cruise, made me laugh aloud with sheer joy. At the same time, seeing Paul was in some way a bracing call not to lose touch with my old self.

It would be a few days before I began to understand how far Paul and I had drifted apart. He was not alone, though. Beside him I saw another familiar face from London. I hadn't realized they were in a relationship. Dark-skinned, in fragile cotton and silk, rich warm colors like clay, Bel looked discontented and sullen. Had there been a row? Perhaps she was simply too hot or too tired after the long journey.

Taking her bag, I led them along Telegraph Avenue in all its chaotic fervor. Black and white together played music on the sidewalk, bongos, flutes and saxophones. Leaflets about concerts, flyers about political issues, head magazines, underground papers, were held towards us. Paul studied new wall-posters urging that a vacant lot the university had abandoned should be brought to life as a "free speech area" and a "people's park". A kaleidoscope of harder-edged leftists called for direct action, for resistance, for uprising. At their feet and to either side, capitalism flourished: craftsmen and craftswomen sprawled outside banks and offices, their handcrafted junk, leather belts and silverwork and strings of tiny colored glass beads displayed neatly on the sidewalk. Dealers called out their chemical wares. Paul stepped inside the bookstores and was thrilled to see *Anarchy* magazine (all the way from Britain) and *Black Panther* newspaper (from North Oakland, four miles away) alongside a dozen hip or radical publications.

At the end of Telegraph we crossed Bancroft and waited outside the university campus. A man was crying out 'Hot tamales! Hot tamales!' again and again, and selling this Mexican snack from a little stall. We bought one each and ate them as a frenetic rush of people flowed around us, crowds of students going in and out of the campus.

There's a lot of tanned naked skin, bare young male chests and dimpled female midriffs, bare feet, loose hair flowing over shoulders. The tenderness of flesh is a vague, disturbing reminder of something: an innocence, an Eden, human frailty.

Angela's Chevrolet came into view among the traffic and drew alongside the hot tamales man. We slammed the doors as she pulled away, Bel in the front, Paul and me in the back. I could tell Angela felt uneasy with these scruffy, probably scrounging, maybe indiscreet intruders into her very private domain. She had expected just one, not two of them. Nothing had been said about how long they could stay. She held the steering wheel with one hand and stared ahead. I needed no reminder that Paul and Bel were not to be told anything at all about Hitch and the ranch.

'Hiya, I'm Bel – Isabelle.' Bel gave her a looking-over. 'What's your sign?' she asked. Angela turned a quick glance towards her. 'Hey, nice to meet you. Scorpio, Sag rising. Yours?'

'Double Sagittarius,' Bel said, 'moon in Cancer.'

Angela nodded. 'Mm. Far out.'

No one asked Paul his sign. As we climbed the hills, he glared at the quiet, well-ordered streets, while Bel and I chatted rather inanely until we pulled up at the house.

At the garden table, the four of us drank China tea delicately, the conversation careful and polite. Then Paul and I left the table to sprawl on the lawn. He pulled off his shirt in a single, easy movement.

'Tell me about Chicago,' I said.

'God, I need a rest. It's lovely to be here, somewhere quiet to just recover and get our breath back.'

'They had amazing stuff on the news. Even party delegates protesting. And the thing with the pig, the Yippie candidate!'

Paul barely smiled. 'There were *thousands* of police, and soldiers as well, and National Guard, guns everywhere, helicopters. You'd have, in one place, people chanting, and in another place, people listening to a speaker – Allan Ginsberg was there, incredible people, even Jean Genet – and somewhere else people singing and dancing and playing music, and then, in another place, people getting hurt, being beaten, on the ground bleeding. Every night there was a battle.'

I could see Bel wanted to keep talking with Angela, while Angela wanted to listen to Paul.

'Some of the kids overturned stuff to make barricades, and set them alight. The pigs kind of went raving mad. Tear gas started to come down like smog, cops in masks appearing through the cloud smashing people with clubs and gun butts. People tried to escape but the pigs blocked their exits so they could have a crack at them.'

'Sheesh! How the hell did you end up in Chicago, anyway? I thought you were in Berlin.'

Paul's brow furrowed. It was the wrong question. You had to be so careful talking to him. 'I thought *you* would be there. Everyone knew about it. SDS [Students for a Democratic Society] were planning it for months, something big at the Democratic Party Convention, and the Yippies were going to join in.' His voice became rasping and passionate

'Who cares about the Democrats?' I asked incredulously. 'That's dead, straight politics. Democrats, Republicans, who gives a shit?'

He glanced at me. 'Well, you do know kids all over America have been campaigning for McCarthy as the Democratic presidential candidate? The peace candidate?'

'They're straight, that's why.'

'No. Well, yes, maybe they are. But he's anti the War. And Chicago also happens to be the very place where the mayor, Daley, ordered his cops to shoot to kill during the Martin Luther King riots.'

'Sounds like Chicago is a bummer.'

His lips tightened. 'Like lots of places in this country. America's closer to revolution than any other country in the world right now.'

Bel fired warning glances at him, which he did not see, or ignored. 'Paul…' she began, 'don't lecture us.'

'A *violent* revolution? No way,' I retorted. 'What, like, a bunch of students take on the American military?' I almost laughed. 'They wouldn't last ten minutes.' I stretched out on the grass thinking there was nothing more to say, but Paul leaned forward.

'Listen! Since Luther King's murder, there's been rioting in over two hundred cities. Yeah, two hundred. All over America. The entire black population under the age of thirty is exploding.' He was raising his voice, 'This *is* civil war! This *is* revolution. It's *already* happening.'

He's talking about that high, high summer, long glorious days and weeks when we saw Grace Slick and Buffalo Springfield and Janis Joplin and Ritchie Havens and Ravi Shankar, and went to concerts, smoked whole tea-chests of grass, fucked endlessly and had just one fantastic time. Meanwhile, political types like Paul had been eagerly waiting for an explosion of violence. In truth I hadn't given much thought to the riots, except that burning your *own* neighborhood seemed like some sort of weirdly nihilistic street theater.

Angela interjected, 'Yah, we know all about that.' Nodding at me for confirmation, 'Don't we, Simon?'

'Yeah, we know about it,' I said. 'It was in the Barb. Black Power. Black Panthers. *Everyone* knows what's happening.'

'Yeah,' Paul acknowledged. 'being so close. When the pigs fired on Eldridge Cleaver, when they killed Bobby Hutton, you must have been able to practically hear the shots from here.'

'But Paul, listen: the Panthers... this race thing. The Panther slogan is All Power to the People. OK, that's cool, but they don't mean all power to *all* the people. They mean *black* neighborhoods under *black* rule. So, black government. How's that gonna work? What, like black autonomy? Black dictatorship?'

Paul was exasperated. 'You don't know *what* you're saying. Black Power is about taking a rightful place in society.'

'Even so, Panthers are not into peace and love. They don't get it. They want to split the movement, black against white.'

'No, they don't,' Paul insisted. 'Look, in a few months SDS are going to team up with the Panthers. *Bring the War home* is going to be the message. That means black and white fighting *together*, right? Just as you want. And since the murder of Robert Kennedy, even white liberals have been in the mood for a showdown. The time is right.'

Angela turned away in annoyance. I didn't want to fall out with Paul. Bel was glaring at him.

'Anyway,' Paul said, 'at least now everyone has heard of SDS.'

'Oh,' Angela replied tartly, 'I think everyone already knows about SDS. Middle-class white kids who want a shoot-out with the pigs.'

Paul answered her with studied calm. 'SDS is about changing the way society thinks.' He conceded it was true that the hard core were forming a new group, the Weathermen. 'It's going to happen.'

I laughed. 'Love the name!'

'*They're* into assassinations, bombings. That kind of stuff. There's a place for that too, you know.'

Angela shook her head, exasperated. 'Look, Paul,' she said, 'it's all a fucking head trip. Maa-aan, what is happening to our beautiful vision? We gotta transcend these power games.'

Paul opened his mouth to respond, then changed his mind. He lay on the grass. 'Maybe you're right. Anyway, it's great to be here. Thank you for making us so welcome.' He had a charming smile when he wasn't talking politics.

'Hey, Paul,' she replied mischievously, 'have you heard the Beatles' new song, *Revolution*?'

He began to sing it, parodying Lennon's scornful '*You say you want a revolution.*'

He sang rather well, which seemed to redeem him in Angela's eyes.

Bel and I stroll through the winding, hilly streets in the September sunshine, relaxed, unhurried, delighting in the balmy air, and walk up to viewpoints overlooking the Bay. We talk easily, as two English people, without the Atlantic of misunderstandings that comes between the British and the Americans. We chat, unselfconscious, we say nothing of consequence, we remark on pretty gardens, and exclaim with wonder at every glimpse of the blue water and the city beyond.

'I didn't realize you were having a scene with Paul. Is it serious?'

'A scene? No!' she exclaimed. 'I do find him attractive. You know, physically and everything. But we have such different philosophies. What about you and Angela?' She raised her eyebrows. 'You're *living* together. I like her. She's interesting.'

'Yeah, interesting! I s'pose she is,' I agreed doubtfully.

'And you're in *love*! That's *wonderful*.'

'In love! More like a fly caught in a web, I think. Or, a cat staring into headlights, unable to get out of the way. It's like Angela has cast a spell on me. Anyway, there's no point in being in love. She's totally hung up on a guy she knows, who's gone to India.'

Bel stared. 'Oh! When's he coming back?'

'I'm not sure. Angela, and all her friends, too, Sasha and the others,

Love 49

they won't discuss him at all. It's like *they* all know, but won't tell *me*.'

'You know what, Simon,' Bel suggested, 'I'd move on. Leave now. Otherwise it'll just be more painful in the end.'

I said that sounded like better advice than I'd had from the I-Ching.

She laughed, teeth beautifully white.

I put it to Angela that, after Paul and Bel left, I might take a trip somewhere, or go back to England. She tightened her mouth angrily. She phoned Sasha to come over. In the bedroom, with the door closed, they talked for hours. Finally they must have resolved the problem, as Angela emerged sweetly agreeable and loving. She urged me to do whatever I felt I had to do. Leave if I want.

* * *

Bel and Paul occupied one of bedrooms usually kept ready for anyone from the ranch. Within days the house began to fill up with books, leaflets, pamphlets and magazines, lying on every chair, table and floor. Most had been stolen from Cody's and Moe's and other bookstores near the campus. Paul read everything effortlessly, then wanted to discuss what he had read, pacing about, declaiming, waving his arms, running fingers through his hair.

In the small hours, often he'd still be awake, studying beside a table lamp, or maybe, without the lamp, just sitting thinking in the darkness. Sometimes I slipped downstairs, and the two of us would talk like old times, agreeing, disagreeing, reminiscing and prophesying.

Not that Angela and I never read! Sitting together, each with a book, we spent many evening hours. Our reading was hip, eclectic, often lowbrow. Angela slipped happily into fantasies, visions of alternative reality, stories set in better worlds. She liked Ursula LeGuin and Kurt Vonnegut (and was currently making her way through *Sirens of Titan*, his trippy universe where all the loose ends of human life tie up neatly, albeit on another planet). Everything seemed equally possible to her.

Books had become somehow communal in these days, swapped one for another, or given as borrowed treasures passed on to someone else. In every house books were on floors and tables, read or waiting to be read, fact or fiction or putting forward some seminal idea, *The Golden Notebook*; *The Magus; Nature, Man and Woman; The Parable of the*

Beast. I'd just finished Tom Wolfe's high-speed *The Kandy-Kolored Tangerine Flake Streamline Baby* and *The Electric Kool-Aid Acid Test*, which opened new vistas over the contours of America's weirdness, and was starting the latest of Brautigan's magical modern tales.

Small publishers and presses, hip cooperatives, radical groups, are turning out thousands of prints, filling the air with ideas, demanding and inspired, madly innovative, experimental, clashing juxtapositions of words and pictures running together, printed at diagonals or backwards, shrieking Freedom. Freedom, at least, from every convention about fonts and margins! Freedom to be, to do, to say, to write, mock, offend, shock, indulge, prophesy, revile, to advocate or to oppose. Some are fun, some serious, some full of turgid passages or hypotheses bordering insanity or illustrated with cerebral, complex diagrams of the soul, of society, of the cosmos. Some laud other cultures (seemingly all assumed to be superior to our own; though the words of that hippy on Haight Street come back to me: 'But do they do acid?'). Herbert Marcuse expounds theories of politics and economics. Chunky practical volumes show how to build a house, illustrated with line drawings of practical young women with long flowing hair sawing wood or fixing timbers. Others express breathless ideas of empowerment and self-discovery, from tooth care without dentists to tapping fountains of sexual energy that lie hidden in the body. Some volumes become instant icons, perfectly titled, like wall-posters of the moment: *The Politics of Experience and the Bird of Paradise,* by R.D.Laing; Carlos Castaneda's *Teachings of Don Juan – a Yaqui Way of Knowledge.*

In the car with Angela, something is sticking into me. Turns out I'm sitting on a book. On the cover, a woman in a short dress emblazoned with the word LOVE, the O cut out to reveal her navel. Beside her is the book's title, *The Medium is the Massage,* and the name of two authors, Marshall McLuhan and Quentin Fiore.

'This yours?' I hold it up for Angela to see.

She glances over. 'Where did that come from? Is it something new?'

I look inside. 'Maybe it's Paul's.'

'*Massage*? Isn't it supposed to be "message"?' she queries.

Every page is a piece of design, the whole thing a typographical circus, a compendium of non-sequitur and meaning-less collage, with a sprinkling of text.

'Maybe it's for kids?' I wonder. 'It's more like a game or a toy than a book. It's far out, it's fun.' Page one, which I read aloud as she drives, it theorizes that because the means of communication will soon include the electric and electronic, the whole of society will be utterly changed, 'you, your family, your neighborhood, your education, your job, your government, your relation to "the others"'.

Angela snorts with derision. 'Is that so? I thought all these things were already in terminal chaos, without the new electronic whatever.'

'What does "electronic" actually mean?' I wonder.

We aren't sure about that. We are sure, though, that the final end of telecommunications will be to unite the seething zillions of human beings in a single ceaseless white noise, a perpetual chattering embrace, only to prove that there is nothing of consequence to say, no one really to talk to except your lover beside you in bed. TV brings the whole world together in unanimous, predictable banality. The din from our planet rises into the cosmos: a yapping, telephoning biosphere.

There's traffic congestion on the bridge and we find ourselves waiting alongside other vehicles with their windows open. I reach out and hand the book to a couple in the next car. All four of us laugh as they take hold of it and look, mystified, at the girl on the front and the word LOVE. But the traffic is moving again. The young woman asks something, but I cannot hear the words.

* * *

Often I go with Paul into the city. We ride the colorful old trolley cars up and down the precipitous streets, hanging on to the outside and catching thrilling views – rolls of mist lying on the Bay, a section of iron bridgework in the distance, a sailboat unmoving on the water. In the cheerful squalor of Haight Street, we find freaks are now outnumbered three to one by straight tourists from around the world, and cops, and journalists working on features about drugs or the underground (though my 'keep clear of the media' hippy is still lounging there). Feeling like a tourist myself, we paused at the city sights, hunted out music and enjoyed San Francisco in a way I'd never done with Angela. I showed Paul where to pick up Berkeley Barbs and other 'alternative' papers so he could try selling a few on Market or down by the Wharf.

We grab a stack of papers each and try our luck on opposite sides of the street. I stand next to a curbside traffic barrier, and start hawking them: *Barb, Barb, Berkeley Barb. Latest issue, Berkeley Barb. Barb, Barb, Berkeley Barb. Latest issue, Berkeley Barb.* The papers soon start to feel awkward and heavy, and pulling one out to sell while keeping the rest neat can be tricky. An endless crowd passes, every kind of person, a few glancing at me and someone stopping to buy every five or ten minutes. People give more than the cover price. Some give nothing. Some pay in Korean or Vietnamese money. Some give food, wine, dope.

A girl in a clingy black satin dress stops to talk, leaning sensuously on the railing beside me, and soon gets to telling me her problems. She has problems, plenty of problems. She's been terribly used and abused. She's resentful, coquettish, egotistical. She's a walking encyclopedia of hang-ups. It's not funny, but we laugh. She's likeable.

She says she's living in a hotel nearby, and suggests we go there to talk and have a coffee. I don't know if that means take drugs, have sex, or indeed – just talk and have a coffee. We pass through the tacky, unwelcoming lobby of a cheap hotel, up dimly lit stairs. There's something distasteful about waiting as she unlocks the bedroom door. The room's carpeted and wallpapered, but small, worn, shabby, with a tired double bed under a thin cover. Puzzlingly, the girl's manner has now changed, she's not smiling or chatting any more. Almost as soon as we're inside, too quickly, without excitement and not a word of explanation, she pulls her dress over her head and throws it on a chair. Underneath it, she's wearing nothing at all.

The girl sprawls on the sagging bed. She has dark hair, thick dark pubic hair, and a few dark wisps around dark nipples. I'm taken aback, rather than excited by the sight. Thoughts scramble through my head: there's something wrong with this, this isn't hip, it isn't cool, it's straight; this is almost like a scene from a porn film. What the hell is going on? I feel distant from reality. I feel like Modigliani – I just want to paint a cool picture of her long, pale, shapely body, its smooth soft surfaces marked with geometric shapes, like something abstract.

'What's your name?' I ask.

'Merry-Ann,' she replies without interest.

'Is that Mary Ann, or Marianne?'

She repeats peevishly, 'Merry-Ann,' emphasizing each word.

'What's your sign, Merry-Ann?' I ask.

'What's my *what*?'

'Your sign, like, uh, your birth sign? Sign of the Zodiac?'

'Oh, I don't know.'

I insist, 'Well, when's your birthday?' She tells me and it turns out she's Aquarius. I try again: 'Aren't you gonna ask what my name is?'

All the while she's still lying there, naked, legs slightly apart, apparently quite bored. 'OK, what's your name?'

'Simon.'

'Where 'bouts in England you from? D'you know the Beatles?' This time there's a faint note of interest.

'Yeah.'

She livens up a little. 'You know them? You know the Beatles?'

'Yeah.'

'Hey, cool. You wanna have sex?'

The no-nonsense offer is exactly the same as Sasha's. Something in me recoils from it. I don't know why, since minutes before I had been daydreaming about something just like this. I fondle, caress and touch her and, mechanically, she does the same for me. The excitement at last begins. She presses herself back into the slack, concave mattress, arches her back, whimpers hoarsely under her breath. As soon as it's all over, I fall down into her soft arms and sleep, and dream vivid dreams of wandering alone and afraid in a hot fetid jungle, a dark forest hanging with dark human hair, a vaginal tang rising from wet ground, a coital odor prickling my eyes.

When I awake, it's late afternoon. The girl has vanished – so have her clothes and her bag. I pull on my jeans and discover that my money too, sixteen dollars, has gone from the pocket. Downstairs at reception I ask who she is, where she is, when she'll be back. They know nothing about her: 'She paid up and checked out about an hour ago. Only stayed one night.' She must have quit as soon as I fell asleep. On the wall a sheet of paper shows the room rates: the most expensive is $1.50.

At least I've still got a few Barbs. I stroll back to Market Street. Paul's gone from his place across the road. When the papers are all sold, I hitch back across the Bay Bridge to Berkeley.

Angela was aghast at my naiveté, denouncing the girl as little thief, a crook, a witch, and despairing that the underground was dying on its feet with hookers and criminals moving in to extract the last drop of life. Bel figured the hotel room pick-up could be some scam she's worked out, and pruriently grilled me about how much or how little I had enjoyed the experience, whether I had ever paid for sex before and how much I thought it was worth.

Angela interjected that the usual price for 'trash like that chick' was 'six bits', and she doubted it was worth that much (Bel frowning as she tried to reckon this mysterious sum in pounds, shillings and pence). Paul was perhaps closest to the truth in guessing it was just some fucked-up young woman, maybe a junkie, who was pretty high when I met her, thought she'd have a screw with me, then wondered if I had any bread in my jeans, and on finding some, just split with it as fast as she could.

* * *

Bel and Paul's plan (or Paul's, at least; Bel seemed an increasingly reluctant fellow traveler) was to head back to Michigan so Paul could attend a conference in a town called Ann Arbor. I'd never heard of the place and forgot to ask what the meeting was about. I'd become weary of Paul's political zeal.

Their last day with us was spent at Mount Tamalpais – Mount Tam. Angela put some bread and cheese, fruit and juice and some cake in a bag. Sirius rolled and wriggled on the back seat between me and Paul while Bel sat with Angela in front. We were stoned before we started out, and as we rode, joints passed between us. Reaching the National Park, we tumbled into the fresh air and walked steeply uphill, throwing sticks which Sirius pursued furiously.

At the Mountain Theater, Angela reminisced about last year's Fantasy Fair. 'Jefferson Airplane, the Doors, Captain Beefheart, the Byrds, all on the same ticket. Two bucks to get in and a tab of acid for free!'

We sat on the ground with our little picnic. A pleasing breeze blew across the hill. 'I can hear music,' Bel said. The rest of us laughed. It was true, though. Soon I too caught the sound of a flute, like a strange bird far away, and exuberant drumming muted by distance. We made our way towards it as spellbound as the Pied Piper's children, stepping lightly on soft, springy turf. A few wisps of sedate white cloud trailed in the sky behind us.

As we climbed, the view opened as though a curtain were being raised. On the next hill sat a large circle of musicians, about fifteen of them. The sound came clearly now, like semaphore.

There was no greeting when we reached them. We simply sat down and one of the group passed us a joint held in a handsome silver clip. We passed it round, and rolled another, and another, and the music still played, loud enough to drive out thought, a sweet chaotic symphony of unrecognizable instruments and melodies. No words were spoken. At last we rose with dazed farewell smiles and turned away. The sound faded as we walked in a trance, none of us wanting to say a word until not even a distant note could be heard.

At last Angela's 'Well, that was far out' seemed to give us permission to speak again, but no one wanted to talk. In the car, too, on the way to the bus station, we remained quiet as if stunned. Dusk had fallen, a bright moon rising nearly full, and for some reason a mood almost melancholy began to touch the scene. Perhaps it was nothing more than a sense of autumn in the air.

We drove directly from Mount Tam to the bus station. With great hugs and kisses we left Paul and Bel with their bags among crowds of waiting passengers. There were tears in Bel's eyes, and an ominous sense of finality about it all.

As soon as Angela and I were back at the house, just the two of us again, I reminded her that I'd also be leaving in a week or two.

Angela awoke at midday and decided on a long, lazy bath. She wanted to lie in the tub 'and think'. I took Sirius for a walk. By an uncanny canine awareness he recognized subtle signs that this thought had come into my mind and stood ready by the door. Despite our inauspicious first encounter, I had grown fond of Angela's handsome, rather terrifying dog. I'd quite often go out with him, down the hill, round a couple of the uneven blocks, and back up again; there were several little parks or open areas where I could let him run off the leash. It could be alarming sometimes, being out with Sirius. He was trained to obey only Angela, and never took the slightest notice of my reprimands or instructions, and I barely had the strength to hold him back, even on the leash.

As we approached the house, I undid the clip and let Sirius run the last few yards. I expected that when I returned, Angela would be out of the bath. To my surprise, fully dressed and with her hair dried, she was in the kitchen with Sasha and Hitch. Sasha kissed my cheek. Straight away, she and Angela went upstairs to the bedroom and shut the door.

Hitch stood in front of me, imposing, decorated with fringes and embossed leather and turquoise set in silver, uncomfortably smiling an intense smile. 'Hey, man! Far out! So! Back to England, huh? Hey, listen, Simon, man, I have something for you. A proposition.'

He placed a cylindrical container into my hand, about the size and weight of a candle, made of some plastic, waterproof-feeling fabric.

'Two hundred tabs inside.' He chuckled. 'Best acid on the West Coast.' He explained that he wanted me to sell them in England. 'Keep what you make on that. Next time around, you gonna have to buy it, dig? But wholesale, see? You'll make a buck or more on every tab.'

'How will I get hold of you?'

'Angela will always know where I am.'

Sasha came downstairs and said goodbye like this: 'Spread the love. Spreead the lurve. Be seein' ya, honey.'

With huge smiles and roars of laughter, a big handshake and a manly embrace, Hitch left and took Sasha away with him.

In those last days, Angela carried on as before: a lot of time together in the bedroom, a lot of grass, a lot of music. After dark, we went in the car to her 'jewel box' viewpoint to look in silence across the Bay, her eyes gazing blankly ahead through the black windscreen.

* * *

On the drive to the airport, Angela's radiant yellow hair hung over a bright red sweater. She looked as fascinating to me as ever. Held up for a long time by traffic on the bridge, we listened to the *Fire Sign Review* on the radio. It was funny enough to have us laughing to tears as we sat in the jam. When we pulled away, the traffic moving again, Angela turned the dial to another station.

It was a 'head' station, at that moment playing the Rolling Stones. Just music, no talk or commercials. We left the bridge and turned beside the Bay, south on 101. It seemed that Angela had chosen a record especially for me as the Stones came singing wistfully

... *Our love is like the water, that splashes on a stone. Our love is like our music, it's here and then it's gone.*

... *I've got no expectations – to pass – through here – again.*

In the end, the parting was too hasty because I was late for check-in. I had to run. There was a quick hug, a kiss, a sad smile and a wave, as if our whole time together had been no more than a one-night stand.

I was nineteen and it was the end of summer. I thought no further ahead than the next few hours. From a window seat climbing steeply, within minutes Angela and San Francisco Bay had vanished. Evening sunbeams poured gold over pure white cloud, like icebergs in a foaming sea, or snow-covered mountains in a gilded landscape, or treetops in a heavenly white forest.

Fall 1968

Time zones in pursuit, Simon slept, falling into visions of cities and airports, headlong dreams of speed and concrete Day and electrically illuminated Night. He struggled to wake, sitting on a low brick wall by the road. The brick was moist and uncomfortable. Shafts of grey cloud hung down across the sky. Gusts of air, damp and chill, caught his face and hair. Everything here struck him as small and cramped, tightly proportioned, streets, cars, shops, all narrow, pinched, faces too, people holding themselves in check. He held out a thumb to each passing car, sometimes standing and trying to look pleasant and respectable, an impossible task; or at least, trying not to look filthy and half-dead. At last a car, featureless, anonymous, pulled in and came to a stop a few yards ahead.

Through the empty, pale land, beneath boughs loaded with autumn leaves, modest, dull browns, it all came back – this little England of his, himself, his life. The speed was soporific. Occasionally the driver spoke, his voice intruding from far away, and Simon struggled to find words.

He leaned back in the passenger seat, legs stretched out, their blue denim patched and decorated with Angela's colored embroidery threads. He remembered these colors when they were still tangles of cotton in her needlework box, and saw her sewing with his jeans across her lap. 'The best embroidery threads,' she said, 'come from England. If ever you go back there, will you send me some?'

Finally Simon had taken his rucksack from her store cupboard. It lay now on the back seat of this car. But travel destroys all sense of time. The journey through the night seemed to have put months between him and America. His head jerked suddenly back into wakefulness when the driver's voice boomed into his thoughts; Simon had nodded off.

* * *

In a suburban provincial street, wide and well-kept, lined with large semi-detached brick houses set back behind handsome fenced lawns,

Love 59

stood the home of David and Mary Shaw. Kindly and good-natured, educated middle-class professional people of liberal and humane views, a little wearied by their duties and labors, Mary and David were now hoping for an unworried decade and a half before David's retirement from teaching. They rarely talked about their life together, but each considered they had been fortunate.

David had been able to climb the career ladder, Mary had been able to find work when it was needed, they had three bright, decent, healthy children (over whose futures they fretted). Even now, more than twenty-two years after their unceremonious registry office wedding day, Mary and David loved each other after a fashion. Every few nights Mary complied willingly with David's continuing, routine desires, finding in them a confirmation of herself and her world: a grown-up woman with a good husband, a comfortable home and a happy family. As he lay on her, caressing her lightly, her mind sometimes reached a fleeting vision, a joyous comprehension of the glorious unremarkable love which raises each family, and, unacknowledged, each parent and each child, far above the everyday.

Despite the news of world-wide turmoil and the air of revolution and unrest, and the iconoclastic mood of the younger generation, Mr and Mrs Shaw did not anticipate any immediate termination of the social order, nor even an end to capitalism. Having been socialists during their own youth, and having protected their country from invasion as young adults, and having voted for a better world at every election since, they complacently accepted the idealism of today's young people, and at the same time were accustomed to seeing the status quo survive.

Their youngest, Ruth, was starting in the local girls' grammar school. The older daughter, Sarah, had just left it with three good A-level passes which had won her a place at university. Their oldest, Simon, had not exactly disappointed them; after all, they only wanted him to be happy. He was, though, one of their biggest worries. He had abandoned university after a single year, got mixed up with the hippy crowd, and had admitted quite without embarrassment that he smoked marijuana. Better, perhaps, that he told them than keep it secret. He had gone to America without warning, rarely written, and they had no idea what he was doing or when he'd be back. The next worry was that Sarah – who had always admired him – would follow a similar path.

Simon dragged his heels with dog-tired steps along the street, feeling like there was lead in his veins and in the rucksack on his back. The driver of a passing police car touched the brake, but summed him up as one of the middle-class and drove on. Simon viewed the police car as a kind of security patrol in the pay of the town's privileged, property-owning super-straight bourgeoisie. He muttered about 'fucking pigs'.

To him, the solid brick houses were fortresses of small-minded materialism, and their inhabitants naive, ignorant, convention-bound fools. That went for his parents too. What the fuck did they know, living in their hidebound darkness, their grim wartime memories, pursuing their petty, pointless materialistic ambitions? They had never dropped acid and seen the world with unclouded eyes and mind forced open, never been disconnected from their regimented daily timetable by getting well and truly stoned so that you didn't even know what fucking day it was. Such people hated drugs, he thought bitterly, and for the most contemptible of reasons: fear. They kidded themselves it was for some moral reason. He spat in a flowerbed at the thought of them. Then was struck by a pang. He shouldn't, perhaps, have spat at a flower.

Mary Shaw saw her child through the window. After eighteen months of absence, the sensation was dizzying, nearly painful – in the lean, defiant young man she saw all the years of his growth, the birth, the crying baby, the endearing boy, and now the strident young adult, and perhaps she even glimpsed into the years beyond.

'It's Simon,' she yelled to David. She met him with almost shrieks of joy, tears welling, and pulled him to her. 'Darling, darling, darling, how lovely that you're back! How did you get here? We'd have come to the station for you. You should have phoned!' she cried. The tears poured from her eyes. 'Oh, darling Simon, how marvelous to see you again!' Simon allowed her to hug him, feeling indulgent. Arguments could come later – why start now and spoil her pleasure?

David too, dashing down stairs into the hall, beamed without restraint, reaching his arm right around Simon's shoulders in a manly gesture of affection. 'It's good to see you, Simon! It's been ages. How are you? How was America?' He laughed with pleasure. 'My *God*, your hair – it's... well, it's grown, hasn't it! It's longer than John Lennon's! Look, dear.' With genuine amazement he showed his wife the flowing blond locks. 'And I love the beads, Simon, very pretty. And that moustache!

Like a South American bandit!' He laughed and stopped himself; remembering that hair was a bit of a sore point with Simon – and why argue as soon as he steps into the house? We can talk about things like that later. He asked instead, 'When did you get back? Did you fly into Heathrow?' in a self-consciously practical, masculine way.

For Simon, nothing had changed; the house was lifeless, the atmosphere heavy with satiety and boredom. In some ways Angela's house had been the same – full of useless knick-knacks, furniture and expense – but here there was more, and added up to mere ornament and clutter, while for Angela and Sasha the house had been a kind of disguise. In this house the cloying material abundance was matched by spiritual emptiness, or so Simon considered. Although it was barely past breakfast time, he sat with his parents in the kitchen and ate a bowl of soup and some thickly sliced bread; he was ravenous. Then came a weary sense of anti-climax. After the long journey to be with them, Simon had forgotten how depressing it is to see one's parents. He made excuses to go to his bedroom and have a good sleep.

That evening his sisters arrived home together and greeted him with astonishment and rapture. In their eyes he recognized that unspoken conspiracy of the young against the old, the child against the parent: they both had some idea what he had been doing these last few months, and wished him well.

As days passed, the American experiences were gathered up, and a place found for them in Simon's memory. But they would not remain there, they were disordered, complicated and could not be stored away. He thought all the time about Angela. Moments that he had spent with her came to mind every hour: the early days after they first met, a first acid trip, visits to Mill Valley, hand in hand on city sidewalks, riding in her Chevrolet, gazing at night across the black waters of the Bay.

Returning to England had not broken the spell.

After a week of abstinence, sexual longing was also scratching at him like needles. Agonized daydreams traced fingertips over every niche and curve of Angela's body. There was another, less familiar longing too, a pain of heart that dragged inside, a yearning to look into her eyes, hear her voice, see her smile. Again and again Simon imagined that figure, yellow, red and blue – hair, sweater and jeans, as she was when he last saw her – beside him once more.

People did not phone across the Atlantic in those days. Those echoing, unclear calls with their clicks and pauses were expensive and only for emergencies. A letter was the way to get in touch. He resisted writing *so* soon. He ought to wait a while and try to master his emotions. Holed up in his room with the door closed, sprawled on the bed, he could not stop his mind drifting to Angela and California, sex and sunlight. He put his old records on the Dansette, the Crystals, Shangri-Las, Chiffons, Little Eva's *The Locomotion*, the Shadows and old Beatles, or fiddled with the radio dial trying to find Radio Caroline, the 'pirate' station on a ship somewhere in grey English seas, unaware that during his absence it had been closed down.

Simon despaired of himself and the world: maybe the 'revolution' had been no more than a brief explosion of light far away on the California coast, in another galaxy. Or had it been, after all, just a hallucination? He felt it disappearing already into memory.

In Britain, it seemed to him now, there was no movement, no underground. The whole scene was just a few public school rebels, fervent little leftist factions mired in the quicksands of rhetoric, straight girls in tiny skirts, rock stars living the high life, and students eager to join the worldwide fun. For the kid in the street, it had become just a hairstyle and a cut of jeans, rounded lapels, huge ties, tight shirts, and collar-length hair, a look cleansed of ideology. Students, students, having a riot. There were no drop-outs. Only posturing and playacting and dressing-up. Nothing really happening.

A torrent of books and articles and broadcasts seemed to be rushing past him. The word 'student' droned endlessly, all that the shorthaired man and lipstick woman on the Clapham omnibus despised and feared.

The Student Revolt would have cost Simon six bob, but he slipped it into his pocket and walked out of the shop. *This week: Cohn-Bendit analyses the May uprising.* Left! Right! Left! Right! Work! Strike! Work! Strike! Struggle! Fight! Live! Die!

Yet, not knowing why, when his parents discussed the race riots in America, he sided with the Black Panthers; when France came up, Simon expounded syndicalism; on China, he was an admirer of Mao's poetry as well as his politics. He knew his father was sincerely interested in the new ideas and wanted to discuss them sensibly, yet Simon could only reject, oppose and dispute. It annoyed him that he too was merely play-acting.

'Is it our fault,' Mary asked David, 'that Simon is like this? So argumentative and disagreeable all the time.'

David shrugged and grinned in wry reassurance. 'Course it is, darling. That's the role of parents. Don't worry, he'll grow up one day.'

'I hope we live to see it,' she said. Then, 'He seems so unhappy, doesn't he? What do you suppose he got up to in America?'

'Oh, taking drugs and sleeping with girls, I shouldn't wonder,' David replied carelessly.

Mary was horrified. 'No, surely Simon wouldn't…'

David had done neither, but he put that down to accidents of history. 'Young men must have their fling,' he informed her.

'Come on, David. Drugs and sex are a bit more important than that. This is Simon we're talking about. Our own child's life.' He gave a grim, helpless gesture of assent.

Later, the thought weighed heavily on her, until she had a headache and, leaving the family in front of the television, went to bed early.

Mary gazed out of the kitchen window. 'Look, a robin! Aren't they lovely? So neat and spruce at this time of year.' Beside her at the sink, holding a dishcloth, Simon watched the robin as it hopped on the lawn close to the house. 'Mum,' he argued, 'a robin isn't neat or spruce. That sounds like you think it's a human being.' There was a petulance in his voice. 'A robin is just a wild creature. Like,' he shrugged, 'like a rat.' She was irritated and stung by his response. Should she ask why he couldn't just be friendly and nice? No point.

She spoke hesitantly, gazing into the garden. 'This girl – Angela – that you mentioned in your letters. Was she your girlfriend?'

He was tempted to say it was none of her business. It felt good, though, talking about Angela. He looked again into the garden. The robin was gone. 'Yes, I suppose she was,' he said quietly.

'Were you… in love?' Mary asked.

More than when Sasha and Bel asked it, coming from his mother the question had an absurd ring, as if he'd been asked if they were courting. Simon smiled, but the smile fell away. 'Maybe. Not sure.' He was conscious of a sort of pain.

'Will you see her again? Is it all over?'

'I think it's all over. I didn't realize I would want to see her again. I mean…'. With a slight snort of amusement, he admitted, 'I'm not quite sure what I mean. Anyway, she's still got a yen for her old boyfriend.'

Mary's eyes opened in surprise for a moment. She nodded sadly, brows knitting. Poor Simon. Her dear little boy was trying to be a man. What a world he was living in. Drugs, demonstrations, men wearing shoulder-length hair and strings of beads. But people still loved, and lost, and were hurt. 'I see,' she said.

* * *

It was hard to imagine how the family could go out together. The girls agreed that it might work better if Simon would try to be nicer. The problem was, they decided, that he didn't *like* anything.

David concurred that Simon was a 'young curmudgeon', as he put it. 'Within a hundred miles, or maybe a thousand, no restaurant could possibly provide the sort of home-cooked humbug, the – what d'you call it? – macrobiotic mish-mash that he goes in for now. And he probably thinks birthdays are a capitalist trick.'

'Basically,' the girls said, 'he's a pain in the neck.' Adding ruefully, 'But we *do* love him. We do, don't we?' They looked around as if canvassing opinion. 'Do we? Do you love Simon, Mum?'

'What a question!' Mary retorted. 'Of course! My baby boy.'

'Ye-es,' David quizzed mischievously, 'but do you love him?'

'Oh, don't be horrible, darling. He just needs cheering up, that's all.'

Whatever lengths they went to, there was a danger that Simon would be surly and ungrateful and spoil the occasion. It was decided that the sisters would make him *promise* to be nice. He'd do it for them.

Eventually David spoke to Simon. 'I say,' he ventured, 'what about if we all go out together for lunch? Or dinner. As a birthday treat.' He waited for the reaction. Looking at his son's bemused expression, anything seemed possible: gratitude, glee, anger, abuse, sarcasm.

Now what? Simon thought. Dad coming on all friendly? 'Hey! That'd be cool,' he said.

'Maybe we can persuade someone to cook up a banquet of brown rice and vegetables and all your favorite things.'

'You know what I'd really love? A proper slap-up meal at the Royal Dorset. Lots of champagne.'

Simon reasoned that a day out with the family would be awful, dinner at a posh hotel could be no worse, and that was what *they* would all like.

In any case, he doubted they would find brown rice anywhere in this town. He considered birthdays a lot of straight rubbish. He didn't want to have a bad scene over it though.

David was dumbstruck. At last he asked, 'What about the food?' And the expense, he thought. Twenty, after all, didn't deserve champagne – that should wait for twenty-one.

'Oh, I don't mind about it that much. They might have a vegetarian dish or something,' Simon suggested, 'or an omelet.' After the effort his mother had made to accommodate his organic wholefood tastes, he daren't mention that he was quite partial to a juicy hamburger if it were forced on him. David glanced to heaven at the thought of paying Royal Dorset prices for an omelet.

When Mary heard, she said anxiously, 'Oh dear, I hope we won't all bicker and argue.' Sarah was frankly disgusted, and slammed into her bedroom. The Royal Dorset! Of all the pretentious, ridiculous, vulgar, ostentatious places. She had really lost faith in Simon. He was just as bad as the rest of bloody adults.

Ruth was thrilled beyond words. The Royal Dorset! It was the grandest, dreamiest place imaginable. Standing in gardens overlooking the sea, the building looked like a fairytale mansion, just like a big cake encrusted with thick curls of white icing. Through its tall windows she had seen huge, glittery chandeliers scattering rainbow sparkles, and women in gorgeous, romantic long dresses and men terribly smart in black bow ties. For an instant of fantasy she imagined music, dancing, elegance and glamour all around as they sat down to eat. She would wear the red Rock 'n' Roll dress with swirly white flowers on it. But – oh dear – her heart sank with a sickening lurch – what on earth would Mummy wear? Would she let them all down? Mummy had nothing remotely lovely enough. Then a much worse thought struck her: *What would Simon wear*? Probably they wouldn't even let him through the door in his messy, patched bellbottom jeans.

Mary wore an elegant, knee-length A-line blue dress, with her string of pearls, sheer stockings and pale blue shoes. David as always was comfortably respectable in jacket and flannels, shirt and tie, but with a gaudy, oversized sprig of flowers in his buttonhole as some sort of private joke about flower-power. Sarah wore an ankle length midnight-blue, almost black cotton skirt with red edging and a white silk shirt and multicolored loosely knitted waistcoat. Ruth did wear her Rock 'n' Roll dress and Simon said she looked great.

He wore desert boots with slogans written on them, bright yellow loon pants that were agony to zip up, accentuating every male bump. His beard descended to a tight green shirt, its huge collar unbuttoned to show a tight purple tee shirt and a dozen strings of colored glass beads. On the shirt was a red and white badge of *Medical Aid for Vietnam* and another showing the Women's Liberation red fist. The blond hair tumbled to his upper arms.

They were treated with exceptional courtesy. Waiters seated them around a circular table in the middle of the room, beneath a huge crystal chandelier. The place had made little effort to modernize, and retained a pre-War polish and style. As the waiters pulled out the chairs, handed gilt-edged menus, and helped with their napkins, Simon reveled in the curious, sometimes half-frowning glances of other diners.

He started to think he had chosen this place especially to shock them. His eyes took in a couple at the next table, and noted with derision the man's garish kipper tie and the woman's extremely short dress with fashionable zig-zag patterns. Glancing back at him, the couple saw only a decent, ordinary family with typical rebellious grown-up kids – harmless enough, well-behaved. And the younger girl was adorable.

The Royal Dorset's set dinner menu offered pale, pastel dishes served with pink champagne. Mary fancied changing it, saying she wanted fish instead of veal, but could not decide between haddock à la bistro and salmon hollandaise, eventually agreeing to the veal after all. David had gone to some trouble to have vegetarian alternatives for Simon, yet maddeningly he too chose the set meal to please the others. For Ruth the waiter brought a glass of sparkling cherry-ade. Sarah, allowed a glass of champagne – being almost the same age as Simon in any case – became giggly and rosy-cheeked after just a few sips.

They picked at shrimp cocktail, chatting and joking nervously, relaxing a little as they spooned cream of mushroom soup, becoming quite convivial over veal à la crème. Simon chewed the meat doubtfully but made no comment at all about cruelty to animals. Here, thought David, was family life in its ideal form, in that happy moment when all have gathered together around a table but no row has yet broken out.

Mary gradually let go of her fears. Ruth, combining *best behavior* and *savoir faire*, glowed with sheer delight. Simon, and Sarah too, struggled with a sort of inner acedia, a peculiar heartsickness that transmutes all that glitters into dust and makes any pleasant, mannered occasion a little disgusting to them.

David remarked that pink champagne probably wasn't the right thing to drink with these dishes, was it? None of them knew, and the wine waiter, perfectly catching the mood, suggested that in fact perhaps a white burgundy would be more appropriate and would they prefer... But no, David declared in a contrary rush of expansiveness, they were more than happy with the champagne.

For 'sweet' the chef respectfully proposed baked alaska. For a few moments Mary debated whether she might not prefer pineapple waikiki, but found at last that she agreed with the chef.

The surprise birthday cake indeed surprised everyone except David, who had ordered it: a light sponge dripping with strawberry-colored icing across which Happy Birthday Simon had been squeezed in thick snow-white letters. The family sang *Happy Birthday* brightly, though with embarrassment, while Simon smiled and blew out the single candle, making a secret wish that he could be free of all this and Angela would come to England and fall in love with him and forget about Jesse.

The waiters clapped. At the next table the man with the huge necktie and the woman with the pop-art mini-dress beamed at Simon. As one waiter sliced the cake, another asked David if they would be wanting cheese and biscuits afterwards. This he turned down, but agreed to coffee, which came with odd, waxy little petit-fours.

Grandly, David invited Mary and Simon to join him in a brandy, the first Simon had ever sipped. On the whole, Simon decided, as his tongue and eyes burned from the fiery liquor, dope made a lot more sense. Sarah dipped a finger in Simon's glass to try it and gasped with horror. Ruth, still bursting with joy, shyly beckoned a waiter and politely asked him for another cherry-ade.

The following morning, Angela's letter lay on the breakfast table; a long white envelope with several stamps and a blue airmail sticker.

Her name and address were written in the top left hand corner, so there was no need for anyone to ask who the letter was from. The round American script was addressed to Simon 'care of' Mr and Mrs Shaw. Even that seemed to mean something.

On yellow tissue paper she had written:

Dearly Simon

Happy birthday to you. A flight, on a postcard pinned up in the bookstore. From here to London Heathrow, only $100. Arriving October 30 at 8.30am. I'll leave Sirius on the ranch.

Looking forward to seeing you. Please be sure to meet me.

Love you.

Angela.

The brilliant yellow a fragment of California. Her handwriting, the mere sight of her signature took away his breath. Simon flushed slightly and became silent. Mary weighed how (or whether) to ask him a question about the letter. Memories and emotions, the paper, the need for privacy embarrassed him. The very touch of it between his fingertips felt like an intimacy. He stared at the words. No 'could you', just an authoritative 'please'. Does 'Love you' mean the same thing as 'I love you'? There was a week until her arrival.

A gleaming new E-type Jaguar picked him up on the A30 and dropped him in Piccadilly. The staff of nearby offices, leaving work, hurriedly crowded towards the tube station. Simon walked against the flow, crossed into Green Park, past Buckingham Palace towards Biggie and Em's squat off Victoria Street. He planned to stay there overnight and go with them on Sunday's Vietnam march.

Biggie was big, sloppy and huggable, his thick sweater in holes, the long hair and strings of beads looking faintly absurd on that massive body of a laborer. He greeted Simon with roars of welcome, and guffaws of appreciation for the Californian tan and sun-bleached hair. Behind Biggie, waiting for a chance to kiss Simon's cheek, his demure girlfriend Em gave shy smiles. There was music, but instead of mellow West Coast sounds, or chaotic torrents of stoned electric guitar, or Top Thirty hits, their stereo scraped out edgy notes of raucous Chicago blues.

Picking up his own guitar, Biggie gestured Simon to sit down, and joined in with the record, yelling the words. He gazed far into the distance and in an instant seemed to forget where he was.

Emma, serene, upright, with her air of unsullied cleanliness, had apparently nothing in common with her boyfriend. With a delicate printed cotton dress draped to the floor, long hair brushed a hundred times, parted in the middle and tied back with heavy velvet, she seemed to have stepped straight out of a pre-Raphaelite painting.

It was strange, to see these two and be so reminded of *class* in the English sense. In America, Sasha told Simon that Angela had class. What she meant was some combination of *hauteur* and *panache*. In that sense, Sasha herself, despite the cocaine wear and tear on her face, had it too. But in England, Biggie was simply working class, while Em was as middle as they come, defying any other meaning to the word.

As the music was raw, so the aroma in the house was sweet, a soothing fragrance of home-cooking and goodness. Em offered Simon a cup of tea, but Biggie urged Simon to come to the pub instead.

There, enclosed by swirling, pungent cigarette smoke and the din of men's voices – Simon hadn't been inside a pub for over two years, and considered them dens of straightness – they sat at a wooden table messy with ash and spilt beer. Biggie tried to confide in him, making oblique revelations. Em, he said, was clinging and jealous. She objected to him going out whenever he liked and doing whatever he wanted. While he, Biggie, was superbly tolerant, fair, understanding and capable of taking the long view, as he now explained. Simon was intrigued: did Biggie mean that he and Em both had other partners? Well, *Em* doesn't, Biggie admitted – but if she did, he would be the last to mind. He didn't believe in jealousy. He believed in doing what you want and damn the consequences. He was looking to have not just a good time, nor even a good life, but a great life, *the* Great Life, the limitless, everything life.

The Great Life. Simon certainly liked the idea. But what about Em? He supposed Biggie's answer to that would be – that only her hang-ups prevented her grasping the Great Life too.

In the narrow kitchen, that evening Simon leaned against the sink as Em chopped vegetables and tossed them into a saucepan. She too spoke confidingly. 'Oh, Biggie's so annoying! He won't help with anything. I cook and clean for him, and everything. But he doesn't care if the place is a mess, just drinks and gets stoned and plays guitar. And I'm worried we'll be thrown out. The owners have started an action against us.'

Squatting had become a big issue – thousands of empty houses in London were being taken over ('liberated') in the name of the homeless. A useful booklet on how to squat had just been published.

'Don't cook and clean for him, Em. Why should you?'

'Oh, Biggie wouldn't even notice. Anyway, I *want* to make a proper home,' Em said plaintively. 'Though I'd rather be in the country somewhere than in the middle of London.' Just then, the front door slammed. 'You see? He's gone out, without telling me.'

Simon commiserated with her, and half envied Biggie. Now he told Em about Angela. 'We lived together in Berkeley, and she's coming to be with me in England.' He paused to let that sink into his own mind as much as into hers, before adding, 'Problem is, *where* to live?'

'What's she like?' Em ventured.

'OK, well, she's older than us. Four years older. She's,' he struggled, 'she's amazing.' He didn't want to say Angela was 'nice'. She was aloof, cool and a little scary. He could hardly say she was imperious, though it came close to the truth.

Biggie and Em had worked with all the freedom squatting gives to do whatever you want to a place. Squatters never have to worry about the value of their home. And unlike most squatters, Biggie and Em weren't sharing with a crowd of others. Their apartment was at the top of a condemned Victorian tenement. Though everything in it was threadbare, they had made it wonderfully comfortable.

Of course, Simon knew they had a spare room with a double mattress on the floor; he'd often slept there and that's where he would be sleeping this night. There was even some furniture, even rugs on the floorboards – and they were almost clean.

Em pursed her lips. 'I'd say you could crash here, but...' She tutted, 'Milly's coming for the demonstration, and she might want to stay for a bit, and, well, it's difficult.'

'Who's Milly?'

'Don't you know Milly? Milly Lewis. She's nice.' It was clear that Em actually wanted to meet his American girlfriend, and sure enough after a moment she said, 'I suppose it'd be OK for a few days.'

'Where will we all sleep?'

'We'll work something out,' she answered.

Em and Simon had dinner together. She put a plate of food aside for Biggie. He saw how it was for her. While Biggie was out, boozing or seeing other women, Em kept house and played Mozart on the piano. She did not seem to understand that it would never be possible to contain or civilize him, or bring him under her wing.

Later, she went to bed. Left alone, Simon lounged on a disintegrating old sofa in the living room. He flicked through books, papers and magazines from a pile on the floor. A key turned in the lock, and Biggie walked in, rosy-cheeked, unsteady and merry.

Sitting down beside Simon on the battered couch, he unwrapped a scrap of silver paper. 'Bombay black, the best. Half opium,' he said. With a long, dirty thumbnail he sliced the chunk of dark sticky hashish into two and put one of the pieces into his mouth. The other, he handed to Simon, who ran his tongue around the small lump a couple of times. It was bitter, oily and soft. He swallowed it.

Biggie put on some music, and unwrapped another piece of hashish, this time crumbly, fragrant and golden. 'Lebanese,' he said.

Two cigarette papers stuck together, another across the end, tobacco sprinkled along the papers, dope warmed over a match and crumbled onto the tobacco, then, carefully rolling the joint, tamping the mixture in at one end with a matchstick, twisting it tight at the other. Into the open end, a piece torn from the cigarette pack is rolled and inserted to make an end like a filter. The ritual over, he put the joint into his mouth, lit it, inhaled and held a lungful of the precious smoke.

To Simon, this whole ceremony seemed so Old World, archaic and complicated. How easy it had been with Angela, a slender twist of paper, a sprinkle of grass, light up and get high. He and Biggie breathed in deeply. They sat without talking, listened to jazzy blues LPs. Simon started to feel that he was melting into the sofa, into the music. At last Biggie swayed forward, muttering, 'Wow, fuck, fuck, fuck.'

Em appeared at the door, her features slightly distorted. She was wearing a demure, opaque white linen nightdress that, buttoned to the neck, looked positively saintly. 'Can you keep the music down?' She spoke with studied pleasantness, but the note of complaint could not be erased. She turned away again at once. Beside her, the towering body of Biggie, flushed, overweight and stoned, eyes half-closed, looked quite devilish. He mumbled something incoherent.

Simon suddenly found himself gazing, as through an open window at night, into the private, crazy psychology that draws people together, the magnetism of hang-ups. He felt fit to pass out, head spinning, mouth dry, sounds echoing strangely, stomach rolling like a cross-Channel ferry. He heard his own voice saying 'Beatles' again and again, unsure if he were repeating it or remembering saying it.

Biggie put on *Hey Jude.*

Simon muttered that he's totally smashed. All else forgotten as a cool sparkling stream of music winds prettily among the hills and washes through his thoughts. At first Paul McCartney sings. Piano notes lie under his voice like strings of little lights trailing around the words.

'*Hey Jude,*' Paul so tender at the start, as Simon muses, Who is Jude? Nobody is called Jude. Is it a symbol? Judas Iscariot? '*Take a sad song and make it better. Reeemember. To let her into your heart.*' It probably doesn't mean Judas Iscariot at all. Jude the Obscure? *Let her into your heart.* Patterns of lines follow steps up and down the octaves, steps, pyramids, over the music under the words – '*Don't be afraid.*' Because people *are* afraid to let someone into their heart. *You were made to go out and get her.*

'*The minute. You. Let her. Under. Your. Skin.*' Under your skin. Skin. Paul's voice is lovely, pure, a summer breeze. John and George harmonize. '*Then you begin. To make it. Better.*' Tambourines like fireworks in the night, sparklers scattering tiny, brief stars, sprinkled lights against soft cushiony darkness. A fresh breeze of exquisite sound blows into his thoughts, a current of air from some far-away window that opens onto the world.

Thudding, remote drumbeats. Cymbals far away. '*Don't carry the world upon your shoulders.*' Rising sounds like warm floodwaters. '*Don't let me down.*' Don't let him down? Does Jude have to do what Paul says? Do I? '*You have found her. Now go out and get her,*' orders Paul. Now John's voice: '*Let it out and let it in.*' That sounds like sex. Or breathing. Or shooting up. Under my skin. '*Remember – Hey Jude – To let her into your heaaart. Then you can start* (John, far away, cries 'Star - ar', the last syllable hanging in Simon's mind for a long moment, an oasis in the middle of the sentence) *to make it better.*'

But he means love. Let it out and let it in. Which is almost sex, almost breath. Paul gets more jazzy, then calms down. jude jude jude judie jude jude. '*The movement you need is on your shoulder*' – '*And don't you know that it's just you.*' It's up to you alone, it's your life.

Hey ju-u-u-ude. It's...('aah' behind the words again) Exquisite, heavenly. Slowly increasing, rising, rising. Instruments, bells. music growing, gathering pace, gathering sound, trumpet, complex, mosaic, a vast symphony spreading beyond the song, wrapping around the horizons. Empty flashes between phrases, microscopic pauses, silence beyond. The sound is alive, a harmonious cacophony. *Ju-uh-oo-oo-ude... Reemember. Under your skin. Yeah yeah yeah yeah yeah heart ah ah-ah. la-la-la-lalala-la.* Choirs endless in unison, hey jude pouring down, cascading. Repeated phrases rolling like waves, breakers rolling to shore, waves in the sun, breaking on sands, 'hey jude' pulling away, away, into the deep darkest blue.

Paul screaming, *jude jude jude you know you can make it*, voices speaking behind him. *Na na na na nanana-na*-crashing to the shore. *La-la-la-lalala-la. lalala-la-hey jude.*

well in a - na

Later like dreaming the night passes in black and white stills. Walking along Victoria Street with Biggie, who is squirting superglue into the locks of huge Whitehall doors. Sitting in a cool Trafalgar Square as restless pigeons rustle on their window ledge perches. On reflection, that really happened. They really did that. On broad wide steps of London stone, laughing helplessly. *Everything will be new and different and fun.*

Freezing cold and hungry they returned to the apartment and Biggie peered into the fridge: He held out something on the end of a fork close to Simon's face and smiled questioningly. A red tangle, looking like, what could it be... worms? Simon frowned.

'Mince?' Biggie said. Simon laughed till the breath wouldn't come and tears streamed down his moustache... he had thought Biggie was offering him worms to eat.

They had fried egg sandwiches instead, and glasses of milk, unspeakably delicious. Then adding ketchup to their plates, and taking more bread to wipe the oily red and yellow.

'Do you want some acid?' Simon said. Hitch had said to get rid of it quick.

The doorbell rang.

'What the fuck! Must be the Thought Police!' yelled Biggie.

'What the fuck time is it?'

Neither knew the time, but while Biggie went to the door, Simon stood by the window in silence and, touching the cold glass, felt the night utterly still and dark. It was nearly morning. He was eager to lie down somewhere and sleep.

Biggie came back with a girl carrying a kitbag and wrapped in a shapeless ex-army jacket over a floor-length skirt, dirty and damp at the hem. Reaching to her waist, glossy hair as dark as blue slate or charcoal hung down straight but for a few tangles. She wore glasses with thick black-plastic frames, and her face, tired and pretty with a no-nonsense expression that made her seem almost plain at this hour, showed that she had reached her wits' end.

She merely glanced at Simon, said a peremptory Hi and at once dropped her bag on the floor, slumped onto a chair and let her head drop onto her folded arms on the table.

'You know Milly?' Biggie asked Simon. Then, to her, 'Want a smoke? Got some fantastic Leb Gold.' With a twinkling eye.

'Cup of cocoa, please,' she replied firmly, 'and a slice of toast. If you can manage it.'

The atmosphere changed at once. They drank cocoa. Milly went to bed in the spare room. As soon as she had gone, Biggie returned to the subject of the acid. Simon found the tube buried in his bag and unscrewed the top for the first time. The two of them leaned over it, speechless with wonder at the sight.

'It's a new batch of California Sunshine, straight from San Francisco.' Simon was startled to hear Jack Hitchins' sales pitch in his voice. He heard himself using someone else's words: 'Two hundred and fifty mikes in each tab. One hundred percent guaranteed Good Stuff.' It was as though those people were still with him, inside him. 'Best acid on the West Coast.'

He picked out a tablet. 'Come to think of it, have a couple of them.' Biggie wrapped two tablets in a screwed-up piece of foil.

* * *

'Hello,' said Milly, surprised.

Simon stickily opened his eyes and found he was on the floor of the spare room, she in the bed. A smile lit up her face. A night's sleep had made miracles for her. She was sunny, healthy-looking, wholesome and youthful, with lovely skin. The dark hair hung round her shoulders like a shawl. For an instant he imagined how his own rough, bleary face must appear to her. Weak daylight came through thin blue cotton curtains pulled slightly apart. It felt late – midday, or one o'clock. 'Have we missed the demonstration?' he said.

'No, plenty of time.' She put on her glasses and inspected him.

'Had a good sleep?' he asked awkwardly. He discovered he was naked.

'Mm,' Milly almost hummed with pleasure, 'really nice. But how about you – that floor looks cold.'

'I didn't even notice. I was just so out of it. What does Milly stand for? Mildred, isn't it? Or Millicent?'

'Or millipede.'

'Not Melisandre, is it? Oh, could be Melissa.'

'Or Milly-ionaire. It's Camilla, actually.'

'Oh! Nice name! Well, Camilla, what about breakfast?'

'Mm, lovely.' She lay back, arms folded back on the pillow, hands under her head, as if waiting for it to be brought by room service.

Simon had hoped *she* would bring breakfast to *him*. Or they could have made it together, that would have been nice and sexy. He stood, yawning and stretching, reached to open the curtains further and peered out at wet roofs. Down below, toy cars moved along toy streets, and tiny human models moved forward in quick, jerky strides.

He turned, aware of Milly's scrutiny. The frank brown eyes were happy, intelligent and gentle. She was pretty! No hippy chick though – madly disheveled, but her dark hair was properly cut, even styled, with a fringe. His eyes held hers for a long half second. 'Coffee and toast, miss?'

Now he took the blanket off the floor and draped it round himself, and became some improbable, blond American Indian. The apartment was quiet, it felt deserted. Had the others gone to the demonstration? When he brought a tray back into the spare room, Milly sat up, pulling up a blue sheet over her breasts. He set the tray down beside her, and sat on the bed with only the tray between them.

'How sweet of you!' she said.

Simon laughed, a little mocking. 'Sweet! That's the last thing I expected to be.' He helped himself to Em's warm wholemeal bread, slices thickly spread with butter.

It felt easy to talk. Perhaps it was love at first sight. He spoke about Angela, and it soon seemed to both of them that he was in love already.

'You'll meet her if you're still here on Wednesday,' he said. 'She's coming to stay here.'

'No, I'll be leaving tonight. I've got to get back to college.'

Milly said she was studying Classics at Cambridge. That's straight.

Very straight. The door opened and Biggie looked in. 'Coffee?' he boomed. 'Ah, you already made some. Sharing a bed already? You randy pair! Good, good, very good! Well, I won't interrupt.' And with a jovial wink he disappeared again before either could answer.

Of course it didn't do to be embarrassed about such things. They laughed. 'I'm sorry. Biggie can be such an idiot!' Simon said. 'I never even thought about it!'

'Didn't you? I did! But I was too shattered to think it for long.'

'Well of course *I* did. It might be very nice – another time.'

'How can you say such a thing if you're in love with Angela?' Milly chided him.

A few minutes later, as they put the tray on the floor, she accidentally let the sheet drop from her breasts. They were smaller and rounder than Angela's, with darker nipples. Simon noticed too that she wore a proper necklace: not strings of little colored glass beads or carved sandalwood or some cheap costume silverwork, but a piece of ordinary, straight jewelry, a slender gold chain that looked beautiful on her bare chest

He passed her a tee-shirt from the floor. Her clothes were piled with his, tangled indecently, her colored cotton skirt and his yellow 'loons', her blouse and his embroidered cheesecloth shirt, and her rucksack pressing into the heap.

Streams of young people flowed in a single direction, and in the air a kinship, a tremulous excitement, a thrill of anticipation, all moving towards Trafalgar Square. Today more than ever, he felt the disturbing thrill of unanimity, being part of the crowd. Hair fluttered like banners, in a sea of denim and patches and badges. There was a mood of defiant freedom, of decisive action, exuberant, exhilarated, excited.

All around, determined to seize this moment, were the missionaries of tough-minded little leftist groups. Some factions on the Left had pompously declared their opposition to the demonstration, others high-mindedly declined to take part because certain other groups on the Left had endorsed it, while yet others had self-importantly made the decision to attend. But *these* black-jacketed crop-headed youths were dreamers of revolution and blood. History, or at least news, was being made, and they would make it, jeans and jackets and boots ready for a march, a run, a ruckus, maybe a scuffle, maybe steal a copper's helmet, maybe kick him in the balls, maybe take a ride in a Black Maria. Some carried furled

Love 77

black banners. Grim, stolid, middle-aged men stood watching from the sidelines, holding up the Morning Star, Maoist journals, papers of the official Vietnam Solidarity Campaign, a multitude of newsletters. Alongside them were the irrepressible capitalists, just as eager to seize the day, quick-buck hawkers offering badges, snacks, International Times, and Tariq Ali's Black Dwarf, and Oz and Peace News.

Biggie and Em walked far ahead and were lost in the crowd. Simon gripped Milly's hand. This was the life! The life *before* Angela, lived anew! At Charing Cross station more teemed ceaselessly from every exit. The leftist newspaper vendors clustered there, concerned more with winning young hearts to their faction than with the war in Vietnam – though their headlines were all about today's 'demo', as they called it. In waves, hundreds crossed the road, halting all traffic, surging towards the square under flags like a medieval crusade. In the distance the fringes of the gathering could be seen, individuals drifting on the edge of a mass.

Seen from inside though, as Simon and Milly joined the crowd, there was space to stroll between clusters of people standing or sitting. Joyful music played, banners were unfurled, the smell of dope was in the air and the demonstration became a huge open-air party extending along every street, not so much an anti-War protest rally as a vast celebration of youth and change, thousands gathered in festivity, waiting for something decisive to happen.

Speeches from tinny loudspeakers echoed around; the whole boring cheeseboard of big cheeses of the leftist establishment were droning earnestly, ignored. Simon did not know who was speaking and did not care what they said. Such people dealt only in rhetoric and clichés and old ideas. That there was a stage at all, and a world divided into speakers and those spoken to, was repulsive and infuriating. From a corner of the square the official march was officially setting off under the guidance of officials. But official routes had been crushed by numbers and spontaneity. Across the whole width of the Strand the mass now began to march slowly towards Fleet Street, prompted to chant, dully parroting *what* they want and *when* they want it, *now – now – now*, an end to Britain's support for the Vietnam war, an end to the bombing, an end to war, *out – out – out*. Etcetera – etcetera – etcetera.

Simon was revolted by the orderly marchers and marshals strolling alongside amiable uniformed police officers, predictable placards and play-acting and boring demands. What *he* urgently wanted was an end to bullshit, an end to people being cogs in a wheel, an end to everything, *now – now – now*. Great swathes of the crowd were in the same mood, and raced free along broad streets. A huge breakaway was in motion, thousands running in a different direction. Phalanxes of police tried to contain them, yet still more demonstrators surged forward. Soon it was the largest crowd ever seen in London, filling the area from Trafalgar Square to Hyde Park Corner in one direction and to Fleet Street in the other, tens of thousands yelling and chanting and dancing and playing music, the whole mass of young humanity squeezing along the West End's broad main streets, hemmed in by complacent facades of unyielding stone. What do *we* want? To unhinge every locked door of entitlement, overturn every seat of power, make every restraining hand afraid, scare every inheritor of privilege, sweep all away. To start all afresh, new and better, equal and just, *now – now – now*.

Simon had no intention of marching along an empty Fleet Street, raging at newspaper offices, or through a deserted West End, boarded against violence, chanting to no one, holding unread banners aloft. He wanted emotion and action and results. With Milly he joined the crush surging endless into Grosvenor Square and pressed against the police barricades, pushing the police back, and back, towards the entrances of the fortress embassy of the United States, its lonely flag fluttering high and proud above the crowd. From lines of vans parked in backstreets, tense, tight-lipped policemen descended quietly in groups, and then came horses to break the crush, forcing the crowd apart, the big animals wide-eyed and panicking, the air a roaring din of philosophy and politics, screaming anger and amusement, hysteria and hilarity and excitement, music and chanting.

A bag flew elegantly from near the front of the crowd and burst open on a police helmet, coating the policeman's face and uniform with white dust. Roars of laughter. Then like arrows came more bags of flour, bursting one after another over the police. The police moved forward on their horses to push the crowd away, but then pennies were thrown and the horses reared and turned as they were struck, retreating and stepping nervously into one another.

Simon moved forward with a thousand others into the line of uniforms. Milly ran, losing him, rejoining him. Police on foot grabbed at demonstrators, one by one, anyone, pressed them down to the ground, kicked them, punched them, carried them away, moved with batons held, the air cloudy and full of noise. Helmetless policemen linked arms, protesters charged against them, and Simon paused in the crowd to throw a protective arm around Milly. Elated, he held her close and kissed her full on the lips. From that moment, she wished their future would be always together.

On a Grosvenor Square balcony a freelance photographer understood and clicked. The black and white image appeared in the next day's papers, a moody, timeless, iconic, inspiring shot. *Make Love Not War* read the captions, and *Love At The Barricades* and *A Time To Love*.

The aura of California clung to them, West Coast sun shining from their skin and hair. Staring at every face, Simon began to wonder if he would recognize her. He could not quite picture her. Had he ever, he thought in panic, really known what she looked like? Had he already missed her? He glanced over his shoulder into the arrivals hall, but dared not turn away from the barrier in case, in that very moment, Angela should arrive. He shifted nervously, looked around uncertainly, craned to see a clock.

Then she stood there, motionless, unmistakable, as fascinating as that first time at Lake Anza. The automatic doors had opened for her and would remain open forever until she stepped forward.

Time and place were wiped from his mind. All else was forgotten. London or Berkeley became one, became meaningless. As their eyes met he fell again into the magnetic pull. Hers as always seemed able to uncover his inmost thoughts. She half-smiled with that familiar, fascinating dizzying mix, disdainful, rueful, conspiratorial, amused, mocking, knowing. He was lost in her, the airport and the crowd suddenly stilled and silenced.

And the same red, yellow, blue! The red sweater and tight, pale blue jeans that she wore the last time he saw her, that looked so good with her golden-yellow hair. Wonderful! Deliberate? Of course. He knew that with Angela, as on a Tarot card, nothing is by chance.

Coolly holding her luggage, expressionless, unmoving beneath the anonymous scrutiny of the crowd, she was locked into a perfect instant in time... Angela, between the obedient doors. To every eye this striking blonde looked magnificently poised and remarkably unwearied by the long flight and four hour delay.

By comparison, as always, Simon felt himself callow, slight, a mere wisp of a person. Yet her arrival – onto his own territory – meant that somehow fortune had singled him out to be a companion for her. As Angela saw him and moved forward, the automatic doors hissed shut behind her. There, where a hundred strangers focused their expectant gaze, her arms folded around him.

'Simon! So good to see you again. Poor dear Simon!' He wondered why he was 'poor'.

'And poor Angela!' He meant, because of the long flight delay.

On the train into London, Angela stared out of the window and tightened her lips. He turned to see what she was watching. Housing estates and streets of small pre-War tract homes littered the ground. Beyond them, dull green and grey fields moved across the horizon. Gradually the rows of little houses extended further until the remnants of countryside could no longer be seen. A sheet of cloud low in the sky, obscured most of what might have been autumn evening sunlight.

'Angela, tell me honestly why you came to England.'

She looked with opaque intensity into his eyes, as enigmatic as a cat. 'To be with you, dearest.'

The effusive Biggie embraced her with an excess of warmth. In contrast, without touching her at all, Em said a shy hello. Casting each of them a sweet smile, Angela sat down as if at home, and asked if she might have a cup of tea. Em asked who else wanted tea. Hearing the unanimous response, Biggie jested, 'What worker and what capitalist does not like a nice cup of tea? It will be a revolution indeed when the teapots of England are smashed.' He caught Angela's eye as she smiled, as if the joke had been made for her enjoyment alone.

For days and nights, warmed only by a two-bar electric fire, Simon and Angela made love on Biggie and Em's floor. But this wasn't Berkeley. There wasn't the joy. She said the room was *awfully cold*. She was melancholy and quiet. Afterwards, Simon lay lost in imagination, half-awake thoughts wandering an endless cosmos. Angela would sleep, her blonde hair lit by the streetlights outside like a bright aura around her head. Her eyes softly closed and her mouth relaxed, as if the true Angela could be known only by finding a way into her dreams.

His wishes had come true: she had come to Britain especially to be with him, and she never mentioned Jesse any more. He no longer feared getting too involved. Yet it didn't feel good. Perhaps it was that they were guests in someone else's place. Perhaps it was the advancing cold of the season. Perhaps it was him. He would look at her, wonder what the problem was, turn over and go to sleep.

They were visited by a succession of his old friends, whom he now saw through Angela's eyes, longhaired, weedy students, hopeless cases, skinny English kids who hadn't ever felt the sun warm their skin, or been to a free concert in Golden Gate Park, hung around Haight Street or driven along Telegraph on acid.

One fine day Simon and Angela sat on the top deck of a number 24 bus all the way from Victoria to Hampstead Heath. As it passed through Camden, he told her that was the hippest and most right-on place to be in London. He pointed out Compendium Books (*'Like Cody's or Moe's, or City Lights'*) and the Roundhouse (*'Like the Carousel Ballroom'*), where the Doors had played a month before (*'Shame to miss that!'*). At Hampstead Heath they walked hand in hand to the top of Parliament Hill and admired the view of London (*'Why's it called Parliament Hill? Can you see the Houses of Parliament?'*). He pointed out where Jefferson Airplane and Fairport Convention had played on the hillside. After a stroll through the backstreets of Hampstead (*'Like the Berkeley hills'*), she declared that she had to live in the area.

The only place Simon could find for them that he could afford was an ordinary little house for rent in the run-down brick terraces close to the Roundhouse. It wasn't in the heights of Hampstead; it was Chalk Farm, at the bottom of the hill and altogether lacking Hampstead's charm and cachet. For all that, the street was attractively curved, with an old-fashioned grocer's on one corner and a traditional pub on another, and the house was in better shape than most of its neighbors – a few of which were derelict, several of them squatted. Further along, an abandoned shop had been turned by volunteers into a thriving wholefoods store called Community Supplies, a fragrant haven of rice and pulses and herbs in bulging hessian sacks, organic vegetables and loose eggs piled high in baskets. It had the air of a meeting place as much as a store, with patchouli-scented longhairs chatting outside.

When Simon reached the house he had come to see, the tenant was moving out at that very moment.

'Hey, man. This your place?' Simon asked him.

'It's for rent. I'm leaving today. Want a look round?'

The tenant gave his name as Rich. Tall, slim, with sharp, smiley eyes, clean-cut features and a great stack of soft brown curls, he wore a fringed suede jacket, wide-collar shirt and thigh-gripping cotton bellbottoms, or 'loons', that were the look *du jour*.

Rich led him across the floorboards of a gloomy, narrow corridor. They peered into a bleak old-fashioned kitchen and switched on a bare lightbulb to look round the cold sitting room. They clumped up the stairs – a narrow strip of carpet running down the center – to inspect two chill, damp, uncomfortable bedrooms. For completeness' sake, Simon opened the door for a glance into a freezing (and unheatable) toilet and bathroom. Angela would hate this. She wouldn't know it was as good as he could ever hope to find. He said he could move in straight away.

Simon lent a hand with Rich's boxes and bags, loading shoes, records and piles of clothes into an old van parked outside. 'So where you going from here?' he asked as he worked.

'Brighton. My girlfriend's at the university. She's got a house in Kemp Town.'

'Far out. Do you want some acid? I've got a stack of California Sunshine. I've got some with me. It's the real thing.'

'Hey, cool. How much?'

Rich bought two tabs and said that, by the way, Brighton was a great place to sell stuff. 'Just walk onto the campus. There's no security. Try the Student Union.'

Angela tugged Simon by the sleeve towards the spare bedroom. She squatted down on the mattress and he sat on the floor next to her.

'Now's not the right time for me to go anywhere,' she said.

'I've been trying really hard to find somewhere for us to live, and I've found a place.'

'Things are different now. Biggie and I are getting on well.'

'Oh. Meaning what, exactly? Sleeping together?'

She snorted at the prim phrase. 'Yeah, fucking, balling, getting laid, whatever you want to call it. How d'ya guess?'

Simon knew he should not be surprised. It was the sort of thing Biggie would do. Somehow he was surprised though, as well as hurt, by

Angela's contempt for him, and further aggrieved that this had happened while he was house-hunting. Then all at once he had several awful worries: he had just committed himself to renting a house; his pride in showing off Angela had come before a big fall; and it was likely she had been slagging him off – badmouthing him – to his old friends.

'I was hoping to love you,' he said. 'And live with you.'

'Well,' she replied with good-humor, 'nothing to stop you loving me.' She laughed and went on, 'As for living together… while you were away, your ol' buddy Biggie asked me to live with *him*.'

'He did *what*?'

'Oh, don't worry. Biggie's like an adorable cuddly toy. Balling him is as much fun as balling a teddy bear.'

Simon cringed at hearing such detail. 'Do teddy bears have balls?'

'Oh, but he's *so* sweet. Emma doesn't give him what he deserves.'

Simon was appalled to realize what he had done to Em in bringing Angela here. 'How's she taking all this?'

'I never asked,' Angela said. 'She's so uptight.' The smile vanished as with sugary kindness she took his hand. 'Oh poor Sim. Why should I live with *you*? You think I should love you, you want me to be your chick, your wifey little chicky, your pretty pretty girlie girlfriend, eh?'

'Fuck off!' Outraged, Simon jumped up and took a step towards the door, but Angela grabbed his hand to stop him leaving.

'OK, OK, take it easy, just kidding. I'll live with ya.'

Biggie stayed out that night. Em didn't say a word to either of them.

In bed, after sex, Angela whispered, 'Of course I want to be with you. In London or any fucking place you take me. I love you. You shouldn't have gotten so upset.'

He could hope for no more than that from her. They held hands under the covers and went to sleep.

* * *

There were no farewell hugs. Neither Biggie nor Em were even there when Angela and Simon left. As far as Em was concerned, Angela had long outstayed her welcome. It made a bitter departure for Simon, followed by a sad arrival at their new home in Chalk Farm.

Angela had literally never seen, or dreamt of, anything quite so bad. The bathroom *was* cold, unspeakably cold, with clattering, spitting air bubbles in the pipes, and she did hate it. The whole house was damp. In the bedroom the floorboards were bare but for a cheap, worn rug in the center, the once-white walls were unadorned, the outlook onto the street dreary and boring. In fact, the whole neighborhood was dreary and boring. The wretchedly dull English people in their wretchedly shabby jackets and coats were definitely dreary and boring.

As Simon had entered another world in California, Angela now saw the flip-side. This was indeed a world unlike anything she had imagined.

Simon signed on at the Social Security office. That dealt with the rent and food. Angela's mother in LA took to sending ten or twenty dollars bills in letters every few weeks. That paid for everything else, including occasional concerts at the Roundhouse (Led Zeppelin, The Who). Simon would walk to the corner shop carrying only half a crown. He was served at a wide wooden counter, and came back with a pint of milk, a loaf of bread and a quarter of a pound of loose tea in a brown paper bag.

They bought a few more records and tapes. The mood of rock had changed, though. In the quiet evenings they played Joni Mitchell's sad, contemplative album over and over, and Dylan's gloomy, cryptic *John Wesley Harding*. The Beatles' new release, *The White Album,* wasn't much good either; even the Beatles, back from India, were slipping.

If there was spare cash, they had a meal of brown rice and veg at Manna, or went to the Camden Plaza cinema – there was a Japanese season at the time. Angela longed for something else. She had said she loved Hampstead and the Heath and wanted to live near them. Yet as the muted, colorful weeks of an English autumn disappeared into grey, humid English winter, they didn't interest her anymore.

'Want to come for a walk?' he'd ask.

She would shake her head. 'No. You go.' He'd kiss her goodbye and walk on his own. In those days, no one seemed to know about the Heath. Sometimes he'd cross it and see not one other person. On the way back, he often stepped into the artists' supplies shop at South End Green, from sheer love of the physical materials, the jumble of brushes and pens, the choice of paper, the colors and painting equipment. This was the time and the season to try his hand at watercolor, and he bought a palette tin. Yet still he preferred the simplicity of pen and paper to capture changing glimpses, movements and moods as he walked.

* * *

Angela lit some sandalwood incense and leaned back in a chair, holding up a book, but did not read. She daydreamed unclear images of exciting or interesting times in strange places. England had turned out to be a flop. A damp squib, as the English say. A wet, colorless monotony.

Simon loved Hampstead Heath, she noticed. He'd go there at dawn, at dusk, anytime. She liked the image of him, wearing the warm jacket on which she had embroidered a scorpion, striding under cold skies. For herself, she preferred to stay at home reading, embroidering, writing letters. She was knitting Simon a scarf, long, loose-knit, in bands of blue and green. Other pleasures were denied her. Even cooking became a chore in that god-awful kitchen. She knew herself to be deeply unhappy, and wondered when – Sasha had said it was written in the cards – Simon would travel.

He lay on the bed, propped on pillows, and watched as she gazed into the book. She wore the thick red sweater and blue jeans, but her hair was less golden than it used to be. He should not have brought her here. But no, he remembered, she came of her own free will.

He fetched his sketchpad and pens, and in a fine black line began to draw, the drape of hair hiding her face half turned away, not reading, the ignored book on her crossed legs, the whole form wearily at rest. He was unsatisfied, and realized it wasn't the effect he wanted. Then he remembered the watercolors. Taking the palette tin from the shelf, he moistened a single brush in his bedside glass of drinking water, twisted it in the bright pigments, and casually swept broad areas of transparent yellow, pyrrol scarlet, cobalt blue onto the paper, filling in the shape of her. The rest of the room he shaded in black and white.

Angela glanced up. His unhip devotion was distressing. She gave a faint smile. Simon had changed. In America she had seen him as light, attractive, clever, quick. Once upon a time he had been bold and bright, and had persuaded her to sleep with him when she was not sure. She had caught in him then some reflection of what she had loved and lost. But now... the light was gone, and she could not believe she had left California, and Sirius, for this. She had to move. Back, or forward, either to Berkeley or to Jesse. But she could not move, could not rouse herself. Of course, they had not been here long. Perhaps things would get better.

'What's that you're doing?' she said.

'Careful, it's wet.' He reached the paper over to her. 'Keep it flat.'

Simon watched curiously as she studied it, and abandoned himself to the fascination she held for him. He desired her always, though sex had become like a present Angela gave him. It was mechanical. He knew everything was wrong between them now. As she had loved him in Berkeley, so she was sick of him in London. He tried to picture a good life, but its details remained out of focus.

Angela pronounced the picture 'Very good', and set it aside.

She began to write on the back of her bookmark. Angela rarely wrote anything, apart from a letter or a shopping list, so he asked if she was writing to someone. 'Maybe I am,' she replied. 'Wait and see.'

Finally she re-read her work and handed it to Simon, a little note on a scrap of paper.

I want to shut up
I want to love
I want to go to bed in a warm room
And sink into dreams
Of him.

I want to wake up
I want to love
I want to shampoo my hair in a warm room
And have a cup of tea
With him.

I want want want
him

The words did not match her feelings. She had never been much of a writer. She was uncertain whether 'him' meant Jesse, a real person far away from her in India and in memories, or Simon, now an almost imaginary, half-forgotten creature of brilliant sex and sunshine, far removed from the boring boy she was living with here. Or both. She did want something though, painfully. Maybe love, maybe sunshine, maybe money. Or maybe only to shampoo her hair in a warm room. Or perhaps it was about nothing, and no one, simply a desire for happiness.

She started to cry. Simon, shocked, wondered if he had ever seen her so miserable. Weeping wasn't her style. In a single instant her quiet tears changed to racking sobs.

An avalanche of sadness, frustration and anger tore through her soul. Through the tears, she began to accuse him, abuse him, raged and wept incoherently at the cards she had been dealt, not just now, but always; not just him, but the whole damned male-female thing; and not just London, but the whole fucking haphazard chaos of life, that ignores your feelings, that has you born somewhere, throws you down in meaningless places, in ugly streets of houses and unheated rooms with pathetic little men. She railed against her loneliness.

He misjudged the venom in her voice, and did not know from what depth it came. He searched for some comforting phrase. He rested a hand on hers. 'We'll make things better,' he said. 'We'll find a way. It'll be all right. You're not alone. We're together and I love you.'

She pushed his hand away sharply. 'No, we won't make things better. It won't be all right. And can't you see *that I – don't – fucking – love – you.*' She started the sentence almost in a whisper and at the end sat up and shrieked at the ceiling, at the pale skies above the roof. Finally she plunged her head into her hands and whimpered 'Leave me in peace.'

He went downstairs and for a few minutes sat at the kitchen table, uncertain what to do. Should he go out? Through the window the weather was clear and light, a washed-out reminder of a summer's day.

There didn't seem any point in sitting here. He wondered if he dared return to the bedroom. The kitchen door opened and Angela walked in, thoroughly composed, hair neatly parted, no trace of tears.

'Simon,' she said calmly, 'you must know, the sort of love you want doesn't exist. It's just a fairy tale.'

He nodded sadly. Yet she seemed to feel it for Jesse, he thought.

With the gas on high, and the oven door open, the kitchen soon became steamily warm, the air condensing on the windows, moisture trickling down the glass.

Angela took off her sweater. She was wearing a tee-shirt underneath. He leaned forward and kissed her head, ran his fingers through the blonde. Angela put her arm around his waist and then, impulsively, she hugged him. 'We do say some horrible things to each other.'

'Yes, we do,' he answered, thinking that it was Angela who said the cruelest things.

'That's only because of stupid stuff, like the weather.'

She rose from her chair, turned off the oven and without another word took Simon's hand and led him from the kitchen back up to the bedroom. There, the two coiled-metal bars of the electric fire gave off a fiery orange glow. She kissed him long and hard, undressed herself and then him. They climbed under the blankets and had sex, and lay together like old lovers, old friends.

Outside, the sky was turning a pearly white. It would be easy to lie here and never move again. Die here warm together between the sheets.

Yet his mind wandered, and in memory he watched again as she wrote her poem, heard again her shriek of rejection, once again lay naked with her on a California riverside, sat beside her looking across the dark Bay at a jewelbox city. He could not remember why he had ever wanted to come back to England. It made no sense to him now. Maybe they should simply return to Berkeley.

He murmured, 'But it's not easy to travel at this time of year. When you haven't got much bread, you know…'

There was a spark of life in her eyes.

'OK,' she said. 'As long as we leave this fucking place.'

'Let's do it. Pack your bag.'

Angela nodded and smiled. He didn't mean this very day, she knew. Yet she felt satisfied, and stretched out in the bed, rested her head on her hands on the pillow and sighed with contentment. Simon caught the thoughtful gaze of her eyes. 'Mm, yes, I think I *do* love you,' she said.

* * *

Onto the kitchen table Simon unfolded a big map of Europe and studied the red and yellow lines traced across it. His finger followed them from city to city, experiences unknown beckoning, and routes untraveled. The obvious direction was eastward; great highways moved that way, reached Istanbul, and continued off the edge of the paper. That journey could not be done in winter, not hitch-hiking. At this time of year it would be murderously cold. North Africa was the nearest place with warm weather. Plenty of good dope there, too.

For once, Angela joined him for a little outing into Hampstead. They browsed in the rambling nooks and corners of High Hill Bookshop, and at The Coffee Cup sat with mugs of hot chocolate and plates of raisin toast succulent with melting, thickly spread butter. At the next table, three elderly ladies in cardigans shot stony glances in their direction and whispered acerbic remarks. Angela was delighted. They walked home holding hands, kicking leaves which lay like golden coins across the path, listening to their soft crashing underfoot. She smiled and kissed Simon's cheek, in a gesture somehow wistful.

When he again unfolded the map, she rose from her chair to look over his shoulder. He explained his thoughts about the route, how long it would take, where they might pass a night, where they ought to stay longer. They could hang around somewhere in North Africa, Simon suggested, and when spring came, if there was any money left, they'd move on, maybe head east.

'Pardner,' Angela grinned, 'we got a long ride to make together.'

So this could be a happy marriage for the duration of our travels, thought Simon.

* * *

They'd need more money, of course. Simon recalled Rich's advice about Sussex University. Alone in Brighton he strolled idly, enjoying being without Angela for a day. He wondered if she'd have been happier there. The town gave pleasure, the way it lay at the foot of the Downs, facing the sea, and had a sort of brightness, and a discreet exuberance. There were plenty of freaks around, too, although in reality these were perhaps undergraduates enjoying three years of freedom and fun before being strapped into straight careers. He caught a bus to the university, three miles out of town. As Rich had said, it was easy to sell acid in the student union. People just lined up to buy it.

With pockets now stuffed with banknotes, he continued into Lewes, the small town near the campus It was much prettier than Brighton, and he wandered happily up and down its 'walks' and 'lanes' of medieval flint cottages, admiring the glimpses they afforded of the green Downs.

He caught a bus back to Brighton, and discovered Kemp Town, with its terraced rows of neat Georgian façades swept over by sea breezes or fleeting mists. By chance, he actually bumped into Rich, who – after a laugh of recognition – agreed to buy Simon's whole remaining stash of acid and sell the tabs himself. He gave Simon £150 for them, in banknotes. Both were pleased with the deal and promised to meet again.

Afterwards Simon stood on Brighton promenade, leaning on the rail, watching slow, surging movements of the wintry sea. Gulls flew free, screaming and circling in the white sky. He could not make out any horizon: in the distance, water and air merged into an opaque curtain. It struck him – banal and obvious, yet a glorious vision – that just beyond it was the rest of the world.

Winter 1968-1969

Christmas brought the usual frenzied television cheer and television snow and, on a visit to the family home, my father's predictable declamations of how wonderful it was that "we" were all together this year.

My mother anxiously asked what my plans were, what I was going to do with my life. Would I be looking for a job? She asked if I had a new girlfriend, or how it stood now with Angela. I had to admit Angela was in England and I was living with her. To allay any concerns I said that Angela had enough money for both of us. My mother was even more troubled by this – and why hadn't Angela come to visit? Through the closed sitting room door I heard my name repeated in a low, urgent voice. Maddeningly, my father seemed to be reassuring her that it was just a phase. I was now twenty years old! How old did you have to be before people would stop saying the way you live is a phase?

I hitched back to London in the middle of a crisp night, tiny stars like pinpricks in the black silk mantle of a midwinter sky. My footsteps struck out a solitary rhythm against the silence as I walked along our street. In the dark room, warm and humid after the frozen air outside, Angela half awoke. 'Come to bed, Simon,' she murmured.

The morning came as brilliant as a New Year's resolution. Angela stayed asleep as I dressed and left the house. Outside, every edge and line – of the curb, the slate roofs, corners of the streets – was sharp and clear in the frosty brightness.

When I returned, Angela was in the kitchen, stirring porridge in a pan. Once more, the oven was lit and its door open to warm the room. She looked up with a smile.

'Hi!' Her voice was unusually cheerful. 'I cooked some oats. Want some?' She moved to find a bowl.

I said, 'It's really nice out.'

'Where d'ya go?' Angela asked.

'Up Primrose Hill.'

Why can't it always be like this? These little fragments of joy.

'That's nice,' she said. 'So, what happened? Did you tell your folks you were gonna travel?'

'No. I didn't. I sort of forgot to mention it. I didn't want to have a row or anything. My mother said she wants to meet you. Maybe when we get back?'

'If we come back.'

'We going for good?'

'Simon,' she replied tartly, 'I never ever want to see this place again.'

* * *

As another year in the straight calendar begins, newspaper columns line up like massed troops of the Establishment, firing denunciations at the chaos. Alternative papers print alternative news. The mood of protest fires even the phlegmatic British soul. In Northern Ireland the touchpaper has at last been lit.

Civil Rights. Free Derry. People's Democracy. Ian Paisley. Jan Palach. Richard Nixon. Yasser Arafat. "Student Riots." "Industrial Unrest." "Space Race." "Equal Pay."

Portnoy's Complaint. The French Lieutenant's Woman. The Little Red Schoolbook.

Music beats across the city skyline as the Beatles play on the roof of Apple Studios…

On such a morning, we slam the front door and walk away without a word to anyone. Angela slips an arm around my waist as she never has since Berkeley. Today we throw away our clocks and diaries. Gazing from a train at the wet fields of Kent, I feel the joyful thrill of uncertainty. Later in the day, in France, we change to the Paris train. As it pulls out of the station, I notice Angela catch sight of her reflection in the window, and smile to herself in the glass.

In impenetrable, veiled dawn the Zaragoza Plain remained obscure, as incomprehensible in daylight as during the long, slow night. The morning was dim, swirling in thick mist. We had become suspicious of lorry drivers after the last one pulled a butcher's knife to show us in the darkness. This new guy was probably younger than us, maybe no more than eighteen years old, his face bright and honest, his eyes dark and melancholy. Could we think he was our own generation? In Franco's Spain, did he even know about acid, about the new revolution? His parents had lost their own war for freedom. Now a different civil war was being fought.

His truck edged slowly forward with a steady roaring of the big engine. The sound became in the end almost soothing. Angela practiced her Spanish, shouting over the engine noise. I didn't know what they were talking about, but at one stage he took a photo out of his pocket and showed it to us with shy pride. It was a photo-booth portrait of a young woman, not smiling, with long black hair primly tied and a dark, remote expression. Could be a sister or a girlfriend. I handed it back. The truck ploughed the dense mist.

We sat by the road and ate bread and cheese, dozed in trucks and cars, never argued and the weather brightened. At Algeciras we were much too early for the day's ferry across the Straits of Gibraltar to Africa. Gibraltar was in view, a massive wedge of rock fixed to the coast.

We went into a cheap café-bar, dark and hot inside. The walls and ceiling had a thick, dusty film of grease. At the other tables, small burly men bent over their plates, talking loudly between mouthfuls. The tortillas were oily, delicious and warming. It was our first proper meal since Paris. We wiped our plates clean with slabs of crumbly yellow-white bread. Angela tucked in like a workman. She looked up, eyes sparkling, and somehow it didn't matter for the moment whether she loved me. We were going to stay together anyway, as long as we kept on the move.

Sitting on the quayside, we held hands and stared idly into the water. Concentric ripples ran away from the concrete walls. In the distance, steamboats chugged through the blue-grey sound. Light spring clouds ran across the sky. The wind blew cool and fresh. Strands of hair strayed across Angela's face. She looked ruddy-cheeked and happy, blue jeans swinging over the side of the jetty.

The ferry, vibrating noisily and overloaded, reached Africa at Ceuta, a Spanish enclave, and the passengers, mostly Arabs, the men in terribly ill-fitting European suits and the women in long plain grey hooded dresses and veils, crowded onto rickety and rusting bare-metal buses.

At the Moroccan border post, our bus juddered to an uncertain halt. The driver slid from his seat and made his way up the aisle asking every passenger for travel documents, taking our passports along with the rest. We were undoubted hippies, beaded and fringed, patched and embroidered, carrying only canvas shoulder bags. With the long hair and round gold-framed glasses, all the way through Spain I had listened to people calling out 'Beatles! Beatles!'

For policemen, passport officers and petty officials of all stripes, we were a rung or two down from regular dirty backpackers. To help with hitch-hiking, my hair was tied in a ponytail and tucked inside my collar. The passport picture, though, showed pale tresses tumbling round a wild-eyed face.

A few moments later the bus driver returned. Beside him a passport officer strode unerringly straight towards me. He turned my head with a single hand and pulled the long ponytail out of hiding. Turning to the other passengers he smirked with self-righteous contentment. They leaned forward and twisted in their seats to discover the cause of his expression. Seeing the ponytail, they nodded at his perspicacity.

He beckoned us to follow as he turned and left the bus. At passport control, another officer grinned. 'In Maroc,' he said, 'no long hair.'

I took a banknote out of my pocket and rested it casually on my passport. 'Can anything be done? We are friends of Maroc!'

Perhaps the note was too small. 'Good,' he said, taking it. 'But no long hair.' I took another banknote from my pocket, but the official shook his head. 'Not interest,' he replied with finality.

'And if I cut it now?'

He beamed with joy. 'Then we welcome you, Monsieur.'

'And if it grows while I am in Maroc?'

He shrugged. The bus driver sounded his horn. The passport officer waved at him enigmatically. In her shoulder bag, Angela had a pair of nail scissors.

'Cut it off at the top of the ponytail,' I said.

'All that way up? Are you sure? Those fuckers. Are you sure there's no other way into this fascist shithole of a country?'

'It's going to be the same everywhere. They hate guys with long hair. They hate women too, so don't argue.'

With quick, savage snips Angela severed the ponytail from the rest of my hair. It fell onto the ground, where it moved lifelessly in the breeze. Passengers' faces peered from the bus, smiling with amazement. His teeth rotten, filled with gold, the officer smiled as if to complete a deal he had not expected to go so well, and stamped the passports for admittance to Morocco. His fellow officers grinned, partly with embarrassment. One of them laughed.

The bus engine was running, waiting for us. The passengers greeted me with laughs and smiles and slaps on the back. As the driver pulled away, I turned and saw my hair still lying on the concrete. Angela's anger seemed even greater than mine.

At a junction of dusty roads we sat on a ridge of earth, our bags slung down beside us. After a while a man came into view, approaching across a dry field. He was thin and small and past middle age, and wore a dirty brown jellaba (a hooded, full-length woolen smock). From his shoulder hung an embroidered bag. His hair was lank, his face unshaven. He walked slowly across the edge of the field, and it became obvious that he was aiming for us.

At last he reached us and, without a word of greeting, sat down right next to me. His eyes scanned the horizon, then the sky. I could see Angela thinking 'Who the fuck is this guy? Is he a nut?'

'Bonjour,' said I.

He sighed, and looked across the field through which he had walked.

'Français?' he asked eventually, rolling the 'r' right at the very tip of his tongue.

'Anglais,' I replied.

His mouth opened in spontaneous astonishment. 'Inglis!'

At once his hand plunged into the shoulder bag and withdrew a disc of bread, flat and dry. He brushed off some dust and ripped it into three, giving us each a piece and keeping one for himself. Eyes twinkling and with a broad smile, he bit into his share with black and yellow teeth.

While we reluctantly chewed the stale, grubby bread, he fumbled again in his bag and this time brought out a long, ornate hash pipe, a packet of kif and some matches. When he had finished eating, he made up the pipe, lit it carefully and handed it to me. We all smoked without another word until the pipe was finished.

Stoned, grinning, Angela then leaned over and asked him: 'Do you speak Spanish?'

Immediately he laughed. He nearly doubled-up with laughter. Angela giggled as he continued and couldn't stop, and then all three of us were roaring and weeping with mirth. I wondered what he was laughing at.

'No,' he answered in English, gasping for breath.

The answer sounded oddly flat. He began to tell us something in Arabic (from his wide-eyed expression I judged that it was a tall story) but at that moment a truck – the cab overfull with four people in it – hurtled around the corner. The old man leaped up, waving his arms frantically at the driver. The truck skidded to a stop and we were invited to come in. Angela placed herself closest to the door, with myself wedged between her female form and the five other men. Seven people in a lorry cab is quite a crowd.

The driver gritted his teeth and with manic wide-eyed grimaces, banged his accelerator onto the floor. We lurched over one another at every turn of the steering wheel, sometimes silent, sometimes laughing, sometimes everyone talking at once. Presently it dawned on me that all of them, like us, were *extremely* stoned.

They set us down in the middle of Casablanca. Night was falling on a maze of crowded streets. Arabic signs made no less sense than their phonetic translations into French. We had lost our bearings, were hungry and tired, and Angela was becoming irritable. I needed a quick solution to our problems if she were not to start blaming me for them. Unexpectedly, a little girl walked up to us and tugged Angela's sleeve. She was not ten years old.

'American *viens avec* me,' she said endearingly, Come with me.

'Where to?' Angela asked.

'Mummy and Daddy house,' the child answered.

Angela glanced doubtfully into my eyes.

'Do your Mummy and Daddy want us to come?' I asked.

'They welcome you. They are happy. They want you,' she replied.

'I doubt that,' Angela said to me.

'Mm. Wanna give it a try?'

'Where do you live?' Angela asked the girl.

'Medina. Come,' she beckoned.

Medina means the old quarter, the heart of an Arab town. Her insistence and our uncertainty caused us to follow. Doubts increased when we had to wait at a bus stop with a huge crowd. We would never

Love 97

find our way back. Back where? We didn't know where we were in any case. When the bus arrived, the little girl pushed and elbowed us onto it. We stood in the crush on board, ignorant of what to pay, whom to pay, where to get off. Outside the bus window, darkness had fallen and every place looked the same, rows of lights and painted metal signs over open-fronted shops, traffic, crowds. The bus raced and rattled along lengthy streets, turned sharp corners, penetrated deeper and deeper into an alien territory of dark alleyways and bewildering script.

At a busy bus stop the girl grabbed our hands and pulled us to the exit of the bus. Angela and I followed as if she were the diminutive adult and we her enormous children, so conspicuous in the Arab crowd. We emerged into a narrow street full of people moving, some fast, some slow, in all directions. Barefoot urchins stopped playing to point and laugh. Adults stood stock still in the rush, staring at us dumbly for a few moments. The girl led us at last to the door of a house. Dusk had given way to night.

She knocked and the door opened. 'Wait,' she ordered us, and scampered inside. The door slammed.

Women and children peered at us from every other doorway. To our relief the girl soon returned.

'Daddy is not here,' she announced with sadness.

'What about Mummy?' I asked.

'She cannot let you in without Daddy,' the girl explained.

'Why?' Angela demanded.

'I am sorry,' the girl replied simply, as she went back inside the house and bolted the door. Although dark, the street was still busy. I expected Angela to cry or become angry. I felt like weeping myself, with disappointment and anxiety. Instead she stood speechless, jaw hanging with indignation and disbelief. Then a grim smile formed. Was she going to look on the bright side? At that instant a slim, sinuous, smiling young man approached.

'I have seen what happened, my friends,' he said in strongly accented English. 'Please to come home with me.'

Suspicious enough of small girls, we were even more alarmed by this new offer from a youth with ingratiating posture and unconvincing grin.

'No, we are all right,' Angela replied, with a surprising lack of haughtiness. 'Thank you though.' If he really had seen what happened, he knew we were not 'all right'.

'As you wish, my friends,' the youth insisted. 'but my parents' home is a few meters only from here if you would please accompany me.'

By a quick nod I recommended to Angela that we try it.

'That's very kind,' I said. 'We shall come.'

He led us to the opening of a small dingy alleyway, unlit, and then into it. This was much worse.

'Wait here,' he cried, running off. We squatted on dirty paving stones. A gaggle of children clustered at the entrance of the alley, peering at us.

Time passed, and a slow shock of fear intensified in the deepening gloom. 'Oh Simon, what shall we do? Where are we?' Angela said. Silence drifted between us. 'In Casablanca. Of movie fame,' she said at last, answering herself with a weak smile.

'Here's lookin' at you, kid.'

I could not show her my own anxiety. 'Let's just leave. Get up and walk away. I don't think we're far from the main road, the one with the buses. Hopefully find some cheap hotel. Want to try?'

'And get even more lost. And ripped off,' Angela retorted.

'Yep. Maybe.'

'And our throats cut too – if we're lucky.'

I shook my head reassuringly. 'Don't let's get paranoid. Let's see what happens. Go with it. Or, it wouldn't kill us to sleep right here.' In truth I was tired enough to sleep anywhere.

The children had wandered off. The street noise waned. 'Well, I don't want to sleep right *here,* that's for sure, if that's what you mean!' she replied indignantly. 'Let's give that guy ten more minutes, then split.'

We sat in silence, becoming more miserable, for another twenty minutes. Then the young man returned, with a companion.

'This my friend,' he said, with the wide smile. Then a deep, sad frown: 'You cannot stay with my family. But,' – the big bright smile again – 'you can stay with his family. We have already asked.' The friend smiled broadly and nodded throughout.

We nodded too, and looked glum. Instead of grateful.

Unaware of how kind they had been, too exhausted now to distrust them, we picked up our bags and followed the newcomer without even saying thank you. He rapped his knuckles on a front door. Pulling a veil over her mouth, an Arab woman flung the door open and hurried away, casting a furtive glance at us as she turned into one of the rooms. She seemed like some crazy lodger, a mad aunt.

Love 99

'That is Mummy,' the young man said in French. He gestured to enter, always nodding and smiling, as several men came towards us along the corridor.

The smiling young man told us his name and introduced us to his father and brothers. Female faces peered tentatively around the kitchen door. These were the sisters, I supposed. If I caught their eye, they would scuttle inside again with a giggle. Rather ceremoniously, we were led into a large room heavily draped in bright fabrics, our bags swiftly taken away.

The father wanted to speak to us – and why not? He was our generous host; just a strange, indistinct figure emerging briefly into the tail end of our long day. I chatted with him monosyllabically in French, smiling often, as a meal was laid out on the table. Only the men – and Angela – sat down to eat. One of the girls waited on us. Angela stared around puzzled, then looked at me questioningly. At last she asked the young man who spoke English: 'Isn't your mother going to eat with us?' This elicited an embarrassed chuckle from him, and from the others when he translated. 'No, no, madam,' the father explained haltingly, 'she eat with the women of the house.'

The meal, a series of nameless, unrecognizable, exquisitely spiced small dishes, then a plate of succulent, meaty stew from a tureen, was delicious, though the conversation became a physical labor. I had strength only to eat and sleep. Instead of looking at our hosts, hearing their words or seeing their house, the day intruded like a noisy film inside my head. We had been in Spain, once upon a time. Vivid recollections roared in my mind, hitch-hiking in the dark, a ferry in bright sunshine, a man handing us bread from his pocket, a crowded bus. How long had I been awake? It must be over twenty-four hours.

Sleep fought me and I could not think.

'The food is good,' I said to the girl, as she scurried past.

'Thank you,' said the father.

The bedroom we were given was in fact a sitting room. A sofa, or rather an upholstered, cushioned bench, ran around all the walls. We were to sleep on this. I undressed and lay down, pulling a blanket over myself. Angela, sensibly, did not take off any clothes.

I fell at once down a slide of dreams, tumbling through pictures of the onrushing road, hearing engines and voices, into a restless sleep.

Straight away, or so it seemed, I was awakened. It was dark in the room. A metallic voice boomed. No one within half a mile could have slept through the noise. It came from somewhere just outside the window. Covering my ears with blankets did not much muffle the sound. Then I opened my eyes wide and stared at the blackness: there was someone else in the room with us. With relief, I saw it was the young man. Covered with a blanket, he sat leaning his head wearily on his knees. I called out, 'What is that?' but he could not hear. The electric wail filled our room.

The voice abruptly stopped, replaced by a vast and ringing silence. I spoke to our host in the darkness. 'What was he saying?' I asked.

'He says it is better to pray than to sleep.'

The morning air was spring-like, and the sky clear blue. The day started with squares of fried pastry and glasses of bright green mint leaves submerged in hot, sweet water. Again the unknown women, giggling and curious, peeked at us from the kitchen doorway. Only the smiling young man joined us to eat. All the other men, he told us, had already left the house. Afterwards he cheerfully carried Angela's bag through the confusing alleys and lanes where we had been so alarmed last night, some now edged with stalls loaded with dried fruits and colored spices or shopfronts spilling onto arcaded sidewalks like one endless market.

Reaching the sudden turmoil of the main boulevard he stood with us amidst a surging mass of people waiting at a bus stop. To our great surprise, he even boarded the bus, staying close to us all the way as it rattled along busy avenues of white apartment blocks to the edge of the city. There he finally shook our hands and wished us good luck, a good journey and a good visit in Maroc, before crossing the road to wait for a bus back to the city. I felt unable to understand the extent of his generosity, or the reason for it.

'What was that about?' Angela ventured after he'd gone, 'At the house? The thing with the women?'

'I don't know. It's what they do, I suppose. Men and women separate. Weird, wasn't it?'

'Freaky,' she agreed. 'But – so why wasn't I with the women?'

'I think a female guest is, y'know, an honorary man. Just guessing.'

'An honorary *man!* Isn't that the biggest insult to a woman?'

A couple of rides, loud Arabic music preventing conversation, raced us along a highway uncluttered by any activity or enterprise. Dusty, scrubby, unproductive farmland gave way to an even sparer terrain strewn with rocks and stones, until we came at last to the edge of a city.

Startling orange trees, their bright fruit hanging amongst the foliage like colored lanterns, lined the main avenue into Marrakech. Skirting the fringes of the Medina, we continued on foot towards the main square, carrying our bags among alleyways, reveling in the dappled sunlight and shadow, delighting in the warm air. Here, the exotic was tempered with the sight of many others like us, and in this city we were not a spectacle.

Beneath an archway, passing under buildings, along a busy lane, we ventured at last through the dark doorway of a cheap hotel. It was soon clear that all the other guests were Arabs. We took a room, spacious, unadorned, and with a small balcony where we could perch on folding chairs looking onto the animated little pedestrian thoroughfare outside.

Every day we woke late and smoked kif, listened to music and lay around, visited the hammam, talked and laughed, had sex, and in the evening strolled to the main square, the Djemaa. There a great crowd circled slowly, illuminated by blazing lamps, choosing from fragrant rows of street-cooks, picking the least unsavory cous-cous stall, sitting at big shared outdoor tables with glasses of sweet mint tea.

Street vendors sold kif piled high like grass cuttings arranged in neat green pyramids, and others came to the dining tables with trays of syrupy cakes, flinging back a cover to reveal 'hash-cookies' beneath the rest. Everywhere the warm, balmy air was fragrant with kif, its scent mixed with oranges and mint and spice.

At the hammam, I lay in a steaming cubicle while the brooding, silent assistant poured pails of hot or cold water over me. Angela went to the women's baths next door, and idly I daydreamed of the soft, naked rounds of flesh in there, myself slipping among the buxom bathers of *Le Bain Turc*. Maybe that's what the assistant was brooding about too.

We were so far away from... we were so far away from it that I could no longer remember what had been bothering me. Our hatred of "the System" seemed laughably remote. Did it encompass the system here too? What did they have here, exactly? Some kind of corrupt feudal Islamic absolute monarchy? Or, rather, was it an innocent Third World nation crushed by the West's fascist industrial-military complex?

Neither of these, for this was but the world of the rich foreigner, a world of delights and Winter Sun, which we dignify as "travel".

As days grew longer and hotter, and February became March, the city became more restless, more crowded with stoned freaks (the longer the hair, the longer they had been here), and the beggars and hash-cake sellers more persistent. Journeys were in the air. Open-air dinner table conversations with friends and strangers in the Djemaa turned quickly to travel plans. Tips and advice, hearsay and opinion, were swapped and noted; a cheap hostel, a cheap ferry, the best day, the best route.

We discussed where to go, and when – and why. What did we want from these places, what did they want from us? Did we have anything for them, except pitifully small amounts of money? Some thought it good for the world to see us: it was subversive. Most admitted that we traveled for pleasure alone, and this drifting, laid-back scene was far better than what we had left behind.

There was, though, some confusion about that. 'A lot of these guys' – gesturing at the Moroccans all around – 'are dope heads, right? But they're not hip. They're straight, right?'

'They're not straight. They're cool. They're good people.'

'No. It's a real *bad* scene here, especially for the women.'

'How can we say that? It's *their* scene, man. *Their* trip, *their* culture.'

'Oh yeah? Same applies to straights back home, doesn't it – it's their culture? Culture, man, fuck that. It's all politics. Everything is politics. It's misogyny, is what it is. Arab women are women like us.'

'That is just so *patronizing*. It's imperialism! People here are *not* like us, and don't want to be. And why should they be?'

What would Paul say? Are travelers bound to be outsiders, merely observers of other societies; are they guests, who must show respect to every foreign custom and belief? Or may they, should they, set out to change the people and places they visit? A lot of the Arabs around us were stoned. But they didn't do acid.

Algeria's western frontier guards demanded another haircut, shouting 'Short! Short!' as Angela snipped. One of them grabbed at her as she worked. She spat directly into his face. He seemed to feel her response had been correct, and took a respectful step back. The other man guffawed till tears flowed.

In the freezing east of the country, we stamped our feet and clapped our hands to heat them. As the road climbed into the Atlas Mountains, we stood in slush as snowflakes whipped in a sharp wind that stabbed like icicle points. White summits ahead marked the Tunisian border.

A French couple stopped at the border and, reclining in their heated car, we descended with them joyfully back to the balmy lowlands.

At the Tunis Poste Restante we picked up our mail, our first contact with the rest of the world for weeks.

Dear Simon

I do hope you are well. You are reading this, so you have at least made it to Tunis, though I don't know when you are reading it so I don't know when or whether I will get an answer. I just want to say, darling, don't feel you are under any pressure to do anything to please us. I wonder if you decided to leave England again because of something to do with us. No doubt, you would say, no, you are just doing what you want. If so, I feel sure that for you, what you are now doing is excellent, tho' it wouldn't do for everyone. Our concern is that you keep safe and well.

Please darling, if you have problems, do let us know. Try to give us somewhere to contact you when you are able. Love from all of us.

Keep well.

Mummy.

Then a PS, in my father's less familiar hand:

It was an unhappy surprise that you left without saying goodbye. Still, you are old enough now to decide for yourself what you want to do. You have our support whatever you decide. This is always your home when you want it. You can always turn to us for anything. Love from all. Dad.

I sat on the steps of the Tunis post office. Traffic roared. Cars sounded horns. Pedestrians brushed past. I rested my head in my hand. *Love from all.* And I didn't even know if I cared about that, or knew what it meant.

You can always turn to us for anything. Half-daydreaming in the din, I pictured my father, his hands open to help; as on the days when I first learnt to walk, ready to catch me, or offer support.

Yet such things are beyond the visible spectrum of family life. Face to face, such love remains always hidden below the surface, forever out of reach. And grown-up children do not turn to their parents for help.

Spring 1969

Rushing darkness followed the sun as, with unnerving speed, it disappeared beyond the horizon. Sand swept across the tarmac. The sky's strange black dimensions soon overflowed with stars, the Milky Way an unfurled banner of the night. The silence of outer space crashed down upon the desert. Perhaps scorpions lurked, or snakes. Later, in the middle of the night, in the middle distance, dogs barked and howled. Where were they? We could make out nothing, nor decide if they were wild or domestic or something between the two. Where was the moon?

In a pick-up truck we crossed the Roman causeway at El Kantara onto the island of Djerba, the first light of the day shining with a springtime tenderness on flat blue waters to either side.

Everything leaves its mark on the soul. Unremembered days make us what we are. Every moment becomes ours, and becomes us. The sound of gravel crunching beneath the wheels, the clean dry air, the luminous blue, thoughts that raced through the mind at that instant, the face of an unknown truck driver half-hidden in keffiyeh, lie beyond memory, as if in a locked chest whose key is lost, but still it is ours. Or a box of old diaries, mislaid somewhere in a house where we used to live.

The first light of the day was warm, the sky clear, and the sea beautiful. That, though, did not please us. Exhausted and hungry, we bickered. As the youth hostel came into view, I told Angela, 'Look, I need to be alone for a bit.' I thought I might sit by myself on the beach.

'Cool,' Angela retorted. She pursed her lips. 'Then I wouldn't have to put up with you.'

'Put up with! You're the one who's always griping and whingeing.'

The hostel, a white house, picturesque and ramshackle, stood at the end of a pebble driveway, surrounded by tall palms, spiky bushes and flowering shrubs. 'Whose idea was it to hitch all night on an empty stomach?' she added.

I turned around and walked away.

Her exasperated voice called out behind me, 'Where are you going?'

I made no reply. *Let her worry.* If I wanted to go to the beach, I was heading the wrong way. The road wound away from the hostel and the town, back towards the causeway. I kept walking.

* * *

More than a day passed before I returned to the pretty youth hostel among palms. On a shaded seat beside the hostel doors, Angela bent her golden hair over some embroidery. She looked up at the sound of my footsteps on the gravel and involuntarily smiled as bright as midsummer.

But no, nothing was involuntary with Angela. She placed down her embroidery and rose to embrace me at the gate. I put my arm around her. She kissed my cheek: 'Hello, silly boy.'

'Now, what were we arguing about?' I asked.

She laughed and hugged me again. 'Nothing. Hey – we're not staying at the hostel,' she said. 'I'm just here waiting for you to come back.'

'How d'ya know I was going to come back?'

'I was sure you would. It's in the cards. And I've got news for you. I found a house to rent. It's real good value.'

A house! This was her way of getting back at me for wanting to travel cheap and light.

'We can move in any time,' she said. 'I already paid the deposit.'

I was aghast. 'You already... but I haven't seen it yet.'

'You'll like it. And the rent is... not too much. I got the blonde chick rate.' She looked me over. 'So where were you last night?'

'There must be a hammam somewhere. I'm dying for a good wash. After that I'll tell you all about it.'

First, though, we strolled along a footpath to look at our house. Angela warned that the outside of it would reveal nothing.

The path passed a hot spring, gushing mysteriously out of the earth. Stonework erected around it allowed women and children gathered there to wash clothes in the warm water. They slapped wet fabrics against flat slabs of stone. A woman kicked away a scruffy little dog, scavenging at the children's feet for scraps of affection. Angela glared at her, and sweetly beckoned the animal. 'Makes me think of Sirius,' she said, though this sickly little mongrel could hardly have been less like that sleek German Shepherd. It trailed her all the way to the house.

Angela was right: the square of windowless walls, pierced by a simple wooden doorway of flaking blue paint, gave no clues as to what lay inside. The mangy dog jumped up at Angela's legs as she patted it, indifferent to fleas, ticks, worms, nits or skin disease. She told it, in English, to wait outside, and it did so, whining plaintively.

Within, the house was like the one where I had spent my night away. Plain white walls enclosed a courtyard, in the center of which an ornate circular pond was empty and dry. Along one wall, the rooms were hidden in shadow, two of them under hemispherical roofs, white domes against blue sky. The other rooms had a flat roof, accessible by a steep staircase of bleached stone. Every room opened onto the courtyard, and inside them was… nothing, just cool space with bare white walls and stone floors. It was a perfect, tranquil haven, a therapy. The empty rooms, especially, I loved.

This would be our home, standing on its own just beyond a sandy outskirt of Houmt-Souk. Behind it the sea lay massive and hazy, idly moving. All around in the sand, tall, ungainly palm trees loitered in the uncertain sunshine.

'Thanks for doing this – making it happen,' I said, rather generously since I had not even been asked if I wanted to live on the island of Djerba. Had I been asked, I would have said *No*.

'Are you ready to tell me where you went for the night.'

I shook my head. 'I need to wash first. I got laid, at least.'

At first she was startled. Then her face tightened angrily.

'By a couple of guys,' I added.

Her eyes widened. 'Oh Jesus Christ, Simon,' she said. 'Why?'

'We-e-ell. It was their idea, but I went along with it.'

'You must be crazy. I wouldn't have done it.' She didn't mean because of AIDS: there was no AIDS in those days. She just meant she wouldn't have done it.

'No, I wouldna done it either. Only I didn't have much choice. Don't worry, I won't get pregnant. Anyway, I got a free breakfast out of it.'

With relief ('So it's all right to have sex with a guy but not with a chick?' I protested), she leaned forward and ruffled my hair like a child. She put her arm over my shoulder in a brotherly way.

'Who were these guys of yours?' she grinned.

I shrugged. 'I really don't know. Just a couple of young fellers. Like I said, I had no choice.'

She laughed aloud. 'What do you mean, no choice? You could have, like, just said...' Her grin vanished in an instant. She stopped breathing and stared. 'No choice. You mean, like, you were... you don't mean you were...'

'What?'

'Not raped?'

'Is that the word?'

'Is it the word? Tell me what happened.'

'Let me have that Turkish bath first.'

The masseur wrapped my body in towels and I leaned back against the marble to think. To think about yesterday. We were arriving at the youth hostel in Houmt-Souk. We argued and I walked away. 'Where the heck are you going?' she shouted. I didn't care, and forced myself not to turn around or respond. I thought: Let her worry.

The road wound away from the hostel and I kept walking, holding out a thumb and glad to be on my own. It didn't matter where the first ride was going, I'd take it. To Tunis would do. I'd catch a ferry to Italy. Anywhere. I just wanted a break from Angela.

Straight away a man in a battered old car stopped and said he could drop me in the next village. There, another driver gestured eastward, and said *Libya*. I slipped into his pick-up and slammed the door. He crossed the low causeway to the mainland and raced noisily along an empty road through featureless country. We had hardly a word in common. Other than an incomprehensible vocabulary of hand-signs, smiles, shrugs and head-shaking, we ignored each other, and that, too, seemed a companionship of sorts. Libya beckoned with promises of sand and harsh simplicity. There was a kind of uprising going on there, the king had fled the country, and we'd heard on the road about anti-western riots. Anyway, it was Angela-free.

The pick-up came to a stop at last on the far side of a dusty village. I gathered from my laconic companion that he could take me no further. *Libya*? I queried. With open palm he gestured further east and spread his fingers, *hamsa*, five, from which I understood we were still in Tunisia.

He drove away, leaving me as alone as I would ever wish to be.

I waited by the roadside under a tree, first standing, then sitting on a grassy bank in its shade. No more cars came by.

The air was hot and dry, narcotic and dreamlike. At last two little girls arrived, played a game, glanced periodically in my direction, and went away. Later, an old woman, pausing every few yards, struggled along the road with a bundle. Her gaze settled on me. I greeted her, '*Labès*.' She did not reply. As she passed, her eyes looked apprehensively into mine, and I realized she was not old after all, but young, and tired. She turned away, only then answering '*Labès*.' She made progress along the deserted way, eventually disappearing from my view.

An afternoon silence fell across the village like a heavy shroud. It was a quietness full of minute tickings and rattlings, low hummings, and the tiny sounds of dry, skeletal insects moving in the rainless underbrush.

I wondered how Angela felt about my departure and what she was doing. Probably she had not thought of me at all and was enjoying a long sleep in a real bed at the youth hostel.

Now two young men ambled along the road, chatting in low voices. They halted, astonished, when they saw me, and gazed in wonder. Feigning nonchalance, they casually took up places on the opposite bank, eyeing me almost shyly while continuing their conversation.

Stringily built, wiry, dark-browed, in Western dress, they seemed not too young nor too old to be up to some cunning trick or clever mischief. I guessed they were about my own age, and would soon ask for money, or try to sell me something. I looked back into the village. There were no cars, only some drowsy peasants on foot in the distance. And the other way, out of the village, the road vanished around a corner into a haze of dry vegetation edged by dust.

'Monsieur, have you postage stamps?' one of them asked at last in a hoarse voice. His manner was forthright, with a hint of cheek. It was easy to imagine him in a year or two working one of the black market rackets up in Tunis. I did not know why he would want stamps, but in any case, I did not have any, new or used.

'*Eh bien*, Monsieur,' chipped in the other, 'then foreign money?' Less bold, less sharp, and less demanding than his friend, he would not graduate to Tunis.

The first youth watched intently. 'But you have Tunisia money?'

'Enough to get to Libya,' I replied.

A look of horror passed over their faces. 'Bad people in Libya!' exclaimed the second youth.

'In Tunisia, they say 'bad people in Libya.' In Algeria they say 'bad people in Tunisia.' And in Maroc, they say 'bad people in Algeria.''

The dark eyes of the first boy looked down as if in shame. 'They all make mistake?' he asked quietly.

'No, they are all correct,' I said.

At this they were outraged. 'What? So, you think we are bad in Tunisia?'

'In Tunisia, people are the same as in my country,' I said.

They missed the irony, but seemed mollified. 'America,' the second explained to the first.

'England,' I corrected him.

'You are Inglis!' they exclaimed, glancing at each other.

The pair sat beside me to chat. They were impressively persistent, and their English wonderfully good. I made it plain that their conversation didn't interest me and I wished them to go away, though it was obvious that I had nothing else to do and no one else to talk to. In fact something like a spirit of friendship crept into my attitude to this spot, the unused road, its dry and dusty earth bank on which I rested, the tree which had shaded me from the afternoon sun which now gave way to evening, the droning insects, and now even these two local lads.

'You want tea, *mon ami*?' one of them asked in a convivial tone, as if it were a habit of ours to take tea together.

It was indeed teatime. 'Well, why not?' I said, and added, so that he could understand, 'Yes, thank you very much.'

As if concluding a transaction, or rising from the conference table, they stood peremptorily. It appeared that the first part of their business was complete. The next part was to get me home for tea.

The older brushed briskly at his trousers with his hand, sending a few particles of dust into the air. I stood too, equally conscious of an important change: I was giving up waiting for a lift and had been invited into a rural Arab home. Procession-like, we made our way into the village. Now walking in a more purposeful manner, suddenly the two seemed older. They were older than me, after all.

'Where are we going?' I asked as we turned off the road along a rutted, potholed dirt track lined with a few unfinished flat-roofed concrete houses. In the dust half-naked children gaped as we filed past.

'*Chez moi, mon ami,*' said the older of the two; my house, my friend.

The familiar tone made me glance at him sharply. 'How far is it?'

'*Mon ami*, it is very nearby to here,' he said. And he was right, for almost immediately we reached a flaking green door in a concrete wall. Inside, we stood in an enclosed courtyard, paved in handsome white slabs. The walls too were gleaming white, everything bright in the sun. Rooms stood around the perimeter, making a square. I'd love to have a place like this, I thought.

'Ma!' The boy called his order: '*Shai!*' Tea!

From far away in one of the rooms a woman's voice greeted us in a pliant, pleading tone.

We sat in the yard, leaning against a white wall. I was curious: I'd have been interested to see inside one of those rooms. The winter sun shone, warm even at this late hour. The two fidgeted restlessly and whispered in Arabic. The situation felt more ridiculous than ever. I wished I hadn't come.

Suddenly a woman peeked out of a doorway and the older boy took the tea from her. She didn't even glance at me, heaping more absurdity onto the situation. As soon as she had gone, the younger of the two leaped up as if inspired and darted into a room, at once returning with a pile of magazines which he showed off proudly. They were French women's magazines, of the type I usually saw only in waiting rooms.

Deftly the pages were flicked to advertisements for underwear. The boys guffawed in excited embarrassment at pretty, nubile white models posing in bra and panties.

'You like? You like?' they nudged. 'You like?'

I prayed that the boys' mother might somehow save me from this awfulness. What was the correct response? Yes, or no? Perhaps I could simply leave. I could say I had to be going. Of course, it would be obvious that was nonsense.

I remembered it; I used to get turned on, too, by ads, or fashion-shoot pictures, in my mother's magazines. But I was twelve or thirteen. At twenty years old I wouldn't want anyone to suppose that I have such a wretched sex life that ads for lingerie are a turn on – even if they are. On the other hand, I didn't want them to think I was homosexual.

With crude, schoolboy gestures, red-faced and smirking, the younger crassly showed his appreciation of a woman's breasts roundly enclosed in uplifted whiteness.

I grimaced disapproval of their lecherous mood and sipped my tea. After tea I'll leave, I thought. Oh God, I wish I was with Angela. I'll hitch back straight away.

On the other hand, that's pathetic. No, I must stay away for, well, maybe a couple of nights, to assert my independence. At least one night. If I return within the day, it'll look like a dog creeping home with his tail between his legs. To go back after a night out has a small ring of triumph about it. Angela would wonder what had become of me, what adventure I might have without her.

Anyway, I can't get a ride out of here. I'm stuck in this village whose name I've forgotten. It's not even on a main road. No – I'll walk back. It'll take me all night. I can arrive in the morning, full of self-pity after a second night without sleep. No, self-pity wouldn't be a good move. Nor would fatigue. I'll hitch, or walk, until I reach a hotel.

Maybe she's missing me already! That would be good. Maybe she isn't so damn certain now about doing things *her* way all the time. While I'm away, too busy with interesting experiences to give her any thought, Angela might be sitting idly, hoping I will soon return. So for once my need would not be greater than hers. Or so I schemed. In truth, I longed to be with her.

Trying with nudges and winks to revive my interest, the two still pored over the pictures, making the same strange laughs and groans that school friends and I had made looking at 'glamour' magazines under our desk lids or in the changing rooms. Are these sounds universal, then?

To break the mood I stood up and wandered around the courtyard, pausing at the doorway to look outside. Evening was approaching. Homeward-bound men walked on the path and in the main street. Women scurried with bulbous, stainless steel pots and wicker baskets.

The older boy's friend will soon go to his own home, I reasoned, and the father of this household will reappear after his day's work.

The woman's voice called. I turned to listen. She was speaking from inside the house without showing herself. The older boy stood listening, then came to me. '*Mon ami*, you will eat with us this evening?'

Thinking it might be better if he called me Monsieur, or even Simon, I replied. 'Thank you, yes! You are very kind.'

'And tonight, where are you going?'

'Is there a hotel here?' There wouldn't be, in a place like this.

He affected shock, almost insult. 'Hotel! My dear friend! How can you say this to me?' Again the voice made me glance into his face. He seemed to have become much older. His dark brows, his shadow of mustache, the wiry frame, suddenly looked manly.

No father arrived, and the younger friend did not go anywhere. Both young men ate with me, while the woman dined alone in the dark room where I had glimpsed her earlier. She had turned on a transistor radio, a bizarre modernity in this home without electricity. A high-pitched voice rattled out of the tinny speaker. Perhaps it was an aged entertainer being interviewed about her colorful life. Evidently it was interesting, as the two youths listened in silence.

Presently, as we spooned cous-cous into our mouths, the older of my two companions muttered reverentially, 'It is President Bourguiba.'

I could hardly believe that this was the iron-handed dictator. 'That is Bourguiba?'

'All the Arab peoples love him. He is President Bourguiba,' added the younger.

I nodded respectfully and said nothing. It would be in poor taste, perhaps, to refer to the President's castrati voice.

After dinner we retired to a room that seemingly served as both a lounge and a bedroom. Paraffin lamps flickered from each corner. It appeared that the young men and I were to sleep in the same room. They told me their names, Abdel and Mahmoud, and questioned me about my travels.

To please them, I told the tale of how we had crossed Algeria in three days because we did not like Algerians.

'*Lorsque*, you have a wife, Monsieur Simon,' asked the younger one, Abdel.

'Yes, yes. Or, she is my friend,' I explained rashly. It would have been better to stick with wife.

'Oh, you are lucky!' they both laughed.

'She is where now?' asked the older one, innocently.

'At Houmt-Souk.'

'But you, you go to Libya?'

This showed that they had been paying attention, and I hadn't.

'She is coming later, if it is safe in Libya,' I answered blandly.

'*Mon ami*, it is *not* safe in Libya! *Eh bien!* Let us sleep,' declared Mahmoud, after a last glass of tea.

It would be easier to pass the time in sleep, so I agreed. Then the night would be over and I could return to my dear Angela. With all her frowns and mind games and pointed remarks and long silences and aloofness yet I adored her and could not wait to see her face again. I cared about nothing else. The lamps were extinguished. A paleness, something less than a light, came through the window from a starry sky.

The two removed their trousers, revealing that their shirts were very long, not western in design at all. With few words, they climbed into their beds, and I into mine. Cicadas outside scratched their persistent, sonorous note. I was not tired, though I had not slept last night. It is strange to be lying here. Where am I? Where ought I to be? Beside Angela in Berkeley? We can never understand. There is nothing to understand. These places and people are incidents in a life, just a life.

I was awakened by one of the Arab youths climbing into my bed. I struggled to think: it was still dark, the stars, the room – nothing had changed except the cicadas had stopped and the night had become silent,

'*Qu'est-ce que tu fais?*' I exclaimed. What are you doing? But I knew what he was doing. His shirt hung oddly over a half-erection. It was the older of the two, now more like a grown-up man than ever.

'Shh!' he coaxed, resting a big hand firmly on my hip to keep me in place. He snuggled next to me under my blanket, both of us on our sides. His hand slipped around me, down over my waist with a deft and purposeful caress, and reached my penis.

Hardly a second had passed since I woke. My mind grappled to comprehend. Yes, he is holding me and stroking my penis; this is incredible. Is it safe to resist? What will happen if I do – or don't? Would he resort to violence? There was no time to think it through.

'No, no. Do not,' I told him urgently, 'Do not do this. It is bad. Let me sleep.' I tried to move away, but he gripped me still more strongly. I managed to turn my head to catch his eye. My words were woefully inadequate, almost amusing, a parody of a girlish refusal. Perhaps I should say I have my period. Mahmoud grinned at my dainty protest. It seemed incomprehensible that he was prepared to assert his desire in this brute manner. Women, not knowing what his desire feels like, must be still more mystified by this. But I knew well what he felt, and that it must be halted at once if it were not to become unstoppable. Should I fight back, actually hit him? It seemed absurd – and inappropriate for a guest. And if I did, he would assert himself all the more.

By now, perhaps as much as three seconds had passed and I was fully awake. His erect penis began to press between my buttocks.

I tried to push it away. It was smaller around than I imagined, but long and thin, with the firmness of hard rubber. At all costs I must stop him. Another second passed. Poor kid – living in this crazy Islamic... No girlfriends, I guess that's not allowed here; or is he gay? I used all my strength as I writhed to escape but his muscular grasp became painful and unbreakable. I realized that this young man was much the stronger of the two us. His thrusting is persistent, mechanical. It'll be like stopping a train. I felt as a woman must, weak, helpless, insulted, scared. He's moaning and whispering in Arabic, then in English 'You are good, good, you are, you are my good friend.'

Frantically I reached to press the palm of my hand hard into his face. 'Don't be stupid! Look, why don't you do this with Abdel?'

'What! With my own brother!' he protested, not stopping his caressing and thrusting.

If I hit him with all my might, grab his ears, stick a finger straight into his eye, what will happen next? Where is Abdel? Would he come to my aid, or would he be on Mahmoud's side?

'Why not? You prefer to do it to a guest?' I retorted. Somehow it had not occurred to me that they were brothers.

Then I realized that Abdel had been watching from beside my bed, and now he too grasped me and held my arms tightly to prevent any further resistance. The idea of *giving in* entered my mind. I wondered if the best course was to succumb to Mahmoud. His hard, slender, bony body made a strange parallel with my own. An understanding passed through my mind, for the first time, of what it must be to *desire* a man, to not resist him, open oneself to him, yield to his animalistic insistence, to humanize it, to satisfy his need, to share in it, to embrace him.

This, though, is different. Between a man's desire and a woman's there is a sense of revelation. As a man enters a woman, whether for the first time, or the thousandth, or the ten thousandth, they confess without a word their different, congruent, private needs that together make something greater than the two of them.

With Mahmoud there is no revelation, but mutual recognition, a conspiracy of knowing *what it's like*. Although he is the aggressor and I the victim, we understand each other – Arab or Englishman, there are no illusions about this. He knows that I know what's driving him. Abdel gripped more insistently with both arms, pressing his weight onto me, and Mahmoud pushed faster and harder as I writhed in a desperate effort to prevent him entering me.

Suddenly something was smeared onto my anus. At first I thought he had come but now he gently grabbed my testicles, massaging them, and as he entered me there was searing pain and a sickening sensation.

This is madness, a pointless inversion of what – so to speak – comes naturally. The easy, obvious geometry of heterosexuality made such perfect sense to me now. (Maybe I wouldn't think so if I were a girl being forcibly entered.) As soon as he had penetrated me, Mahmoud's breathing changed, sighing now as if from relief. His movements were slower. I knew that pleasure, too.

'It is hurting,' I gasped, 'Stop!'

He moved his hand to my chest in a reassuring gesture.

'Ah, you have not done this before. It is painful the first time. Not much longer,' he said, with something like kindness in the voice.

Pain at once became anger, resentment, rage that I was should be used as a mere receptacle. At the same instant his movements became more frenzied and more agonizing. With a final gasp he stopped. Abdel let go of my arm.

'I have finish,' Mahmoud said weakly. He slipped out, rolled over and off my bed. He let out a great sigh. 'You are kind,' he said.

Immediately Abdel lifted my blanket and climbed into the bed beside me. 'Now me!' he said, disagreeably assertive.

That was definitely the limit. This one had not caught me by surprise, and I could resist in earnest. 'No,' I said.

'You let my brother,' he complained. His body touched mine as he snuggled against me, holding me firmly as the other had done. His penis was already hard: it was fatter and shorter than Mahmoud's. I was determined not to put up with him, and pulled away, prepared myself to strike him, to punch his face with all my might, to poke out his eyes, even were I to lose my own in the process. But with a few quick movements of the pelvis, clinging like a dog, pushing not into my anus but against my legs, he ejaculated. The warm silky liquid spilled onto my skin. Somehow I didn't mind. It no longer mattered. This was nothing after Mahmoud's painful invasion.

'Finished?' I asked, trying to push him away.

'Oh no!' he replied, and still he clung to me, as if we were fighting beneath the sheet. His hardness rapidly returned and in frantic movements he rubbed himself against me as we struggled, coming again within a few moments. The thought crossed my mind that he must, after all, be very young to be able to do that, surely no more than fifteen.

Abdel rolled out of bed and dried himself on his long shirt. 'Oh,' he sighed. 'You are kind!'

'Have you ever done this with a woman?' I asked the darkened room.

'Oh yes,' their voices answered at once.

I doubted it. 'Who?'

'A woman in this village.'

'It is my turn next,' said Mahmoud.

'What! No, that's all. Finished,' I said with certainty.

He stepped towards the bed. 'But you let my brother twice.' By now I had learned all I wanted to know about being on the receiving end of male desire. I got out of bed and grabbed his forearms. Now I would play the male. I must hurt him, injure him, punish him. I lunged to grab his face and in some way damage it. My fingers began to squeeze his face. At once I halted and reflected. There were two of them. I had discovered that Mahmoud was not as feeble as he looked. And if there were a commotion, other people would come to their aid, not mine.

Perhaps what they had done was normal, acceptable in Arab culture. But Mahmoud was alarmed and backed off. He pleaded, 'My friend, let us not fight with each other,' warding me away with raised arms. 'You are right. I am sorry, my friend.' He sounded tired.

'Will you sleep now?' I asked.

'Yes,' he said, and both of them returned to their beds.

My eyes stayed open, staring nervously at the dark shapes of the two beneath their blankets. There could be no more sleep tonight, that was sure. I found a position away from the moisture on my sheets. The silence increased, dreams colored the darkness, at last engulfing me.

There had been no more disturbances – I had survived the night. I could return to Angela. In joy at the thought, I lay listening to the sounds of birds and distant voices. Only the soreness of my anus prevented perfect happiness. My hosts were awake but said nothing. On my thigh their semen clung in dry flakes. Mahmoud sat up and pulled on his trousers with a mere glance in my direction.

Love 117

I grinned ruefully. 'Good morning.' There was no anger, somehow, only pleasure at the thought of getting away from them.

They smiled, relieved by my attitude. 'Good morning! You want tea?'

Today, Mahmoud looked my own age, twenty, and the younger boy about seventeen. They dressed and went out of the room: I heard them speaking with the woman, their mother. I pulled a handkerchief from my jeans pocket, and wiped the vaseline and semen from my behind.

We sat outside the doorway of the house, on the pale stone step, to have breakfast. The home-going men of the night before passed us again, dispersing now to their day's work. The woman brought each of us a bowl of dry powder which we ate with our fingers. It would have been impossible to eat without some tea to moisten the mouth.

'I must go now,' I said.

'To Libya,' Mahmoud said.

'No, I go to Houmt-Souk.'

'To see your girlfriend,' explained Abdel.

The transistor had been turned on and Bourguiba's voice pierced the air. I went to the dark kitchen to say goodbye to the woman. She sat on a straight backed chair listening intently. It was not polite, perhaps, to speak to someone at this pious moment in the day.

She half rose and nodded with a smile. 'Bourguiba,' she said bashfully, pointing at the radio.

'All the Arab peoples love him,' explained Abdel.

They shook my hand, smiling without memory or regret. 'Good travels, *mon ami*!' Mahmoud called, with a cheerful wave.

Under the domes and arches of the baths a dignified silence reigned, except for the pouring of water and the slapping of wet flesh. I considered my naked body, sore and soiled by the experiences of the night. I wanted only to wash away the traces. I strolled from a cool room, through the warm shower, to a room moist with scorching steam. There I gasped from the heat and boiled my flesh as if in a laundry.

With every pore fully dilated, and not a corner or crevice, not a mucus membrane untouched, I felt yesterday's skin and oil scalded off. Reeling, steam-cleaned, exhausted by the heat, I staggered to the half-naked masseur and flopped onto his low table. Yet still the resentment had not been washed away, and I began to fear that the masseur might use me to relieve his own desires. Without a word he began to handle me as if I were something inanimate and he were a muscular tradesmen setting about his work. Shoving my limbs easily into place he clicked and pulled and smacked me, wrenching me into further looseness. Back in the cool room he handled me like a baby, wrapped me in clean towels and leaned me tenderly against the cool marble.

No one, but no one, knew where we were. We ourselves had only a vague idea. There was no news beyond what we could see with our own eyes or glean from the trickle of tourists. Angela occasionally began letters to friends but didn't complete them.

We'd walk to the main market square in Houmt-Souk to pick up food – the produce was wonderfully fresh, ripe and good – or wander the narrow lanes of the souk. Stallholders had fun teaching us some Arabic (with the help of a slender, optimistic booklet called *How to Speak Arabic Without a Teacher in 4 Days*), as well as how to judge if an orange is ripe and juicy by weighing it in the hand and feeling the skin.

Around the marketplace, rotund wives, wobbling within large sack dresses that brushed the dust around their feet, hauled food and charcoal in heavy bags. Market vendors surrounded themselves with wicker baskets and rolls of cloth and rugs, gleaming metalware, silver jewelry, and, for the rare visitors, a few dreadful souvenirs.

An enterprising merchant set a hand-operated juice machine on his stall, and we'd pause there for a glass of his carrot or orange juice, He marveled that we were still in Houmt-Souk. Eventually he stopped remarking on it, instead detaining us for the usual Arab conversation.

He'd start with a cheery, '*Labès*, all right?' and grasp my hand.

'OK. You?' He continued to hold my hand.

'Thank God. And you, madam?', with a respectful nod at Angela.

'*Labès*,' she'd smile.

'You are well?' he'd ask, as if troubled by her equivocal reply.

He was relieved to hear 'Yes, yes, very well. And how are you?'

'Thank God.'

'And your family?' Now it was our turn to insist.

'Thank God. My wife is well, and thank God, my children are well.'

'That is good, good, very good,' I'd agree (as a non-Moslem, I was

not expected to thank God).
'Well, then, good bye!'
'Good bye.'
'God willing!' And he would let go of my hand.

We so often heard similar conversations that I wondered if it was ever permissible to say, 'Shit man, feel lousy today,' or 'Hey, in a big hurry – catch ya later.' Not that we ever did feel lousy or pushed for time.

Time is one thing we have. No commitments, no obligations or demands get in our way. Each morning I lie awake, unhurried, comfortable, in our bed on the floor, musing in dreams and memories. It is luxuriously warm and peaceful. I hear little quiet sounds of the day like faraway music. I put one hand over Angela. She is still sleeping. I close my eyes. Sunlight fills the bedroom. There are no seasons here. Although the calendar presently lies somewhere between winter and spring, this is pure, endless summer. We have recaptured the light, a summer to last forever, the sunlit path we should never have left. On our island, there is no sense of there ever having been a winter at all.

Here the daylight itself is a joy. We abandon ourselves easily to sex, in the morning or afternoon, or at any time, less frenzied than before, but lingering, exquisite, sometimes on our mattress, or out on the flat roof which cannot be seen. We sit on a blanket on the floor and eat cous-cous – with fruit for breakfast, with vegetables for dinner. The past, parents, politics, are unimaginably far away.

It's *doing* that wastes time. Not Doing stretches it endlessly, makes each moment longer and longer, until every instant stretches so far that you cannot move on to the next, and time has stopped. When you're happy, time becomes a cushion in which you recline. For time is nothing anyway but mind and imagination. Walking together to and from the town, without hassle, without issues or obligations, we'd hold hands and talk and laugh. Passing the stonework around the hot spring we'd wave at the women gathered there, and they would wave back, hardly bothering to cover their faces any more. We'd see the horse hauling its small tanker of petrol, and laugh each time at that.

Time passed unmeasured. My hair was long again. At home, Angela would sit at the side of the house where she could watch both the desert and the ocean. I sat on the sunlit side opposite, looking towards treetops and rooftops, drawing, painting, or with eyes closed in daydreams.

Or we'd go to the seashore, where little dry flowers and reeds grew like rugged individualists in the pale sand. Angela sat among them while I bathed, the sand and water warm, the breeze cool and refreshing.

Or we would stroll slowly, slowly, slowly talking on the dusty path, and forget altogether about time passing. Then we would laugh and point at some stray cloud, small and white in the dazzling sky, and exclaim: 'Oh, it must be raining in Europe.' Once, I caught her stealing a glance at me. It was a look of love, the purest and simplest, with a curious, questioning smile. Surely this would remain, as clear as a photograph in the hand, when all else of Angela was gone.

In the market square, local men and boys clustered around a big, bearded American as he tinkered with a shining, polished black motorcycle, miraculously dust free in this dusty little town. He showed off to them proudly, and told them it was a 'fuckin' Norton 750, man, best fuckin' machine on the whole fuckin' planet.'

We bought him a Pepsi and he revealed chinks of light from the world beyond Djerba. He said Paul McCartney had married 'that rich bitch photographer heiress chick' and John Lennon had married 'that crazy weird Japanese chick'. In the cause of peace those two had spent a week in bed in the Amsterdam Hilton. He offered us a peanut butter and jelly sandwich. 'Brought a whole stack of 'em along for the ride. Still almost good as fresh.'

'What brings you *here*, man? Take a wrong turn?' Angela asked.

He laughed loudly. 'Liked the look of it on a map, is all. Little island at the end of the line. And dig that causeway thing. 'Cause you know, man, I just really, really want to get away from all the fuckin' hype and bullshit. Hey, you headin' back for Woodstock?'

We admitted we would not be returning to America just for a concert.

'No, but this is gonna be the hugest gig in history. *Everyone's* gonna be there. Except me. And you two.' Again he roared with laughter. 'Hey,' he turned and rummaged in the bike's big black leather panniers, 'speaking of, I mean, like music.' From the bags he drew out handfuls of cassette tapes. 'Ya want these?'

'Don't you want them?' I asked, amazed.

He grinned at Angela. Pointing a finger in my direction he asked her, 'Don'cha dig that cute way of speakin'?' He hammed-up a prissy upper-class English accent, nothing like my own. 'Don't you want them?'

'Well, don't you?' I asked again.

'I'm finished with 'em.' He held up a few of the tapes and, squinting as if they were on the horizon, read their handwritten labels aloud, 'The Band. Al Kooper, *Kooper Session*, that's pretty good. Albert King, *Blues Power*. Canned Heat. Shugger Otis, *The Blues*. Here's another Albert King, *Years Gone By*. BB King. Sleepy John Estes. You dig this stuff?'

Angela opened her eyes wide and nodded. 'Wow! You fucking bet we dig it. Problem is, we don't have anything to play 'em on.'

'Uh-huh,' he grunted. 'Well, I guess,' he turned again to the panniers, and pulled out a small Sony tape player. 'Want it?' Unceremoniously he handed the machine to her.

Angela was delighted, flashed him a smile. 'Hey! You sure?'

'Yeah, it's cool.'

The crowd jumped back in awe as the engine started with a lion's roar, and stared in speechless wonder as he maneuvered the bike into position. He turned and grinned, then seemed to remember something, reached into a breast pocket and handed Angela a screwed-up scrap of paper. 'Mescaline.' Only at this stage did he introduce himself with a quite formal handshake as he gave the name 'Kano'.

'Kano? Like volcano?' Angela asked.

'Yeah.' Lifting his hand in the peace sign, he added solemnly, 'Love and peace.' With another guffaw and the hint of a wave, his hand moved to the throttle. 'Later.' A cloud of dust hung in the air behind him.

Some boys in the Arab crowd raised their own hands in the peace sign and said, *Love and peace*.

Angela and I smiled and nodded at each other. 'Phew! Now that does give me itchy feet,' she said.

Where was he going, the biker? Where was there? Only certain places had any currency. They were not even places, but names, games, images, words – and cachet. It could be Greece, or Turkey, though these were cheaper jewels, mere halts on the trail. The biker must ride East, fleeing 'fuckin' hype and bullshit' towards the uninhibited liberty of Goa and Kathmandu. The grail was India.

That evening, we played the biker's tapes. To the sound of BB King we took out our map and followed the roads across Italy, through

Greece. From Istanbul they continued on some other map which we had not yet bought, to Persia and Afghanistan and beyond.

'You know what, though?' I said doubtfully. 'Angela, listen. Ferries, buses, hostels, food. It all costs money. We've got fifty-two dollars left.'

'We can get some bread.'

'How?'

'Well, *I* don't know. We'll just get some.'

'Cool, but *how*?'

'I don't *know*, Simon. Don't hassle me. So fucking negative all the time. Look, let's just go. To Greece, maybe, see what we find, OK? Maybe we could score a kilo of shit and send it to someone.'

'You mean, in Greece? Doesn't seem the best place'

'All the time, fucking negative,' she repeated. 'Turkey, then.'

'No, no. Not Turkey.' I was adamant. 'Very heavy. You can go to jail for twenty, thirty years.'

Angela frowned. 'OK, not Turkey. Somewhere. What about here?'

'No! Everyone knows us here. They'd talk about it.'

She said, 'OK, *you* think of something.'

'If you did score a kilo, who would you send it to?' I asked.

'Hitch, maybe?'

'Hitch isn't gonna want a kilo of dope! A ton, maybe. Couldn't Sasha just lend you some money, or give you some? Write to her.'

Angela pursed her lips. 'I can't ask for any more favors. I'm not doing anything for her any more. What about your guy in Brighton?'

'Rich? I don't really know him.'

I was relieved when she dropped the subject.

* * *

I relaxed in the courtyard, leaning on the sunny wall at the foot of the stone steps, watching a praying mantis. It caught a fly and, with elegant movements, ate it piece by piece while the insect still struggled. Angela sat on the shady side of the courtyard, in thoughtful repose. I looked across, fascinated by her face, the shape of it, the tan skin, the golden hair. And how I loved that rather taut, skeptical expression.

In the cool hours as evening turned to night we sat at a café in the open, half lit by a few bare electric bulbs. President Bourguiba's shriek being over, the Arab men, some with their wives, were taking the air, strolling or talking. We listened as they exchanged the stock blessings and greetings, the formulaic replies thanking God that all was well.

Angela's voice disturbed my reverie. She handed me an aerogram, pulled from a pocket in her skirt. 'I didn't write Sasha. I wrote Hitch.'

'When did this arrive?' I unfolded the thin, sky-blue paper.

'I asked him to write "care of" the youth hostel. I picked it up a couple of days ago.'

'And you didn't even tell me!' It was in Jack Hitchins' usual style. I could almost hear his voice in my mind, yelling the words.

Hey kids howarya!!! Snakes in grass, step carefully!! Tunisia Mail NOT reliable. Use Italy or Greece. When you have souvenirs, send to Ozzie – not me. He can wire funds. Better still, Guys, find some other way to make bread. Top dollar paid for pretty English boys. Ten bucks for ten minutes. Or sell blood, ten bucks a gallon. Harvest oranges, ten bucks a ton. Nice to hear from ya. Everything as usual here. Sun shinin.

'Not very encouraging, is he?'

'I don't think he's saying *don't* do it. Just, be careful.'

'Who's Ozzie?'

'He's actually Turkish. Been to the ranch. I met him there.'

'So what does he mean, send it to Ozzie?'

'This guy Ozzie, he lives in Germany. He's a businessman. He has a factory in Munich. Plastic molding or something.'

'Really?' That sounded as straight as it gets. 'I'd have thought Sasha might have sent you something, now she knows where you are,' I said.

Into my hand she placed a tiny square of tissue paper with miniscule handwriting on one side. 'This was inside Hitch's letter.'

My dearest Queen and Angel. We love you and miss you. Sirius is well and having a doggy time on the farm. Send your next address and let's write. Yours ever lovin.

'Nothing about money,' I said.

'No.'

'Well, we don't have to go East at all, if we can't afford it.'

'Yes, we'll go.'

On the path back to our house by the sea, a three-quarter moon cast a simple white light on the palms. It was a peaceful evening. I did not want to disturb it, but had to pose the question, 'Why is it so important, the overland trip? To be with Jesse again?'

'No!' Angela shook her head. 'Jesse...' She sighed deeply, glanced down, paused. 'I don't know any more. I do want to see him, but... I don't expect anything to happen.' She was almost whispering. 'But you know I thought, once... Well, that's not to be. Even so, I would like to say hello. Or goodbye. He won't let me to do more than that.'

She reached out and held my hand. Her tone of voice tonight, frank and unguarded, wasn't at all like her. Perhaps she talked in this way with her real friends, never to me. Either she was telling the truth. Or lying. Maybe she herself did not know. It made no difference anyway. She was in love with Jesse and had to go to India to see him. And I had to go with her.

Summer 1969

A young man, trim, clean cut and handsome, leaned on the ship's rail beside me. Gradually the ethereal daylight revealed Corfu veiled in morning mist. The island's coast of small bays and steep, olive-green slopes faced across the splashing turquoise waters to gaunt Albanian peaks on the other side. The young man spoke, gentle Bible-belt accent, in a reverential whisper.

'Ain't that byoodaful.' He shook his head in wonder: 'Like Nam.'

'Vietnam looks like this? I didn't know.' Soundless, the ship drifted past the island and into the dock at Igoumenitsa on the Greek mainland.

Angela and I had hitched through a whole day, yesterday or the day before, to Tunis, where I found a postcard waiting at the Poste Restante. An overcrowded car ferry took us through the night across the Mediterranean to Italy. All over the wooden floorboards of the decks like bundles of cloth, the passengers slept crammed without regard for modesty or privacy. In the middle of the night, Angela lay breathing heavily. She looked so grim and determined even in sleep. As she slept I took out the postcard again and by the faint glow of some deck lamps read, or remembered, the words.

Dear Simon
I often, OFTEN think about you, and our strange night and lovely morning, and our beautiful anti-war kiss! That was before Angela came back into your life and took you far away. No one seems to know where you are. I assume you are having a wonderful life and too busy, or too stoned, or too much in love, to keep in touch! I finally had the idea of asking your parents. They said they hadn't heard from you in three months. They miss you VERY much. I hope you remember me.
Love, Milly.

From Igoumenitsa the road climbed above sweeping valleys, dry golden hillsides descending to soft pastel greens and yellow wildflowers. The air was sharp and clear, the sea and sky a ravishing, luminous blue.

It hardly mattered where we were going. Every step along the road was pure joy, an end in itself, every place where we stood trying to hitch a ride became a destination, somewhere where I could happily have lived or died.

In each car or truck that stopped, the same upbeat, repetitious, high-pitched plucked strings of Greek pop favorites played endlessly, accompanied by the same wavering, melancholy tenors, moving our fingers to click and the driver to sing along.

After that introduction to Greece, Athens came as a shock. It was the biggest city we'd seen since London, but with vaster, faster avenues, more immense, more airless, more grandly named squares, inhuman with noise and heat, the air a suffocating stew of vapors scorched together as if in a crucible of concrete and stone.

As we walked through the heart of the city, I caught sight of Kano, the American biker from Djerba, thundering past close enough to touch. Astonished, we called out, and chased him in the surge of traffic and pedestrians. Held up by a traffic light, he saw our wave.

Big hugs, laughter, and he led us to a crumbling five-story hostel in a Plaka backstreet at the foot of the Acropolis. Kano had a little room here but was leaving it this very day, and had a ticket for the overnight ferry to Crete. We climbed narrow, winding stone stairs to a flat rooftop, and in the balmy air sat facing the majestic, elegant white ruin illuminated on its hilltop.

Kano suggested we take his room. 'Fifteen draks a night – that's fifty cents,' he explained. Another fifteen drachmas would pay for dinner at the taverna across the lane.

'I was in Stamboul,' he told us. 'Whoa! If you're heading that way, I found a far-out place to stay – like, a hotel, man – with dorms, and shared rooms and stuff, or you can crash in a kind of tent on the roof, that costs only one US quarter a night.' He told us the name. 'Yeah, four nights for a dollar. I'll write it down for ya.' As he wrote, he assured us Istanbul was 'fucking cool, tons of dope, great food, everything cheap.'

Puzzled, Angela said, 'We heard it's a bad scene for dope in Turkey.'

The biker acknowledged that was true. 'You have to keep your wits and know who's cool! But ain't it always that way?'

Then Angela confided her plan to buy a kilo of hashish and send it to a friend to raise a few dollars.

'That's a good idea.' He nodded and became much quieter. 'There's a hotel in Stamboul. The Blue Minaret. Across from the Blue Mosque. One of the managers there, he's dealing. Be sure you have the right guy, yeah? Tall, fat, balding, big floppy tache, soup stains down his gut. Been there for years. The stuff comes in half-k bricks. Red Leb or Bombay Black. A half-key of Black is, well, I think it's, like, thirty-five bucks.'

'Seventy dollars a kilo!' Angela clapped her hands with glee. 'We can triple our money every few weeks! Easy!' She looked across at me with eyebrows raised, as if to say *See? Was I right?*

'You know what else,' Kano revealed, 'on the way to Stamboul you can earn most of what you need to pay for a brick. Like this, man: when you reach S'lonika, stop by at the hospital and sell blood. They pay four hundred draks every time. That's fifteen bucks. Two of ya, thirty bucks. I did it – sold blood. But when you come back to Greece with the dope, don't take that S'lonika road. They search everyone. There's a sweet little alternative route, a border crossing in the country near a place called Edirne. No searching. No one around.'

'So you went to Istanbul, and came back to Greece?' I asked. 'You not heading East?'

He shook his head vigorously. 'Not me! I wanna get off that superhighway. Tomorrow I'll be in Crete. Holed up in a Matala cave. You know about it? Bunch of freaks there, man, living in caves on the beach. That's the place for me.'

'I'll bet there's no peanut butter there, man. No jelly.' Angela warned.

Kano smiled. 'If I can just wean myself off those fuckin' sandwiches, I'd be a free man at last.'

* * *

Istanbul came as a still more violent burst of urban madness, worst of East and West, an anarchic squalor of crowds squeezing like a living, human paste through narrow market streets, and dented, aging American cars honking wildly along ugly boulevards. Spanning the waters which divide Europe from Asia, the city seemed to gather the washed-up jetsam of both continents. I dared not imagine its prisons. A taxi, one of many disintegrating Oldsmobiles or Chevrolets, rocked and rolled through seething backstreets and dropped us at the Blue Minaret Hotel, a concrete building, run down yet unfinished.

A large, rotund, unsmiling man stood behind a makeshift reception desk. Taller than average, with a few thin threads of black hair across a glistening scalp, and a bold, bushy mustache streaked with grey hanging below chubby cheeks. He had none of the joviality associated with tubby men. A white nylon shirt, tucked into shabby trousers, was speckled with yellowing oil spots. A nest of hair growing from navel to neck showed through the fabric's thin sheen. He agreed he was the manager.

'Nice place,' I remarked, and looked around at threadbare modern furnishings and peeling, discolored walls hung with improbable images of Mecca and Ataturk. His eyes shot at me with suspicion. I went on, 'How long you been working here?'

'Thank you, many years.'

'Is there a room free here?' I asked.

'Who sent you?' he said.

The question caught me off-guard. I had expected everything to go smoothly, from saying hello to booking a room right up to actually buying the dope. 'No one.'

'Hotel Hashish,' he unexpectedly announced.

Angela and I tittered. The jail sentences being handed down now in Turkey for possession of hashish would last half a lifetime. Just saying the word felt indictable. Why bother with this, I asked myself, why not just keep heading east along the road. If we *must* head east. With or without enough money. A few days ago I lived in heaven in Djerba. This was madness.

The guy did seem to be the one Kano had mentioned. On the other hand, he was strangely uncool. He said drily. 'Don't worry, quite safe here! How much you want? All best quality, very safe.'

He brought us a single broad flat slab of hashish, dark and soft, its powerful, familiar scent like some kind of herby confectionery. The size of a pitta bread, it weighed half a kilo. Angela had decided that would be enough, and she took it as a good omen that our "blood-money" exactly covered the cost. We left it in a plastic bag in our unlocked (and unlockable) hotel room while we walked the city center.

Cars blared their horns ceaselessly, ignored by surging crowds. Muscular, mustachioed men, in main streets and backstreets and market lanes, grabbed at Angela. I was pushed aside when I tried to intervene. She, though, surprised them with her nail scissors, jabbing the points as only she would, without pity, into the stomach of her persecutor. They did not cry out, but withdrew, seething, a hand over the trickling wound.

Whenever we stood still, curious men and children approached, sometimes standing between us, staring and listening. When we walked, we were mauled and jostled, and followed by men and children trying to catch our attention, 'Hello mister'. Everywhere policemen's whistles blew, trams rattled.

At the Pudding Shop, Istanbul's crazily popular pastry café, we joined a crowd of freaks heading east, and some returning like veterans as if from paradise, and ate delicious little snacks.

Back in our hotel room, we shut the door and listen for anyone coming up the stairs. The manager has found something suitable for us: an antique mirror eighteen inches square, a thick sheet of silvered glass within a frame of dark, richly carved wood held together with tiny nails.

With the mirror on the bed, he uses tiny pliers to pull out the little nails. His expression is inscrutable, he concentrates on the job in hand and the thick, hairy fingers move with surprising dexterity. Beads of sweat appear on the high forehead.

The mirror glass lifts easily from its frame. There's plenty of space behind. He lays the pitta-sized slab, still in its bag, inside the frame and replaces the glass. It doesn't fit quite as well as before, but he manages to dust the wooden joints with glue, jiggle everything into place and replace the nails. It seems faultless,

Is it our imagination, or does the scent of dope still linger in the air; can we smell the stuff even in its plastic bag? But he has not finished. Using ordinary grey window putty, he packs the little gap between the glass and the wood. Now he stands upright and hands us the mirror. Angela and I sniff at the edge – and agree there is no dope smell now. And no sign at all that the mirror has ever been dismantled.

It's lying on the bed. It's just a mirror. To us, like a ritual object for some strange, secret magic, it contains luck and danger, courage and fortune. The manager takes our money and says nothing. Will he now go to the police, who will give him another gratuity? They could even recover the hashish for him to sell another day. Or for themselves. We ask if everything will be all right. He puts a finger on his lips and says 'Don't worry.' At the door of our room, at last he smiles and shakes our hands. Gold gleamed at the back of his mouth. Kano didn't mention that.

Kano had recommended Edirne. We found his little border town on the map, on the main road not to Greece but to Bulgaria, and hitch-hiked there between huge yellow fields of sunflower heads, millions together, heavy eye-faces staring into the sun. From the center of the little town we continued on foot, crossing a wide river and taking a rustic, unfrequented lane which led us for several miles back towards the Greek frontier. The afternoon was warm and bright. We walked through a village, past peasants working by the road. They looked at us curiously, as if to comprehend an image somehow distorted, or gazing across a chasm at something half-familiar. Women waved to us from a field, but hid their faces when I smiled back.

Without hesitation, the Turkish customs officer pushed our other bags aside and immediately unwrapped the mirror. His eyebrows rose and he seemed almost to recognize it – were they a common item in Turkish homes, perhaps? First glancing into our faces, he exclaimed 'Ah, so!' He tapped the back, listened, tapped again and appeared to be thinking. They had long, long prison sentences in Turkey. People our own age were in jail for possession of hashish. Some are still there, growing old in their cells.

His mouth tightened a little, yet the customs officer affected nonchalance. He asked casually, 'What is inside? Opium, morphine?'

Was it so obvious that there was something behind the glass? And did we look that heavy? 'No,' I said. The back of my neck felt damp with sweat.

He gave a brief shrug. Maybe he thought, what the heck, they're leaving the country anyway. 'Good,' he said, not smiling. He put the mirror down and waved us to go. He knows though, I thought. We wrapped the antique mirror again and walked out into the sunlight.

Beyond Turkish customs the road continued like a pleasant country lane, through an archway on which was written Türquiye, the crescent sword of Islam nailed above, and towards another which declared Hellas, where the fluttering blue and white flag on a high pole announced Church and State.

Over the border into the West again, for the West is a receding dream, always in the next country along. Until you reach the California state line. Or the misty cliffs of Big Sur. On this day, the West began on the frontier of the Christian world.

The afternoon heat dragged like an extra weight, the long walk had made us tired, the near miss at the Turkish customs left us anxious and drained. We considered taking a rest right where we were, between the frontiers. We could continue our journey in the evening, or even at night. There was no hurry. A large tree cast cool, enticing shade beside the road. We did so many things wrong. We did not stop under that tree.

In three or four minutes we reached the Greek border post. There was a deserted cafe and gas station, and another small customs office, quiet in the drowsy officialdom of the afternoon siesta, almost unguarded. Flags shifted lazily in the warm air beside a sign, *Douane*.

A truck stood at the gas station. 'That's our ride to Alexandroupolis,' Angela said. In the police department a man stamped our passports. We're in Greece. He pointed us to the customs office, a wooden hut.

As Kano had said, there was no one there. No one sat at the tables of the café opposite. I turned to glance back: the policeman was watching us, but having seen us arrive at customs, he disappeared into his doorway. All was still, afternoon sunlight and silence.

We could have walked on, but hesitated. We did so many things wrong. We did not walk on. I tried it in my mind, and with a nod in the direction of the road suggested it to Angela. She shook her head: 'Might look suspicious.'

The whole fate of things, and the destiny of every single individual, are larger and smaller wheels in the same machine.

The present is made of the past, and contains the future. Nothing is new. Everything grows from its forgotten origins. We make mistakes because of mistakes we already made.

We should have walked on, and that's what Kano expected. As we paused uncertainly, a customs officer appeared, fastening his belt. Had he just been to the toilet? Or having a nap? He nodded lazily and his hand gestured Angela to open her bag – not in an office, not on a bench, but right there on the wooden porch. He sat himself down too, slumped on the step beside the bag. For a moment he did nothing. I felt calm. Angela too. Maybe we should have been more impatient and irritable. A soldier came from somewhere and gave us each an apple. Mine tasted very sour – unripe – but I could not throw it away while he stood there watching. Why was the soldier watching us? That seemed unusual. Maybe because he knew the apples were too tart to eat and wanted to see what we would do. The atmosphere remained warm, lazy and careless.

The customs officer plunged his hand into Angela's bag and straight away found her tampons. He did not recognize them; tampons did not exist in Greece (or Turkey or Tunisia) at that time, and Angela's supply had all been brought from Britain. As the officer's eyes widened, Angela explained with gestures how to use a tampon. At last he understood, a flush spreading across his face. Looking away, he continued his search. And it occurred to me that he really was searching for something in particular, rather than just checking, or even looking.

Puzzled, the man finished with Angela's bag, and turned to mine. He pulled out a few items at random, clumsily dropping my toothbrush on the ground. I picked it up, wondering whether to be angry, or irritated, or forgiving, or to ignore the accident. What would be the most natural, normal reaction? I twisted my mouth irritably and said nothing. Then he saw the mirror, lying separately, and at once sighed 'Ah!' and gestured towards it. He had found what he was looking for.

Angela handed it to him. The customs man fumbled with the wrapping, so she removed the paper for him. 'Beautiful,' she said.

I wondered why she had said that, and suspected it was a false step. The customs man glanced at her, but she was smiling sweetly as if waiting for his agreement. He nodded.

He moved the mirror up and down in his hand. Feeling its weight. These antique mirrors are very heavy. The glass and the wood are thick. Especially heavy, of course, with a pound of hashish inside. Much too heavy. A pound too heavy.

I looked along the road, the little road where we could have walked without going through customs. Sunlight and silence. Angela stood up and said she needed the bathroom; briefly catching my eye as she left.

Was our good humor suspicious? Surely people are rarely in a good temper with customs officers? But no, on the contrary, customs officers must be most familiar with politeness through gritted teeth. Perhaps our teeth were not sufficiently gritted. I sat tense, aware of every move, made by myself, the customs officer and the watching soldier. For an instant, it seemed the customs officer and I were acting in a play. The calm and the sunshine were ironic. The soldier had seen it before.

I mustn't do anything which might indicate anxiety. Or rather, which might give away that I have something to be anxious about.

Having weighed the mirror in his hand, the officer smelled around the edges of the glass. For some time, it seemed. Why? The Turkish officer too had suspected something. Why? Had the hotel manager given us away? Had the Turkish officer phoned his Greek counterpart: *Hey friend, couple of hippies on the way. They have drugs hidden in an antique mirror.* Was it simply the weight? Were these mirrors, always packed with dope, a familiar sight at the customs? I knew there was no smell. Now he tried to glimpse between the glass and the wooden frame. I knew what he would see there – a thin line of putty.

My breathing stopped and my heart pounded. Would there be putty in an antique? Obviously not fresh putty. And there was a smell after all: of fresh putty. He's close, but is he really suspicious enough to press on? So far, nothing was happening or appeared about to happen. So far, life remained normal. The sun still shone. At this point he might decide to drop the whole business and let us go down that little road.

He decided not to leave it there. He worked with his fingers at the nails in the mirror's wooden frame. He's thinking about opening the mirror, taking it to pieces. But the nails don't shift. Might he still stop here, and go no further? He reached into his pocket and took out a small screwdriver. He began to work at the nails.

He spoke to the soldier. So the soldier is not merely the audience of our little play. He already took a part, in giving me this inconvenient apple, which I'm still holding in my hand. Perhaps it is I who merely watch. While he is gone, I throw the apple away. Did throwing the bitter, half-eaten apple give anything away? In what felt like less than three seconds the soldier had brought two other screwdrivers and a pair of pliers. All set now to find the dope.

The customs man looked up at me. His eyes were piercing, pleading, as if he wished me to find some way to have not arrived at his door. I sat as still and calm as I could. Am I looking calm? This isn't the end yet. Should I be calm? Every straight tourist would be agitated by having a souvenir antique taken to pieces.

The customs man looked guilty. 'Is there hashish inside?'

'No,' I said, firmly, with a startled frown. No, no. Firmly. Too firmly? He looked away, down. Why does he say *hashish*, while the Turkish officer said *opium*?

He started to take out the nails. Where the heck is Angela! I could see like a drowning man all too clearly what was happening. For now it was happening. Was there something that I, or Angela if she were here, could do at this stage to save us?

After starting to remove the nails he would not stop until he had removed them. And there was no chance at all that he would remove the nails from only one, two or three of the four corners. This means he will take out the glass? Yes, when all four nails have been taken out, he will remove the glass. So, is there any chance left to us?

Surely it is not my destiny to be busted. In a minute we'll walk down that road, amazed at our narrow escape. In one second of calm, I was amused that I could still be hoping to get through customs unscathed.

He was working slowly, taking care not to damage the mirror. My body alternated detachment and panic. I turned and saw the soldier still watching. He noticed the apple lying on the ground. I shrugged as if amazed at what the customs officer was doing. The soldier continued to gaze at me, and I saw myself through his eyes: a skinny, naïve kid, a long-haired foreigner, a hippy hitch-hiker with tatty luggage.

The nails were out, and laid down by the customs officer's side. These are the last moments... I mean, he will surely find it.

A Citroën 2CV suddenly drove up, juddering and squeaking as it slowed beside the *Douane* sign. Our officer looked up, distracted. Inside the car, two bright, nervous, cheery faces, also young foreigners, also long-haired, also a guy and a girl with open, naïve, hippy smiles. They sat enclosed by overstuffed embroidered cloth bags, fabrics, packed up to the roof of the car. It was just an interruption. He waved them on, and the car jerked forward, moved away along the quiet road into the Greek sunshine like a holiday snapshot.

The officer picked up his tiny screwdriver again. Holding it between thumb and forefinger he pushed it into the putty. My eyes strained to watch. Definitely he had stuck it in far enough.

He moved the screwdriver a little. Pulled it out. And smelled it. I sat motionless, petrified, a mouse in the headlights before it is struck. He smelled it for less than no time before turning to me. His eyes looked at me tenderly, as if at his own beloved son, with a terrible sorrow.

He spoke with simple resignation. 'Hashish.'

We both came back to life. My mind raced ahead now. What to do next, what to say? How to get Angela to say the same thing.

'Hashish!' I exclaimed at once, with shock and disgust. I shook my head to deny it, and reached across as if to smell the screwdriver for myself. He nodded and gave it to me.

One sniff, and a huge unmistakable aroma filled my consciousness. The familiar, beautiful smell of some good dope.

'Yes!' I looked at him amazed. 'But you know, this mirror isn't ours. It belongs to an English girl we met in Istanbul.'

Now it was his turn to look amazed. I moved away and turned to look for Angela, as if to get support for my story. The soldier had gone. Angela, returning from the toilet, had stopped alongside a car heading the other way and was talking happily through its open windows. The truck, our ride to Alexandroupolis, had gone.

'Angela,' I called. She looked up.

I took a step towards her. 'Angela, the customs guy has opened up that mirror and found some hashish inside.' My voice was incredulous. The young couple in the car stared in horror and left at once. I spoke slowly and pointedly, word by word: 'Angela, that girl – that girl in Turkey – who asked us to take the mirror to England – has really landed us in trouble.' Angela listened intently, her lips pressed together.

'Hashish!' she cried out, 'But that's impossible! She was a nice girl.'

The customs officer also listened, watching and waiting.

As we turned to face him, Angela immediately explained that the mirror belonged to someone else. She took from her handbag a piece of paper on which was written a girl's name and an address in England. It was not in Angela's handwriting. I stifled my astonishment.

The customs man held his breath. He stared at the scrap of paper between Angela's fingers, puzzled, and reached up to take it from her. Now he let out his breath, frowning at the words, turning the paper over in his hand. It was clear he had doubts that we were smuggling. He looked me up and down.

Angela reached out for her piece of paper, but he did not give it back. We were at the beginning of another chapter in the story. The bust was over. Now tension fell away as we began to tell him, and each other, of a girl in Turkey who had asked us to take the mirror to England. But he shook his head and shrugged. It was a whole new stage: we had been detected. The customs man could not change that. Our story was useless. It was a 'Tell it to the judge' situation. He beckoned someone.

Young policemen and soldiers were everywhere, and the sad customs man, with his unkempt hair, and trousers slipping below a middle-aged belly, seemed to have become one of us rather than one of them. Angela cried. Some were making fun of us, asking Angela why she was crying.

One called out, 'Why you did it?' Another squirmed with pleasure and chanted, 'Ten years in prison! Ten years in prison!' He clapped with glee, then suddenly grimaced with contempt. An older officer rummaged through my bag. Pulling out the sketchpad, he turned the pages with careless, puzzled impatience, dropping precious drawings on the ground. I tried to gather them as they were stepped on. Another hand found the tape player. In anger I lashed out to stop it being taken, but the hand slipped away with its prize.

'What are we going to do?' Angela asked me quietly.

I said – to myself more than to her – that all was not lost, because this was merely part of life. A person doesn't own their life, or create it; it is revealed to them, one day at a time. Life and Life Only. An event, just a single line in a vast unwritten biography. And so on. That sort of thing. She didn't listen.

* * *

We were instructed to remain at the café opposite the police department. Just as before, sunlight and silence. All was calm again. This time, the peacefulness seemed no more than a clever trick, the fleeting instant of perfect stillness as, for example, when a glass can be made to balance on a match. We sat in the shade at an outdoor table, Angela facing me. We looked at each other without speaking, her piercing eyes regarding mine, mine hers. At last, and until we could be taken away to different places of detention, Angela and I were bound together, though in a union unrecognized and unholy. Ever afterwards, we would share this lovely, tranquil, dreadful moment together. The child I had been, my parents' child, was no more. The whole scene, taverna, blue sky, her brilliant hair, everything was ineffably beautiful. Outwardly, nothing had changed, yet all the world was cast in a new illumination.

'What blew my mind,' I said, 'Was that name and address you had, already written down. How did you do that?'

Angela smiled wanly. 'It was the girl in the car. I got talking to them and she wrote me her name and address.'

'Wow!' I shook my head, uncertain what to think. 'Might she get in trouble – I mean, if they check it out?'

Angela shrugged. 'Won't affect anything. It's nothing to do with her.'

'What about our stash?' I asked.

'I got rid of that,' Angela said. 'It's in the restrooms.'

'Might they find it?'

'No. It'll still be there when we come back this way.'

'When do you think that's going to be?' I looked into her eyes with fear. 'Not ten years?'

She looked away. 'Not ten years. It mustn't be. Maybe we'll be acquitted. We must be, Simon. I can't go to prison.' As soon as the word had been uttered, it was clear we would not be acquitted. My greatest fear was not imprisonment itself, but that it would end our relationship.

'Is there anything we can pray to?' I said quietly.

The question was rhetorical, but she shook her head. 'No – except maybe a lawyer.'

'Yes, we need a lawyer, don't we?' I realized.

She nodded unhappily.

'Don't admit anything, don't sign anything,' I suggested.

Angela looked doubtful. 'Maybe it's better not to come across too obstreperous,' she said.

I nodded. Probably she was right. 'Still, don't sign anything. And what did you do with the mescaline?'

'I threw it on the ground, over there.' She pointed to a patch of stony soil, near the police station, where some hens pecked and scratched. A waste of good mescaline. We thought about what a tripped-out chicken would do, and smiled. And the luck of some dopehead needing the bathroom and finding a small plastic bag of kif and oily black hashish.

Over the road, next door to the customs office, people were moving around inside rooms which had been deserted when we arrived. From time to time, one of them would look at us through the window. Angela and I talked through our simple 'story'. The dark haired girl in the car became The Girl – we figured it would be easier to describe a real person. Where had we met her? Every day, in the Pudding Shop, at about lunchtime. Had we known her before? No, was the simplest answer. What did she eat? Same as us, would be best. When did she appear with the mirror? Yesterday. What did she ask us to do with it? Take it to England and post it to the address. Why? Sending it from Turkey was too expensive. Why did we agree? Ah, if only we hadn't.

Fear of the immediate future pressed against my mind. In a few minutes, or hours, whenever they decided to call us, we would go over the road and enter a room, where the door would be closed behind us and I expected to be physically hurt. What would they do to me in that room? Everyone knew about Greece since the military coup. Would I be beaten? Or worse? Worse still, would they hurt Angela?

Yet I felt detached, almost content: because for the moment nothing was being done to us. Angela was calm too, waiting as if without any concern. We could have been at any outdoor café anywhere.

'What I don't get,' she said, 'is by *what right* they keep us here.'

She was perfectly serious. The more we tried to explain that to ourselves, the more it seemed we struggled even to grasp that Law exists. At first I am affronted by this seeming denial of our natural, animal freedom to wander away as we wish. Then, it troubles me that, somehow, Law *is* natural to humans. For we are not animals in nature's freedom. And nor are they free from the cat laws and dog laws of their kind. Even birds are not as free as a bird. *Are birds free from the chains of the skyways?* cries Dylan. Is there no freedom, then, for anyone or anything? Yes, there is freedom – to fly around inside the cage.

'It's their country, I guess,' was the only answer I could think of for the moment.

'Huh. Well, I don't get that either,' she argued. 'It's all bullshit. Who does a country 'belong' to?' She gestured quotation marks in the air. 'It's just a piece of the good Earth. I don't see any lines marked on it.'

'Yeah,' I nodded. 'OK, so it belongs to the folks who live in it?' I suggested. 'Or were born there? Or, I guess, a country is like someone's backyard, it belongs to the people whose name is on the title deeds.'

She laughed slightly at that. 'No!' She shook her head. 'No one, that's who. Who writes the title deeds, and who makes the law of the land?'

I saw what she was getting at. 'It depends, maybe, like, if the lawmakers have been elected or not?'

She snorted. 'Nah! Either way, law is just barrel-of-a-gun stuff. Winner take all. And countries, it's the same thing. It's all the will of guys with power. I mean,' she said, 'the laws we're supposed to have broken are *nothing to do with us*. Dig? We're not part of their medieval religious patriarchal fucking crap society. They're not *our* laws.'

'Freaks don't make laws,' I pointed out. 'If they did, they wouldn't be freaks.'

'Yeah – because freaks expect nothing from anyone, except that they treat everyone else as human.'

This brought the fruit-picking commune back to my mind, that I traveled with in California, no doubt still making their way from farm to farm. Do they have laws? Nothing written, though they're hedged around with what it's right to do, or not right. No crimes either, beyond the sin of idleness while others work. Even that's forgivable if you can play the guitar. If they had laws, there was no sanction except expulsion.

A man wearing a police uniform leaned out of a doorway and whistled. He gestured us to come over. The time had come.

My heart beat faster, for the physical pain would be soon. 'That's how they'll be treating us,' I said.

We got up from the table. Hand in hand, we strolled across the road.

Staring at the stones on the ground. The light of early evening making shadows. As I take each step, I seem to watch myself, as if looking at a picture, an old motionless image of myself, distant, unreal, hard to place.

In the long moment of the walk, I had time to wonder why we hadn't stayed in Djerba, and whether Law would be OK if it really did reflect the will of the people, and how things between Angela and me would be affected by this turn of events, and whether we would have walked across the border without difficulty if only, if only, we had rested a few moments under that shady tree.

Hens ran across our path. They live always in this space. Istanbul, where we had been that morning, lay buried in memory. The café tables, the police station and the road between them became the entire world, as we walked into the waiting hands.

Facing us, our interviewers, or inquisitors, were three men sitting behind a long desk. All three were middle-aged, bloated, with black hair slicked back and thinning, eyes sagging, mouths taut. Their questions were in English and we answered in English. Angela's torn scrap still existed, and now lay on the desk with other papers.

Angela sat beside me on a wooden bench. For hours, we repeated our story in greater and greater detail, dull, repetitive, calm.. There was nothing else in the room, just a bare stone floor and plain white walls.

Was it some sort of trial, or pre-trial? I could not tell. And the men, were they policemen, soldiers, lawyers or magistrates? I did not know. Everything was slow and subdued. There were no threats nor anger, no suggestion of violence.

Sometimes Angela was sent out, and they asked me some questions. Then I went out, and she was asked.

A man's voice called me back inside. Angela looked worried and harassed. She clutched my arm and said they had been asking her to sign something. One of the three men nodded. 'She must sign. You too.'

He handed me a sheet of paper with a printed heading, a long handwritten passage and an official-looking circle of blue words rubber stamped at the bottom. It was all in Greek. I pointed out that we could not read the statement, so we could not sign it. I said it was like signing a blank check, and handed it back. All three exploded with anger, or pretended to. Yet still I was not hit, not even threatened. To everyone's surprise, just at this moment the apple soldier entered the room with two bowls of rice pudding, one of which he politely handed to Angela, the other to me.

The intrusion disconcerted our angry inquisitors. Puzzled, Angela took a little of the pudding on the tip of the spoon. While the men resumed shouting she asked me what it was and I said, 'Rizogalo. Chilled rice pudding. It's nice.' But she did not think so, and handed the bowl back to me.

I insisted, 'Eat it, it's nice.'

She answered, 'Have mine, if you want, I can't eat now.'

'Save it for later.'

She frowned with incomprehension. 'Later?'

Realizing that we were not listening, the three men became quiet and watched us. 'It is one o'clock,' one of them said at last. From their manner and their faces, two of the three appeared sorry for us. Maybe they were convinced of our innocence. Yet it made no difference what these men thought. No doubt their job was to question us, establish the facts of the case and make a report in the form of a statement for us to sign. If so, we had wasted their evening.

Angela said, 'Can I phone someone?'

'The girl?' one of the men said.

'No...'

'The American consul? Not at this time,' he said.

'No,' Angela said. 'I want to try to get a lawyer.'

'No, it is the middle of the night. We have notified the consulates already of your arrest, and they have arranged a good lawyer for you.'

'So where is he?' she asked peevishly.

'Probably in bed with his wife,' he said.

Angela and I slept, or lay awake, fully dressed and without bedding, on the stone floor in that same room. A soldier periodically peeked through the window, maybe to see if we had escaped, or were getting up to any of the tricks for which hippies were so notorious. But we did not.

In the darkness the customs officer burst into the room, accompanied by another man. It was five in the morning. The other man shouted in English that he was the chief of police. Whether he meant for the whole of Greece or just for the tiny border post at Edirne, he did not say and we did not ask. Beneath ferocious little eyes hung grey folds of tired skin, and his belly wallowed over his trousers, but the shoulders were pulled back proudly, and on his chest and arms straps and stripes and badges spoke obscurely of rank. A pistol hung low beside his buttocks.

I immediately wondered how often anyone, even he, saw his body naked. The two men shouting in Greek and English as we tried to smooth the restless night out of our hair and crumpled clothes. The chief yelled that we were going to Alexandroupolis.

'Quickly, hurry, hurry,' the customs man shouted, while the chief shouted, 'A taxi is waiting.'

Angela asked the customs man to please stop shouting and he became very quiet and sad. To the chief she merely flared her nostrils and sneered. He too, pursing his lips, became silent, but flapped his hands as if to shout silently.

'Why the hurry?' I asked. The idea of the taxi intrigued me.

He replied, 'They are waiting for you. The court. You will be tried.'

'Who is waiting for us at five o'clock in the morning?' I asked. 'What time do courts start work in Greece?'

'The journey takes two hours. We must start now. Do not argue.'

As we approached the taxi, the chief said we had to pay for the trip ourselves. At this I balked. I put down my bags, and at that instant imagined myself ready to be beaten rather than pay the taxi fare. 'No,' I said decisively. 'A man does not pay to go to his own trial.'

To my surprise the fat police chief promptly opened the cab door and propelled me inside. Holding the door handle, he looked at me and said: 'If he is innocent, he wants to pay. If he is guilty, he should pay.'

At this, the taxi driver started the engine. Another policeman slipped in beside me on the back seat. Angela got in on the other side. The police chief and customs man squeezed comically into the front passenger seat together. The doors slammed and we pulled away.

Rather a clever remark, I thought, that the policeman had made about the taxi fares, and I gazed at his shaved neck in front with more respect. Outside the car, neat, leafless vineyards stretched across the countryside. To the left lay a broad, hazy river plain, while on the right hills rose into the distance. Half-way to Alexandroupolis, they let me out to urinate. I stood alone by the roadside, my eyes wandering over the landscape as the rivulet of my piss flowed down to nourish some weeds in a ditch. The new day's first sunlight picked out contours and colors. It was another beautiful morning. In the car, as we started off again, I could not hold back a certain happiness.

* * *

The police cell at Alexandroupolis, large and gloomy, with a metal door and a floor of rough stone and bare concrete, seems more like a storage area than a room: I am being stored inside it. In one corner, two dirty, stained blankets and a dusty cushion are my bed; in the other corner, a rank lavatory hole without water is my bathroom. I push the blankets around the edges of the floor to keep out mice (one or two do squeeze through). Having the light on all night deters cockroaches, or at least lets me see any that have woken me by crawling over my hands or face.

Being in a small locked room without anything to look at except the wall itself is thought-provoking. At first I find myself looking around the cell as if better to understand it. But there is nothing to understand. Nothing. It's so simple. I stare at the wall, the uneven stone. I rest my gaze on the slightly sloping, slightly damp floor. I look at the lavatory hole and contemplate what the sum of our days will be. In the wall I study meaningless contours, and wish to look beyond. Instead, my gaze turns to an inward distance, and I see once more the green fields of England, scenes from childhood, the salty movement of the sea, and re-enact moments with Angela, rewriting might-have-been events and should-have-said conversations. In the end there remains an inner discomfort, a psychological ache, and I marvel at the invention of the prison. What a clever way to make people unhappy! What cruel, imaginative and unusual punishment!

The dash from the border cost seven dollars, leaving us with twenty-nine dollars. The reason for the early start turned out to be that the 'chief of police' – just a local police officer, after all – wanted to get into town early on private business, and realized we could pay for his ride.

Angela and I were handled like a delivery of postage, logged into a book without anyone speaking to us, pushed away in separate directions: Angela along a corridor and me down some steps and into a windowless cell. Two days later, I have not spoken to anyone since – until now.

Metal scrapes and grates, it chimes and rings and clatters as it is slammed into place; keys turn, and the cell door is unlocked. A big man shuffles into the room; he's wearing a comfortably worn-in jacket and shabby trousers and open neck shirt with hair bursting forth at the nape. I might assume it's another prisoner, except that he's carrying a chair in one hand and a bag in the other. He does not greet me, and now I wonder if this is a prelude to physical violence. He sets down the chair in the middle of the room, under the light bulb, and opens his bag. My worst fears are confirmed as he produces a pair of scissors, long, gleaming and deadly sharp.

But no, I'm wrong. He's a barber, come to give me a short back and sides. After two days alone, it's strange and pleasant to have someone in the room with me. The space his body takes up, and the living warmth it gives out, fascinate me. I feel like holding his hand, maybe hugging him. But he ignores my eyes, makes not even a greeting, throws a cloth over me and works in silence, clipping and combing. That too is enjoyable, like a massage, or a caress as I watch the hair gathering on the stone floor around the chair, a reminder of the distant Moroccan and Algerian frontiers, long ago. Why this obsession with men's hair? Yet we too are obsessed with it: hair is the symbol of our generation.

Then he brings out a cut-throat razor and I submit, leaning back as he wields the blade on my face and neck. The barber finishes and does not even show me the result in a mirror, simply turns and calls, loud as a hammer in the solid, square sounds of Greek, for the guards to come. Before leaving, with a start he seems to notice my existence for the first time. He tells me the trial will be tomorrow.

After dawn – I don't know what time it is, but I've been awake half the night – I dress in my smartest clothes: embroidered shirt, frayed sweater and patched jeans. I can only hope last night's haircut and shave make me look quite straight. It's a pity there is nowhere to wash.

I sit on the floor and wait for the future to begin. A policeman unlocks the cell door at about midday and leads the way to a truck. We drive around a corner to pick up Angela. From across the street I see her, standing beside a policeman; she looks my way, too, but does not recognize me with my new haircut and unbearded face. I recognize her, though, like vertigo, like a roaring in the ears.

As she gets in, there is no kiss, we do not embrace. Our eyes meet and hands touch. She sits beside me and we start at once to rehearse our story, as the truck moves at a stately pace on a busy road through the town. I nudge Angela and point out of the window: we have driven down to waterfront and through the glass we see the shining sea. For some reason I grin at that. Now her eyes twinkle too, and flash a glance far into mine. She leans and whispers in my ear, 'I love you.'

* * *

Four men entered with great pomp ('the judges and prosecutor', the translator murmured), and a reverential silence fell while they took their seats at a raised bench overlooking the courtroom, which had become full of people apparently unconnected to our case. There was no jury.

One of the four at the bench, dark and overweight, with a kind voice asked me to tell 'the story' in my own words, I told him about our travels, and about the girl, and the whole room listened. The story seemed perfectly believable. I even began to believe it myself.

Angela told it all again, with more emotion. It struck me that even Angela must seem little more than a child to this roomful of adults.

With sincere curiosity I was asked, 'Why did you want to go to Turkey in the first place?'

I said, 'We are traveling around, and seeing the world while we have the chance.' But I feared the translator failed to catch the nuances.

'Yes, but why would you agree to do a favor for someone whom you had known no more than a few days?'

Such questions do deserve answers. 'Among young people like us,' I said – Angela gazed at me cryptically, anxiously – 'students,' I added –

'such things are normal.'

The customs officer appeared, now with his hair tightly brushed into place, shirt neatly tucked in and the trousers properly done up and reaching his waist, though he kept pulling his neck to one side as if the buttoned-up collar irritated it. The translator whispered: 'He says that you were most surprised when he discovered the hashish, and both of you immediately told him about the girl in Turkey.'

Good, good. Always, *hope* leaps forward eagerly.

The translator continued, 'On the other hand, he says, you seem familiar with hashish and recognized the smell.'

Another of the four men at the bench, this one lanky, thin and hollow, with a deep voice and ornate sharp face, made a short statement to which everyone listened attentively.

The translator explained that this was the prosecuting counsel, or prosecutor, and that he was recommending three years in prison. Our lawyer spoke again, more serious now and with a hint of concern on his brow. The judges listened less attentively, stood before he had quite finished, thanked him and left the room.

Angela and I were silent, stunned, quite in the dark. When I raised my eyes to hers, Angela shook her head – in disbelief, in despair. Our lawyer approached, breezy, grinning as he told us there was a good chance of acquittal. Certainly three months or less.

We stood as the judges came in. They made a long statement, ponderous and thoughtful. The translator summarized it succinctly: 'You have been found guilty and sentenced to thirty months in prison, with confiscation of the mirror and destruction of the hashish.' Angela's face drained of color. I struggled to comprehend what lay before us. That was all. The trial was over. The lawyer shrugged matter-of-factly as he chatted with other men. Policemen held our arms and urged us away. Only then did the lawyer hurry to wish us farewell. 'So they did not believe us,' I said. He turned a hand enigmatically. 'They believe you!' he cried. 'That is why thirty months. If they have not believed you, then it must have been thirty years!'

Angela was allowed to sit with me on a divan in the police station. We talked or read, or held hands, before two and half years apart. I drew a picture for her to take to prison. She said we needed to find out about making an appeal, and that our lawyer wasn't much good, was he? I didn't know. Nor did I know how to find another one. Sitting alongside one another, our conversation exhausted, we wrote letters. On pages torn from Angela's notebook we wrote to a few friends, and our parents, and I wrote to Milly, too, to tell them what had 'happened'.

* * *

White sunlight hung in crystal air, shone on pale hills, shimmered on silver water. Twisted olives stooped in rows like old soldiers. Along the narrow roadway, figs clung to dry, ancient stone, groves and orchards stood silent in the nestling corners of valleys, or basking their branches on warm hillsides.

That we knew, for we passed this way just days ago. This time we saw nothing, traveling along the same road in the darkened world of law, enclosed, windowless, electrically lit, attended by armed, crop-headed policemen in an immune, opaque, parallel part of society.

We shared the van with other prisoners, enough to make a crowd. The air we breathed together was the rank odors of cigarette breath and rancid underarm sweat, farting and, near the end, even vomit. Angela was the only woman, and the two of us sat together. I asked myself what Mr Natural would make of this. For a moment I saw all that had happened as just one square in a cartoon strip life. Angela must have been thinking the same way, for to my surprise she smiled and said, very brightly, 'Keep On Truckin''.

'The Prison,' writes Lawrence Durrell in *Prospero's Cell, a Guide to the Landscape and Manners of the Island of Corfu*, 'is a pleasant whitewashed building standing back from the sea.' When the doors of the van opened, and we were roughly urged out onto the tarmac, that's what we found. Beside us stood a pleasant whitewashed building on the edge of town. The sea was not within view.

To breathe fresh air again was like sipping champagne. Waiting for guards to make the next move, we stood outside a wooden gate set in an arch of stone. We wondered whether there could yet be miracles. Our feet still stood on the earth outside the prison, so there was still hope.

However, the gates opened. We were led inside to the prison's small concrete reception area. Prison officials pointed at Angela and an argument ensued between them and the guards who had brought us here.

'What's happening?' I asked, and a prison warder understood. He answered in faltering English: 'No woman here.'

The row went on as the other prisoners were dolefully checked-in and had their pockets emptied. Then, furious, the guards gestured Angela to return to the police van we had just left, one moving to take her arm. She frowned, looked worried, yet still haughty, and pulled her arm away. 'What is happening?' she repeated.

She was to be taken back to Athens, where there was a women's prison called Averoff. Her facade shattered and she grabbed at me in panic, weeping furiously as we hugged and kissed in a terrible embrace, her tears running onto my cheeks and hair; I tasted them on my lips.

A guard pulled Angela away. I looked on in horror, following into the roadway – with morbid interest in our emotion, guards did not stop me – and watched as she was placed inside the van.

Its doors stood open for a moment. 'I love you,' I dared to call. This time, it had to be said, though it seemed a weak, pointless parting remark. She nodded miserably as the van door slammed shut.

I turned into the prison. Vines, rich with leaves and fruit, hung over the doorway.

I look around, my head spinning. I might almost be tripping. The yard is dazzling white. There seem to be a lot of people about. A warder is leading me inside the building, still reminiscent of a youth hostel, and I realize I am grinning like an imbecile or a flower child.

He takes me past the cells, which are closed not with doors, but with floor-to-ceiling gates made of black metal bars, like railings. Each cell is a dormitory, clean and light, with tile floor, bare white walls and high ceiling. We stand at one of the gates and he unlocks it, and takes me inside. There are seven beds on each side of the room. Each is simply a thin, lumpy hair mattress unrolled onto three wooden planks resting on metal supports, and each is a man's domain, enclosed by a few tokens of his private, personal world, little intersecting spaces.

The men stare at me. This is not a case of straights and freaks. Here all are straight, but these straights are crooks and liars and thieves and con-men and low-lifes, burglars and bag-snatchers, marginals who hate society, or have been chucked out of it. Most are tattooed, muscular, their torsos thick with hair, and their arms slashed with parallel lines of self-mutilation, something which, I am told, is a mark of pride.

One of these spaces is now mine. The warder's final word is that I am lucky not to be in the Big Prison, the bigger building next door (for where we are now, he explains, is the Small Prison). In the big prison, he says, foreign drug-dealers and drug-takers are serving long sentences; twenty, thirty years. I sit upon my bed and the others inspect me.

One says in halting English: 'How you like this place?'

'I like it, it's nice,' I answer politely, unthinking.

Amused, he translates my remark at the top of his voice for the others to hear, and all burst into a roar of laughter, clapping and stamping with mirth. Some are calling out in English, but I understand nothing.

The first half-hour inside a prison covers a long span of time, longer than a day outside. The baggage search, the walk to the crowded little reception office, the parting from Angela, seem already far away in some distant morning. I make up my bed and lie on it exhausted.

During 'open' periods, we could leave our cells: we could use the cold showers, or take a walk in the little courtyard, pacing up and down. The robust proximity and physicality of the showers alarmed me. After the experience in Tunisia, I was afraid of men's frustrations. I soon saw what took place: despite unanimous anathemas against homosexuality, certain prisoners demanded services from certain others. Hissed, insistent, no-nonsense transactions took place in the brutal, ambiguous terrain between coercion and compensation. The relief given was quick and unsentimental, the payment trivial.

Most men, most of the time, paced up and down in the yard, not speaking, in pensive exercise. Some spun worry beads around their fingers. During these hours, discipline was relaxed indoors as the outer wall was more closely watched. While other men took the chance to stretch their legs and breathe deeply of the island air, I slipped upstairs and stood at the bars of another cell. It wasn't the thing to wander into other men's cells – but a foreigner could get away with it. I had discovered that from upstairs the view reached far into the countryside.

Villages clustered on distant unimprisoned hillsides. A tiny group of white cottages shone in the sunlight, though the mountainside on which it rested was hardly visible, a hazy shade of purple which faded into the sky. Birds flew. Little paths and tracks wound half-hidden across the landscape. I could see a stony footpath, and by a leap of imagination, could feel my feet walking along there. And, walking on that path, if I turned my head I could see the red roof and white walls of the prison, small in the greenery of the middle distance. But I did not look back, for fear of seeing myself at the barred window. Instead I looked ahead to where the fields led into hills. Cool leaves lined the track, and the silent sound of insects and birds.

* * *

A letter! With dried flowers folded into the paper.

Simon my love, hello
The first night was spent in Patra jail and the flowers are from there. I saved them for you. My shell has been thickening ever since I arrived. Blue Meanies wear dresses here. So do we, a uniform of a baggy dress made of mattress ticking material. All the prisoners are Greek except me. I share a room with the two who are well-educated and can speak English. The younger one has been here for 10 years already. She murdered the boyfriend who raped her. The older one shot her husband at Athens airport. Our room is Institution Green and Yellowing White. There is a table and benches, a bookshelf with just a few books. One corner, with bread and tomatoes on a shelf, fresh every few days, is designated as the kitchen. The three beds are in the other corners.

The other women are crowded into rooms on either side of ours. Some of them are clearly raving mad. Many are not 'mad' but, still, are deep in mental problems. One woman tells everyone about the day she poured gasoline over her sleeping husband and set fire to him. She got 43 years. Another woman cut her husband into 33 pieces, she proudly tells you over and over. She got a year for each piece.

A lot of the women are here for murder, with fantastic stories of what brutal monsters their husbands were, how much they hated them, and how they finally did away with them. These women will be here forever, political prisoners in the cause of, maybe not women's liberation – these people aren't into liberation – but at least a woman's right to fight back. There are prostitutes here, too, but they are a world apart. They speak only to each other.

Some real political prisoners – opponents of the military regime –

truly are apart, strictly segregated. I'm sure they're the most interesting people here.

Our food is grossly inadequate. Some days only bread and potatoes. Nothing else. And there are roaches crawling around when it's served.

A letter came but I wasn't given it – was it from you? If you can, let me know how you are. It was so good that you said goodbye to me properly before I left, and called out.

I love you too, Simon. I miss you.
Angela.

The envelope, already open when I receive it, is criss-crossed with Greek lettering, rubberstamped by different departments of the prison authority. I read her letter again. Funny, we don't have a uniform here. Maybe the freedom to dress as you choose is more treasured by women, or has more significance in a women's prison. She says she loves me, and I must try to believe it. Simply to hold Angela's letter is a reminder of her face, her body, having sex. Then I think of her changing into the prison dress, putting it on, and taking it off, and writing to me.

I'm not surprised Greek wives resort to murder. Anyone would take a butchers' knife to most of my companions here and cheerfully chop them into 33 pieces.

Angela describes her prison surroundings so well. I can't see my own as clearly. I look up from her letter. Men are sitting despondently on their narrow beds, lost in thought. Beside each bed a man has his suitcase and his dreams.

And his spit can: all but two or three of the men have a tin can by the bed into which they spit, drop nose-pickings, flick ash and cigarette ends (they are allowed to smoke at certain times, and all do) or put unwanted secretions or dregs of all kinds until the can is full to the brim.

I look back at the paper, the flowers from Patra, and Angela's handwriting, and am lost in dreams of my own.

There was another letter on the same day. Eventually I learned prisoners were allowed no more than two letters a week, so I started to hope nobody would write in case it delayed one of Angela's letters. The other was hard to figure out – from England, the neat handwriting on the envelope looked vaguely familiar. It too was already open, of course, and as soon as I began to lift out the page from inside I remembered – I had treasured another letter in that handwriting. Her postcard was still tucked somewhere in my bag, if it had not been taken by Guards.

Dear Simon
I have just read your letter with absolute horror. Do you want me to come and be with you? I could stay in Corfu somewhere, maybe there's a campsite, and come every day (are you allowed visitors?) and talk with you, or listen, or sit in silence if that's what you want. Or if not, then just stand outside the prison and touch the wall.

You are stupid. Is your beloved Angela behind this? One or other of you must be to blame for dropping you both into this shit. Tho' blame won't help now. To think of you, of all people, in jail – like 'a robin redbreast in a cage', which as I'm sure even a benighted philistine like you must know, 'puts all heaven in a rage.' (William Blake).

Certainly I'm in rage to think of you, O charming, lovely footloose boy, behind bars, maybe badly treated. Or maybe there's something, some person – a warder or a prisoner – or some view of the experience, that you find valuable. That would be like you, that's what I like.

It won't last forever. If things are bad, keep your mind fixed on that. Or, for all I know, it's really groovy behind bars: non-stop parties, cool dudes, far-out chicks smuggled in, great dope. From what we hear about Greek prisons, though, that's not the scene.

Are you eating OK? I have a feeling wholefood macrobiotic vegetarianism may not have caught on in Greece yet. Can I send you something, or maybe even bring stuff?

I simply want to say I love you, but I guess that would turn you off. So I'll just say I want to help you get through this. Write and let me know how. What about some books to read?

Peace and love and freedom.
Milly.

For a moment I had to sit on the edge of the bed, my mind blank, struggling with some wounded, wordless emotion. I felt touched by Milly's concern, but she felt far, too far away. Even if she had been in Corfu, it would not have felt any closer. I took out Angela's letter and re-read it, tenderly running a fingertip over it where she had written her name.

* * *

Time moved slower than I had ever known it could. Every minute resembled every other, and as they accumulated, sixty to an hour, by noon I could hardly remember if seven o'clock in the morning had been on the same day.

Later, the evening is long. Bob, give me the *chains of the skyways* any day. For that means only the rules of society. As I adjusted, though, to the boredom, things began to move faster again. Several days would pass all together in a bundle. A mindless rhythm set in, Greek pop music blared from loudspeakers and it all seemed to be just one record, and I lay on my bed in the crowded cell, feeling the time pass like a viscous, gritty suspension running over my skin .

The electric light stays on all the time. At night, it shines eerily into my dreams. There are no dark corners, even in dreams nowhere to hide, or to be alone. Then someone rigs up a clever thing out of a twist of paper shaped like an ice-cream cone. Hanging from a long thread hung over the light socket, the cone can be pulled up at night to cover the light bulb. I don't know if this is an old trick or a brilliant new invention, and no one can tell me. But the guards seem familiar with this device and make no attempt to remove it. Surely it will burst into flames one night, overheated by the bulb... but yes, that's obviously what happened before, and soon it happens again, and we spend a few more nights half awake in the light before again, someone makes a new light cone.

We sleep, we lie awake. Worry beads click. Some men snore. One guy snores so bad he gets a shoe thrown at him. It strikes him squarely in the face and he wakes with a shout of pain. The others laugh, then yell at him for keeping them awake at nights. He is both angry and apologetic: I understand he is saying he can't help it. Gradually we nod off, once more half-dreaming, half-sleeping. Some fart, some belch. They scratch. They masturbate, holding the blankets away from their bodies, trying not to make a noise, though some sigh deeply with miserable contentment at the final moment. At first I do the same, day dreaming and night dreaming of hippy chicks in tight jeans or flimsy skirts, knickerless, legs apart, of Angela, of Milly, of all women and none, of the female form, of girlish thighs, buttocks, breasts. After a while I hardly bother to think about them anymore. I just jerk off as if brushing my hair or cleaning my teeth. The guy in the corner snores as bad as ever.

We are awakened by angry shouts, by the clank of metal. It's morning. The entrance to the room is not a door, but a gate; it's now left unlocked for a while and we can wander into the courtyard for exercise. If we stay in bed, pairs of guards pull back the bedclothes and literally throw our bodies off the mattresses. But there is no reason to wake or get out of bed, there is nothing to do. Time seems to put on the brakes, or change down to a lower gear as soon as I hear the noisy morning clatter of the guards yelling at the gate. Dreams seem to pass in real time. The waking hours are like those slow-motion nightmares where you are paralyzed, panicking, stuck to the earth, trying to run, to escape.

* * *

The prison courtyard is small, as small as the back yard of our terraced house was in London, but enclosed by walls as high as the yard is wide, and without any interesting features. As soon as the cell doors are opened, men stream outside. At this time, a tiny cup of Greek coffee is served – looking like something steaming and unpleasant dredged from the bottom of the Bosphorus, but tasting strongly of coffee. I savor the drink, lingering over each sip, then chew up the grounds. Several men turn down the drink, some saying it is bad for their hearts.

At the morning coffee break, just when the tiny cup of swampland mud is poured, a young prisoner from another cell suddenly approaches and grasps my arm. He implores me silently, like a mute laboring to form words. What does he want? He does not look violent, or homosexual, but crushed, with plaintive, intelligent eyes.

At last speech comes to the surface. 'English', he says. Then, 'I Greek, you English.' I nod encouragingly. He carries on, 'You girlfriend? Me not.' He points towards the gate, and struggles to continue: 'I. Go. Out. Today.'

I smile, and nod again. Because people do come and go. They are released. 'Efto gallo, that's good.'

He shakes his head. No, I have not understood.

Finding more English, he lowers his voice and gazes into my eyes. Speaking as if to an old friend, he comes closer and tells me, 'My life the way how I used to live…'. I nod, and he carries on quietly, 'To look always that picture.'

Puzzled, I try to make sense of the words. He turns away exasperated, and flees into one of the cells. Uncertainly I begin to follow him – he seemed quite desperate to get his message across – but at that moment my name is called on the tannoy. I must go down to the office at once.

A parcel has arrived, my first, and among the contents I glimpse (for it has already been opened and rifled) ballpoint pens, a new notebook of lined paper and a bar of Cadbury's chocolate. What joy! At first I suppose it must be from Milly. Then my heart tightens painfully to see the handwriting on a letter inside the box.

Along with the parcel, another opened letter is handed to me. I carry the box and the letter back to the cell. On the way, I see that several other men, too, are being given mail this morning. It must have arrived all at once. I assume our post is kept at some censor's office in Athens until a prison van happens to be coming to Corfu. I wonder what is in their letters, what Greek words expressing what Greek sentiments from disappointed, dark-haired Greek fathers and mothers, dutiful sisters and brothers, faithful, unhappy wives and forlorn children.

The first letter, inside the parcel, is in my mother's hand, and I dread to read it. The second is in Angela's rounded American script. This one I am eager to read, but an apologetic sense of shame forces me to take out my mother's letter at once.

Darling
Poor dear Simon, what can we do to help? I hope the guards will let you have the box of treats.

We desperately hope that you are at least in good health, that you are eating, sleeping, and keeping the physical well-being that might help you to survive this experience. We phoned the British Consul but he advised us not to go to Corfu. He said that we would only be able to see you on an ordinary prison visit, and that that would be upsetting for all of us. He said it would be better to send you letters and food, and that, at least, we intend to do. Still, if you would you like us to, we will come at once.

We know you have been happily getting on with your wanderings and adventures, mercifully free of parental interference, and we reckon by the number of letters we receive that you don't yet wish to re-enter the life and love of your family.

Both of us can understand that. We too were twenty years old once (the difference is there was a War on), and we do wish you a lot of luck and happiness. But it seems you have met instead, at least for the moment, bad luck and unhappiness. We love you and want to help. Please let us know if there's anything we can do.

Daddy is having problems at work, with a new colleague he does not get on with who is making life hard for him. The stress and worry was already taking a toll on him, not sleeping, constant indigestion, and also – nothing to worry about – seemed to affect his heart when we got your letter (a long time after you sent it, by the way).

I think at first he felt it was almost the last straw and he could not go on. We had a couple of days, after we got your news when he could not face going to work or even speaking to anyone. I was worried what he might do. Then, though, a change came over him and he decided that the tragedy that has befallen his son is what really matters to him. Stress at work is not the issue now. In a funny way, having something even more important to worry about may have done him good. It's hard to say.

You mentioned making an appeal. Do you know when that will be? Daddy is willing and even keen to come and help at any time, and in particular to speak at your appeal. Would that be useful? The Consul seems to know nothing about it, and your lawyer seems to have lost interest too. He says you have a new lawyer. If that's true, please get him to contact us urgently. We are completely in the dark here.

We have not told the girls what has happened. And when other people ask if we've heard from you and how you are, we just say we have heard, and you are now living in Greece. Which is all perfectly true.

This girl whose mirror you were carrying sounds like a perfect crook. She is not the sort of person you should be passing the time of day with at all, and I hope it will be possible for the police to trace her and bring her to justice, even though it's you (and Angela) who have suffered the consequence of her dishonesty so far. We have confidence in you. You may be a rebellious young man now but you were always an honest good-hearted boy, and somehow, we think, that is the real you.

Enjoy the parcel and write soon to tell us what we can send, whether we should visit and if you want Daddy at the appeal.

With all our love, darling, and wishing you health and happiness.

Mummy and Daddy.

The music stops and a crackly announcement is heard. We are instructed that we will be remaining in our cells for the rest of today. Rumors fly around the room, and through the bars, that a prisoner has killed himself.

We don't find out who it is, or how he died, or at least, I cannot understand the hectic guessing and gossip. In the yard outside, self-important policemen in uniform and others, presumably also police, in suits, laugh and chat, light up cigarettes.

We crowd at the windows and bars as guards carry a body out into the yard. Strangely, it is dressed all in bright red, as if attired for some ceremony. With shock, I see that the body is the young man who spoke to me earlier at the coffee stand. He said he would leave the prison today. No, he is not dressed in red after all. He is wearing normal clothes – the red is his blood.

I don't know what one has to do to remove the life from one's body. Even dead, this body is alive. Under dark furrowed brows his gentle eyes appear still to be open, as if he still struggles to explain, and utter some thought to me, while from his arm the very flesh hangs out of a wide red gash. The Greeks think it was brave and manly of him to slash himself so decisively. I recoil, afraid that I may 'look always that picture.' If the parcel had not arrived at that moment, would I have saved his life?

I turn to Angela's letter. Her handwriting pleases me like a kiss. The paper is bright yellow-orange, the color of the sun torn from a notebook.

My love,

Are you allowed outside much? You have been heavy in my thoughts. Letter from Ozzie: he got the news from Sasha. Feels it's somehow his fault! He expressed real concern – it surprised me, I don't even know him – and sent money and food, and says he will organize another lawyer for us for the appeal, and let my father know what's happening. Isn't that weird? I haven't thought about Ozzie in years. Nor my father.

Really, Simon, the only person I want to be with is you. Want to talk to you, have you hug me again. You are the only one who matters to me. I ache for your happiness.

Last week I had a nightmare that Sirius was shot trying to protect me. Two days later I was uneasy for him again. If anything happens to him now it'll be more than I can bear.

There are women here who still manage to look like streetwalkers, even here. They ain't young or sexy, these gals. In fact the young, pretty chicks are nearly all in for adultery. Did I say adultery?!! Is that a crime? Yup, in Greece it is.

All the women here are very unhip. I have no interest in changing them (we scientists know a lost cause when we see one). Shall we give up hoping to make the world a better place? Truly, it's beyond help. Maybe a nuclear war is what we need after all. Blow the whole caboodle to kingdom come.

A quote from Santayana: 'Everything in Nature is lyrical in its essence, tragic in its fate, and comic in its existence.'

I end now to retreat into a book. I love you and long for you. Be well, and a little happy, and write again soon.

I love you.

Angela.

Birds flying overhead are a reminder of better days.

At last she truly loves me, thanks to prison. It really seems quite clear that she does. Does she think of Jesse at all anymore? As I pace up and down I imagine her eyes and her touch, and wonder if birds flying overhead are a reminder of anything.

* * *

We pace, pace up and down, up and down between the walls, from one wall to the other, eyes looking half down, half down and half nowhere, working over our thoughts, our thoughts and our memories, our memories and our dreams. Inside the cell, or in the yard, we pace up and down and think, think of our trial, our case, our family, our lives and our dashed hopes.

After breakfast I go upstairs and look out of the window. The weather is unusually clear, the air perfectly limpid, a precious substance of unflawed translucence. The hill on the horizon, and the village resting on its slope, are sharply in focus. Then, not far away, I see a man working on the flat concrete rooftop of a house. He wears blue and white, as if dressed in the Greek flag, and holds a long-handled shovel. My bare feet step right into his shoes and for one long moment I work outside under the open sky.

For some weeks the chocolate bar, which is divided into a dozen small squares, brings about a regimen of troubled self-discipline. I eat half a square every day. It is important to keep the chocolate wrapped in its thin shiny foil and purple wrapping paper. These coverings become like ritual, magic materials, and the chocolate itself, always in danger of being stolen, or of melting, is something beyond treasure, meta-gold, the product of alchemy.

Each day I look forward with subdued excitement to the time when I shall allow myself to eat another half-square. I say nothing about it to anyone. In the afternoon, while the other men doze, unwrapping is done with meticulous care – for reasons of luck, the paper must never be torn.

The half-square, I place in the middle of my tongue, near the front. I do not bite the chocolate, but allow it to dissolve. This takes much longer. Sometimes, though, I hold it between my teeth and, in an exquisite agony, refrain from biting. I have been experimenting with other places on my tongue, and at the side of my mouth, and at the back, to find the perfect place to let the solid liquefy deliciously into pure sweetness. This is as near to dope as I have been since coming to Corfu.

The chocolate produces a sort of euphoria, mixed with disappointed longing. While I hold the chocolate in my mouth, a heavenly satisfaction appears at the center of my thoughts, and clears a small space for itself. I descend into this space and think only of the melting joyful moment. To hold on, and not let go! But the moment is always going, and changing and cannot last, and no sooner is it gone – the half-square lasts about half an hour – than a gloomy despair falls upon me.

Then I, too, doze in the afternoon silence. There will be more chocolate tomorrow, if it is not stolen.

Up and down in the yard, up and down, to and fro, I paced through my thoughts, not pausing except to turn on my heels and come back, and come back, and come back. Pictures from the past, or from vivid half-dreams, filled my mind. No one spoke to me.

One day, the door between the yard and the reception area stood half-open. I stopped walking. The guards were nowhere in sight. I looked through and saw that the gate from the reception area to the Outside was also standing open. I could actually see the lane. A mad, impulsive inner voice urged me to act quickly, to run out at once, without thought or hesitation, and be free. Could I really escape? Another inner voice cried out not to be an idiot. Would I be shot? Where would I go? What about Angela? As I looked out, an aged woman clad in deep black was walking past, her face furrowed, the eyes staring down; In her left hand, resting on her right arm, a bunch of brilliant yellow flowers.

She was in mourning, perhaps. For someone dead long ago, perhaps. Perhaps she was making her way to lay flowers at the cemetery next door to the prison. She was coming, though, from the direction of the 'big prison'. Perhaps she had visited someone there. A brother or a son.

Such people did come to leave food parcels for their relatives. Men in 'the small prison' survived on the food brought by their wives and mothers, and picked unhappily at prison meals.

At half past eleven the first meal was slopped into bowls by surly guards. I did not want to live on the curious blobs of pasta oozing starch, or thick-cut potato fries limp with orange-tinted grease, or gluey dollops of rice. I was reluctant to eat more than a little of the strange, fibrous, dry bread we were given, that was like rolls of doormat. Sometimes torn threads of meat like tangles of hair floated in the accompanying watery soup. I sat on my bed and ate slowly to make a meal of it, for even food such as this made a little high point of pleasure. And I would sometimes remember my mother's cooking and Angela's, or, better, eating in the street, sitting on doorsteps eating fresh white bread and strong cheese and fresh tomatoes. And I would sometimes dream of a good life Outside, and imagine... *we're free, and our time's our own, and we'll be always happy, happy together, happy, free and in love.*

Dear Bob Dylan, as one of your friends in the prison, I can tell you the *chains of the skyways* are claptrap. Freedom is the freedom to walk out of this place. That is the pure joy of life. Yet for the free man, a purer freedom is the freedom to stay home on a working day, forget the rent or to go with a woman when the impulse strikes him.

Beyond that, advertisers reveal a far greater freedom, a transcendental physicality, leaping, running, glowing with the unrestrained vigor that comes from a certain yoghurt or breakfast cereal. Freedom is driving fast along a dreamlike, flawless open road over a majestic landscape free of people, free of speed limits, free of police.

Free of law. But those are mere dreams of freedom. In the real world, We Must Survive is the first law and all must obey. To survive, we must live together. To live together, we must not kill, we must not steal, we must honor our parents... We must and we must not. All who dream of freedom soon run up against the walls that cannot be scaled.

Even in the vast open spaces of time, we are confined by seasons, by the tides of the moon, each week its day of rest, regular as a metronome. Janis Joplin scorned such petty restraints, 'It's all the same fuckin' day, man.' Life as a torrent, not as an ebb and flow! A constant rushing TODAY. Far out. Come visit me, Janis, here in the prison, and I'll show you a fuckin' day, we'll wrap this fuckin' day around us and feel its coarse weave irritating our skin 'til we long to throw it off.

This is the flip side of the endless days in California and on our island, Djerba: Prison too stretches time endlessly, makes each moment stay with you like a mouthful of unwanted gum, that you chew and chew, till you want to spit it out but there's nowhere to spit. Grab it with your fingers and it stretches longer and longer like playdough, so every moment of time stretches over the horizon, forward and back.

Completed days are counted and treasured like coins in the counting house, counting out his money, payments into a pension, coins amassed towards the rich freedom that will be paid out one day.

Afternoons pass same as the mornings. Nothing happens, but still they do pass. In the evenings I look forward to sleep. Looking forward is exciting and enjoyable, so I delay sleeping to enjoy looking forward to it for longer. And I savor the thought that if I do sleep, I shall wake, and when I wake, time will have passed, be it five minutes or five hours, so the end will be that much closer, and the freedom.

I did not dash through the open gate. I clung to the bars upstairs and watched the sun set, casting colors across the sky. In the evening calm, a man cycled by, glimpsed between trees, between houses, between bars.

A lovely, ordinary world, and its setting sun. Somewhere Outside, just out of view, people were walking, couples strolling. I pictured us among them. For they walk in my memory, and there we still stroll together somewhere, Angela and I.

* * *

The music is pure Greek open-air taverna. It plays loud and tinny most of every day. Blue sky above dazzling white walls, the blue edged with barbed wire. I notice a living green stem with flowers – convolvulus or ivy or honeysuckle – creeping over a wall and reaching for the black bars of a window. It holds my attention and, enchanted, I stand adrift, breathless, admiring the tender wild leaves, green hearts twining, and the purple flowers. Purple! A few flowers among the heart-shaped leaves. Minutes drift past like sails on a calm sea.

I sit on the side of my bed and compose a list, and send it to Angela:

- *Stand in the hall putting on your coat. Open the door and step outside. Shut the door behind you. Enjoy an evening stroll.*
- *Open your door with your own key. Go to the kitchen and make yourself something to eat.*
- *Go into your bedroom, undress, turn off the light and get into bed.*
- *Sleep until you wake.*
- *Pour cereal from a packet into a bowl. See the piling up in the bowl. Pour on as much milk as you like. Pick up a spoon and eat. Take as long as you want.*
- *Check the mail, open your letters.*

People arrive and people leave. They start their sentence or have served their time. I am tense with anticipation of a trip to the Outside, for the Appeal is coming. The British Consul called on me, and knew more about the case than I do myself. He, at least, knows the name of our new lawyer. He tells me, too, that my father transferred 'a sum' but it was spent 'on incidentals'. He says I'll be given any balance on my release.

Release has a contemplative, abstract quality, like some philosophical concept unconnected with the real world. I have spent the summer here, and feel quite at home here, within these walls, enclosed by the larger fence of my view from upstairs. Now, when I look out, the sky is overcast, sometimes it rains. Angela has become simply a collection of letters, and the hope of another, each one a treasure to me.

As long as we stay in prison, I am sure of her love.

* * *

My Simon
After a week of disturbing dreams about you, I got your latest this afternoon. Your list of 'freedoms' cheered me immensely. I love you.

Last week there was a day of rain – did you get that too? – and I saw in my mind the grey skies of England. I feel as if I will be free soon and long to see the sad soft colors, red berries and old gold and faded, melancholy browns of an English fall.

I think we should go back there just to rest and recover from all this. Nowhere better. Tho I admit my head's in a mess about the future.

Er, hum... Simon, I've put on a LOT of weight from all the starchy food. I know you don't like 'em too buxom. You like 'em pretty skinny, dontcha? I've noticed that. But as of this week I've stopped eating. TOTALLY STOPPED. It's about time I pulled myself together. So I have been fasting. This is my fourth day without any food AT ALL and I'm not hungry. I just miss chewing.

We shall be freed at the Appeal. This I believe, and must believe. What to do when I am free. It's not even a question of Jesse anymore. Just a matter of ME. This period of my life has fucked my mind. I must go somewhere and see myself, meet myself, spend time with myself. And other people? Yes, I want to be somewhere with someone else as well, but the only real idea is Sirius. Everything else is up in the air and will not come down to earth till I get out of here.

Did you hear, Ho Chi Minh has died. I don't know what importance these things have to us anymore. I'm the village eccentric round here. Barefoot, hairy legs, no bra, nose in a book all the time. I realized: there's no revolution going on – nothing's changing and we're just a tiny blip, one deranged generation of crazy-people. I look forward to being on the road again – with you. God I miss you Simon. Will see you soonest. Write again. Know that I love you.

It's worrying that she is not eating. She has not signed off with her name but with a little heart. In the center of the heart she has written a tiny letter *A*. I raise the paper to my face and touch the heart lightly with my lips.

Fall 1969

Even as our cheerful new lawyer introduced himself to me, breezily remarking that Angela had already been here in Komotini for several days, I saw her through the window. The lawyer's voice continued unheeded and forgotten. Into the room she stepped, into my very presence, with her wonderful control and poise, white smile and clear blue eyes.

Her rigorous diet must have worked; she had not put on weight. For an instant I was speechless with confusion, delight and pain. Half stranger, half lover, her physical closeness amazed me.

With perfect calm, she greeted me, 'Yassou, Simon.'

'Hello Angela.'

'Nice tan. Looking good.'

She reached out a hand and, with fingertips, I touched it with mine, the one person who knew me truly, my dearest human being, faultless example of femaleness, body and soul. She looked steadily into my eyes as if examining the emotions inside them.

We must remember ourselves and be normal. The lawyer was still talking, his warm, amiable tones like a low hum as he explained the legal basis for our appeal. He gestured Angela to sit on the chair next to mine, and so we sat, and faced him, and I tried to concentrate on what he was saying. I still had not understood, and it did not matter, who had asked him to take our case, and who was paying his fee.

Leaning comfortably in his smart suit, the lawyer had a pleasant, sympathetic manner. It seemed that he neither knew nor cared about the facts of the case. He openly schemed with us to make a good presentation for the court. We must try to act – or stop acting; we must show ourselves clearly as two innocent young offspring of the respected bourgeoisie – for was it not, as he said, in fact the truth? Through innocence and ill-luck and a foolish desire to be rebellious, not to mention a misguided vanity that we were grown-ups who knew how to take care of ourselves – we had committed a foul deed. After all, he asked, was not that also the plain truth of the matter?

At this I bridled, brows knitted; but he threw back his head and held up a hand to forestall our protests. 'A foul deed,' he repeated. 'Bringing an illegal drug into Greece, bringing into our fine and pious country this vile, energy-sapping, soul-destroying cannabis. Bringing our country into disrepute.'

Now he raised his eyebrows, adding *sotto voce*, 'At this point you apologize to the Court for the mishap, quite unintentional and quite unknown to you, of tainting the goodness of Greece with this... dreadful substance. A little acting may be needed, but only by me. If the Court asks your opinions on this drug, this is what you will say about it: you have come across it before, among degenerates at university in your own country, among whom it unfortunately flourishes in these days; and you know it to be loathsome and harmful to the mind and the body. I will tell the translator what to say.'

He leaned forward. He seemed clever, intelligent, sophisticated. 'Now, I wonder,' he said, 'are you simply victims of your own youthful folly and naiveté? Or are you victims of a sinister third person?' He pursed his lips, pondering. We said nothing, and he answered his question: 'The Court cannot know for sure. No one can ever know the whole truth about things. Perhaps an element of doubt remains in the mind about this. However, of this we *are* perfectly sure – that such things do happen. And of this we are also sure – that young people are not as clever as they think they are. And, even more important, of this we are also sure – that according to the testimony of the customs officer, Miss Angela instantly produced a paper with the name and address of a young girl whom she claimed to be the real owner of the drug. Instantly! And this also we may wish to take into account, tempered always with a sensible degree of skepticism – that the customs officer said at your trial that you appeared astonished by his discovery of the drug.'

He went on, 'The police and prosecuting authority, I shall point out, failed to make any effort to contact the girl and establish the real truth of this matter. So, what is the real, the whole truth?'

The smile gone, and looked at us. 'The truth is, that two foolish, kind, thoroughly respectable young people, of good families, with their lives before them, are in trouble in a foreign land.'

A wave of despair swept over me, as I saw how he knew and understood the falseness of truth. In a way, whatever the legal argument, he would appeal only to the humanity of the judges.

He turned away to make notes, and we had a short time to talk. Angela grasped my hand. 'I'm so worried, Simon. Terribly worried, about the appeal.'

I no longer had any hip philosophy to console her. She let go and pulled something from her pocket.

I was puzzled. A pair of socks! 'I made them for you,' she said.

I took them, and could have wept.

The lawyer remembered something he had brought for us, and from his briefcase pulled a copy of Life magazine. It was all about Woodstock. The festival, the nation, the generation. The mud, the music, even the drugs. Pictures of our own people, dancing, decorated, stoned, unclothed and carefree in the rain, and we could have been among them instead of here. The positive tone of the article made us suspicious. Angela said, 'They just realized what a big market hippies represent.'

But already our moment together had ended. As we were led away, the lawyer said 'By the way, Simon, I have an extremely useful letter from your father. A very intelligent man. Most of what I have just said comes from his words. I had it translated and shall show it to the Court.'

When will I see her again? At the Performance? We need more time to rehearse! No, this isn't the school play. Later, a guard at the Komotini police station opened the cell door with more presents from Angela: some shampoo, a pair of shoes and a recent copy of the International Herald Tribune. Where had she got these things?

I seized the newspaper, thrilled at the feel of it. The main story was a grisly one. Lieutenant William L. Calley, who led the massacre of civilians at My Lai, in Vietnam, last year, had just been charged with the murders. The war was now raging across the border in Cambodia. But in Greece, 'the war, the war' was not spoken about, nor was peace, nor love. The only issue prisoners discussed with any passion was the exile of King Constantine II now that the military junta was in control. The prisoners felt that without its king, Greece was hardly Greece at all. That mattered to them above all else.

A long corridor dark with wood paneling led into the square courtroom. This is not the Greece of holiday dreams. Around the heavy woodwork mists of shadow moved; a somber darkness lay in the room, barely penetrated by the light outside. The judge – to our surprise there was only one, and again no jury – heard the arguments of both sides as we stood in the quiet room, the moments passing, or remaining still, like the uncoiling of a spring in another dimension than time.

The lawyer's voice, and the prosecutor's, sounded beautiful, the chunky, soft Greek words like squares of cloth. I fancied that they were reciting poetry, or carving it in the heavy air, poems as sculpture.

At last the lawyer handed up a letter to the bench, and I recognized my father's handwriting. The same blue seal had been stamped upon it as on the letters I received in jail. Stapled to it was a second sheet, the translation, but for some time the judge studied the original. He looked up towards us, Angela and myself, standing in the dock, as if he had not realized until that moment that we were here in the room with him. Like the customs officer at our first trial, he looked sad and guilty behind a transparent mask of pomposity. The mask became thinner, until suddenly he seemed like a man with a bus to catch, who could not wait to get away from here. He abruptly pronounced that our sentence was reduced to six months, and stood up to leave. All rose to their feet as he strode from the room. That meant freedom in just one more month.

* * *

Darling
There has been no way of getting a letter to you for weeks, so I'm asking the British Consul to read you this message. With luck he may be able to give it to you.

We learned of the Appeal success, or partial success, by phoning the Consul at Thessalonica. It was such a relief we were a little hysterical. We were disturbed that no one had bothered to tell us the result, or even the date of the hearing. We received nothing, not even from you. As though it were nothing to do with us.

Anyway, never mind, soon you will be out of there, and no doubt after a period of recovery will want to carry on with life. We'll hope to see you here as soon as you're able. It's a shame that you're going north just as winter starts, but not as much of a shame as being in prison!

Now, about money. We are sorry we can't be of any further help. In fact, it will take some time to recover from the expense of the last few months. As the Consul will tell you, as well as the hundreds of pounds in cash we have sent you, of course there have been all the other things, phone calls, cables, parcel postage, not to mention, especially, translators' fees and lawyers' fees.

If you do feel stuck for any small sum, we will try to help as we don't want you to suffer any more or get into any further difficulties, so don't be afraid to ask. It's just that the immediate shortage has rather bogged us down and we are in some difficulty ourselves.

Anyway the important thing is that you are soon to be free and that is all that matters. Do write to us as soon as you can to let us know what you will be doing.

Some letters we sent to you have come back unopened. There was one each from Daddy, Ruth, and me.

We'll understand if you don't want to spend your birthday with us, even though it's your 21st. We'll toast you in your absence! Perhaps at least we might see you at Christmas?

Love and best wishes from all of us. Keep well.

Mummy and Daddy.

PS. Ruth and Sarah are absolutely desperate for a line from you.

Lawyer's fees? I thought Angela's dad, or Ozzie in Germany, or someone, was paying for that. Has the lawyer pulled the wool over our eyes, and taken a fee from both our parents? I can't be bothered to think about it. The cash is a puzzle, too. If they sent me money, where is it?

Yes, it might have been kind to tell them about the appeal. I just forgot. Well, as she says, never mind, we'll be out in a month. That's as good a time as any to be heading north, south, east or west, whatever the weather. As for turning twenty-one, nothing could be more irrelevant.

On returning to Corfu, my good fortune was the talk of the Small Prison. The popular view was that someone had been bought. I imagined the whole sentence as a single day, and thought continuously about what time it was on this 24-hour clock. Nine minutes, eight minutes to midnight. Then one minute, and finally, none.

A man shouted with anger, roared, and banged his fist down on the planks of his bed. 'Deka chronia! Deka chronia!' (Ten years, ten years). The others looked at him with eyes expressionless. Then his manly rage died, and he sat down on the side of the bed like a child, a little boy. Another prisoner jocularly commented, 'Deka chronia makaronia' (ten years macaroni), and some smiled wryly.

Then to their surprise, at this the man leapt up again and seized the can of saliva and phlegm, nostril-pickings and cigarette butts from beside his bed. In two strides he had reached me and emptied the contents over my head. He knew but a word of English and yelled it now: 'Fucking.'

A single second of utter silence rang deafening as a bell, broken as the other men shouted and laughed in extreme horror and elation. Some stepped towards me as if to help, then held back, halted by the sheer disgustingness of the sight.

The man's stale mucus and congealed fluids slid over my head and face, and hung from my nose and eyes. I turned away towards the blank wall behind me. I did not want to be seen like this. We had nowhere to wash inside the cell. There was a hole-in-the-ground toilet with no tap. All sound subsided as now the men waited for my rage. Any of them might have killed the other man.

Miserably I turned back towards him, too dejected and humiliated to feel anger. In a quick movement without aggression he pulled off his shirt and bent forward to clean my head and face, wiping the repugnant mess onto his own shirt. Tears burst from his eyes and dripped down onto his face. The other men looked on transfixed. He did not stop, wiping until every drop was gone, though I felt dirtier than I had ever been. Finally I said to him the one word of abuse we shared, 'Fucking.'

'Fucking filaka,' he replied bitterly. Fucking prison.

My name was called. Every face in the cell gazed at me as I picked up my bag. On being released, prisoners were allowed just one minute to say goodbye, but I have no farewell speeches to make here. Yet as I turn to the door, a hand grabs my arm, and I spin round, fearing some new assault. I don't know the man's name, though I have been with him in this room for half a year.

He held out his hand, and in it I feel the enduring strength of the man and his people. I don't know what he felt in mine, perhaps merely weakness. 'Yassou, English.'

The others too, shook my hand, even he whose dried spit still smeared my face. I felt pity sicken me, the senselessness of their crimes and their punishment, the suffering of their loved-ones and of their victims and of all. In the office, against every wish I felt something similar for the guards, the pathos of these absurdly uniformed working men, their loathsome career choice. One of them handed over my bag and what remained of my things, together with a few unexplained banknotes that had been added to my possessions. Andreas, the guard most abusive of his power, wrinkled his brow with awkward amiability as he led me to the door and unlocked it nonchalantly.

I was standing Outside. From this angle, the village on the hill could not be seen. I turned to the barred window from which I had so often looked out. There was no one there anymore.

A uniformed policeman on a motor scooter collected me at the gate and, astride the pillion seat, I clung on to him as he drove to a small hotel facing the waters of Corfu's port. He checked me in and without ceremony left me there unguarded, waved goodbye, amiably promising to meet in the morning to put me on a ferry to Italy.

* * *

A room of my own! My own shower and toilet, clean and private, and a real bed with pristine white sheets and coverlet. I open the window to the full and watch the boats, the water. On the edge of the bed I sit, marveling at the scene. I open the door, and close it again, just for fun: it's hard to believe I have the key. For a moment, I play with the lock. So simple! Freedom and the lack of freedom is no more than that: a key and a lock. I smile and whisper aloud, 'Alone at last!' Yet on hearing my own voice I find a sob bursting from my throat, and slump down, bury my head in the bedclothes and weep.

My dried tears, and another man's dried saliva, I wash from my skin in the warm shower, and the months of hard-to-reach grime, the dirt, some patina of pain which clings and clings to the skin. I want to wash it all away. I will be clean, I will be fresh and new, I will be myself again. Even hot water does not seem to be enough, though in prison we had only cold. I return in memory to the baths of Djerba, all filth erased, scrubbing with savage vigor. Later I shall wash myself in scalding steam, in wind-blasted sand, in snow, in ice, in total silence and solitude.

Afterwards I remain naked, and keep the light off at dusk, and stare in wonder at the delicious darkness of the room, feeling it with my eyes. This we never saw in prison. Even our paper covering for the light bulb was no more than a lampshade. Leaving the light off, I face towards the window, and sit like someone watching television, looking at the night sky and the streets.

Tomorrow, or the day after, I shall be with Angela again. How will it happen, and where? Will we resume our journey to Jesse, or is that finished now? I slip between the exquisite sheets, place my head on a soft pillow, and sleep.

Seagulls coasted easily alongside. I wanted only to watch them without thinking. I had brought some pastries and fruit for Angela, in case she were on board. I searched the ship twice, or more than twice. She was not there. Disappointed, I sat on the bare wood of the deck and ate them myself.

In Brindisi, I waited at the port, marching up and down as in the prison. Always I carried a gift, anything she might like, a flower, a leaf, a drawing, a fruit. Sitting on the edge of the quay, feet dangling above the oily water, my thoughts hung in the air, waiting, waiting for her.

At café tables I sat with a view of the docks. Backpackers, longhairs, hippies passed close by, brushed against me, sat at the next table, stood in doorways inspecting postcards and foreign newspapers. Yet they seemed to move in a distant world, where one chooses from a menu of sweet dishes. Their coming and going was all air and laughter. For them, these days would be forgotten, or become simply 'Italy.' Under a colored sunshade I ate Italian ices and stared at ships beyond the harbor, sailing from Greece like cut-outs pasted on blue paper.

All of a sudden, there she was. Among the passengers streaming off a ship that had just docked, Angela stepped onto the ramp and paused. For an instant my eyes were drained of sight. My heart trampolined, it took off like a rocket, and I laughed aloud, clapped, and exclaimed 'Yes!' to the people at the next table.

I rose to my feet and called out. 'Angela! Angela!' She looked over the quayside crowd and café tables, and saw my wave; and even from that distance her eyes grasped mine like a magnet. The movements so uniquely hers as she carefully stepped down and walked towards me.

She rested her face against mine, skin touching, and clasped my shoulders. We studied each other's faces, at first expressionless, then smiling, then laughing, then again hugging, tears blurring our eyes.

In the next instant, the ecstasy evaporated. For beneath the joy it was not joy we felt, but anger, fatigue and misery. Straight away I led her to the station and reserved a sleeper on the night train to Milan. We did not think about the price; between us we had enough. She hardly spoke, before the journey, or during it.

'And Sirius?' I asked, 'Did you hear anything more?'

Angela roused herself from thought. 'Yeah. Dead. Shot by a farmer.' She showed no emotion.

'Oh, dear!' I bowed my head in sorrow. Angela leaned forward and kissed my cheek. I squeezed her hand. 'I'm sorry to hear that, Angela.'

In Milan, golden leaves had been swept neatly to the edge of the sidewalk. The overnight journey had taken us from late summer to mid-autumn. This time, I could not be bothered to kick at the leaves. In the breeze they flew around and were left behind, like days from the past, memories of childhood.

We walked in the old quarter, sat next to one another in the cathedral, ate pastries in a square among a flock of pigeons, went into a bar for a coffee. There was a juke box and I sauntered to look at it.

I said, 'You realize? Hundreds of records have been released, been hits and vanished from the scene, without us ever hearing them. I expect whole groups have come and gone.'

Angela smiled weakly. 'Guess that shows how unimportant it is.'

'Here's one,' I announced, half to myself. I put in a coin and pressed the button. 'It's Dylan. Must be from a new album.'

'Dylan played England in summer, did you know?' The record began to spin. 'Is this Dylan?' she frowned. 'Sounds like some old crooner.'

'There's a new Beatles, too.'

'What's awful,' said Angela, 'is going back to England. Like it was all for nothing.' I wasn't sure who had decided we would do that. We listened to the song, *Lay Lady Lay*, then walked to the station.

Winter 1969-1970

Friends had no space to spare. In truth they were worried what troubles Angela and Simon might bring – maybe the attention of the police. Paul and Bel weren't around and had split up: Paul had disappeared from view somewhere in America; Bel was in Vancouver. Obviously, Simon didn't ask Biggie and Em (who anyway were now living on a commune in Wales, he learned), but it was a friend of Biggie's, a girl called Jan, who said they could crash at her place.

She lived in Kentish Town, in those days a drab, down-at-heel proletarian neighborhood being taken up by dope freaks, drop outs and hard-up students. In Jan's cold hallway, an aroma of hashish engulfed them: familiar fragrance of their own people, their own world. But it made Simon think of the last time he had smelt it, at the Komotini border post, as the customs officer pulled the screwdriver from the putty.

And inside the living room, not their own people after all, lounging wordless and stupefied. One of them absently handed Simon a chillum, hashish glowing red. Rock music played, too loud to speak. There was a lot of hair, dazed expressions, and a cool nod of greeting. Drawn curtains, dust and discomfort and cold, wasted English hippies melting into tattered embroideries and cushions; it was not what Simon wanted.

Light, light and love, peace and quiet, happiness, time to reflect and breathe. A flash of the Djerba house filled his mind for one instant, its washed, hard surfaces, the white walls dazzling in sunlight, the luminous emptiness of the air. 'I wish I was there and nothing since had ever happened,' he murmured to Angela. He remembered that flat roof where they sat naked in the sun and laughed, and listened to the tape machine.

Where was the tape machine now? Lost, left behind somewhere, taken by someone. Angela smiled sweetly in reply, though angry with herself and with a destiny which she conceived as something deliberate and conscious. They found themselves squeezed between two freaks heavily scented with patchouli, leaning on a grubby sheepskin thrown over a stained mattress on a torn piece of discolored carpet that harbored long pieces of brown hair mingled with unrecognizable specks of dirt.

The hair might have been Jan's. She had a thin, nervous face framed by lank hair just that color, wore an ankle-length cotton skirt and was too tired to care much about appearance. Her place was the top floor of a decaying Victorian terraced townhouse, the whole street wretchedly like 'distressed gentlefolk': once the home of a respectable, well-to-do family, now pauperized and forlorn.

Here Jan offered them a tiny space, an oddly shaped box room with an old mattress on the floor. During the day, Jan was 'temping' – doing a temporary office job obtained through an agency – as a receptionist for a small business. The rent and electricity meter took about half her income, the journey to and from work another large part. Little of the prosperity created by an entire century of urbanization and industrialization accrued to her or to anyone else in this part of town. Jan expected no more from life. She had somewhere to live, listened to good music and smoked plenty of dope. That was enough; in any case there was nothing else. People came and went, and mostly were still there in the morning when she left for work. Over the door she, or someone, had painted in pink paint: *All Things Must Pass*. Jan couldn't wait.

So much had changed since they left last year. The Rolling Stones' Brian Jones was dead. Riots in New York had sparked a rage for gay liberation. The uprising of Ulster's ghettoes had become full-scale guerrilla war. The certainties of privilege were disintegrating in plain sight. In London an exuberant anti-authoritarianism was everywhere, in streets and offices, universities and factories, and its opponents also in full cry. Dozens of brilliant albums had been released during the last year that they had not heard, The Who, Neil Young, Cream, King Crimson, Led Zeppelin, roistering Captain Beefheart, Pink Floyd, Velvet Underground, pounded day and night.

It took Simon a week to remember to sign on for social security, and a few days more to remember he ought to visit his parents. That they must be desperate to see him was a burden he resented. He hitched to the south coast alone, unwilling to hear their advice or their sympathy, unwilling even to breath the stifling air of their respectable carpeted house. He did not want to see his mother's tears of relief or be told how much his father had worried or how much his sisters missed him. He did not want to be offered a glass of sherry or invited to have a shower.

Simon was even more horrified to find that his father now sported longer hair, and his mother wore a button-up dress that didn't reach her knees. How ridiculously fashionable! *But do they do acid?* The idea was absurd. Would he even want his parents to get high on LSD? Ghastly thought. *Of course, ultimately, the revolution includes Mum and Dad – doesn't it?* Their whole cast of mind was a nightmare trip of discipline, deference, moralizing, hierarchy and prejudice.

Yet when the three of them, David and Mary and Simon, walked together on cliffs by the sea, it was Simon who was moved to tears. His mother took his head in her hands and pulled him to her, saying 'My darling'. As they walked a little further, his father put an arm around him with infinite tenderness and patted his back softly.

As the family made themselves comfortable in the cozy living room, the TV news came on. There had been a killing at a huge rock festival in California. The Rolling Stones or Grateful Dead or someone had hired Hell's Angels – paying them in beer – to run security and keep control, as if the bands wanted the hip scene to own the Angels' thuggishness and boast a whole alternative society with its very own police force. The footage wasn't clear: Jagger was on stage inanely urging people to calm down, while Angels in their colors swung pool cues and grappled with what looked like an enraged black man in a pale suit. One of the Angels raised a knife, the crowd moved back chaotically and the black man fell.

David muttered, 'So much for love and peace.' Simon felt a savage mix of defensiveness and despair, though he thoroughly agreed. His father had hit the nail on the head.

Back at Jan's place, Simon allowed himself to get as stoned as he had ever been, inhaling deep from the chillum, or swallowing any tablet given by one of the others without even asking what it was. He wandered in the street and in his mind, a soaring wild disorientation as paving stones and brick and black tarmac and grey light became fused with his soul, and he seemed to find himself at one with the dysfunctional humanity and tribal longings within the heart of the city. Night fell and Simon saw it as a fine, hard sheen on the world. Stars twinkled like knives. Ideas cramming his mind, Simon walked and walked through miles of streets. Finally he returned to the house. Angela would be lying asleep on their floor mattress, quiet and peaceful at last, though something in her face was troubled. He sat cross-legged and watched her breathing, then lay down beside her without closing his eyes, the darkness full of color.

Damp winter pierced the stoned world, streetlamps and headlamps reflected from rain-black pavements, wet clouds hung low over the red tile roofs, and frost crept into their relationship. As he looked out of the dirty window, now there was no view of a village on a hill under sharp daylight, though he saw it still, and Simon wondered again if birds were free, after all, from the chains of the skyways. It depended whether you were in chains yourself. Somehow, he still was.

The music went on and on. Sometimes they wanted silence, and Angela would take Simon by the hand and walk him onto the Heath or round the block, scarves tied and coat collars turned up. They talked about prison, and the prisoners. Sometimes they made light of it all. Other times, Angela would sit on a bench and weep: not for herself, she assured him, but for her beloved Sirius.

Jan made toast or slices of bread and butter and Marmite and cups of supposedly health-giving Maté ('too yang') or chamomile ('too yin') and infused a whole Culpepper of weeds and worts into water poured from a whistling aluminum kettle, or boiled pans of brown rice. She washed dishes at an old glazed white earthenware sink, rinsing cigarette ends and ash and matches out of cups before drying them with a dirty cloth and putting them back on the rack. To eat, they sat on the floor, and served rice and vegetables at a low table made of wooden planks resting on a couple of house bricks.

'What are you two doing with yourselves?' Jan asked them. 'You planning to stay here forever?'

'Well, we're on our way to India.' Simon pursed his lips and tried to think. 'I don't know if we're still going there. Guess we are.' He looked to Angela for agreement, but she had been distracted by something.

'It's thataway,' Jan pointed out of the high window, over the rooftops.

When Jan went out, they sat on the mattress, holding hands. Angela asked tetchily, 'Why *are* we still stuck here, back where we started?'

'We started in California, not here,' Simon answered. 'Remember that girl? That blonde hippy chick, with the house in Berkeley?'

She grinned. 'And that skinny English kid, that will o' the wispy thing, with long, long hair and bare feet and a cute accent?'

'Well,' Simon said, 'he and she – have been through a lot of heavy changes together.'

Angela stared, as if struck by some thought. 'Simon, y'know, it was *not* together. I feel a very different person from the Angela you spoke to in Tilden Park. Have you ever heard this l'il nugget of wisdom? – 'I know what I have given you; I do not know what you have received."

He had never heard it.

'What changes have you been through, Simon? And I? Have we experienced entirely different things?'

He nodded. 'For sure two human beings never experience the same thing. Even when they *are* together, and love each other.'

'*Love* each other! *That* again. And,' Angela retorted, 'who knows what that even *means*? You realize two people who "love each other"' – she made quote marks in the air – 'live two totally separate lives?'

'Anyway, look, are we still going to India, or not? Maybe in spring?'

'I need to think about that,' she shrugged.

The following morning. Simon awoke before Angela. Slight, occasional trills of birdsong cheered him, and a ray of sunlight pierced the windows frosted with wintry condensation. He switched on the electric fire.

Angela woke and watched him sitting by the glowing metal bars. Her voice startled him, the first words of the day: 'We're going nowhere, Simon. We shouldn't be living together.'

Her tone was utterly sincere, yet his response sounded light-hearted. 'Aw, man, one day, we'll look back on this as a bad winter. Want some breakfast?'

'No, no, man. Living with someone is supposed to be good, summer or winter.'

'S'posed to be, is it? I should ask for your money back if I were you.'

'Simon, I don't want to be horrible to you. But we can't share a life, you dig? You can share a home, share a car, maybe even share time, but not share your life. I have my *own* life.'

'So I just want to share a home and share some time. And a bed. That's all. That's living together.'

She sat up and shook her head emphatically. 'No, man, that's like, just hanging around waiting for the curtain to come down. This isn't a relationship any more, it's a habit.'

Simon moved to the bed and sat there, and took her hand. 'This is just a mood, Angela.' She did not draw away. 'You think too much,' he said. 'You are thinking about… mathematical theorems. But if it should happen, by any chance, that you should instead think about… making love…' He raised his eyebrows with comical suggestiveness. She put her arms round him and urged him down, under the blankets.

Afterwards, for a while, her mood seemed to have passed. But later, she said, 'Sasha's coming to London. I'm going to live with her instead.'

To hide his shock, he looked away and stared at the grimy windows.

That really would be the end. Simon tried to picture life without Angela. With Angela, he resided in some fantastic realm, from which the rest of the world and its people appeared as shadows. In this realm, Angela was queen and empress.

Yet he knew that to others, he and Angela appeared as nothing more than a sad couple, damaged, wretched, penniless, sleeping on a friend's floor. Sasha alone, for some reason, had some other view of them.

He got out of bed and stood by the window. Icy wind came around the window frame. Outside, rainwater lay cold on grey slate and concrete reaching to the horizon. A single white cloud stretched across the whole sky. If I can just hold on, survive all this, he thought. One day, somewhere, I shall live. Everything will be right, in that future.

As luck had it, Milly phoned Jan that very week to ask if she had an address for Em in Wales. Jan mentioned that Simon and Angela were staying with her.

Milly was incredulous, then pained that she had not been told, then ecstatic. 'They're back? The appeal was successful, then? They're free?'

Jan had forgotten Simon and Angela's imprisonment, and never knew about the appeal. 'Oh yeah, yeah.'

'How are they? Are they all right?'

Jan had no idea. Frustrated, Milly said, 'Hey Jan, is Simon there now? Can I talk to him?'

Simon gave her the bare outline of what had happened, the date they were released from prison. He apologized for not letting her know.

'Oh, Simon! You should have told me!' Milly was back in London for the Christmas vacation, staying in a shared house south of the river. To him, she sounded frank, down-to-earth, guileless and – what was that quality in her voice? – she was not on any kind of trip. 'Do you want to come and see me? Or, don't suppose I could visit *you*, could I?'

'That would *not* be a good idea,' he answered.

Simon made his way beneath London on the Northern Line, changed trains to reach New Cross and walked along streets of Victorian houses exactly like the ones he had left behind an hour ago. He rang the bell and it wasn't Milly who answered the door. Some other young woman showed him up two flights of stairs.

He was astonished. Milly may have changed, or his memory of her had departed from reality. He knew her now for what she was – an intellectual. Smiling a little diffidently, though the gaze was animated with freshness and intelligence, she appeared sunny, healthy, bright. The surprise being, most of all, how attractive she was. He didn't remember that; and the softly curved breasts, the glossy dark hair and gentle brown eyes. And she was wearing a dress! Not a flowing home-made robe, or workmanlike denim overalls, or something from a surplus store, but something well-fitting from a straight clothes shop. He wanted to touch that finely woven wool and feel the girl underneath. He went to her and kissed her forehead.

Milly too seemed startled by what she saw. 'You've changed. A lot.' She guided his arms around her and said, 'Give me a proper kiss.'

It was like embracing a beautiful stranger in the street.

'Can you stay?' she asked.

'If you want me to.'

'I want you to.'

They moved in sheer delight, and Simon discovered he was happy in this room, in this bed, with life, with Milly, truly happy for the first time in a couple of years. The candle burned out and they lay in darkness. Late at night she asked him about the prison, and he told her.

'Stay with me forever,' she said.

'No. And don't fall in love with me,' Simon commanded.

'It's already happened.'

'Since when?'

'Since you made my breakfast at Biggie's. Remember that?'

Simon chuckled. 'You know – it's not as romantic as you think. I was actually hoping you'd make my breakfast.'

Of course, she had known this.

'Anyway, don't,' he repeated. 'And if you already have, then stop.'

Milly's voice became serious. 'What is this thing between you and Angela? You don't really love her. You don't even like her.'

'It's not about that.' He looked for words. 'The way I feel, about Angela,' Simon said, 'my feeling for her – this love, or whatever it is –

it's a massive, unassailable thing, a fortress. It dominates everything.'

Milly furrowed her brow as if struggling with the unhappy image. He noticed how quiet it was: the house had become utterly still. Even in the distance there wasn't much traffic. His voice fell to little more than a whisper. The very room itself seemed to listen. 'I'm inside with Angela, and high walls keep the world at a distance. From the battlements I see the green landscapes and pretty meadows outside, and you, Milly, and all the good things in life, are out there. Only Angela is in here with me, we are locked together. That is my home, my world. Whether that looks like hatred, or like love, it is always love.'

Milly touched Simon, but for the moment he did not want to be touched. 'With other people,' he continued, 'I spend time, and I am fond of them, or even, maybe, *love* them. But all that is in the sunny meadows beyond the walls.' He stopped, and turned towards her in the darkness.

A tear rolled down onto his chest from her face. 'I'm sorry,' he said.

Milly said, 'Well, it sounds like the Real Thing all right. It also sounds like a bloody nightmare. Why the medieval imagery? You might just as well still be in a prison, with barbed wire on the walls.'

'Except this prison feels like a privilege, not a punishment.'

'One thing, though,' she asked, 'is the castle your *love* for Angela, or is it your own *self*? You say Angela's in there *with* you. So is it her world as well?'

Simon had not thought of this. A castle, a fortress, is defensiveness, isolation; also power. Maybe the metaphor had been pushed too far. After all, Angela had said she didn't want to carry on with their relationship. It was late, time to sleep.

Maybe it was all ego, being with Angela. Ever since those first days in Berkeley, he was 'the lion tamer in the lion's cage.' More metaphors!

'You know what?' Milly mused. 'This castle thing of yours is just a fairytale. Well, mister, now the *good* fairy has arrived and she's coming in there with you, and we're going to light some fires and warm the place up. Throw open the windows. Say goodbye to the bad fairy, she's moving out. We'll knock down her horrid stone walls, plant a nice little garden, invite everybody, and live happily ever after. A fairytale ending.'

Simon grinned sadly and shook his head. 'Sorry, Milly, I don't think so.' Whether his own metaphors worked or not, there was no chance at all of her fairy story coming true.

He caressed her and thought – this is like that other kind of love, in which people are happy together. The sort that Angela is looking for with Jesse. Oh, had he forgotten to tell Milly about Jesse? Another time.

The phone in the hall rang and rang. Milly's room was in one of those shared houses where people write their name on pints of milk and packets of butter and nobody can be bothered to answer the phone because it probably isn't for them. Either someone would take the call eventually, or else the ringing would stop and an abrupt, blissful silence take its place, together with an uneasy awareness of the conversation that was meant to have been but didn't happen. This time the ringing went on for five minutes. At last one of the girls took the call and yelled up the stairs, 'It's for Simon. Anyone here called Simon?'

He couldn't think who knew he was here. Jan, maybe. Nobody else.

'Hi,' said a vaguely familiar, half-forgotten American voice. 'It's Sasha. I'm in London. How are ya?'

So she had already arrived; Angela's wait was over. She and Sasha would live together, and he would stay on at Jan's.

'Hey, Simon. Do you remember being with us at the ranch?'

He thought back to those faraway, innocent, sunlit days. 'Yeah.'

'With the Tarot cards?'

Simon remembered the Tarot cards incident.

'Well, I still feel the same way. So, hey, Simon, what do you say?'

'To what?'

'Get over here and let's ball. Come and get laid.'

'What?' Had he misunderstood, or had she really just said that?

'Screw, fuck, get your rocks off,' she shrieked. 'For chrissakes, you know – do sex.'

'Wow! Except, you know, I'm getting laid over here.' He hoped the others in the house weren't listening to this. His voice reverberated around the high-ceilinged hallway.

'I kin dig that,' Sasha answered curtly. 'But I b'lieve you said you'd make me come a hundred times? Or was it a thousand? Well, tomorrow night's good for me if it is for you. Moon's in Cancer.'

'Oh. Moon in Cancer, eh?' Simon paused. 'OK, see you tomorrow.'

Sasha mimicked his accent. 'Oh Kay,' then, giggling again, 'Bye-ee.'

With part of his mind, Simon never stopped thinking about Angela. He always had a sense of where she was and what she was doing. In any case, he knew she was at Jan's apartment. Yet when he arrived there, it astonished him to find not only Sasha and Jan, but Angela too.

She stared at him with some strange mix of resentment and curiosity. Simon felt as if they were alone in the room. The bond between them was overwhelming. Surely anyone could see lightning crackling from one to the other. The attraction seemed stronger than ever now that he had been sleeping with Milly.

He greeted Sasha with kisses on the cheek, exclaiming how far out it all was. 'Yeah! Fuck!' she replied. '*So* many changes since last time!'

Angela said, 'That's for sure!'

They seemed to be acting out parts, and speaking lines written for them by R. Crumb.

An overflowing salad of beansprouts and wheat grains and chopped nuts was served, and a thick, spicy lentil stew, with a succulent baked dish of sliced potatoes and cheese, and a thick, sweet dessert made of dried fruits. The four of them sat on the floor, cross-legged around a bedspread laid as a tablecloth. Candles flickered, incense burned, music played. After dinner they smoked a couple of joints and laughed a lot. Angela helped Jan clear away the plates. Simon turned to Sasha.

He had never talked with her like this before. Strange as she was, Sasha's mind was sharp, her smile quick, her eyes intelligent and alert. It struck him now that Sasha had an air of success; she was, after all, a wealthy businesswoman. Wasn't she, in fact, the guiding hand behind Jack's success? Yet she had the opposite of fame – the romance of secrecy. Her business demanded discretion, watchfulness, even disguise.

Jan threw down some quilts and blankets to make a second bed on the floor. Sasha and Simon were to sleep not six feet away from Angela. The lights were put out and Sasha knelt facing him on the mattress.

Angela turned her back to them.

Simon unbuttoned Sasha's shirt and they unzipped each other's jeans. Her brown pubic hair was revealed. His arousal was quick and she pulled him forward greedily. Yet as soon as he had penetrated her, she lay perfectly still, legs apart, as if in some yoga position. Whatever he did, Simon could not make her express anything. Perhaps – he wondered – she felt uncomfortable about Angela, who was presumably trying to ignore that in-out slurping sound and Simon's deep purposeful breath. And Simon thought of Angela's feelings – jealousy must be torturing her now, stinging enough to die, burning like napalm.

He had promised Sasha he would make her come and whispered into Sasha's hair, 'Is it good?' She remained silent, eyes closed. He whispered, 'OK, so is it bad?' She opened her eyes, stroked his back and shook her head to say that it was not bad. Suddenly Sasha arched her head back, quivered for an instant and sighed. Had she come? It did not seem to matter; at least, not to her. Grasping Sasha's tanned body in this cold, mean room, as if he had entered a lost paradise of California, of sunlight, of acid, of money and the good life, he too came silently. At once a vision of Milly came into his mind and he missed her, and wanted urgently to get back to her, as if she alone knew the secret of true happiness outside the gates of Eden.

In the darkness, Angela reached over to him. Still lying half on top of Sasha, lingering inside her, he held Angela's hand. 'Oh Simon,' she whispered. 'Life is complicated, isn't it?'

'It is.'

'Sleep here with me, won't you?' she implored him, 'Not with her,' whispering the plea into his ear.

And he spent the night between the two of them, but curled up against Angela, trying to get comfortable and trying to keep warm.

In the morning, Sasha asked Simon to take her somewhere. Anywhere. It was a balmy winter's day, the air humid yet refreshing and agreeable. They strode across the Heath for a second breakfast in Hampstead. Dressed for a Californian winter, in tight jeans and a thin cotton jacket, she pressed against him and complained that it was damned cold. Her hair, tied with a velvet ribbon into a thick auburn mass, bounced with each step. In dark glasses, walking tall, indifferent to mud on her clothes or suede boots, her nostrils reddened by cocaine, she looked stunning and mysterious. A scent of patchouli oil drifted in her wake.

Simon, with hair and beard trailing long and unbrushed, was not so much dressed as decorated. The jeans were made almost entirely of scraps and patches, felt-tipped with symbols and slogans and lines of text. The bright green and blue woolen scarf Angela knitted last year wound around his neck and hung over a quilted Chinese jacket which someone had left on the floor at Jan's, and which Angela had covered with embroidery and pinned with badges – the yellow flames of Medical Aid for Vietnam, the red fist of Women's Liberation, the black and white CND sign. He wore scuffed desert boots, and his wrists were enclosed with long strings of tiny glass beads and a whole heap of cheap, thin silverware.

He offered the jacket to Sasha, but she refused it. After a steep climb they stood together at the top of Parliament Hill looking across London, neat pale buildings spread out like a printed picture on a cloth, a Canaletto city beneath a moist sky.

He pointed out the dome of St Paul's Cathedral.

'People call this Kite Hill now, and come here to fly kites.'

She looked around. No one was flying a kite. A man and woman on bicycles struggled up the hill, and passed without pausing to admire the view, freewheeling down the other side.

'At the Summer Solstice,' he said, 'there's a crowd of people up here. At dawn, the sun rises just there,' he pointed to the spire of a church in Highgate. 'Right there. But it's usually too cloudy.'

'Do they come on the Winter Solstice, too?'

'Only true believers.'

She gazed rapt at the spire as if impressed by some thought. 'That's a ley line, for sure.' She pointed to Highgate, then turned, 'over there,' pointing to a circle of trees on the next hill. 'Then right here, where we're standing!' she exclaimed. Facing London, she tried to follow the line as it made its way into the city. 'And look,' with a sweep of the hand to east and west, 'see how other lines come into London. Yes, wow, they converge at St Paul's! Far fucking out!' Eagerly, she led the way, striding quickly over the turf to the next hill, and the next.

'I never thought of you,' he said, 'as someone who likes walking.'

'Did you think of me at all?'

'Only as a person who would not like walking.'

'Shit, man, you didn't think of me as a sexy bitch with a gorgeous butt who you'd just love to screw the pants off?'

He turned to her. 'No. Is that how you think of yourself?'

'Just *kidding*, man! Fuck, you English have no sense of humor. No irony,' she mocked.

'We seem to have the Heath to ourselves today,' he observed. 'A wet weekday in winter doesn't draw the crowds, does it?'

Sasha put her arm through his and, like that, they walked side by side.

'I'm starting to like you,' she said, as if surprised by the thought. A moment later: 'You know, it's funny. Did anyone ever mention you look a whole lot like Jesse? Not quite the same coloring, but, yeah.'

He recalled that Sasha herself had mentioned it, in California. 'Angela always used to say that. She hasn't talked about Jesse lately.' The tangled, leafless branches hung around them like heavy ruches of lace fabric. Sasha stared up at the intricate canopy of twigs overhead. Simon didn't expect a reply and at first Sasha didn't give one.

After a while, though, she said, 'I always dug that guy. I wished he would've stayed with Angie. Anyway, we can still work with him.'

'So, what do you mean, is Jesse like, a business partner of yours?'

'Yeah, well, not exactly. Shouldn't be telling ya, man, but what harm can it do? You're going to meet the guy yourself soon.'

Simon tried to make sense of this, and told Sasha that Angela didn't want to live with him anymore.

'Yeah, I know,' she replied. 'That's why I'm here.'

'You mean, that's why we had sex?'

'Why shouldn't people have sex? You promised we would one day! Sex doesn't need a reason,' Sasha shrugged. 'Anyway, in the end,' she declared, 'there are no events, just patterns. All our separate lives are just lines in the whole.'

'The hole?'

'Yeah, like, the whole picture, man. The big picture.'

He led her to Cyrano's, a spacious, comfortable vegetarian wholefoods diner with country-kitchen décor, newly opened on Hampstead High Street. After a horrible coffee there, they strolled down the street, Sasha pausing to look in boutique windows. Simon hadn't been in the area for a while and the latest designer fashions came as a shock: ready-made imitation hippy styles, flared jeans already patched and frayed, tight, big-collar shirts printed with swirling mock-psychedelic patterns. This really is the end, the end of our thing, he thought: straight commerce making it chic to look like a drop-out. He remembered Angela, in Berkeley, saying 'Capitalism can cut the balls off anything.'

None of it bothered Sasha, though. She turned into the doorway of a shop. 'I'm cold,' she announced to the assistants, all of them dressed in tight little button-up tops and ankle-length cotton skirts. 'Do you have a jacket I could wear?' It sounded as if she would like to borrow one.

One of the girls rose above the uncertainty of the others, and offered Sasha the most beautiful casual cashmere jacket. It fitted perfectly.

After the merest glance in a mirror, Sasha handed it back to the girl. 'Thank you. Would you cut out the label for me? I hate labels.' She laughed at her own remark, and turned to Simon. 'I mean, who wants to be labeled?' She paid a hundred pounds in cash.

'That was too expensive,' Simon chided her, outside.

'I have a theory,' she answered, half blithe, half serious, distracted, 'that when you spend money, more money rushes in to fill the vacuum.' Sasha now wearing her cozy new jacket, they stopped at the bookshop and wandered through the jumble of rooms. Sasha found a slim paperback with a pop-art cover, called *Alternative London*. Simon flicked through it and was reassured: the movement, radical groups, self-help, disengagement, alternatives, every kind of hip stuff was taking off all over the city.

Next door to the bookshop, Sasha looked at a storefront window displaying pictures of local property for sale or for rent. She beckoned Simon to step inside with her. 'Do you have a nice little cottage I could rent, right on Hampstead Heath?' she asked one of the staff. The naiveté of the question made Simon smile, embarrassed for her.

To his surprise, the answer was 'Yes'. Even the agent looked astonished. He drove them to see it, and by lunchtime Sasha had become the tenant of a small redbrick house hidden down a lane on the West Heath, opposite the old Bull and Bush pub and beside Golders Hill Park. Greenery, trees, a spread of delicate snowdrops, masses of bright yellow and purple crocuses, clusters of daffodils just about to burst open, were on every side. They peeked into all the rooms: two bedrooms, a sitting room with a skylight, a spacious old-fashioned kitchen-dining room, and in the bathroom, the biggest bath he had ever seen. All the rooms were arranged in a line, with a corridor alongside, like a railway carriage. It was called Heath Cottage, and Sasha trembled with delight.

'God, this is what I always wanted!' she cried. 'A neat little cottage half in the country, half in the city. I'll take a walk on the Heath in the morning, have coffee in the park, lunch in Hampstead, a drink in the pub in the evening, and eat dinner quietly at home with Angela – and you too, Simon, if you want to stay here. That's how I want to live, for ever and ever.'

'Angela won't like that, if it's you and me sleeping together.'

Sasha shrieked with ecstasy. 'You gonna fuck both of us, boy,' she yelled out across Hampstead High Street. 'Till she begs to have you all to herself!'

Simon pulled Sasha's head towards him till he could whisper into her ear. 'Next time don't just lie there, do something.'

'Lie there!' Sasha protested loudly. 'Hey man, that's Tantra. You don't know about Tantric sex? You *control* the desire, man, harness it and reach a spiritual high way higher than any, like, regular orgasm.'

Unimpressed at the thought of a spiritual high instead of a regular orgasm, Simon grimaced. 'Tarot cards sounded more interesting,' he said drily.

'You total fucking heathen. You Philistine. You – hey, take me out to lunch,' she ordered. 'Somewhere nice. I'll pay.'

Spring 1970

Jan pronounced it 'pad of the year', and officially only Sasha could call it home. Angela and Simon were her two houseguests, and everything went as Sasha had planned. The growing light of spring was a therapy and a return to reality, that Berkeley reality of leisure, music, dope, acid and sex.

Angela became ravishingly beautiful. It wasn't an illusion: the freedom from care toned her skin and limbs and eyes and hair. She drifted around the house in flowing cotton, indulging him. She and Sasha hugged each other for no reason. Underlying it, though, lay a reflective mood. The music that year, as spring turned to summer, was mellow and calm. They played and re- played a track (*Teach your children*) on the new album from Crosby, Stills & Nash, and a new Beatles' song, *Let It Be*. In the evenings, Angela made clothes for Simon and Sasha: a yellow shirt for him, a purple smock for her.

After a few weeks, Sasha left them on their own. She had to go to California on business, and afterwards rarely turned up at Heath Cottage.

Hand in hand, palms together like teenage lovers, Angela and Simon strolled into Hampstead, maybe for a cake at Louis, or to pick up a few groceries, or to step into the bookshop and sit there awhile on the bare wooden floorboards leafing through the latest books and head comics.

They ventured into the derelict Hill Garden where, right behind the cottage, rampant honeysuckle and roses entwined the broken pillars and wooden canopy of a romantic Edwardian pergola.

A path passed beneath the pergola's little stone bridge, and as they walked beneath the bridge, Simon often glanced up to see who was standing there. No one ever was. One day he half-imagined that he saw himself on the bridge, as an old man leaning on the parapet, looking down, as it were, from the perspective of years. Angela followed his gaze to see who he was looking at, but there was no one.

Simon assured himself that this mirage could never become real. He would be living happily with Angela by then, in some earthly paradise.

By then, Jesse would be long forgotten. The world would be infinitely better by then. By then, capitalism and socialism would have been replaced by sharing and cooperation, love and respect. And he wouldn't still be in London in that ideal future, that happy world-to-come.

Angela's vision of the future was rather different. She had started writing to Jesse. She was preparing herself for a reunion. He was living in Ahmedabad, and Angela told him she'd be there sometime this summer. She laughed merrily and declared it was all clear in her mind now. Jesse's brief replies were cool, remote, terse, yet he did say he looked forward to her visit. She touched the paper with fascination; for just days ago Jesse himself had touched it with his own fingers.

His breath had been breathed just here, onto this airmail paper. She stared at it expectantly.

As the day approached, this time Simon didn't just slip away. He made farewell calls, sometimes deciding whether or not he ever wanted to see certain people again. He visited his parents, once more without bringing Angela to meet them. The thought of their naïve son again traveling the world with *that girl* filled David and Mary with dread, after the disaster of his last trip. They could do nothing but hug him, kiss him and wish him well.

He decided to call on Milly for what could be the last time. He might as well end it with her. He told Angela he was going to Brighton for the day – he could stop off to see Milly on the way. Besides, he really did need to go to Brighton.

Angela was suspicious. 'Why Brighton?'

'To see that guy Rich.'

'Why not just phone?'

'I'd rather talk to him face-to-face. The stuff I want to discuss, you can't talk about on the phone. Anyway, I like Brighton.'

'Not seeing that chick Milly, are you?'

'No,' he answered. Her instinct was uncanny! 'Why would you even think that?' He made a gamble: 'Come with me – do you want to come?'

She shook her head. 'What, to Brighton? No. But I want you to make me a promise.'

'What kind of promise?'
'That you won't see her. Please don't see her.'
He touched her hair, and her cheek. 'I promise. I won't see Milly.'
'Really promise?' she said with surprise.
'I really promise,' he declared solemnly, and kissed her fingers.

Sunlight shone prettily beneath the heavy branches of big, leafy trees in Milly's street, and a choir of blackbirds trilled. In the front gardens, hundreds of bright roses were blooming. As he neared the house, Milly saw him from a window and dashed downstairs in joyful greeting.

He told Milly he'd soon be going to India with Angela. He'd be away for ages. Pained, she held him in her arms.

'It's a shame I never met the beloved Angela,' she said.

He said it was a shame, but in truth would not have wanted this good and gentle girl to come face to face with Angela's eviscerating gaze, or be the object of Angela's merciless tongue.

They lay in the bed and had sex. Afterwards Milly made lunch of beans on toast in the shared kitchen. She shook her head, a sad resignation in her eyes. 'Just because you're going away, doesn't mean it's over between us,' Milly reminded him. He said he agreed, but thought it probably was.

Angela was not at home when Simon returned. Into the doorframe he slipped a note, in fact a sketch – it showed the two of them, himself and Angela, sitting in the sun on the Heath behind the house, together with the words *I Am Nearby*, and a heart like on a letter she wrote in prison.

Eventually Angela came and found him, and they sat just on the grass exactly as in the picture. 'Did you see Milly?' she asked.

'Yah.'

'You shit. I knew you would. Did you sleep with her?'

'Yeah, of course. What did you expect?'

She grimaced bitterly. 'Of course.' Nothing more was said and he guessed she would be willing to overlook it.

Neither of them was prepared for Milly's unannounced arrival at the cottage the following afternoon, though.

The meeting itself passed off politely. She came inside the house and Angela offered her tea. They all sat down with their cups of tea as if perched on a cliff edge. Milly said brightly that she had heard so much about Angela. Angela answered with careful charm and offered a slice of cake.

Milly's sweet, girl-next-door ingenuousness jarred painfully against Angela's tight-lipped deliberation and control. Simon waited with dread for Angela to launch some sharp comment at Milly, but she held back. Sensing the strange discomfort in the room, as soon as her tea and cake were finished, with a smile Milly rose to leave. 'Well, must get on,' she said. 'Lovely to meet you. It's been really nice. I'm glad I dropped by.' Simon went with her to the door.

Milly looked into his eyes. 'I shouldn't have come. It was silly. We already said goodbye. I should have left it at that. But I had to meet her, this girl you love so much. I wanted to see the two of you together.'

'Never mind,' Simon answered softly. 'It's OK. I'm just sorry Angela wasn't nicer to you.'

Milly shrugged, and in a whisper said, 'I'll write to you, if you'll write to me. Just once in a blue moon.'

'It's a deal,' Simon agreed.

They put their arms around each other and kissed, and held each other tightly for a brief moment.

Then she turned and stepped into the lane outside. 'See you, Simon.' A wave as she started to walk away, and a last word, 'Don't forget to write.' Although she smiled, he saw moisture in her eyes.

In the sitting room, Angela waited. 'What the hell,' she began, 'have you two been doing out there? It's been five minutes.'

'What? What d'you think we've been doing? Having a screw?'

'I think,' she answered tautly, 'that you've been kissing that girl right here *in my house*,' the last words rising almost to a shout.

What Simon felt was mainly surprise. 'You're flipping,' he said. 'It's not your house. And' – he had to raise his voice to sweep aside her interruptions – 'sure I kissed her; we were saying goodbye.'

'Don't think you can kid me, man. I was listening and you hardly said a word to each other.'

'I guess you had your ears pretty wide open, huh? Didn't it occur to you to mind your own fucking business? Besides which,' now Simon's voice rose, 'we spent the *whole* time saying what a drag it was that you weren't friendlier to her.'

'What!' Angela shrieked. 'I was friendly to the point of servility. She just came walking in here.'

'So? She wanted to visit me. I live here too.'

'No. She said she had come to see *me*, because you've told her *so much about me*. Why did you talk about *me* with *someone like that*? Like, what did you say about me?'

'That you're on a huge fucking ego trip.' Simon said, turning to leave the house. He grabbed his jacket and the little rucksack and stormed out.

Angela had the last word: 'Yes, get the fuck out,' and slammed the door behind him so hard that rabbits all over the Heath must have scattered. Glasses in the Bull and Bush must have tinkled on the tables.

At a fast step Simon marched up the hill towards Hampstead, his hair streaming behind him. His passport was in the rucksack. He'd go to Yugoslavia, he'd go to Turkey. he'd go to Tunisia, he'd go to America. He was free, free. He'd go to Milly and throw himself into her arms. Angela could fuck off to India and her fucking Jesse and he'd never fucking see her again.

But no; his pace slowed. He could not finish three years of living together like this. Besides, he did not want to finish it. All he truly longed for was that things would be good between them. As he passed Whitestone Pond his anger was already subsiding. To part like this would be the end of him, it would be an emotional disaster. It was only a row, he must not leave and ruin everything. Still, he kept walking.

Angela caught up with him at the tube station. Simon heard her running and turned as she called out. He pretended to be uninterested in making it up. 'What do *you* want?' he sneered. So, she was the weaker one today, he thought with pleasure.

'Simon, please stop. Let's talk a little. Don't go,' she said.

'Talk about what? Milly? Or Biggie? Or Jesse?'

'Simon, no.' She was a little breathless. 'About us. Us.'

He was still walking, and had almost reached the lifts that would take him down to the trains. 'Oh yeah. What about us?' His voice was mocking. He knew he'd have to give way before he reached the lifts.

'About how we do really, really love each other,' she said. He stopped and she touched his shoulder. People moved around them. Falteringly, she said, 'It's only that... I'm so hung-up. I know it's stupid, but I'm jealous.' And she smiled at her own folly.

Slowly they began to make their way back up the hill. She reached for his hand, and he took it.

Her voice was plaintive. 'OK, I'm in a mess. It's true, I do want to see Jesse. But you are more real to me now. You're better for me than anyone, and I don't want to lose you. Jeez, I'm confused, I wish Sasha would come back and help me figure things out.'

Reaching the house, they went straight to bed. He desperately wanted to please her, and succeeded.

When Simon opened his eyes, he said, 'The thing is, I'm afraid when we get to India, you'll make it up with Jesse, and that'll be the end of me.'

She sighed and stroked his hair. Through the skylight, he could see the hazy blue and white. A bird flew overhead. 'Whatever happens with Jesse,' she said softly, 'it won't affect my relationship with you.'

'Will we still do this?'

'Yes. Jesse won't affect that.'

Like that they started, walking along the street together at the beginning of their renewed journey. An impulse made Simon say he'd forgotten something and had to dash back. Angela stood waiting with the bags, while Simon went by himself for one last look inside the house.

He stepped into each room in turn. He felt he was saying goodbye to himself, or at least, to everything he had been until then. The departure last winter now seemed somehow false, as if he had been a mere child then, and must have known he wasn't capable of cutting the strings. This time, he walked into every room, and in each one saw all the rooms he had ever lived in with Angela. Heath Cottage had become a chamber of memories, hopes and illusions and disillusions. Now his presence in the house rattled like a pebble in an empty box. Simon talked to himself in the hollow silence, said goodbye, and heard his voice strange in his ears. 'She will live with him and forget about me, and I shall be alone.' But Angela waited for him outside.

Summer 1970

Between dirty white sheets, inside a cube of dirty white walls, supremely comfortable. She breathes into my hair, 'Simple Simon, the simple life is so simple really, isn't it?' It's midday and we're in no hurry. I answer that it is, simple really, and run my hand over the naked skin. She seems fonder of me since we started traveling again, happier with me. I must not wonder why. This is joy, these moments jewel-like, more beautiful than real jewels, as lasting, to value for ever. We don't speak about Jesse, and keep our thoughts of him hidden in the back of our minds. There is all the time in the world, time to breathe, time to make love. Jesse is not expecting us yet.

Hitch-hiking through a waking dream of drivers and roads and the roar of engines. Nights pass somewhere with open eyes, sparkling mind. We cross a plain, and some mountains still gleaming with snow. We sleep on a dirty beach and nothing matters. We stay without paying on a campsite, sleep on benches in a railway station, sit holding hands on a cliff beside a lake, walk all night in darkness.

We hold up signs to some places, words from a map, copied with a black ballpoint onto scraps of cardboard we find by the road. Cars flash past, some fast, some slow, each making a sound, murmuring like lines in a long, long poem. Let's stay, I suggest, at the Blue Minaret Hotel, and see if we can figure out if that slimy manager turned us in. If he's amazed to see us, and thinks we had been busted, we'll know it was him.

We do not stay in the Blue Minaret. Our carefree joy drains away as we penetrate the domain of Islam. Trains grate and groan across Turkey towards the Kurdish east, carriages crowded with mustached, muscular men. They hassle Angela, reach out and hold her buttocks, squeeze her with firm grip. When I try to stop him, one man nonchalantly pushes me in the face, almost gently, though it would leave a raw bruise. Angela surprises them with the points of her nail scissors, jabbing into the stomach of her persecutors and the blood trickles onto their shirts. They take it like men, continue to fondle her, grinning with evil glee.

Through Iran the harassment continues and the cockroaches become bigger. In Mashad, Angela's torment is at its worst. The devout throw stones at us as we pass a gorgeous blue mosque. While running for cover we find other freaks boarding a bus to the Afghan border.

And so in curious repose, we talk to one another, far away from any country, or any time. At a dingy tea-room, dark and oily, the bus halts for a break.

'Hey, man.' It's one of the freaks. He joins us.

He hands me a chillum, wrapped in a piece of rag moistened with saliva. Holding it to my mouth, I inhale deeply. Straightaway, lightness and heaviness besiege me all at once. The dark tea room becomes a new and undiscovered wonderland, as if I am only now entering it. I look around and think, I could live here. In this tea room. The light in here is beautiful.

I pass the chillum to Angela.

'Hey, d'ya hear wha' happen the Chinese cat on the bus?' our companion asks,

Angela replies, 'Ya mean that Chinese guy? On the bus?' Her voice and expression sound weird. I glance curiously; it's obvious she has been knocked sideways by this dope.

I have no recollection of anyone Chinese on the bus.

There's a long silence as we all take another toke.

'Yeeeah...' our companion eventually says, more like a sigh than a word. 'He freaked out.'

'Who? That Chinese guy? What happened?' I ask.

'Yeah, what happened?' Angela says.

I take a good look at Angela – why has she repeated my question? She smiles with inane pleasantness, beaming as if she has cracked the world's funniest joke.

Unsteadily, not meaning to, I half fall onto her. 'Jeez, man,' I tell her, 'you're stoned.' Her soft arms and shoulder are like a cushion. With repressed mirth, she props me up again.

'Steady, big fella,' she says, with absurd seductiveness.

The two of us laugh as if this is the sequel to the world's funniest joke. Angela slaps her thigh in uncontained exuberance. Our companion sits quite unmoved, waiting in a daydream until we might calm down. He stares at me, and I try to straighten my face. As he's handing me the chillum, he says, 'Hey, you look just like that guy in that poster. You know that poster?'

I don't know what he's talking about, but Angela exclaims, 'Yeah, yeah!'

'Yeah. So what happened to the Chinese guy?' I insist.

'Well, he ate all this shit and freaked out,' he explains, sipping his Afghan tea to moisten stoned, dry lips.

'How much did he eat?'

'Two hundred grams. Yup. Two hundred fucking grams. Best Bombay Black. Ate it. Yeeeah...' and a philosophical shake of the head.

'What! You're putting me on,' I exclaimed. 'I kind of thought that amount would kind of, it would kind of fucking kill you.'

The guy nodded. 'Yeah, well, I think he *is* dead, man. That's what they say.'

Angela pursed her lips in an unsuccessful effort to stop grinning, and said 'Holy fuck. Stoned to death, huh?'

I said it was 'Too much.'

'Yeah, way too much,' the guy concurred.

Angela said it was 'Too bad.'

He said it was a fucking waste of a hell of a fucking lot of fucking good dope. We nodded our agreement. He added, 'You look so fucking much like that guy in that poster. You could be him.'

'Yeah?' I affect surprise. 'OK, I will be.'

Angela giggles and he looks at her with a shake of the head. 'But you,' he says. 'Definitely not the same chick.'

'Nah,' she agrees, holding back a grin which bursts to get out, 'not the chick pic. I mean the pic chick.' She can't keep it back. The two of us splutter hysterically. Tears roll down my face.

At every stage there are more freaks. At every town along the road, a pull of people, a crowd drifting always with its back to the West, away from the afternoon sun, just a few heading in the other direction. Outside Tehran there's a campsite with a special room for 'hippies'. Sleeping in there is cheaper than hiring a tent-site. In this crowded, filthy dorm freaks compare notes. One or two play guitars or flutes, and nobody cares if dope is being smoked there. On the wall someone has written, 'This is the road of excess, but where is the palace of wisdom.'

We long to reach the other side of the Islamic world: it's a bummer.

We want to sweep it away, along with the western crap. Islam is another way to be straight – a worse way. Islam to us just means misogyny and brutality. Can anything free the world from all this? All these nations, these millions of pieties and certainties and repressions, these lifetimes of narrow-mindedness? In truth, just a few drops of acid could change this whole world and everyone in it, drive it mad or drive it sane. One hundred and fifty millionths of a gram can change an entire life.

A Pathan tribesman stands close by, grim faced, his knife in his belt and rifle across his back, as I stand in a street waiting for Angela. A local woman passes in between us, concealed within the bulbous cloth of her chadoor, but a breeze presses it against her shapely thighs and buttocks, and I see that the Pathan has also noticed. Then a western girl passes between us, making her way along this street in Kabul in tee shirt and miniskirt, and I feel embarrassed by what we are doing here. My eyes follow her. Then I notice the Pathan looking at her in just the same way, and again he notices me, and our eyes meet in a flicker of amused recognition: we have that much in common, at least, though we may both have to deny it, he for his reasons and I for mine. Later I mention it to Angela and we have our old debate, whether the traveler may feel entitled to change the place he visits, and reach the same conclusion. Societies will rise and fall, but the animal in us will go on forever. It is a human animal though, so must always make society, with rules to live by. Rules about men and women.

A bus full of freaks climbs through the Khyber Pass. Long haired, colorful, crazy. Loose-limbed, jeans torn and frayed, each on a trip: some latter-day cowboys, others ragged wildflower children. Girls in fine cotton, caught between modesty and freedom.

Locals ride these buses, too, but hardly any western straights. Of course, there are degrees of straightness, and one freak's straight is another straight's freak. Straight travelers garner memories and anecdotes, and revel in a sense of adventure. Freaks are in pursuit of good cheap dope or a hiding place, or a teacher, or looking for simplicity or knowledge, wisdom really, far away from the 'big ideas and distorted facts' of the West. Our own grail is Jesse. We both know the time has come, for beyond the next country lies India.

Not understanding our surroundings, no one's guest, unsure of the meaning of words or gestures, we discover the strange reality of just being. So that is possible, after all: you can be something even without any connection to the world around.

Traveling is just a dream, each place a different part of the mind. The shadowy figures that you pass are not real... those robed women: dare one think of soft, dark, smooth skin beneath the cloth, can one imagine pulling aside a wisp of dark hair and whispering in her ear? Learning her language and she learning yours? Will *they* become part of the movement? Will they ever stand tall as human beings, as free as their menfolk, and equal? March beside us? And those turbaned men gathering to pray, how little do I share with them? Can they too become freaks, will *they* ever become part of the movement? Those poorest villagers, lost from view, how much further does their poverty reach down into the earth, far beyond our own trivial notions of poverty? Will they march beside us, or we beside them, every man and woman upright and equal and free?

In time, after enough miles have swept through our hair and blown away behind us, the world turns into a mere flow of forms and textures, an ephemeral collage in which we are a piece, a palpable fantasy in which all people and places are dreamy dream symbols. And then at last it is the world which is moving, while we stand still, just *being*: our bus is motionless and India is coming towards us.

The bus rattles round hairpins at breakneck speed from Kabul to Peshawar, over the Khyber Pass. Views open on one side, then the other, our vision thrown out suddenly across deep valleys ridged with stony peaks. A knife-edge of sharp light cuts across the landscapes. Steep from the road edge, slopes climb into rock and bracken. On such a hillside a young turbaned man with a rifle sits aloof on a horse gazing at the bus of westerners: our eyes meet in a fleeting instant.

For him, we in our bus, constantly and forever passing on this road, are the fleeting, dreamlike image. The movement is a conceit of rich westerners, a sunspot, a brief flare of energy in one despised, enviable corner of the world. Yet there *is* something happening here too, and all around the globe, a thrill of awakening. Maybe radicalism here seeks some opposite goal. Maybe the tide of his dreams runs in a contrary direction from ours. Or maybe that young man will journey with us one day. Anyway, the bus passed long ago and I see him no more.

A mighty silence canopied the land from horizon to horizon. Within this invisible covering, a frightening heat accumulated. A breeze touched my skin occasionally, like the last drops from a beaker falling onto a dry tongue. We walked at the edge of the lonely road, no sound but that of our sandaled feet crushing dusty weeds on the verge. From a tree, a cloud of gold and green parakeets dashed out screaming and made a vast circle of color in the steely haze of the air. Beyond, the land seemed abandoned, fields unworked. I could not understand – do people live here? Where are they? Unnervingly, two large black birds followed us, flying above our heads with lazy wing movements. They stopped at a tree, but two more took their place. As the border came in sight, they fell back, leaving us to go on alone. Did they know it was a frontier?

We had crossed Pakistan in a day, not descending from the train all the way from Peshawar to Lahore, sustained by the spicy snacks and hot tea eagerly reached up to open windows in the hands of hawkers at every station. Men with contemptuous eyes hassled Angela. She responded as in Turkey, but Pakistanis were more outraged by their punishment, less manly, whimpering at the sight of their own blood.

From Lahore station, a bus was waiting to take us straight to the Indian frontier. We spent a night in the city, though, at the Lucky Inn, and next morning over breakfast learned that the bus service had been suspended and the border between the two countries was now closed.

We made the journey anyway, hitch-hiking and walking to our goal, prepared to wait beside the border until India would let us in. When we arrived, without any explanation the frontier post was open after all. Officers sat at leisure inside a large tent of thick pale canvas. From the roof hung a fan, moved by pulling a rope, and skinny servants pulled the rope in big slow movements, creating a gentle balm of breeze for everyone inside. An official poked his chin forward and raised his eyebrows. 'Have you completed the Currency Declaration Form? How much money have you?' I was asked.

I had not completed the form and answered vaguely, 'Oh, you know, a few dollars, and a few pounds, some rupees. That sort of thing.'

'Ah! It is not allowed,' explained the official, 'to bring Indian rupees into India.'

'Oh dear,' said I, 'in that case, I haven't got any rupees.'

'Good!' The official said, shaking his head from side to side.

Angela asked him, quite hypothetically, if one had had rupees, what should one do with them instead of taking them to India, at which he laughed merrily, saying that was very good, very good indeed, and wishing us a pleasant journey. 'Oh – and when you return through here,' he advised us, 'say you entered India with travelers checks only. Then there will be no form to complete for the departure.'

Almost in the instant that we crossed the border, the landscape became richer, darker, laden with foliage and heat and time. For a while we continued on foot, quietly. I could imagine the country like a great animal, almost hear its deep, slow heartbeat. Yet eventually the sense of having reached our goal began to fade, for no end can be finally reached.

Our objective now was Delhi. The city of Ahmedabad, where Jesse lived, lay south of the capital. Angela wrote a letter to him, to say we were in India and on our way to see him.

The village railway station was a precious article of Victoriana, perfectly preserved, with an insular sense of its importance. The uniformed staff, each spruce and proud and with his job to do, carried out their tasks with straight-backed diligence as if the chaotic world outside had no reality, as if the station and its employees and the railways would endure, while all else would crumble and rot and pass away. In truth, surely it would be the other way round: this comedy would end, while the sultry heat and the flies would last forever.

A clerk sat serene and expectant behind an arched window, the word *Tickets* written in tiles above the glass.

'We would like tickets to Delhi, at the student price,' I said to him.

'Have you student concession?' he asked.

'Here are our student cards.'

The man took them away and we waited. After a full ten minutes he returned. 'You must take these to the student concession office.'

'Where is it?'

He gave directions. It was ten minutes on foot. When we arrived the office was closed, a sign pinned to the door, Closed on Sunday. I turned to Angela: 'Is it Sunday?'

Tight-lipped, she said 'Yup.'

We made the ten-minute walk back to the station and to the ticket window. Now, there was a queue, so we waited in line for ten minutes. I spoke to the man again: 'It was closed.'

'Yes, yes,' he agreed, 'it is closed on Sunday.'

I was exasperated. 'Why didn't you tell me?'

'Sorry, sorry, you asked me where it was, not when it is closed. Yes, it is closed on Sunday.'

'So when is the office open?'

'The student concession office will be open on Monday.'

Despondent, we walked away. I slumped down beside Angela on a bench. After ten minutes, a passer-by paused directly in front of us.

'How do you do, lady and gentleman,' he began.

He was dressed in a shabby western suit instead of Indian clothes. 'Hello,' I replied suspiciously. Angela remained silent.

'Do you object to me speaking with you?' he asked.

A reflex of politeness led me to say, 'No, not at all.'

'Well, young sir,' he began with Dickensian flourish – perhaps he had learned English from Victorian novels – 'If I may ask, where are you going in this manner?'

Two other passers-by stopped to listen, standing as close to us as old friends. Were they with the first man? Angela glared at them. 'We are going to Delhi,' I replied.

Ah! Delhi! they nodded sagely. One of the newcomers interjected, 'And what is your mission in India?'

Under her breath, Angela muttered 'Mind your own business,' but I replied, 'We are on an educational tour of the country.'

There were admiring intakes of breath and the three men turned to each other with understanding, murmuring 'Ah! On Educational Tour.' One announced more widely, 'They are on an Educational Tour', as if he wished to take possession of the fine phrase. Two more young men stopped to inspect us and listen to our amiable interrogation.

'And may I ask, sir, if there is no objection to my impertinence, what is your relationship with this good lady?' asked the first.

'Good grief,' responded Angela. It was the first time we had had this perennial Indian conversation, to be repeated many times more during the year we would end up staying here.

Should I ask the reason for his question? Or, Who wants to know? 'This lady is… my wife,' I replied.

Angela turned to me sharply. 'Why'd you say that?'

'To protect you from hassle.'

She snorted. 'Weird way to get married. Very sudden.'

The five men listened intently, but uncomprehendingly, and spoke to each other in low voices. Within days, we would be experts at the responses demanded of us, and would learn to say that Angela was my sister; for no young wife, probably pregnant and certainly already burdened with small children, would set off on a pointless journey like this; no young married man would admit to being so irresponsible as to expect her to do so. If we were rich, of course, perhaps. But rich people do not go on an educational tour, and they travel by air, not train. However, a grown-up brother and sister, still unmarried and childless, if they were crazy enough, might keep each other company on such a journey of respectable exploration far from home.

When we had finished our private exchange, and they theirs, one man said, 'When do you expect to travel to Delhi?'

I laughed bitterly. 'Tomorrow, when the student concession office is open.'

The men looked on amazed. 'But do not wait!' one exclaimed. 'You can obtain a student concession today from the Station Master.'

'Really?' I exclaimed, jumping up as Angela stared in disbelief. The other men concurred, assuring us that this was so, and I hurried back to the ticket window. The clerk inside sat waiting just as before. I asked, 'Is it possible to obtain a student concession on a Sunday?'

'Yes, yes,' he replied. 'From the station master.' Following his directions, we hurried to the Stationmaster's office. But it was closed. As I knocked, and looked through the window, a voice told me to wait. I knocked once more and the door was opened by an irritable man whose corpulent form stretched to bursting the buttons on a long white shirt. 'The Stationmaster is praying,' he said with a dismissive wave.

'And the assistant station master?' I suggested. 'It's for a student concession.'

'Assistant cannot give student concession,' came the reply.

'Anyone else who can give it?'

'Yes, yes, of course. The deputy stationmaster is also empowered to give concessions.'

'And is available on Sunday?'

The Indian headshake, 'Yes, yes, of course.'

But the deputy station master was also praying. Perhaps less devout than the station master, or of a different religion, he urged us to wait, saying it would take only a few minutes. When he returned from prayer though, the deputy stationmaster said, 'I must eat now, so please wait.'

'And the stationmaster, is he free now?'

'He also must eat!' was the cheerful response. He returned in an hour, utterly indifferent. Angela and I had to write formal letters to the stationmaster, who himself had just returned to his office. He read our written requests for student concessions with the greatest of care, and immediately granted the requests, issuing us with student concessions within one minute.

Wearily we returned with our written permits to the ticket window.

'We would like two tickets to Delhi, at the student concession price,' I said.

'You have student concessions?' he asked blandly.

I handed him the forms. He inspected them and at last named a price as if offering to buy them. 'Thank you, sir,' he said in conclusion as I stared at the tickets, and in tired disbelief at the ticket clerk.

Astonished that I still stood there, he nodded his head from side to side. 'Thank you, sir,' he said again. I held up the tickets to show Angela. With a shrug, she said, 'They have showers on these stations, don't they? Man, I need one.'

Sauntering animals, hurrying men in dhotis or white pajamas, women in saris, whining scooter-rickshaws, groups of street clowns and acrobats, tinkling bicycles, overloaded buses, rustic wooden carts drawn by bony buffalo or staggering, hungry horses, wandering chai-wallahs saddled with urns, busy dabbawallahs delivering lunchboxes, smart Ambassador cars pushing forward with a sounding of horns, and roaring, gaudily painted lorries, jostled for space across the whole width of every road. At the margins, yelling touts and traders and hawkers, rickety drink-stands squeezing sugar cane or limes, street barbers, open-fronted shops and cooking stalls stirring big metal pans, and simmering spices and smoldering incense scenting the hazy air.

Each day brought a greater sense of venturing further into a labyrinth from which there would be no exit. It seemed that somehow I alone, or we together, I knew not which, had tumbled into a well, a whirlpool, of insane color and seething fecundity, dense with life of all kinds, and death; and on every side, a dizzying torrent of human beings, living and intent upon survival, others crushed underfoot and resigned to any fate. In the midst of all was a baffling stillness, a timeless tranquility in the heart of the chaos, and there the mind sought refuge from the din.

Among the dense weave of streets and lanes were gaps and openings, rough tracts of bare earth used as open-air latrines, or where foundations were being dug, not by hard-hatted drivers of bulldozers and mechanical diggers, but by disorganized crews of scrawny, ragged men and exhausted boys working with hand shovels, or where shaky scaffolding stood against makeshift new buildings, and teams of willowy young women climbed up and down wooden ladders bearing bricks loaded on their heads and sometimes, too, babies on their backs.

On a crowded Old Delhi thoroughfare a man lay on the sidewalk. Not like the Haight Street hippy, and not like a Haight Street sidewalk, yet in my mind I heard the voice – *But do they do acid?* – cruelly incongruous, irrelevant to this man, to these people, to the plight of India. This was an expressionless creature nearly skeletal, the skin drawn tight over his skull and naked ribs and fleshless thighs, curled in the dirt as if asleep though his shining eyes stared wide awake. Thousands of striding legs thronged to either side or stepped over him without a pause.

'That guy, look,' we stood aghast, 'he's dying. Isn't he?'

'What blows my mind is, no one doing anything to help him.'

'What can they do? There's nothing, is there? It's too late.'

'Wait here!' I ran to buy a glass of milk from a dudhwallah just yards away, and placed it on the pavement beside the man where he could reach. But he did not move. I saw with shock that he was not old. For a moment I had foolishly assumed that only the old die. I dipped my finger in the milk and put a drop on his lip. Now at last passers-by noticed; I felt a fool as they turned to look at me with disgust.

Slippery as mercury and filthy as an alley cat, a small boy darted from the crowd, grabbed the drink and poured half of it into his mouth. All at once, the strong hand of another boy appeared and clasped the glass, sprinting out of view. The first boy had vanished. The man still lay in his place. 'Come away, Simon. We can't help him. It's too late.'

'What's the answer to all this? Charity means nothing – why help one person when a million need help? That's about your *own* conscience. It's not about the real need. It's ego. It's almost selfish.'

Angela looked disturbed. 'No! It was good, what you did. But a glass of milk wouldn't save him. That guy should be in a hospital.'

'Yeah, but – that's crazy too. The whole system. How can he even get to a hospital?' Yet if they *could* see what acid shows! This place, this heaven, this hell, it's fucked. 'Is Paul right? Politics? Revolution? Is that the way? A great uprising of violence is what this place needs.'

'No, man. That's your anger talking,' Angela shook her head. 'You know why no one here takes any notice? They're used to it. They know it's hopeless. One life, one destiny, one among millions, means nothing. India won't change. India will eat up any solution you think of. India shows the weakness in everything. There's no answer at all.'

Jesse had written back to the Delhi American Express Poste Restante. His letter said only, 'Don't come yet.'

We decided on Kathmandu as a place to wait until he was ready for us, Angela brooding, puzzled, uncertain. Before leaving Delhi we bought chappals – leather thong sandals – and asked a sidewalk tailor, working at an old Singer treadle machine with his bare feet, to make up white cotton copies of our blue jeans. He finished them the same day. Cool, smooth and comfortable, they were a liberation in themselves.

Our route was via the sacred riverside city of Benares, also called Varanasi. On the overnight train I could not sleep, having to vomit or shit every few minutes. Urgently I stepped over bodies in the gangway, lolling among their luggage. In the dirty toilet I squatted, puddles of water and urine flowing between my toes and under my feet. A giant cockroach scuttled towards me as I balanced over the toilet hole, my trousers pulled down and rolled up. Disgusted and frightened by the huge insect, I slapped my bare foot onto it, but it ran unharmed beneath my sole, its hard smooth body rubbing against the skin.

I longed to sleep, or rest, or stop feeling ill. The convulsive waves of nausea and diarrhea had started even while we waited on the platform as the huge train approached. Suddenly I felt sick. Images of filthy restaurants in Afghanistan and Pakistan, and plates being washed in ditches, flashed back to mind. Yet common sense asserted that since Afghanis and Pakistanis seem to thrive, and Angela too was perfectly well after eating in the same places, the fault more likely lay in myself. As I sat in the carriage, sweat trickled from me, soaking my thin cotton clothes and falling in droplets all around my body.

Emitting dark swirls of gritty smoke, the train meandered capriciously through the broad Ganges plain, sometime rushing forward with easy power, sometimes screeching to a juddering halt in large, low vistas of empty countryside. At each station I staggered to the water pump on the platform and poured cold water over my body and into my mouth.

Angela looked on with disapproving, slightly disgusted sympathy. A young Sikh took pity, squeezed into a space beside me on the wooden seat, and at the next station brought a shining metal tumbler of lime-juice, sweetened and diluted. It had an instant effect, and for an hour I felt well. Then vomiting and diarrhea returned with new force. He urged me to go to hospital, and not wait until 'the liver is damaged.' At each stop he pressed the lime juice upon me, and I followed his advice to eat or drink nothing else, while he and Angela ordered samosas and bhajias and twists of paper filled with nuts, and tea served in clay pots, from vendors who reached up to the windows at every station.

The two of them chatted merrily, the young man glowing with pleasure. Yet he remained modest and respectful. The merciless hassle which clung to her throughout the Moslem world had ceased on crossing the border into India.

At Varanasi station he would have helped us to the hospital, but Angela wanted to fly to Kathmandu straight away, and the helpful young Sikh parted from us with concerned farewells.

'Makes you think, doesn't it?' I said. 'That guy. Same age as us. Total straight, right? Do we want to turn guys like that onto acid? Or leave 'em as they are?'

She shook her head. 'Yeah, really nice guy. But suppose some Sikh girl wanted to be like me, travel the world with her boyfriend. Suppose it was his sister. Then what? Would he try to forbid it?'

'Yep, that's true. It's that *sister* question. Liberation is not just your own liberty, but other people's. Otherwise it won't change a thing.'

I had been clinging to her shoulder for support, but at that moment had to rush to the toilet. My whole digestive system from mouth to anus seemed to be turning inside out like a pair of socks. Afterwards I lingered exhausted in the shower, slumped fully-dressed on the floor as gallons of cool water cleaned my body and my clothes.

A taxi took us from Kathmandu airport straight to the city's hospital, where I was seen at once by an amiable doctor who spoke public-school English and gave me an injection and a generous, uncounted handful of pills. I began to feel better within an hour. The illness was diagnosed as giardia and the tablets were to be taken several times a day for weeks.

Along the unmade streets of the town, thousands of hippies wandered. At a corner, some were boarding a minibus to the stupa at Boudhanath. We'd never heard of it, but riding anywhere would be easier than walking nowhere. About five miles out of Kathmandu, the stupa turned out to be a domed circular shrine enclosed by a dusty village. The Buddha's painted eyes, peering narrowly from the four sides of a spire over a massive white dome raised above the level of the rooftops, stared in four directions across the fields. Any worker looking up and gazing at the village would see the Buddha's eyes staring into his own.

In the circle of simple packed-earth huts and cottages around the stupa, on one was pinned a small handwritten note in English: *To Rent*. It was nothing more than a few rooms joined to other houses. We moved in straight away, right then. Weak and tired, I sat in a sunny corner near our new home. The golden spire of the stupa glinted. Buddha's unblinking eyes looked down. Day after day I sat in my corner and the eyes stared with unwavering and unspoken comment, both stern and compassionate, castigating and encouraging. Devout Buddhists walked around the stupa, always clockwise, sunwise, turning with one hand each of the hundreds of prayer wheels which were set into its wall. The prayer wheels spun, clockwise too. Always circles, circles and rhythms. I returned to my place and smoked dope. Poor Angela also spent hours sitting and waiting.

We slept on the floor, beneath a hanging mosquito net like a four-poster bed. In the morning, we listened to neighbors scraping and washing the insides of their throats, retching and gargling. We descended to an outside lavatory (beside a well) for our own ablutions, and I would spend most of an hour in the dark, acrid toilet struggling with my guts before emerging exhausted to start the day with a pipe of ganja. I strolled the narrow paths between rice fields; the paths led around paddies, up and over hills, far away from the hippy trail which seemed to have brought the West with it to this remote place.

Kuncha, the owner of our little wattle-and-daub duplex, lived in another part of the jumbled circular terrace of dwellings. Her kitchen was a windowless dungeon next to a stable where she kept a few animals. Kuncha squatted low in the smoke-filled kitchen before a wood fire, pots upon pans of rice and steaming vegetables. Her eyes and white teeth flashed in the smoky darkness, greeting us as we passed the doorway. She had several children, though which were hers and which were neighbors' remained always unclear. One of the children became ill with diarrhea and open bleeding sores. I gave him some of my antibiotics and he quickly recovered. Kuncha wanted to thank me, and stood in front of me, speaking, as it were, from the heart, while I listened without understanding a word. After that she always beamed at me, and I treasured her affection like something intimate between us.

Kuncha liked Angela too. Angela endured the eye-gritting smoke of the kitchen to squat beside her, drink rancid tea and be shown how to cook the plain, oily and dull Nepali food. She reported that the children used the floor as a toilet and that sign language didn't go far enough to find out what she most wanted to know: where was Kuncha's husband.

Yet Kuncha, as much as all her neighbors, looked askance at our disgusting foreign habits. Such as, feeding animals. So many of the dogs at Boudhanath were sick. One mangy bitch, belly bloated and hairless, used to cry in a low voice day and night. We wondered if she had cancer. While locals kicked and cursed her, we brought her meat and gave it to her under their disapproving gaze. A man nonchalantly swinging a stick whacked the wretched creature. Enraged, Angela – still grieving for Sirius – seized the stick, pointed at the dog, then beat the astonished man furiously. He tried to retaliate before realizing that he was no match for this mad blonde giantess, and running away yelping as the dog had done before him. Locals watched without expression, while freaks paused to debate the rights and wrongs of her act. One called out, 'Yay! Revenge of the underdogs!'

Angela wrote again to Jesse but there was no response. We walked or took the crowded minibus to Kathmandu to visit the Poste Restante, but neither of us received any letters. We'd sit with the freaks on the post office steps, talking and passing round joints or chillums, before sauntering in dung-splattered market streets jostling with Tibetans and Nepalis (distinguished by their hats), as well as snuffling pigs, cows meandering as if in a daze, and swarms of bicycles sounding tinkling bells. Gusts of fragrance, mingled with less pleasant smells, moved in the air. Sometimes Nepalis swept around our large pale bodies, like a shoal of fish letting a liner pass. In the encircling distance, Himalayan peaks, white, massive and silent with a silence that seemed to dwarf all this noise, rose through the cloudy horizon.

A hippy crowd, us among them, gathered daily at Himali Cold Drinks, a milk bar close to the favorite spot of a vast bull who lazed and strolled in the crowded market lanes, or at the dingy Blue Tibetan restaurant, where we'd peer through the heavy fug of incense and dope for people we had met before.

In every building, in every room, aromas mingled spices, oil, sweat and incense, most often sandalwood or rosewood, but some unfamiliar, sweet or sickly sweet, others almost acrid. One type of Tibetan incense, a stubby wedge, threw out clouds of pungent fragrance more like fumigation than perfume.

The final stop on a visit to town was the government hashish store, a dank upstairs room in a crumbling terraced cottage, its doorway marked by a pinned-up playing card. We'd buy a few tolas (a tola is just under half an ounce) of charas (hashish) or ganja (grass).

The sole item of furniture in our home was a small table. Using a window ledge as a chair, one of us would sit there and prepare chillums to smoke alone or with other freaks who were neighbors or passing by. There was enough dope in crumbs swept onto the floor to pay for the whole trip to the East and back, if we had but gathered them up.

A mosquito net covered the window – there were shutters but no glass – and the tender green top leaves of a marijuana plant swayed outside. All summer it grew, gigantic weed, climbing past the upstairs window.

Angela sat sometimes on the window ledge, gazing through the net at the myriad world of tiny paddy fields beyond the village, and at the gigantic horizon where mountainous banks of white and blue and purple cloud, swirling in slow rhythms, crashing together or tearing apart, opened to reveal the real mountains, vaster still, the brittle Himalayan peaks tactile and close. The wind that turned those immense clouds came as a soft breeze into the Kathmandu valley, gently arousing the tiny topmost leaves of the cannabis plant. Over the weeks and months the view moved across a spectrum from wonderful, to beautiful, to ordinary, to boring. Then one day it was enough.

* * *

There had been no more letters from Jesse. Yet Angela maintained that she was certain they would soon be together again.

We left as suddenly as we had come, walked out of the house with our shoulder bags, uncertain where to go next. Now at last Kuncha put her arms around me and pressed her face to my cheek, and stepped back to look fondly. 'Bye bye, Sai Mung,' she said.

Our Air Nepal pilot flew around Boudhanath stupa, mandala-like from a window seat, as a token of reverence. Our house, the familiar fields, were tiny below, and there – one last time – was Kuncha, looking up at the plane, a hand shielding her eyes from the glare. That, down there, I asked Angela, pointing out the house with Kuncha in front of it, beside the stupa – 'Is that it? Is that the simple life?'

She shook her head. 'It's the same there as everywhere. There's no simple life.'

Angela never came to the ghats, the crowded, majestic stone steps rising from the vast Ganges, the holy river. Perhaps she went at other times of day, without me. She was troubled by the heat, and the dirt, and about Jesse, and rarely went out of our small hotel room in Varanasi, the waterside pilgrimage city to which we had returned and where, this time, we lingered.

She had written to Jesse yet again, giving the hotel as our address, and no longer expected a response, yet kept waiting, like someone whose only hope for the future is the chance of winning millions on a lottery. I too was waiting, waiting for the next stage. I drifted, let India wash over me and through me, and loved the near-nakedness of loose cotton and the steam-bath climate.

A thick humidity suffocated the streets. Glancing up, one could barely see the shape of the sun through the moist atmosphere. After 'pre-monsoon showers' the air was briefly cooled and the city flooded. Scooter-rickshaws, tiny open-sided taxis built onto the back of motor scooters, wound their way around or, with big splashes, straight through enormous puddles. When we went out together, we stepped into the warm water lying in the street, and would stroll together, pausing for a lassi, a sugarcane juice or nimbu-pani (lime juice and sugar in water) or some mangoes. We bought thin, embroidered kurta shirts and had more white cotton trousers made, thinner and looser.

Exhausted by the stifling air, people lay down on the edges of the pavement. Cows, also irritated by the heat, ran angrily down the street from time to time, scattering weary pedestrians. In our room a big ceiling fan turned as if with heavy limbs, circulating hot, turgid air slowly around the room. Angela had the idea of wrapping oneself in a sheet which had been soaked in cold water; it was instantly refreshing, but became too warm in minutes.

Yet the street-theatre of Indian city life continued, the processions, dances, marches, music, bells and drums, carried along the road by a shouting, chanting crowd. The sound, loud and savage, felt like a hymn to the terrible heat, though perhaps it was to fate, or destiny, to the cycle of the seasons, or to some wild goddess of the sun.

At dawn I walked to the ghats. On the way, the sidewalks were lined with sleeping and waking bodies of those who spent the nights in the street. Approaching the river, I was one among hundreds or thousands heading to the water's edge. Street vendors, sleeping beside their wares, were stirring, opening their eyes to another day of sitting in the same place, selling the same goods, using the same phrases, their souls molded by repetition, each day a wretched mantra.

At the riverside, calmed by the quiet peace that dawn possesses even in the midst of noise, people gathered to wash and defecate and pray. For all I knew, all three were alike holy. Fat women and thin entered the water draped in their saris, to bathe in the sacred stream. Their modesty was nominal only, for when they emerged the thin cloth clung invisibly to them. Men leaped more boldly into the grimy soup, naked or in their undershorts, gargling and cleaning their teeth (without toothpaste) with the same water that had just washed another man's feet. The rush of the broad current swept all away, the dirt of body and mind, and the ashes of the dead, whose corpses burned on pyres in mid-stream.

Angela sat on her bed, cloaked in a thin sheet, head leaning forward, hair hanging with sweat. 'Is it gonna get hotter than this?'

I shook my head. 'I don't think it can. If it gets hotter,' I said, 'people will drop dead in the street.'

'That wouldn't stop it getting hotter. Maybe people do drop dead in the street,' she said. 'Shall I tell you what I want?' She leaned back on the wall. 'I want to get away from this goddam place. Where do rich Indians go on summer vacation? Where did the Brits go when they ran the show?'

'They didn't leave India. They went into the hills.'

'We were in the hills already, if you mean Kathmandu. I don't want to go back there.'

'No, man, not those hills. Kashmir and Simla and places, that's where they went. Classy summer resorts. Come on, pack your bag. We'll go.'

I was serious, and left her again as I went to find out about trains to Kashmir. I learned there was a direct service, taking thirty hours, with one hundred stops en route. The next would be tomorrow afternoon.

During that night the heat seemed worse than ever. In the distance, rumbles of thunder hung in the dark air. We tossed restlessly, Angela occasionally going with her sheet to run it under the cold tap. But I must have slept, because I dreamed. Perhaps it was the delirium of the night, but I awoke with a start, the sweat running as a warm fluid around my body, down my neck and sides. Even though I could not remember the dream, it left me uneasy and afraid.

Angela, for the moment, slept. Her breasts and pubic mound beneath the sheet, the legs splayed, tempted me. But no, her 'new attitude to sex', as she had started to call it, seemed to be turning into a kind of hostility towards my desires.

I dared not sleep again, but walked to the ghats in the night darkness. There the living lay uncomfortable on the sidewalks and an eerie light glowed from the smoldering dead.

As the sky lightened over the river, early groups of pious bathers were already descending into the water. At that moment, the monsoon rains began in earnest. At first tentatively, then with assurance, raindrops that would fill a saucer splattered onto the ground, onto the people, and the animals. A mood of joyous relief swept through the streets. Suddenly the shabby black umbrellas were up, dhotis and saris tucked higher, and the day dawned up to its ankles in water.

Angela was awake, grimly packing, and had resolved upon waking that instead of heading for the hills, we should turn south towards the heat and find Jesse, whatever he thought about it. I was glad.

She explained, 'I had such a weird dream. What a night! Man, it was hot last night. I dreamed I was struggling through some steaming jungle, could have been in India but it could have been Africa, and I was looking for the source of the Ganges, which I think was also the Nile. And in the dream the Ganges flowed from the south, just like the Nile does, and didn't flow from hills, but from some hot, flat place. And when I woke up I just knew what it was saying and what I had to do.'

* * *

After each downpour, the air steamed and a pearly sunlight gleamed on the drying surfaces. The railway journey, without the illness of the earlier trip, was a joy. The windows were raised, wide open to the humid breeze and the flat, hazy view on the downwind side (hurriedly closed if the engine's hot, gritty smoke should come down the train on that side).

The secret of traveling is to be in no hurry at all. The train journey took thirty-five hours on the wooden slats of third class. We stopped at Delhi, spent a night at one of the hippy hotels, and boarded another train to Ahmedabad, where Jesse had made his home.

In the last hours, Angela became quiet, looking out of the window at the meaningless expanse of bare land. At last she said, that her longed-for reunion might be better if she could arrive alone.

On the other hand, if she arrived alone and Jesse wasn't there, or wouldn't let her in, she'd be in trouble. To be a woman alone in Ahmedabad could be a problem. All the way from California to here, she had wanted to avoid traveling on her own. What did I think?

Yes, I had to agree. To meet Jesse alone would be best for her.

'And if he doesn't want me, or is away?'

For a moment I pictured a scene, of this man Jesse, of whom I knew nothing except that I looked like him, answering a door and telling Angela that – after her ten-thousand-mile voyage – she couldn't come in; and she would turn away from the door, and make her way to me, accepting her fate and prepared to forget Jesse forever.

Even to visualize such things was pointless. I said, 'I'll take you there, and leave you there, and come back if I'm welcome.'

She reached and touched my cheek and smiled a small smile, and said, 'Dear Simon! Whatever happens, you'll always be welcome to come to me.'

Fall 1970

Brightly painted scooter-rickshaws waited outside Ahmedabad station, touting for business. We took one on a long journey across town to Jesse's street, a wide road lined with big houses surrounded by scrubby patches of garden and bare earth. Angela peered at the buildings as the scooter puttered along.

Jesse's house had five steps leading up to a wooden porch. The scooter stopped outside and I paid the driver, who glanced up with the faintest curiosity – tourists usually went to hotels, not private houses – before roaring away.

When I turned back, Angela was at the door talking to someone, a young westerner in jeans and check shirt, who did not look like a freak, and did not look like me. Perhaps we had come to the wrong house. I almost hoped so. The guy kissed her on the cheek and held her hand.

As I stepped forward, he came down to meet me. Yes, now I saw the resemblance. In the bones, the figure, a lightness of body, of step, of eye, a paleness in the color. But his color was whiter, sharper than mine. Eyes blue, like mine, but much bluer, metallic, sparkling. And hair platinum blond, the color of milk, in a neat college cut. I wondered if he was partly albino. Firm, muscular arms of smooth pale skin. No beard, but a handsome, drooping mustache of thick white hair. Around the eyes, some amiable creases, and the mouth a genial, sincere smile.

'Hi!' He held out a hand to mine. 'Simon? I'm Jesse, Jesse Quin. Good to meet you.'

He had presence. He was likeable. He was fascinating to look at. The two of them standing together, Jesse and Angela, made an astonishing sight, her coloring vividly golden, his as silver as the moon.

Not concerned that we had arrived uninvited and unannounced, Jesse introduced us to two others who lived in the house, a young Englishman and a young Indian, both handsome and rather fey and, like Jesse, wearing clean, casual western clothes. They described themselves as students. Angela had not expected that. In all her imaginings of being with Jesse again, there were no other people present.

The house stood large and square, the interior cool with spacious rooms. From high ceilings were suspended large wooden fans, like majestic birds with wings outstretched, turning at a leisurely pace. Rugs with the colors of stained glass lay on washed tile floors, and sumptuous red and blue embroideries studded with mirrors hung from the walls.

Jesse showed us around. I found myself staring at the face, the hair, listening attentively to the voice. There was something so unusual about him; not just his intriguing, eerie paleness, but his deliberate, well-paced movements, too, and concise speech. Somehow, between each of his words was a silence. I noticed an absence of things – of clutter, of restlessness, of nervous talk.

It was a fabulous house. Once again, someone in Angela's intimate circle seemed to be extremely wealthy. In the lounge, behind cushions and canvas chairs, a wall of shelving was jammed with LPs and 78s; hundreds of them – maybe thousands. Despite the uncertain electricity supply, Jesse's sound system looked as good as any I'd ever seen. Double doors led out to a tiny lawn with a border of tropical flowers.

Another room, designated 'our studio', appeared to be part-workshop, part-gallery, filled with paintings, large, intricate, intriguing, depicting the melée of India's streets, shifting crowds, haze-filled train stations, intriguing slums and markets, overwhelming everyday scenes under clouded skies.

'Wow! Are these your work?'

He said they were.

'I love them!' I told him at once (which he acknowledged with a modest bow of the head). 'Is it oil paint?'

'No,' he said, 'pastels. Oil pastels on canvas. Do you paint?'

'I draw, but I've never used pastels.'

'Try them while you're here. I'll give you some tips, if you want.'

Jesse's 'Library' was like some classy clubroom with rugs, a divan and armchair and a couple of low tables. On dark bookshelves reaching the ceiling were politics and poetry, economics and art, as well as books from hip self-reliance manuals to Herbert Marcuse, Buckminster Fuller and Alan Watts to Baba Ram Dass, from *Light on Yoga* to the *Whole Earth Catalogue*. I even saw *Frommer's India on $5 and $10 a Day* among the rest.

'*Look* at this!' Angela exclaimed. 'Where d'you find all these, man?'

she asked. 'Is there like, a hip bookstore in Ahmedabad?'

'In *Ahmedabad*? No! Mostly I buy 'em from Cody's in Berkeley. Mail order,' Jesse replied, as if that were obvious.

Along a corridor, the bathroom was a bare stone chamber where you could empty buckets of water over yourself, or even – in the case of the men – have them emptied for you, Jesse employing a man for that purpose; he called out, and a slender, middle-aged dhoti-clad figure stepped from shadows to introduce himself respectfully. The man was joined by a woman, her grey hair tied tightly back, dressed in a sari over a fitted blouse revealing a few inches of midriff. 'This is Dipesh,' said Jesse, 'and Madhu.' The two stood demurely side by side, the pair of them now inclining their heads in a troubling show of deference. The wife, Jesse explained, did the housework and cooking.

Jesse's bedroom was large, with folding doors opening onto the little back garden we'd glimpsed. The walls were a rough, plain white, and the bed a double with a thick mattress, draped with colored Indian cloth. Small birds flew around indoors, staying close to the ceiling. The thick leaves of an exotic bush pushed through the doorway into the room.

Jesse did not show us his friends' bedrooms. Opposite his own bed, shutters opened to a spare room with a charpoy (a bed of criss-crossed rope on a wooden frame). Angela and Jesse stood in his room while I inspected the spare room, unsure whether I was invited to stay.

'Why, Jesse,' I overheard Angela's most peevish voice, '*why* did you not reply to my letters?'

I heard him chuckle. 'You're here for just ten minutes and already carping and criticizing. And that, my dear Angela, is the reason for my doubts about even writing to you. As you have now arrived uninvited, as I knew you would eventually, of course it is lovely to see you. If you remain calm and quiet, and good-tempered, it will be lovelier still.' She murmured a reply that I could not hear.

A few minutes later, Angela found me and said in a low voice, 'Hey, let's go outside for a minute, I'd like to discuss something.' We went to the other side of the house, where there was no garden, just bare earth.

She leaned her head close to mine, as close as we'd been for many days. 'I know this is hard for you, Simon.' Her sensitivity came as a surprise. 'But I was wondering...'

'Ah! I thought there would be a "but"...'

'No, listen. I wondered if you would be able...'

'To fuck off?'

'No, let me finish. Not to fuck off. But to give me and Jesse some space. We talked about that, right?'

It was true, I had agreed to leave them alone. Now she made clear that Jesse had invited me to stay, and that was fine, but for herself she would be grateful if the following day I would leave.

Of course, there was a kitchen too, and a dining room, the two separated by folding doors fixed open. Jesse and Angela and myself, and Jesse's housemates, gathered at the large kitchen table. A joint was lit and passed round. There was awkward talk about the weather, the heat, our journey. Only when speaking to Jesse did any of us feel quite at ease. Angela sat beside him, and smiled happily as they looked at one another.

Slipping ignored into the kitchen, the cook began a steady chopping and peeling and clattering and a slapping of dough. Her thin arms gathered all the waste and tossed it through a door onto bare earth beside the house, where it quickly vanished, eaten by wandering animals.

The air became scented with appetizing fragrance. Jesse's man, now in pristine loose white cotton short-sleeved shirt and pressed trousers, came in and set the table.

Surreally familiar and unfamiliar, the scene might almost have been in a San Francisco restaurant. Balmy evening air drifted pleasantly through the room and we ate lightly spiced vegetables and the most tender rice, delicious chutneys, dal, yoghurt, and finally an English-style fruit pie with custard. Madhu and Dipesh served us, carrying dishes to the table, even spooning the food onto our plates and discreetly removing used crockery.

* * *

A soft light slivered into my room from theirs. I could hear their voices, low and intimate. Angela giggled sometimes. Then the rhythmic panting of sex. In anguish I got off the charpoy and paced up and down, up and down, as in the Greek prison cell, breathing low to make no sound. A mood of despair rose through me. Then I caught a glimpse and held my breath: in the gap between the shutters I could see the gold of naked skin, their flesh moving like a metronome. Their feet were straight towards me. She lay underneath, legs wide apart, and he between. Very clear to see, Jesse went in and out of my beloved Angela, his loose testicles brushing her buttocks with every push.

I turned away. This I never thought to endure! I should not have seen that, should not have been tempted to look. Angered, humiliated, I lay on the rope bed in a rage of misery and frustration.

In the morning, with a curious smile, perhaps with a touch of guilt, or of coy pride, she came in to see me. She was wearing her short, thin kurta shirt and seemed to me very desirable.

'You OK?' she asked.

She leaned forward to kiss my forehead with something like pity, and went back to the bedroom.

Then Jesse came in, dressed in a handsome lungi (a cloth wrapped around the waist), greeting me with a gentle good morning. He was holding a thin blue air letter.

I nodded, and gestured him to sit on my bed, but he remained standing. 'She's been hung up on you all the time I've known her,' I said. 'I guess I sort of knew it would end like this.'

There was sympathy in his face. 'Don't worry. I don't want her.'

I felt an urge to discuss it with him. It seemed that Jesse was one of those people in whom it is easy to confide. 'Not easy, lying here, while... Stupid to get jealous,' I admitted.

He looked straight into my eyes and merely nodded, yet conveyed a world of fellow-feeling. 'I think it's me that was supposed to be jealous.'

'What do you mean?' I was puzzled but he smiled sweetly.

'Here, this came a long while ago.' He held out the letter, addressed to me in a round American hand.

After he'd left the room, I unfolded the aerogram.

Dear Simon. So glad you made it. Thanks for everything. Love, Sasha. PS. It's not the end.

As I read and re-read, mystified, I looked again at the California postmark. With a wave of something almost like fear, I saw from the date that she had sent the letter even before we started out from London.

Waiting on a crowded platform for the next train to Bombay, traveling once more with no companion, no lover, was strangely joyous. For a little while it seemed that all torment, longings and jealousy had been physically discarded, and I imagined myself returned to the carefree, footloose life before Angela. Only two or three hours into the journey, though, I began to miss her, and learned that there could not, after all, be any return to that innocent time.

At the Rex Hotel, one of the dirt-cheap flophouses and guesthouses near the Gateway of India, freaks occupied every room. Some sat in the street outside playing music while others hawked acid, Bombay Black, and ganja. Signs on VW buses, parked nearby, offered rides to Goa for a share of the cost. A guy had a cassette player to sell; I bought it along with an assortment of tapes, good old pop and rock, the Yardbirds, Jethro Tull, the Move, Beatles, Rolling Stones.

Stretched on the bed, gazing at the ceiling fan, I listened to the music and pondered my situation, reaching no conclusions, and slept. Now feeling rather alone I wandered in the noisy streets, paused at a sidewalk stall for a creamy fresh dessert, or sat in Dipdi's Fruit Juice Bar, nearly opposite the hotel, with a glass of their specialty, fresh fruit in milk.

Walking from the hippy area I was accosted by little girls, too young even for the first sign of breasts, who asked if I wanted to have a good time. I was waylaid by young men who asked if I wanted a good time with their sister – 'Only twelve!' they promised. Women in saris, who were in fact girls of my own age, asked me if I wanted a good time. Certainly I wanted a 'good time', but in them I saw a horrible time, of despair, wretchedness and squalor.

In the clamor of spicy backstreet eating houses I joined laborers at oily tables and ate, as they did, with the fingertips of my right hand, pressing rice and vegetables into mouth-sized balls. Except for such glimpses, I knew nothing of Indian life.

Around a table at Dipdi's, on the steps of the Rex or hanging around on the sidewalk, sometimes the question was asked, a little puzzled, just how poverty and caste – we didn't even know about debt-bondage and dowry murder and child laborers chained to looms and young wives burned alive in the *sati* rite – fitted into our India trip. We declared them a bummer, to be swept away when religion and capitalism fell by the wayside. Hindus, we were told, believed misfortunes were their own fault – karma, an inheritance from themselves, a legacy of forgotten former lives. Freaks liked the idea, though viewed it distorted through a western prism, as if karma were a never-ending *Judgment Day*, akin to *poetic justice;* or *just deserts* on a cosmic scale. Others declared karma a fascist trick to keep everyone yoked to their station in life.

Yet India hinted that it was impervious to our ideas. It seemed immutable. Its lunatic religiosity, its infinite patience, its inhuman indifference – and unplumbed sufferings – were destined to outlast everything philosophers could dream of. That India was at a different stage in its development could not be denied, but was it ahead of us or behind? I lacked a perfect faith in the power of acid to right its wrongs.

A constant traffic of wide-eyed freaks on the move between Goa and Kathmandu passed through Bombay, reporting that they had visited hill stations in the north, or stayed on a houseboat in Kashmir, or spent time in an ashram, or traveled south to Kerala. It did not matter which direction I chose. Apart from missing Angela's caress, all was easy, the steamy weather sensuous, the mood unfettered. Every tie was cut, and England fainter than a ghost.

A long, bone-rattling bus ride to Goa set me down at Calangute Beach, final frayed end of 'the hippy trail' beside the Indian Ocean. Flimsy shacks stood on the sand, palm trees rising between the little houses. The ocean glimmered with sparkling, enticing coolness. Freaks strolled everywhere.

As I walked along the shore, a voice called. Freaks on the porch of a house invited me to smoke some dope with them. Big chillums were filled. Some, before inhaling, raised the chillum to their forehead and shouted the sadhu's cry to the destroying god Shiva, 'Boum shankar!'

They told me of a house for rent. I weaved a route through the trees to the cottage. The fishing family that lived there named a monthly rent in rupees that, for all I knew, would normally be year's income to them.

'What about you? Where will you go?' I asked.

They pointed to a much smaller shack nearby: they would live there. In the meantime, they cheerfully handed me a plate of rice and fish. I lay down on their porch and slept till morning.

Winter 1970-1971

Yes, it's free, say the women. We don't know who built the well but it must have been a long time ago. We don't know who it belongs to, but anyone may take from it.

The wells fascinate westerners: that they are surrounded by women, that they give inexhaustibly, that they sustain life, that they descend into darkness, that they are at the center of every neighborhood. Because of the daily routine of fetching the heavy buckets, filled to the top and splashing over the brim, water flows beneath all our thoughts.

The sight of water slopping from pails brings washing to mind, and the thought that the women at the well will wash, loosen their saris. The hippy girls too will slip off their skirts and wash. I don't struggle to push the thoughts away.

Washing at the well is frowned upon by locals, as something uncouth, immodest and antisocial. Some westerners do it anyway, using their pail as a washbasin and splashing soapy water into the well. A few – always men, never women – even fall, or jump, down a well. This they do when there is no one there, in the afternoon, or at night, are discovered later and end up in the hospital at Panjim.

You need water to have a shit – a little pot of water, which you hold in your right hand and pour between your buttocks while wiping clean with the fingers of your left hand. That's what Indian mothers teach their children to do, and that's why Indians don't touch one another's left hands, and why they eat only with the right hand. But they greet each other with a gentle *Namaste*, tenderly pressing their palms together, so transferring everything from left to right.

There are no flush toilets. All Goa's beach houses have a separate shack, made of palm fronds, which serves as a lavatory. Inside, you squat on a raised wooden platform and your shit drops onto the sand below. A space in the back of each hut allows domestic pigs, wandering loose among the houses, to push their snouts inside and eat the shit, which they apparently consider delicious. Simple system! Disturbing, though, when snouts begin their snuffling before you have finished.

Love 221

Among some peoples pigs are unclean, forbidden. This could be why: they eat shit. Hindus, Moslems, Jews and Jains don't eat pigs, so the animal is hardly seen in India. For the Goans, who are Christian, the pig is the God-given model of efficient economy, turning human waste back into nutritious food, and once again clearing up the digested remains and again turning it back into food.

Some westerners, mostly Australians and Americans, don't need water to have a shit: they insist on using paper, cut pages from the Times of India. Pigs eat shit happily, but hate the press. So, thanks to hippies, shit-streaked newsprint blows among the trees.

Calangute has a town center of sorts, with unmade, sandy lanes and a couple of streets with shops and eating places shaded by palm trees. A battered local bus with hard seats travels from here, windows open, horn roaring at every bend, across a long bridge over the wide Mandovi River, to Goa's capital, the once-Portuguese colonial town of Panjim.

I call at the Panjim Post Office to put a package in the mail and ask if I have received any letters. Some people write. Never Angela. One day there is something, not from Angela, but in my mother's familiar hand. She wishes me Happy Birthday from all the family – I was twenty-two years old a few weeks ago – and makes a sad, agonized attempt to find common ground, give 'news' and keep in touch. My father, she hints, never recovered from his effort to help me while I was in jail. He is having treatment for heart disease.

The clerk has found something else, an air-letter. It's from Milly: there's *so* much happening, she says. Come back and get involved! It's important! Students at the college started a women's group and issued a list of demands for equal rights for all students, male and female. She sets out her theory, that women's rights are the key to equality for all, for this reason – that the weak must in future no longer depend on the goodwill of the strong. The weak will organize, and the weak will not be afraid of the strong, and will take the law into their own hands, and make new laws. Women must show the way, because women are everywhere, in every home throughout the world, and women are the very symbol of the weak versus the strong. And so, all who are weak will be inspired to organize. Her views have a little ring of straightness about them. I'm not sure about Law as our ally.

The way Milly describes it, London now has the fervor of Berkeley.

She shies away from the personal in her letter, except to sign off *With my love*. My mother has written *All our love*. It's disconcerting not to have been forgotten.

I stroll among Panjim's market stalls, linger over a drink and a spicy snack, buy the latest Times and Illustrated Weekly of India. Then I board a bus back to Calangute, where I read the newspapers and from them learn India's vocabulary of oppression, disorder and resistance, *Naxalites* (Maoist guerrillas) and *begar* (forced labor) and *lathis* (long police batons for beating angry crowds), the euphemistic *Dalits*, *Harijans* and *Scheduled Castes* (the seething underclass of "untouchables"), and, too, India's intriguing numbers, which measure people and rupees in *lakhs* (one hundred thousand, written 1,00,000) and *crores* (ten million, or 10,00,00,000).

Inside the house, at the small table, I take a pair of nail scissors and carefully cut a square from the inner pages of a newspaper. I wrap a flat, soft slab of hashish tightly with plastic and tape, place it firmly into the empty square, and roll and fasten the bundle for posting. On a label I write the address in College Row, Brighton, England, agreed with Rich. On my next visit to Panjim I go to the post office and mail the package, paying the rate for printed papers.

Christmas Day. No colored lights. The festivities do not touch us here. Strange, because the local people are Christians, but for us on the beach, none of that exists. Just an almost imperceptible hint of extra silence in the air. We have already celebrated the Winter Solstice, thousands who stayed up all of one un-wintry night around bonfires on the beach.

My home is at the Calangute end of Baga Beach. Calangute Beach is busier than the rest, closer to the one hotel, where almost all the guests are well-to-do Indian men staying on their own. These visitors, it is felt, come not for the sun and sea, but to ogle hippies. Wearing shirt and trousers and polished leather shoes, they rarely walk beyond Calangute. The second half of the distance from the hotel to the river is Baga. Then comes the Baga river and, across it, Anjuna.

On each beach a different fantasy is being lived. The Calangute crowd affect hippy style, are vegetarians, meditate, talk I-Ching and mysticism, see themselves as messengers from the future, vanguard of the hip revolution. In Baga, many play out dreams of being Wild Men or Noble Savages. Fish are caught and cooked whole over beach fires by loincloth-clad ex-junkies. Beyond the river, the real freaks make their homes, skinny, dreamy, quiet, mad, in love, everything calm and silent but for the waves, end-of-the-road, in the world of Dreams-Come-True.

Kathmandu, Goa, these are the destinations. Many who take the road seek only a cure for life in the West, nor do they wish to know anything of life in the East. They travel not to arrive, but to leave.

* * *

The sunlight, the endless beach, the lapping ocean, are the whole world now. Hardly noticing time, wearing little or nothing, I pass whole days walking or swimming, sometimes wading to Anjuna beach. There is a dull pain, a weight inside my chest, whenever Angela comes into my thoughts, as if my heart were literally heavy. Otherwise, all is good, apart from the need for sex. I imagine myself in sensuous embrace with any of the nearly naked hippy women all around me. I daydream that Angela will return; I try to believe she is going through a phase, that soon she will come to me, and we shall lie together in the porch and eat fresh fruits and have sex continuously without ever stopping.

I have no watch, no clock, no diary, no calendar. Night is simply the dark time of day, when the breaking ocean waves sparkle with phosphorescence and millions of stars cascade over the velvet skies. Day is the sunlit period of the night, when the never-ending deeps of space become blinded by the dazzling glare. I don't need to plan an acid trip or set time aside for it. If I want to, I drop a trip in the morning. I don't need to be in my house to sleep a long sleep afterwards, but lie down anywhere, among the palms.

The palms writhe seductively, lift their branches like showgirls with their feathers, all the heavy greenery and grasses wave with rubbery picturesque malleability in the silky breeze. At the wells women dressed in colors gather like flocks of birds.

At last, a letter. Angela is angry with Jesse. She writes that she's not getting on with him, he doesn't take anything seriously, he's wrapped up in his own life. I have no idea what she means, and write to tell her so. I draw a picture for her, of my little house on the beach. She writes again, once more about her discontentment with Jesse. I fantasize that she will leave him and come to me, and it will be like Berkeley again, and this endless sunlit winter will be endless summer. We will take acid, and swim in the waves, and all will be good again, and Jesse will depart from our thoughts as if he had never been.

Then, I open a letter one day and read that she is coming to me. It's no fantasy. She is really leaving Ahmedabad.

The first desperate embrace, with her tears of joy, and almost anguished cries of greeting, seemed a good omen. Yet as I led her from the bus station, her next words were to warn that we would not be sleeping together.

'I'm just so confused about what I want,' she said. 'It's so good to see you again. But I don't want to get even more mixed up by having sex with both of you. Can you dig that?'

I said I could dig it, and laughed because I did not believe her. I wondered, though, what she meant by 'both' of us? She was not with both of us; she was with me, no longer with Jesse. In the sun, stripped off, and stoned, she'd fall into the good and easy life of Goa. It would be sex as usual, and I was nearly delirious with impatience for it.

On the way to the house, she repeated that things were not the same now, and would never be. 'We have to get to know each other all over again, in a different way. I'm Angela. You're Simon.'

'Me Simon, you Angela! What's happening?' I smiled 'Is it some kind of game?'

'I don't know what that means.'

She was not pleased with the house. Straight away she complained that it reminded her of the prison.

I took her hand – I didn't want to argue; I wanted my dreams of love and sex to come true as soon as possible. 'It's not like prison, Angela. Look around. It's totally beautiful and we are totally free.'

The palm fronds over the porch hung down 'too low'. They made the house 'too dark, too shady.'

'That's to keep it cool,' I explained. 'Isn't it just so great to live in a house with palm leaves for a roof?' But she was not happy, and I remembered it had been the same with the house in London. And Jesse had said, when I overheard them talking on that first day in his house, that she had been there only ten minutes and already she was carping.

I said, 'Come on, I'll show you how nice it is here.'

The house stood about fifty paces from the sparkling, hushing waves of the ocean. With the sea view open in front, it was secluded by flowering bushes on the other three sides. The porch provided a place to relax and admire the ocean view. The house was one of few with electricity, so I could play my cassette tapes.

'Doesn't it take you back to Djerba a little bit?' I asked.

She went into the house, sat on the floor and cried.

I knelt beside her and put an arm around her shoulder. 'What is it, Angela, my lovely Angela, what is the matter? Tell me.'

She allowed me to comfort her, accepting hugs like punishments, but did not reply.

Angela chose the small room, or rather, she chose not to share the main bedroom with me. Then she became angry that I had the better room. 'Look,' I said, 'there's no need for this. Let's both just sleep in the same room. Why not? We have seen the world together; let's just be grown up.' And I remembered her *I changed my mind* on our first night in Berkeley, when she *wasn't ready* for sex with anyone but Jesse.

She shook her head. 'We're friends, OK, that's cool. But I'm worried you think we're gonna sleep together. That's not going to happen. And anyway,' she said, 'I stopped taking the pill.'

I let her have the larger room. Every night, I lay awake as visions of Angela, naked on the other side of a thin wall, tortured me. Stopped taking the pill! So she was trying to get pregnant by Jesse. Yet she was so confused that she had left him and taken refuge with me – but had not started the pill again. I believed she should, and ought, and surely would, and really *must* be willing to have sex with me, or do *something* for me.

It was not be. 'We aren't a couple, Simon. We're friends.'

The household labors were tacitly divided. While I collected four buckets of water, she made breakfast. At Calangute market, she chose the groceries and I carried them home. She cooked, I cleared up.

In the afternoons, she remained in the porch in melancholy mood, staring at the sea, as I wandered on the beach, far away. In the evening we shared the sunset together, sitting on the sand as the orange circle flamed into the waves.

That, sure enough, was a little like the old days. But everything else was different. Now it was my house, she the guest. Now, we did not walk hand in hand, and there was no Sirius, bounding ahead. Now we never had sex, instead of having it all day and all night as we did then. Now we spent most of our time apart, not together. I called on people I had met on the beach, ate with them, smoked dope with them. Angela did not come with me, and didn't even know where I was. Sometimes I'd see her by chance, clothed in thin, loose cotton, walking slowly, meditatively. If she turned towards me, smiling with recognition, then my heart would leap to the heavens and to Berkeley.

Sleepless with frustration, I paced in my room. I stepped onto the porch to feel the night air on my skin, and stood gazing at the starry darkness, and the pale surf shifting at the edge of the black sea, and listened to the ceaseless breath of the waves.

Back inside, I peeked through Angela's half-open door, hoping for a glimpse of her naked body. She was covered only by a sheet, every contour clear, and awake, her eyes open.

'Hi,' she said quietly. 'I heard you walking about.' I stepped in and knelt on the floor by her mattress.

I wondered if she might be relenting, and want sex. 'What do you think about, all the time?' I asked.

'Light the candle for me, will you?' I lit the small candle that stood in a saucer on the floor. Its pale light made curious shadows of us, dark giants moving on the wall.

She turned her face towards me, dull and expressionless. It occurred to me that she was depressed, not something that had ever crossed my mind before. I thought she wanted to say, Mind your own business, but instead she said, almost in a whisper, 'Jesse is so difficult. He doesn't care about things. I want his baby, I want to raise his children, I want to live with him. He doesn't want any of that. I want to care for him. He doesn't want that.'

I listened just to please her. 'What does he want?' I asked.

'Nothing. Not from me, anyway. Did you know he was gay?'

Startled, I said, 'He can't be. He has sex with you.' I recalled too clearly those testicles tapping Angela's buttocks as he pushed into her.

'Yeah, but he's doing it with those guys in the house as well?'

'I did wonder about them. But I thought –'

'Well, he is. He says he's struggling with his sexuality. That's how he puts it.'

'Should you be telling me this?'

'You asked me what I was thinking about.'

'You didn't have to tell me! And what now?' I asked.

If Jesse were homosexual, surely she would have to give him up. She looked at me unhappily. As the candlelight shifted, somewhere in Angela's careworn face I caught sight of the unimaginable, the first marks of ageing. Of course, I wasn't nineteen any more either. It was obvious, and I already knew, our Berkeley days would never be recaptured. Already they had become locked in our past. No matter how much I longed to touch them again, feel the Telegraph sidewalk under my feet during that thrilling summer, breathe its air, I never would.

Dawn would soon break and yet another day behind us. I so wanted to see yesterday's dawn once more. They were being lost, our mornings and evenings, vanishing forever. I pictured Angela as an old woman. The lines were unmistakably there, the future in waiting.

She continued wistfully, 'We were together once, Jesse and me, and I loved it. A long, long time ago, in Berkeley. I wanted him to need me then, and I want it now. But he just fucking doesn't.' Her voice had become a whimper of utter misery. 'That's the trouble, Simon. I loved it with him. He left. And then you came, and were very, very nice, and I tried to enjoy being with you, but really I still wanted Jesse. That's all I ever wanted. That's the whole story. Now he lays this on me: that he's fucking *gay*. And still I want him, 'til it hurts.'

Tears, real salt tears, burst from Angela's eyes. With something like shock, I reached forward to brush at them with my fingertip. I set a quick, chaste kiss on her forehead. I could not do more, unclothed.

Would this go on forever, I wondered; in thirty years, grey, middle-aged, would we both be wanting what we can't have? Oh, we'd have got our heads together by then, and discovered the secrets of a good life, and learned how to be happy – right? In thirty years?

Even now the minutes are trickling away. We shall be old, and maybe even mocked by the new young. Or will they be on our side? On the other hand, youth is just a transient, sparkling moment. Age is the great thing. The passing of years, that is the big adventure.

In thirty years? Maybe we would all be dead. Maybe that would be best for us, our whole generation. Let the straight bastards have things their own way. They'll have blown the world to pieces by then.

Angela nodded. 'I must go back and try again.' She meant back to Ahmedabad, not to Berkeley. The tears had stopped, but I could not quite make out her expression in the darkness.

'I'll come with you –'

'No,' she interrupted, alarmed, holding up a hand.

I smiled. 'Don't worry. Just for the ride, I was going to say.'

'Just for the ride. You're good. Why didn't I love you?' she said. 'It's so idiotic that I don't.'

I asked nervously, 'Didn't you ever? For one minute?'

She squeezed my hand. 'No, not really.'

'In the beginning?' I asked, pained, hopeful. 'Or all the times when you said 'I love you', was that always a lie?'

She remained perfectly still, frowning, then shook her head. 'Not a lie. Not a lie, just life. We were together. We lived together. Like you said, we've seen the world together. That's worth something, isn't it?'

An emotion pressed my chest, pulled at the sides of my mouth, at my cheeks, ached my eyes. I shook my head to refuse it, shake it away.

She saw my grief and moved to put an arm round my shoulder, her nakedness against mine. 'I'm so sorry. Dear Simon. Love's a funny thing, a terrible thing.'

'A stupid thing,' I retorted angrily.

Two tabs of acid was four times the normal amount for a trip. I swallowed them with a glass of water, in my bedroom before dawn, while Angela still slept. At once there was a fear that my feelings about her might give me a bad experience. The first mild sensations grew quickly into a crashing waterfall of confusion and color. I moved into the porch, where the moonlit night had turned into a wild pattern of pulsing hexagons and after-images. Angela seemed far, far away, and of no concern at all as every cell became preoccupied with matters much closer to home: only my own body, and my own self residing within it, were real to me, all else a spectacle. For so it is. The acid was working and my mind racing.

The sea, the sand and the sky's pale promise of imminent dawn appeared as something printed on a curtain rippling in the breeze. In the distance a local man worked in the half light. A dark row of wooden boats, pulled up on the sand, came more clearly into view.

Gaudy traditional designs on their prows obliquely reminded me that this humid, imperfect place is the home of a community, his community. Somehow it belongs to them, and they belong to it, the thousands of unknown creatures, human and others, male and female, who *live* here, *make a living* here, who are *alive* here right now, curled in sleep close by, their nests hidden among the trees. They are of this place as much as the wild flowers and the palm trees and the fish they catch.

Yet I too am alive here. Thoughts streamed round each other, sometimes in concert, sometimes in opposite directions, sometimes rising to the crescendo of an idea, a realization. About life in the right place, every place is a *human* place, the world is a human world.

The hanging, eternally collapsing roof of our porch waved and swirled like a flag in the air. I heard a sound inside the house; Angela was out of bed.

In the indoor gloom she looked bizarrely small and sad.

'I'm tripping,' I announced at first.

'Good,' she said. 'All OK?'

'Yes, yes. I've got something to say. You know...' already I could hear it sounding foolish, but it was too late to stop the words coming out, 'I've been thinking.' Overwhelmed, I paused, 'Wow, man. Phew.'

She listened with a tolerant grin.

'About... perfection,' I continued. 'The right place to be. The right thing to be. About aiming. Aiming for the Perfect Thing. Perfect Place. That's it! So right. So simple. Nothing else worth aiming for. Dig it.'

She nodded sagely. 'Fucking acid freaks,' she said. Her hand reached out and touched mine. 'Be happy, dear one.'

I started to laugh. 'Anyway, you know what I mean,' I said, and found I had somehow returned to the porch, and stepped onto the beach.

I could barely walk and had to sit down before I reached the ocean's edge. In front of me the water turned and shattered like harmless, transparent, ephemeral jewels. Each wave a sound, a gentle whisper of song, music, color. Blue, blue... the Blue dome above sheltered me. Color seemed a very pure form of existence.

A westerner came into view, a young woman carrying a blanket. I felt – in truth I could feel it – the exquisite freshness of the morning on her skin. And the blanket under her arm. She herself a human bundle of nerves. Inside her, a thread, a current, a light that is her own light, our own light, why we are separate, why we are all different. Ego. That's so good too. At one moment we are united. The next moment separate, divided and different. Time and place for it. Why come together? To satisfy a purpose. To use each other? That's the idea. Call it love.

Man The Tool-Maker. Uses everything and everybody. Every coming together serves a purpose. There's a job to be done. We are all a tool for someone else to use. That's the genius of the human species: using each other. Community. That's clever – who thought of that?

Man The Tool-Maker falls in love. Another tool? Another way of using people? Oh, *that* wouldn't be love. But yes, on another level, (what level?) it's cool, we are that other person, the user and the used. Because, the real purpose – of love, community, and (of course!) sex (the 'stupid fucking thing' about love) – the purpose of all our longings – to be together, a couple, a family, a society, a species – to be part of 'one stupendous Whole', to be a little microcosm of the great big thing we call Everything...

...is that Man the Tool-Maker must go forth and... breed like lemmings. Love is the way.

To make the world stay together. Bind us to our mate. But, no, we're clever, we are. We can love without breeding. Ha, ha – you think *that's* clever. Here's one cleverer: love even in childless freedom is a way of using one another for the good of all. Society.

The sun's early rays had become warm, an exquisite caress. People were arriving on the beach in ones and twos from beneath the shadow of the trees. The whole world was changing like melting plastic, my own body as well. I moved step by step along the shore, with fantastic slowness, looking at the malleable faces and frightened eyes of those who passed, each cautious Ego. Afraid, all afraid, they, we, I. Each one of them brought a renewed sense of clarity and revelation. A thousand realizations in every second, ten thousand in a thousandth of a second, an infinite number of realizations in an infinitely small particle of time.

I knelt in the water. Cool myriad droplets, from single breaking wavelets, hung in the air, not quite motionless, descended at leisure, splashing over my thin cotton trousers.

Time, all relative, matter of perception, faster your mind works, slower time seems, time at a standstill. I am alive, all in the mind.

Love 231

Except... I must think. About love, and ego, and being alive.

Ego is a glass box. (Hello, I'm in here). Imprisoned senses touch the glass. Imagination looks out longingly.

The real world – stones, waves, sky – is all out there not being alive. Imagine the world. Without being in it. No, not looking at it from some hidden place in your mind. Utterly without you. Yes, it exists like that *all the time*. A lifetime is less than nothing to the lifeless world. Youth! Thirty years! Old age! Ideas, inventions, technology, advances, breakthrough, up-to-the-minute froth. Pah, nothing! One day the beach will be empty of humans, and the waves will still turn.

I stood up to walk. On the ocean, fishing boats drifted with their massive nets. Working on board, local men, men of this place, making their living. The sun was warm and promising. A whole day – and all for free. Like water from the well.

The long beach gave me enough space, space to be, to be myself, myself uncrowded. I stood on Baga Beach, toes in the water, facing the sea, listening to its soothing *hhh-sss-sh, hhh-sss-sh*. Birds floated with easy grace. Alive, and living here, making a living here. Not wasting this perfect, pointless day, lest they die and the days go on without them.

I noticed that the air was illuminated. Not just the beach, the sea... but the air itself, full of light, as if I could see and feel this translucent substance, surrounded by it, inhaling it. Indeed, light seemed to fill me with each breath, or to sweep through me as if I were invisible, transparent, empty. There is no 'Simon'. That is just a word, a curtain to cloak that which is real. The letters of that word and all words seemed to unravel and evaporate, revealing... nothing within. Light bathed me, passed through me, all around me light. It seemed this moment of time was to be mine, and I was free to live in it forever. I looked along the beach, the empty sand, and...

...the beach reached me, ran through me. Amazed, aghast, now I noticed the sea. It was motionless. A wave stood completely still, caught in mid turn, its corkscrew shape clear, divine. I inspected its curved perfection at infinite leisure. Lingering forever, fascinated, ecstatic, I adored the beauty of it, and in utter rapture held it gently in my mind, and all at once saw too the simple balance of forces that it was.

And as I watched, the softest of breezes blew right through me, yet the very air seemed stilled in the instant.

Now with miraculous slowness it began once more to move, a slow spiraling, elegant, lazy turn. The wave with ineffable ease lifted more water, pulled the liquid up from the ocean to become part of itself. Somehow I knew that feeling.

Then, suddenly, the glorious moment was in the past, the wave moved at a normal speed, it turned and broke upon the sands, the surf scattering towards me. I was not invisible, the beach again passed beneath my feet, and the breeze merely caressed my body. Sunlight warmed my skin, but did not pass through me. It had lasted, then, that radiant moment, less than the time it takes a wave to turn. Yet I was uplifted as never before. The Earth became glorious to me, a garden, exquisite, my Eden, my home, my place. I am made of it, dressed in it. Perfect, perfect world.

Tiny in the distance, human beings moved on the shore. Then, among them, I recognized Angela, walking towards me with easy, rolling stride, a long faded purple skirt and a loose white kurta flowing around her, her breasts and hips moving beneath the fabric. My head spun with thoughts of her femaleness. I had no physical desire, just a puzzled awareness. Like a child who has not noticed it before, I did not understand the troubling difference between us, male and female. Created he them.

I waved as she came close. Yes, microcosm of the whole goddam show.

Angela smiled beautifully. 'Still high?'

I nodded.

'I thought we could watch the sunset together, if you want to.'

'Sunset? I thought it was morning.'

Surprised, she said, 'Didn't you notice the sun is over this side?'

I looked around. It was true, the shadows were drawing away from the ocean. How could that be? Had the wave remained motionless all day?

And she sat beside me on the sand, held my hand as the sun crept towards the horizon like the hour hand on a clock. In the very instant that the last paper-thin slice of the orange ball had vanished, wild brush-marks of lurid color leapt up to streak the horizon clouds.

Angela stood up. 'Want to eat? I'll make ya something.'

Eat! I forgot to eat! I wanted nothing, except that this moment would last till the end of time. While Angela returned to the house, I stayed out.

All human beings slipped away like the tide. Daylight dimmed and faded. Animals and birds too, except one or two scavenging dogs, disappeared. Yet it was not dark. The moon rode up ghostly behind the palms and the palmy roofs and made silver of everything, a silvery bond glistening on the reflecting sea. The sand became as snow in smooth white drifts, immaculate and untouched.

Timeless, lifeless, yet all the world seemed animate and intimate. The snow-dunes shifted and breathed, the sea's silver edge voiced soft, sibilant verses, the trees, beyond the quiet bushes, stood awake as I danced ecstatically without music, a madman on the shore.

Spring 1971

We made our final journey together, Angela and I, on the boat from Goa to Bombay, cruising close to the shore for a leisurely twenty-four hours. We didn't speak much, though sometimes we sat on the deck and she reached out to hold my hand. During the night I dreamed I was on a ferry to England. The thin, cool spray of the English Channel splashed over the sides as I stood alone on the deck, refreshing my face and dampening my hair. When I awoke, the moisture on my face and hair was sweat.

After a day in Bombay, I went with Angela to the railway station and set her on the train to Ahmedabad, paying someone to climb through the windows as it waited in the station and save her a seat.

I arrived at Jesse's house a few days later. It was clear he had already tired of her. Angela went to bed very early, he very late; he rose early in the morning, while she remained asleep until morning was over. Occasionally, he did not go to his own bed at all, sleeping instead in another room. I hardly ever saw Jesse's housemates. They seemed to be there only at night. During the afternoon and evening, Angela remained at the house while Jesse often went out. She wanted to help in the kitchen, but Madhu complained to Jesse, who asked Angela to let the woman get on with her work.

I felt elevated, remote from their concerns. I bicycled or walked in the hot, unpaved streets, in noisy fragrant markets and squalid alleys.

Each morning after breakfast (usually leftover spiced vegetables), Jesse retired with a cup of coffee to his library, where he reclined on the divan and read the Times of India. I joined him, not to interrupt, or chatter, but to enjoy his presence and browse the bookshelves. The latest arrival was a beautiful edition of the Tao Te Ching.

Sometimes we talked about India. I told him I was starting to think a bloody overthrow of the whole rotten hierarchy, was the only way out for the impoverished, wretched, put-upon masses.

'Well, that's a point of view, I guess!' He shook his head. 'Here's *my* plan for India. Land reform, criminalize the caste system, compulsory free secondary education for all.' He thought for a moment whether his list was complete. 'Oh, and mandatory jail for accepting a bribe.'

'Man, *none* of that's *ever* going to happen! Everyone, police, politicians, landowners, business, *everyone* will make sure it doesn't.'

'Oh, I'm sure it'll happen in the end.'

'And what about servants? If there's no caste and free education? You'll have to cook your own dinner, man. Wash your own dishes.'

He chuckled. 'Yah, but y'know, live-in help is just a job. There are twenty million of them in India. There's nothing else to do.'

'You're cool with it?'

'You know what *would* be weird? *Not* having any. In a neighborhood like this? People would point in the street, and talk: rich guy with no servants. At least a cook and a bearer, that's the minimum.' People surely point at him anyway, I thought, with that white hair. He went on, 'Best thing you can do, employ good people, pay well, be nice. Oh yeah – and help them learn English. That's their only hope.'

Jesse's man and woman moved silent and unseen, half-glimpsed, like beneficent spirits, every room always just-cleaned, clothes neatly folded, meals cooked and served without a word. Any greeting was answered by a deferential smile, a murmur of *Sahib,* a polite little bow of the head.

One morning Madhu brought me – on a tray! – a letter from Milly. She had written once again about Women's Liberation. There had been a huge march through London, the first ever, not so much *demanding* as *expressing* the equality of the sexes, she said. It sounded like fun, and an important step. I wished I had been there, and Milly said I should have been. How, I wondered, could such a march ever take place in India? How could all castes march together, side by side? How could Madhu and Dipesh join in? These questions defied the possibility of answers.

After an hour in the library, Jesse went to the studio, opening windows and doors. It turned out that he worked from enlarged photographs, painstakingly copying them with pastels, smudging and smoothing, and touching in miniscule details. I too used Jesse's pastels, and he found time to teach me how to get the best from them, in his studio, or outdoors, against the russet, hazy background of an Indian sky.

When we became hungry, we cycled to a simple back-alley eating house he liked. Pedaling beside one another on heavy old sit-up-and-beg roadsters, Jesse and I talked and joked in amiable ease. At a table in the dark, spicy air, I asked what he wanted from Angela. In Goa, she had told me Jesse wanted nothing at all. Now he said it himself.

'Why should I want anything from anyone? I don't want anything.' We ordered bhajis. Heaped on saucers they came at once, the triangular pastries hot and oily. 'All I want is she'll leave me alone, exactly as I am.' We picked up the food with our fingertips, nibbled at the spicy filling and sipped cold water from shiny metal beakers. 'Simon, what I don't get is what *you* want from her. You imagine living with her in, what, a nice little house? In an English city? An American one?'

'No, no! With Angela, but on the road. Or, in green countryside. I can almost see it, a community, I don't know, somewhere peaceful, rural.'

'A *commune? Angela?*'

'Not a commune. A community. Working the land, friends around. Kids, music. Someplace nice.'

'Oh, right.' He smiled, his eyes like blue stained glass. 'Community. Hey, nice! What, *Angela?* You think she shares that vision?'

He was mocking me! I felt slightly insulted. Still, it was a pleasure to talk about Angela with someone who knew her even better than I did.

'Well,' I conceded, 'you're right, it won't happen. That's a fact. So…' And for once, I did really wonder what the future held for me.

Jesse swallowed a mouthful. 'You know she's trying to get pregnant? Soon as it's confirmed, I'll be free of her.'

'What about the baby – your baby?'

'If you're living with her on a commune, maybe *you'll* bring it up.'

'Angela told me you two were happy together in Berkeley. She doesn't understand why you left.'

'She understands,' he countered. 'I had to get away for a lot of reasons. Before '67, the whole scene, the Acid Tests, was great, exciting, beautiful, it was fun, we all loved each other. Then things became heavy, and then the war. Sasha asked me to come to India.'

'Sasha? What's Sasha got to do with it?'

'Simon, there's much more going on than you know. Sasha plans to make acid in India. Here in Ahmedabad. It might have worked. There are two hundred thousand students here. Angela was in on that. But when she wanted something else from me… well, that I can't give.'

I stared in bewilderment. In all the time we'd been together, Angela never mentioned that she and Jesse had been, in effect, business partners, working with Sasha. Maybe I should have figured it out. In London, Sasha had said something about working with Jesse.

'You did live with Angela, though? She said you did.'

'Yeah,' Jesse gave a little laugh. 'We enjoyed it for a while. It's about perspective. What's near to us looms large. Anyone can love anyone, or hate them, if they come close enough. But everything keeps moving, right? Time passes, things continue on their path, and – well, that's it.'

At the mention of *time*, I found myself telling him what had happened on the beach, that radiant moment, when time halted in its tracks, and everything became transfixed and transfigured and filled with light.

Jesse stopped eating to listen. 'Maybe you're kind of scared you saw God on Calangute beach?'

'No, I saw what it is to be a living thing.'

As we left the café he put an arm around my shoulder. 'It's going to be cool. Things will work out fine. I'd like to show you something.'

We pedaled through the traffic, dodging shoals of pedestrians, weaving around hooting, reckless rickshaws, stately cars and swarms of jingling bicycles, and the enigmatic chaos of a million lives.

He led the way to an abandoned temple, overgrown with greenery and wild flowers. It was as quiet a place as I had ever been, yet full of sound. Birds, bees, butterflies and dragonflies made their journeys around the building. Within, the temple truly was silent, solid stone. Yet something pressed on the mind's ear, the sound of puja long ago, repeated thousands of times, memories of bells and chanting. Around its various chambers stood lingams, sturdy erect stone phalluses, on which the devotional marks looked like colored semen spilling down onto yoni, the stylized vagina shapes which accompanied the lingams.

'Wow – these people worshipped sex!' I declared.

'No, man,' Jesse said. 'Fertility. Family. Continuity.'

We wandered apart, lost in the foliage. Carved figures were having sex, lone female figures of stone enticing me, in the soporific humming silence, to make an offering onto their spherical breasts, their dimpled, rounded bellies, between their parted thighs. I longed instead for the embrace of a woman, not Angela, nor any other goddess either of stone or flesh, but someone sweet and good.

Summer 1971

The train moved across the great land, between fields desiccated and fading in the gathering heat of the season. An exultant happiness soared within me. I am alone. This train, these clattering wheels, are a flickering mirage. But I am real, I am alive and new.

At Srinagar, a letter on yellow tissue paper was waiting.

Dearly Simon
I have been stupid. Unbelievably. This is not the way for me. One can grieve for the past, but never return to it. Jesse will remain here forever. He doesn't want me. As it was in Berkeley, so it is here. I am pregnant with his baby, our child, which is what I wanted. But my eyes have been opened: all I want is a good and happy life for my baby. I am coming to you, my Simon, if you will have me. Everything will be as before, only a thousand times better. This time, we shall love each other for real. I know what you must think of these words, but darling Simon please believe me, this is the truest thing I ever said. You are my future. Trying to make the journey back, instead of going forward, was a terrible mistake. The Jesse I longed for was an illusion. You and I have spent these last years together, and I know now that I love you with all my heart. I am longing to see you and return to you.
Yours always, Angela.

A boatman rowed slowly alongside the wooden deck of my houseboat, offering wall-hangings for sale. I leaned over and bought one as a gift for Angela, and he pushed away, oars splashing calmly as he disappeared into the dense silence, white mountains rising behind. The hanging was very beautiful, the fabric embroidered with irregular little squares of color like mosaic, set with dozens of tiny mirrors.

Straight away I realized I'd never give it to her. There would never be a time or a place for gifts. There was nothing more we could ever give each other.

Instead I met her at Delhi station and helped her to the airport, hailing a taxi and carrying her bag to the desk. It was quite impossible to detect what she was feeling. We kissed long at the moment of parting. I held her, knowing that when I let her go it would be for the last time, not wanting to give up her warmth, her familiar body, our time together, not wanting to leave our love and our days behind, our happiest moments and unhappiest, and let her slip into the past.

Finally Angela said, 'Goodbye, Simon.'

I kissed her cheek. 'Goodbye, Angela. Good luck with the birth, and with everything. I hope it all goes well.' I held back from saying, *I still love you*. She passed through a barrier and disappeared into the crowd.

I waited at the airport until I could watch her plane rise steeply into the hazy sky. I stared as it became tiny; and then, quite suddenly, it could not be seen any more. She was gone.

Years later, Simon did see Angela again, when he and Milly visited California with their son, Samuel.

Her small timber house stood far from any neighbor, the forest pressing against a patch of cleared land beside a dirt road in Mendocino County. She made them welcome in the effusive American style, though with a just-discernable trace of frost towards Milly.

Angela held and admired Simon like a precious vase. 'You still have a mustache, at least!' The smiling sentimentality didn't seem like her old self. 'And is that grey hair I see? Dear Simon. Well, well!'

Neither she nor Milly had any grey hair at all. Angela had become fat, though. She was sluggish, had a double chin, moved wearily. Was this the Angela he loved? No, this is another, another time.

When she introduced them to her son, Simon studied the boy for any sign that this was his own child. It was impossible. A likeable, ordinary youth, Noah had inherited a quite uncanny resemblance to Jesse, with the same crystal-blue eyes and straight hair nearly white. He was in his late teens, and Sam not ten, yet Noah was charming and patient with the younger boy. The two amused themselves roaming around the untidy yard, while the grown-ups sat indoors with cups of tea.

'We went to Berkeley,' Simon said. 'Wow, it's *so* different.'

Angela nodded. 'Aren't we all, man.'

He chuckled at that. 'It's still great, though. We saw some fantastic-looking kids on Telegraph,' he said. 'Not freaks. Punks.'

'Brilliant, weren't they?' confirmed Milly. 'Hair standing on end, dyed red, whatever. Safety pins through their noses!'

He grinned. 'I felt like saying to them, *Look on me and weep.*'

Angela understood. 'Ah, well. They'll find out soon enough. All growing up ends in disillusion.'

'I heard about that firebombing at Cody's. What an insane thing.'

'And just to stop people reading Rushdie's book! Something weird is happening in the world.'

'Yup. Do you still see Sasha and Hitch?'

'Yeah, of course! Sasha comes up here sometimes. I owe everything to Sasha. She bought me this place, you know. Sasha,' she explained, 'is Noah's godmother. Oh, and they sold the ranch. Jack has a venture capital business now, in Palo Alto. That was Sasha's idea, too. They have a lovely house there.'

'What about Jesse – are you in touch with him?' he asked.

With only a brief hesitation, Angela replied, 'Jesse is dead. A couple of years ago now. Nearly two and half years. He had AIDS.'

Simon gasped audibly. 'Wow! My God! I'm terribly sorry!' He did not hug or console her.

'No, it's fine,' she assured them. 'I'm fine. I sent him photos of Noah sometimes, over the years, but Jesse told me in India he wouldn't be interested and it was true. He never wrote. Just one letter, just one, right at the very end. Hey, Simon, you OK?'

Milly too was looking at Simon questioningly. His forehead rested on the palm of his hand.

He sat up. 'Yeah, yeah.'

'You're not upset about Jesse, are you?'

'I don't know. I really liked him.'

Angela remained calm. 'You know, I never realized that.'

Milly asked, puzzled, 'AIDS? Was he gay?'

'Yah, yes. Yes, he was.' Angela's composed, imperturbable features seemed to hold back something concealed – a reservoir of bitter tears.

'You say Jesse wasn't interested in Noah, so...' Simon stopped as the dreadful realization took hold of him.

Angela turned away and shook her head. 'That's right.' She breathed in deeply and let out a long sigh. 'Noah never met his father.'

Milly was frowning darkly. 'Poor kid.'

'Don't worry, Noah's OK,' said Angela. 'Don't mention Jesse to him, will you?'

Simon asked, 'Did you go to the funeral? I guess Jesse had family somewhere.'

'His folks flew the body home to LA. But none of them knew about me or Noah. It wouldn've been right to go to the funeral.'

'What, they didn't even know about *you*?'

'Nope.' Angela recovered herself at once. 'And how're *your* folks?'

'Pretty good. Except for my dad's heart problems. They adore Sam.'

Angela cut slices of her carrot cake, as delicious as ever. Simon watched carefully. A lank strand of blonde slipped from behind her ear. How on earth, he wondered, did she become so overweight and unhealthy?

'Hey, let me show you something.' She took Simon by the hand, the soft flesh cool and damp, and led him along a corridor to a picture on the wall. Milly followed. In a small frame, mounted on sunny yellow card, was a still-recognizable sketch of Simon and Angela, a heart, and the words, *I Am Nearby*.

'What is it?' Milly asked.

Angela glanced, wondering how Simon would answer. He said, 'It's a note I wrote once, when we lived together at Heath Cottage.'

Milly caught Simon's eye. Why, she wondered, would Angela keep that on display?

'And this,' said Angela. She turned. There on the opposite wall hung his yellow, red and blue watercolor portrait of her. He wondered how on earth these things came to be here. Where were they when she was in India? He did not ask. It didn't matter anymore.

They called the boys into the house. The pair of them rushed in noisily, the screen door banging shut behind. Little Sam could not contain his enthusiasm for the moist cake, picking up pieces and pressing them into his mouth.

Milly glared at him, which he knew meant 'Mind your manners'.

'Mum,' he protested, 'you should make cake like this. Ask her how.'

And Angela gave Milly the recipe. Ever afterwards, though, when Milly baked Angela's carrot cake, it never tasted as good. Milly said a vital ingredient must have been left out.

Leaving the house, driving back to the city, Simon stopped the car at an ocean viewpoint near Mendocino. He took his drawing pad and pastels, and they walked for a few minutes on a clifftop path. Sam ran on ahead.

Milly said she thought Angela was over-attentive to her boy, fretting around him, indulgent.

'Do you think she still loves you?' she asked.

Simon shook his head. She loved the child, she loved Jesse. 'She told me, ages ago – she never loved me.'

'Well, I don't believe that,' said Milly. In a lower voice, looking down, she asked, 'And are you in love with her at all?'

Again Simon shook his head.

'But as she was?' Milly insisted.

He took Milly's hand and pulled her towards him, kissed her cheek. 'Don't be silly. How can you be in love with someone as they were? A person as they were doesn't exist.'

'Don't they?'

After Angela's plane had vanished into the haze, I returned from the airport into the Old City, walking in the teeming streets. For once I did feel rather lonely. To pass the time I took the express train to Agra, to visit the Taj Mahal. I strolled barefoot through the vast, perfect tomb, this elegant shrine to the agony of remembrance, now crowded with jostling tour groups herded by guides.

I walked away, to a minar, a solitary tower that overlooked the bare countryside to the south. After a few moments, I left the tower and walked further. Dry fields and tough shrubs and bushes surrounded me. The blazing sun and the soil threatened to parch me, turn me into dust, so that on a breeze I might be scattered over this unchanging land.

Among some rough bushes I discovered a tiny windowless stone room, its doorway open and uncovered. It was a mausoleum. I crawled inside. The grave lay in the center. The room was cold like a fridge, and utterly silent. A narrow ray of light came through the entrance.

There was no room to raise my head, so I squatted down. The walls, the ceiling, the floor, the grave, all were entirely covered with brilliant mosaic. The mosaic pieces were unbroken, every one of them vivid in ancient blues and reds. The colors surrounded me, close to me, cold stone and deathly still.

Alone and at peace, hidden and unfindable, I sat in rest beside the tomb of an unknown human being. When did this person live, when did they die? Now at last was a time for silence. Yet even here silence eluded me, for I heard the sound of my heart. A deep sigh came from my living, breathing body.

Who will decorate the inside of my grave, one day?

After some minutes I crawled out again into late afternoon sunlight, and sat on a hilltop overlooking the surrounding fields. From the distance, from a village timelessly forbearing, unvisited by tourists, a plaintive music hung in the wind.

This was the India I could never know except as an outsider. Our revolution will never reach this place. In that village, the India of western imaginations cannot be found, and the road to the East does not exist. Three seasons, hot, cool, and wet, turn forever round, uncontemplated, like a clock with no hands. Relationships, emotions, stir the hearts within these hidden communities. One man seeks admiration, another wealth, never leaving the village to find it. And there too, never looking elsewhere, a man and a woman fall in love.

The End

www.andrewsanger.com/Love

Love 245

Proper names have been spelled as was correct in 1967-1972. Some have changed since that time:

BOMBAY
The city was officially called Bombay from 1534 to 1995, when it was changed to Mumbai. The name Bombay is still current though, for example by long-established institutions such as Bombay High Court.

MAO TSE-TUNG
The given name of the former Chairman of the Communist Party of the People's Republic of China was written as Mao Tse-Tung under the Wade-Giles transliteration system which was used until 1979. In that year the government of China ruled that Pinyin was the only acceptable system of romanization, under which the name is spelled Mao Zedong.

MASHAD
This Iranian city, now more usually transliterated as Mashhad, was previously spelled as Meshed or Mashad.

MOSLEM
Nowadays usually spelled Muslim, the word Moslem was the norm until the 1990s. The American Moslem Society (www.masjiddearborn.org/), founded 1938, still keeps the earlier spelling. The Young Men's Moslem Association, founded before World War II and based in Egypt, also retains its original name. Some Islamist organizations use the spelling Moslem, e.g. Hamas, in the official English translation of its charter.

PANJIM
The capital of Goa is more often known today as Panaji.

PERSIA
After the Islamic Revolution of 1979, it became more usual to call the country by the (now official) name, Iran.

SIMLA
Now better known as Shimla, this hill station was usually called Simla until the 1990s. The name Simla is still in use by Indian Railways.